THE FEUD

THE FEUD

KIMBERLEY CHAMBERS

preface
publishing

Published by Preface 2010

10 9 8 7 6 5 4 3 2 1

First published in Great Britain in 2010 by
Preface Publishing
20 Vauxhall Bridge Road
London SW1V 2SA

An imprint of The Random House Group Limited

www.rbooks.co.uk
www.prefacepublishing.co.uk

Addresses for companies within The Random House Group Limited
can be found at
www.randomhouse.co.uk

The Random House Group Limited Reg. No. 954009

A CIP catalogue record for this book is available from the British Library

ISBN 978 1 84809 140 5

The Random House Group Limited supports The Forest Stewardship
Council (FSC), the leading international forest certification organisation. All our titles
that are printed on Greenpeace-approved FSC-certified paper carry the FSC logo. Our
paper procurement policy can be found at www.rbooks.co.uk/environment

Typeset in Times by Palimpsest Book Production Limited,
Grangemouth, Stirlingshire

Printed and bound in Great Britain by
Clays Ltd, St Ives PLC

In memory of Lee Mouser
1962–2002

My daddy told me I never should
Play with the gypsies in the wood

ACKNOWLEDGEMENTS

Firstly, I would like to express my gratitude to everybody at Preface and Random House for believing in me and my books. A special mention to all the reps, who have done a wonderful job in getting my name out there.

A big thanks to Tim Bates, who is a great agent and friend and Rosie de Courcy for giving me an opportunity to make something of my life.

As always, I would be lost without my amazing typist, Sue Cox, and a special mention to Trish Scott for her help with technology.

Seeing as the majority of this book is set in the rave year of 1988, I must mention Jenny Munro, Tina Mouser, Sherri Fuller and Tracy Mackness. With the lives we lead back in those days I'm surprised we're all still alive, let alone still in touch!

And last, but certainly not least, I must acknowledge Chas and Dave. Gutted you split up boys, but your music will live forever!

PROLOGUE

Summer 1970

As Eddie Mitchell ran his fingers along the side of the baseball bat, he could feel the beads of sweat forming along his forehead. It was one of those muggy days, where flying ants appeared. It was far too hot to be suited and booted and stuck in the back of a Transit van.

Eddie listened intently as his father repeated his instructions. 'We don't want an all-out war, so nothing too heavy, boys. This is a little warning for 'em, and if they don't get the message, then heavy'll come later.'

As the rest of the family discussed the feud, Eddie sat in silence. In his eyes, the O'Haras had taken a fucking liberty and deserved more than a little warning. For as long as Ed could remember, his dad, Harry, had run the pub protection racket in the East End. No one messed with the Mitchells, no one dared, and then, like an unwanted disease, the O'Haras appeared on the scene and tried to muscle in on their patch. Eddie was the youngest member of the family firm. His dad ran the show, along with his uncle Reg. Then there were Paulie and Ronny, his two elder brothers.

'You OK, son?'

Smiling with anticipation, Eddie nodded at his father. The O'Haras were a travelling family who had recently moved to the East End from Cambridgeshire. Eddie hated travellers. In his eyes, they were uncouth, lowlife, inbred scum. In particular, he hated Jimmy O'Hara. He was the strongest of the sons, the loudest, and flash didn't even begin to describe him.

'I wanna be the one to take out Jimmy, Dad.'

Harry eyed his son proudly. Even from an early age, Eddie was the one full of promise, and Harry knew without a doubt that one day his youngest child would be head of the family business.

As the Transit van pulled up outside the pub, the Mitchells clutched their weapons.

'Right, let's do it,' Harry said as he sprang from the van.

Barging his brothers and uncle out of the way, Ed followed his father into the boozer. 'See you? You're dead, you piss-taking pikey cunt,' he screamed as he spotted Jimmy O'Hara and lunged towards him.

As the pub erupted into full-scale mayhem, Eddie was grabbed around the neck from behind.

'Do him, Jimmy, fucking do him!' he heard a voice shout.

As the knife slid down the left-hand side of his face, Eddie felt anger, not pain. With blood spewing from his face, he went for O'Hara like a rabid Rottweiler.

'You inbred pikey piece of shit!' he screamed, as he threw off the geezer behind him and repeatedly thrust the baseball bat against Jimmy O'Hara's head.

In that moment, Eddie completely lost it, and if his family hadn't dragged him away, Ed swore he would have committed murder.

Harry, Reg, Paulie and Ronny managed to clump and scare the rest of the O'Haras and, aware that Eddie's face was almost sliced in two, they quickly bundled him into the back of the Transit van.

'Let me go back. I'll kill him, I'll fucking kill him!' Eddie screamed.

'Your face is fucked. We need to get you stitched up, son,' Harry said seriously.

Ed was seething as he held the side of his face together. He was covered in claret from head to toe. The wound was so deep, it had even soaked through his suit.

Aware that his mouth was full of blood, Ed spat a mouthful onto the floor. As he turned to his father, his expression blackened.

'I'll get me own back, Dad, if it's the last thing I do. Even if the O'Haras lay off our turf, this feud ain't over. It will never be over between me and Jimmy, not now – not ever.'

ONE

1971

Joyce Smith smiled as she carefully lifted her best dinner service out of the box. She rarely used her expensive china, but today was a very special occasion and she was desperate to impress.

As Joyce entered the living room, her smile immediately turned to a frown. That lazy husband of hers was still glued to that filthy, stinking armchair of his. 'Stanley, get your arse up them stairs and get yourself ready. You haven't even washed or shaved yet and they'll be here soon.'

More interested in the 3.45 at Kempton, Stanley leaped up and down. 'Go on my son, get in there. Go on my son, you can do it!'

As his horse got pipped at the post, Stanley threw the *Sporting Life* up in the air in temper. 'Stupid, bastard nag!' he shouted.

Annoyed that her husband was ignoring her orders, Joyce picked up her broom and clumped him on the head with it. Why he betted, she'd never know. He always bloody lost. 'I won't tell you again, Stanley. Now get up them bleedin' stairs and smarten yourself up.'

Stanley knew better than to argue with his wife. She wore the trousers, and he just complied with her orders.

'Your nice blue shirt and best slacks are hanging on the wardrobe door; put them on,' Joyce ordered.

'Anyone would think the Queen Mother was coming for tea,' Stan replied, as he ran up the stairs.

Picking up the duster and polish, Joyce did her best to tidy his dirty little corner. She had a quick vac round then, to finish, sprayed a whole can of air freshener around the house. That's better, she thought as she studied her domain.

Joyce was very proud of her three-bedroomed council house. It was situated in a road off Upney Lane, but she always told people that she lived in the upper-class part of Barking. Obviously, she would have liked to have bought a private property in a better area, but on Stan's bus driver's wages, that was never going to happen.

A proper little homemaker, Joyce was always buying new ornaments and furniture to tart up her surroundings. Her neighbours all said that she had the poshest house in the street and Joyce loved the compliment. Being known as the posh woman suited her down to the ground.

Stanley mumbled and cursed to himself as he shaved and got changed. Not only was he annoyed with the jockey and nag that had just lost him money, he was also annoyed with his daughter, Jessica, for messing up his usual plans.

Apart from the one in four Saturdays when he had to work, Stanley loved these afternoons. They were like his day out of prison, when he'd escape Joycie's moaning and spend the whole day in the pub or the bookie's with his pals. Today, he wasn't allowed to go anywhere. His daughter, Jessica, was bringing this new boyfriend of hers around for tea and Joyce had insisted he stay indoors and play happy families.

Like most dads, Stanley was quite protective of his only daughter. Jessica was only seventeen and still lived

5

at home with them. Petite and blonde, Jessica was a very pretty girl with a sunny nature. She'd had boyfriends in the past, but there'd been nothing serious until this latest one.

His son, Raymond, was forever bringing different girls home, but Stan wasn't worried about what he got up to. With Jess it was different. He knew what it was like to be a hormonal young man and he would hate anyone taking advantage of his little girl.

Stan checked his appearance in the mirror. From what Joyce had said, this new boyfriend sounded like a right Flash Harry. Call it father's intuition, Stanley just knew he wasn't going to like him very much.

Joyce stared out of the window as she plumped up the cushions. They should be here any minute and she couldn't wait to meet this Eddie. For the first time in her young life, Jessica had fallen hook, line and sinker and Joyce was ever so pleased for her. Joyce's own life had always lacked excitement and romance, and she wanted her daughter to have everything she hadn't. Sometimes she wondered why she'd even married Stan and then she remembered her mother's harsh words: 'You're twenty-two now, Joycie. Look at all your mates, every one of them married. Even that fat Doreen from across the road has found herself a husband. Young Stanley's from ever such good stock. I know all of his family, even his aunts and uncles. You don't wanna be left on the shelf, do you now?'

'But I don't think I love him, Mum,' Joyce complained.

'Well, it's up to you, Joycie. I wasn't in love with your father when I married him, but we made the most of it. Love comes later, dear. Take my advice and marry Stanley. If you say no and leave it any longer, at your age there'll be little else to choose from.'

6

Six months after that little chat, Joyce reluctantly agreed to marry Stanley. Jessica arrived a year later, closely followed by Raymond. Love between her and Stan had never really blossomed, but Joyce threw herself into the children and in her own way was happy with her little lot. Romeo and Juliet, she and Stan most certainly weren't, but they jogged along quite nicely, especially since he'd stopped wanting sex.

Joyce loved reading and what was lacking in her love life she found in the pages of Mills & Boon novels. Now she hoped that Jessica and her new beau would fill a void in her life and inject some much-needed romance.

Seeing her clean-shaven husband walk towards her, Joyce smiled at him. 'That's better! What a difference to see you in a nice shirt and slacks. See Stanley, you do scrub up well when you try.'

Stan tutted and flopped in his armchair. 'Scrub up well! I feel like a bleedin' pox doctor's clerk,' he moaned.

Joyce shooed him out of his chair. 'They're due in five minutes. Stand up, or you'll crease your shirt.'

Stan jumped up as though he had a firework up his arse. He wasn't the bravest man in the world and over the years he'd realised that it was easier to comply with Joycie's orders than to argue with her.

'Where's Raymond?' he asked.

Twitching the curtain, Joyce explained. 'Gone round his mate's. I told him not to come back until later. He's been a cheeky little sod lately and, as for that racket he keeps playing upstairs, I didn't want him to give a bad impression of us in front of Eddie. Quick, here they are, this is them. I'll answer the door, you go and get some beers out the shed to offer Eddie. Now, Stanley. Quick, chop-chop.'

As they approached the house, Jessica squeezed Eddie's

7

big hand. Clocking Ginny and Linda staring at her from the house across the road, she waved proudly. Jessica couldn't stop grinning. To say Eddie was a looker was an understatement. The expression tall, dark and handsome could have been created just for him. She was dying for her parents to meet him, especially her mum. The only worry she had was the age gap between them. Eddie was thirty but she had told her dad he was only twenty-five. Her mum knew the truth and once her dad got to know Eddie and like him, she would tell him the truth as well.

'This is it, number eleven. Now, remember what I told you about my dad. He still thinks of me as his little baby, so if he's not overly friendly, please don't take it personally.'

Eddie kissed her on the nose. 'You worry too much, Jess. I'll have a chat with your old man, just leave him to me.'

Unable to contain her excitement any longer, Joyce flung open the front door.

'Ed, this is my mum. Mum, this is Eddie,' Jessica said, beaming.

Eddie shook Joyce's hand and politely kissed her on both cheeks. 'It's a delight to meet you, Mrs Smith. Your Jessica's told me so much about you.'

Joyce giggled. 'All good, I hope?'

'Most definitely,' Eddie said, winking.

Joyce led them into the living room. 'We'll have a nice cup of tea, Jess, and let the men have a beer,' she said.

Jessica smiled as she noticed her mother had got the expensive china out. 'Where's Dad?' she asked.

Joyce offered Eddie a sandwich. 'Gone down to the shed to get some beers. Speak of the devil – here he is now.'

Eddie put his sandwich down and stood up as Stan

entered the room. 'Dad, this is Eddie who I've been telling you about,' Jessica said nervously.

At five feet eight inches tall, Stanley felt inadequate as he shook Eddie's strong hand. He thought of the jockey who had lost him the race earlier and, for some reason, felt like his twin brother.

'Would you like a piece of homemade fruit cake, Eddie?' his wife asked.

Stan flopped into his armchair and studied the object of his daughter's affection. He'd been right all along. He didn't like the look of him one little bit. Jessica had told him that Eddie was twenty-five, but the bastard looked old enough to be her dad. He was broad-shouldered, with dark hair and was wearing tailored grey trousers with a long black Crombie coat. As he turned his head, Stan noticed the massive scar that ran from the outside of his left eye to the corner of his mouth. Stan knocked back his bottle of Double Diamond and opened another. Eddie looked an out-and-out villain. He certainly wasn't the sort of chap he envisaged or wanted his beautiful daughter going out with.

As the conversation flowed, Stan could tell that Mr Fucking Charming Bollocks had Joycie eating out of his hand.

'That fruit cake was amazing, Mrs Smith. So much better than the cakes I'm used to,' the smarmy bastard said.

'You're ever so quiet, Dad. Are you OK?' Jessica asked, as she handed him and Eddie another beer.

Knowing that he was expected to join in the conversation, Stanley cleared his throat. 'Jessica said that she met you at a local party. Do you come from round here, Eddie?'

'No. My family are out of Canning Town and I live

up that way. I share a flat with me brother, Ronny. It's nothing special, we live above a pet shop along the Barking Road.'

Stanley carried on prying. 'And what do you do for a living? If you don't mind me asking?'

Eddie smiled. The old boy didn't like him, he could sense it a mile off. 'My dad owns a load of salvage yards. He's retired now, so me and my brothers run them for him.'

Stanley felt fear wash over him. Canning Town? Salvage yards? Surely he wasn't one of the Mitchell boys – please God, no.

Dreading the answer, it took Stan a while to pluck up the courage to ask the all-important question. 'Before I met Joycie, I used to live in Canning Town myself. I remember a lot of the old school. What's your father's name?'

Eddie smirked. 'Harry Mitchell. You probably know him, most people do.'

Stanley took a large gulp of his drink and started to choke. Unable to breathe properly, he fell off the chair and onto all fours.

Aware of her husband going redder and redder in the face, Joyce stood up and repeatedly thumped him on the back. Embarrassed that he'd made a show of her in front of Eddie, she tried to make a joke of it. 'He spends so much time watching them bleedin' horses on telly, he's started to behave like one now. Giddy up, giddy up,' she said, laughing.

Feeling as though he was about to have a heart attack, Stan managed to heave himself up and stand on two feet. 'Went down the wrong hole,' he gasped, as he legged it from the room.

Joyce smiled at Eddie. 'You'll have to excuse my Stanley. He's not used to having visitors, but he's a good man

10

deep down, and once you get to know him, I'm sure you'll like him.'

Eddie grinned. He doubted that very much. 'I'm sure we'll get on like a house on fire, Mrs Smith. Now, is there any chance of having another piece of that wonderful fruit cake?'

Joyce beamed as she handed him a slice. What a charming chap, she thought.

Stanley sat in the shed and tried his best to compose himself. Canning Town had a notorious reputation for producing villainous families and they didn't come much worse than the Mitchells. Bootlegging, pub protection, illegal boxing. Rumour had it that over the years the bastards had had a finger in every pie going.

Stanley remembered Harry Mitchell as though it were yesterday. He'd been standing in a pub in East Ham having a drink with Roger Dodds, his old school pal. All of a sudden the door had burst open and the pub had fallen silent. A man in a suit and trilby hat walked towards them.

'Which one of you is Roger Dodds?' he'd asked menacingly.

Crapping himself, Stan had nodded towards his friend. Seconds later, Roger Dodds had his face slashed and his right eye taken out with a broken bottle.

The man in the trilby hat had then ordered a Scotch, downed it in one, apologised for any inconvenience and casually strolled out of the pub.

That man in the trilby was Harry Mitchell. Apparently, Dodds's father had fucked him over for a load of money and that was payback time.

Deep in thought, Stanley didn't hear the shed door creak open. It was Eddie. Stanley leaped up. 'What's going on? What do you want?' he asked nervously.

Eddie stared at him. 'Calm down, you'll give yourself

a cardiac. The girls were worried about you. They said you'd be in the shed, so I thought I'd check you were OK.'

Stan nodded. 'I'm fine now. It took me a while to catch me breath, so I came out here for a sit down.'

Desperate for some fresh air, Stanley led Eddie away from the shed. He locked the door, then was horrified as he felt a massive arm go round his shoulder.

Eddie smiled. He could almost smell the old man's fright. 'Actually, I wanted to have a quiet word with you, man to man, like.'

Stan looked at him in horror. He'd only been dating Jessica for a month; surely he wasn't going to ask his permission to marry her.

Eddie stood in front of him and looked him straight in the eye. 'The thing is, Mr Smith, I think you should know that I'm really serious about your Jessica, so I wanna get a few things straight. I'm not twenty-five like Jess told you, I'm actually thirty years old. I've also been married in the past and I've got two little boys, Gary and Ricky, who I dote on. Obviously, they don't live with me – they live with my ex-wife, Beverley. I've been straight with Jess from the start and I think it's only right I do the same with you. As I said, things are moving pretty quickly between me and your Jess, so I just wanna know that you approve of our relationship.'

Dumbstruck, Stanley stood with his mouth open and was horrified as a fly flew in and hit the back of his throat. Half choking, he spat it out and ended up on his knees for the second time that day.

Eddie helped him up. 'So, are you OK about me and Jess?' he asked again.

Stanley nodded. 'No problem, Eddie, and thanks for telling me,' he mumbled.

'There you are,' Joyce said, as Stanley returned, ashen-faced.

12

The polite conversation carried on for another hour or so and was only stopped by Eddie giving Jessica a secret nudge. Jessica looked at her watch and stood up. 'God, is that the time! Mum, Dad, we best be going now. Eddie is taking me to the pictures tonight. We're going to see that new film, *Love Story*. All the girls at work reckon it's brilliant. I've been dying to see it and we don't want to miss the start.'

Eddie stood up and put his arm around his young girlfriend's shoulders. 'Mrs Smith, Mr Smith, thank you so much for your hospitality. It's been a pleasure to meet you both. Don't worry, I'll take good care of your Jessica and I promise to have her home by a reasonable hour.'

Overcome by the romance of it all, Joyce stood at the door waving them off. 'No snogging in the back row,' she giggled.

'Stop it, Mum,' Jessica said embarrassed.

Joyce shut the front door and sighed a happy sigh. What an attractive, polite chap. He was like one of them Mills & Boon men, sophisticated and handsome. Thrilled for her daughter, Joyce decided to have a G&T to celebrate.

'Well, what did you think?' she asked Stanley, as she sat back down.

Stanley said nothing. He was too frightened to voice his opinions, in case Joyce told Jessica and it got back to Eddie.

Joyce kicked off her shoes and put her slippers on. 'Did you see his shoes? He's definitely worth money. Look, I know it's hard for you, Stan, but Jess isn't a little baby any more. Most of my friends were married at her age. I want her to have the best in life and that Eddie's got class stamped all over him. He's got lovely manners and he'll take good care of her, I know he will.'

Stanley cracked open another beer. He'd had the day

13

from hell and all he wanted to do now was watch *Ironside*. 'Do you mind if I watch the telly now? And if you're gonna keep on about it, no, I wasn't overkeen. In my opinion, Eddie's far too old for our Jess, and, no, I didn't notice his bloody shoes.'

Joyce laughed. 'I knew you had a hangup about him. I know he's a bit older than her, but you're such an old fuddy-duddy. I bet if she'd have brought Prince Charles home, you'd have found fault with him. You just won't let go of her, will you, Stan?'

For the next hour, Joyce wouldn't shut up. It was Eddie this and Eddie that.

Unusually for Stanley, he completely lost his rag. 'For Christ's sake, Joycie, I'm no man's fool. The bloke's a wrong 'un and I know it. He's thirty years old, a divorcee with two bloody kids. As for them going to the pictures, I don't believe a word of it. Jessica's probably round his flat as we speak with her knickers around her ankles. They're probably right in the middle of creating more kids for the smarmy, villainous bastard.'

Furious, Joyce stood up and hit him with the broom. 'How dare you talk about our daughter like that? She's got morals, our Jessica. What are you, some bloody pervert?'

Seething, Stanley jumped out of his chair. He rarely gave an opinion in this house and when he did he got called a bloody nonce. More than anything else in the world, he wanted to pick up Joycie's broom and smash her right over the head with it. Maybe that would make the stupid, naive woman see sense. Filled with self-loathing, Stanley ran to the serenity of his shed. Once inside, he sat on his wooden bench, put his head in his hands and cried.

His old mum had mapped out his life for him at a very

14

early age. 'Stanley, always remember son, it's better to be a live coward than a dead hero.'

Stanley wiped his eyes with his hanky. He feared for his Jessica. That Eddie was cold and calculating. He had those horrible dark eyes, dead man's eyes. There was sod all he could do about it though. He was far too weak a man. What the Mitchells wanted, the Mitchells got, and who was he to stop them?

TWO

Back at Eddie's flat, Jessica fumbled with the zip of her boyfriend's trousers. Realising she still had her knickers around her ankles, she quickly stepped out of them.

Eddie threw her onto the double bed. He expertly entered her and held both of her hands down with his own. He liked it that way; it gave him total control.

'Aw, baby,' he moaned as he shot his seed and pulled himself out of her. Not wanting to be selfish, Eddie used his index finger to pleasure her.

'Oh Eddie,' Jessica cried, as she reached her climax.

Confident that she was satisfied, Eddie rolled onto his back and lit up two cigarettes. Handing one to Jess, he grinned. He'd been told in the past by birds that he had bigger fingers than most men's cocks, and he certainly knew how to use them.

'Did you enjoy that, babe?' he asked, as he studied the smoke rings he was blowing.

Jessica propped herself up on one elbow. She loved taking in his naked body and his handsome face. 'I always enjoy it, Eddie, you know I do.'

Eddie put his arm around her and kissed her gently on the forehead. 'So what do you reckon your parents thought of me?' he asked.

Jessica laid her head on his chest. 'Mum loved you. She thought you were great. Dad's more old-fashioned, but I'm sure he liked you in his own way.'

Eddie smirked at her take on things. The mother he'd had eating out of his hand, but the old man, he knew, had hated him on sight. Gently easing Jessica off him, Eddie jumped out of bed.

'I'm gonna have a quick bath and then I'll take you out for a drink.'

'OK. Save me some hot water so I can freshen up, too.'

Jessica smiled as she watched his muscly long legs and gorgeous naked buttocks walk away from her. She'd only met him four weeks ago at a mate's birthday party. Their eyes had locked and that was it, they'd been inseparable ever since. Jessica couldn't believe her luck. Eddie was rich, handsome and an absolute bloody catch. She'd had boyfriends in the past, even had sex with a couple, but none of them compared to him. Eddie oozed charisma. He treated her like a lady, so much so that he insisted on paying for absolutely everything and picking her up every day from the shoe shop where she worked.

'No girl of mine is putting their hand in their purse or getting on buses,' he told her bluntly.

Her workmates were filled with envy. None of their boyfriends even had a car, and when Ed had first pulled up in his gold Mercedes 250C, their jaws had hit the floor.

'Jess, he's gorgeous – and look at his posh car. You are so lucky,' they'd crowed.

Jess giggled to herself. Ed had a big personality, a bulging wallet and a massive willy. No woman could want more and she was a very lucky girl indeed.

Jess thought about her mum's life. She'd hate to be married to a bus driver and live in the same council house

17

for years like her mum. Her mother didn't want that either. She was forever giving her good advice. 'Jess, with your figure and stunning looks, you can get anyone you want. Don't make the same mistakes as I did and end up with someone like your father. If a good catch comes along, take my advice and grab him with both hands.'

Jessica was aware of how attractive she was. She had long, blonde ringlets, a cute, pointed chin, an amazingly slim figure and men went crazy for her dimpled cheeks.

'The bathroom's all yours, sexy,' Ed said, walking towards her.

As Jessica walked past him, Eddie stared at her fantastic tits. When he was married to Bev, he'd played around with other birds. Meeting Jess had knocked him for six. She was a major piece of eye candy, had a terrific personality and, since they'd got together, he hadn't so much as glanced at another piece of skirt.

Eddie did up the top button of his shirt. As he secured his tie, he thought about the sex they'd had earlier. He hadn't used a rubber today, he'd forgotten to buy any and it didn't bother him at all. In Jess, Ed was sure he'd found the woman he wanted to spend the rest of his life with and the quicker he put her in the club and stuck a ring on her finger, the better.

Eddie looked up as his brother, Ronny, slammed the front door.

'Am I glad to see you.'

'What's up? Can't you spend a day without me?' Ed asked sarcastically.

Ronny walked towards him. 'Don't muck about, this is serious, Ed. The O'Haras are in the Flag. They're mob-handed and we're gonna need backup if we're gonna

18

sort it. They looked like they were about to smash the pub up. I think they're trying to muscle in on our patch.'

Eddie's features blackened. He'd never laid eyes on any of the O'Haras since last year when his face had got slashed to fuck. He'd caved Jimmy's head in with a baseball bat that day, and the families had avoided one another ever since.

Ed had ended up with forty-seven stitches in his face, but Jimmy had come off worse. He'd spent over a month in hospital, and had to have numerous scans and tests to rule out brain damage.

The feud between the two families had been halted since then. Ed's dad, Harry, had arranged a meet with Jimmy's old man, Butch.

Harry had said, 'Look, we're all trying to earn a few bob here and no one needs all this extra aggravation. I'll do you a deal. You stick on your patch and do what you've gotta do and we'll stay on ours. If you agree to the deal, we'll let bygones be bygones. If you don't, and I find out your boys have stepped one foot in any of our boozers, I promise you there'll be a fucking bloodbath,' Harry had said.

Butch shook hands on it. 'You have my word, you'll have no more trouble from me or my lads,' he promised.

As Jessica walked towards him in a white halterneck catsuit, Eddie kicked Ronny to urge him to keep schtum.

'You look gorgeous, darling.'

Jessica smiled. Any new clothes she bought now she kept round Eddie's. She had to look the part for her new man.

Ronny was pissed off. What was more important, family business or fucking birds?

'Where are we going?' Jessica asked excitedly.

19

Eddie decided to give Canning Town a wide berth. He didn't want Jess to see the other side of him. He was a lunatic when he got going and he knew if he came face to face with Jimmy O'Hara, he'd throw him straight through the pub window.

'I thought we'd go to East Ham for a change. A bloke in the Burnell Arms owes me some dough and needs a little reminder. If it's any good, we'll stay there; if it's shit, I'll take you out for a nice meal instead.'

Jessica nodded happily. As long as she was by Eddie's side, she didn't care where she went.

Eddie handed her his keys. 'Go and sit in the car, babe. I just need to have a quick chat with Ronny. It's business, you'll only be bored.'

'Bye, Ronny,' Jessica said as she left the flat. That was one of the things she loved about Eddie. She knew he was a bit dodgy and she found his little business chats and his life in general bloody exciting.

Eddie made sure she was out of earshot, then turned to his brother. 'Don't ever say too much about what we get up to in front of Jess, will yer?'

Ronny shook his head. 'Fuckin' hell, Ed. You can't put birds in front of family business. You always used to put your family first when you were married to Bev.'

Eddie stood his ground. Ronny wasn't as good-looking as him, and his bird, Sharon, was a big old heifer.

'Look, Ron, family comes first and you know it does, but there's no point in storming in the Flag tonight. We don't know where Paulie is, for a start. Listen, the O'Haras will be well pissed up by now. If you were in there, they'll definitely be expecting a visit from us. They're probably staring at the door as we speak. Our best bet is to leave it a week or two. Let them think they've got away with it, and when they're least expecting it, we'll pounce on 'em.'

Ronny shrugged. Maybe he should go and find his other brother, Paulie. He'd round up a few faces and maybe they could sort it without Eddie.

Eddie read his mind. 'Don't start organising things behind my back, Ron. I'll speak to Paulie tomorrow. We'll sit down properly, put our heads together and hatch a plan.'

Ronny nodded. He knew deep down that Eddie was talking sense, but he was still annoyed. Both he and Paulie were older than Ed, but they never got to call the shots. Even his old man put Eddie before them. It was as though they were the lackeys and Eddie was being primed as his father's successor.

Ronny let out a loud sigh. 'Look, Ed, I like Jessica and that, but is she gonna be hanging round here all the time?'

Eddie smirked. He knew Ronny was fucking jealous. 'Yes, Ron. For your information, Jessica's here for the foreseeable future.'

Eddie slammed the front door as he left the flat. When he'd split up with Bev, he couldn't be arsed buying a place of his own, so he'd moved in with Ronny. He hadn't minded sharing with him, they'd got along OK, but since he'd met Jess, he could sense things were getting a bit awkward.

He opened the car door. 'Sorry about that, darling.'

Jessica kissed him on the cheek. 'Don't worry about me. I know your business is important – you do what you have to do.'

As he drove towards East Ham, one part of Eddie's mind was focused on Jessica and the other on business. The O'Haras had taken a bloody liberty. The British Flag, better known to locals as the Flag, belonged to the

Mitchells. It was their headquarters, where they'd meet and discuss work matters. The O'Haras used the Chobham Arms in Stratford, and Eddie wouldn't dream of taking the piss in their pub. Whatever happened, they had to be taught a lesson. He'd speak to his dad tomorrow, see what he had to say.

Eddie pictured Jimmy O'Hara's ugly face. Word had it that since their little fall-out, O'Hara's finances had gone from strength to strength. Jimmy was the middle son. He was only thirty-two, and owned salvage yards out in Essex. Ed hated the cunt with a passion. Jimmy thought he ruled the world and the silly big prick even had the cheek to call himself King of the Gypsies.

'What do you think of them, Ed? Do you like them?'

Realising that he hadn't listened to a word Jessica had said, Eddie apologised. 'Sorry, babe, I had a police car up me arse and I was concentrating on that. Do I like who?'

Jessica laughed. 'T. Rex. My brother Ray is obsessed with them. He spends hours in his bedroom playing their records and he's even started wearing eyeliner like the singer, Marc Bolan. He's in a band himself, with three of his mates. Ray plays the drums and they've done a couple of gigs locally. I went to see them play one night and I was shocked – they were actually quite good.'

Eddie shrugged. He'd never had much experience with blokes who wore make-up. 'You sure your brother ain't an iron?'

Jessica couldn't stop laughing. 'You must be joking. He's a right lad and he's got a different girl on his arm every week. Raymond's one of life's go-getters. He'll make it big somehow, I just know he will.'

Eddie pulled up outside the pub. 'How old did you say he was?'

'Sixteen. He leaves school this year and my dad wants him to learn a proper trade. Raymond's having none of it, says he wants to be a rock star and he's not interested in doing nothing else.'

Eddie got out of the car and opened the passenger door for Jessica. 'Don't worry about your brother, he's bound to grow out of it. Now, what is madam drinking tonight?'

As Jessica followed Eddie into the pub, she noticed how all heads turned their way. She clocked the whispers and loved the way people fell over themselves to acknowledge and be acknowledged by her handsome man.

'I think I'll have a glass of wine,' she said happily.

'Eddie! Long time no see. Christ, you're looking well. What a lovely surprise to see you. Now, what would you and your beautiful lady like to drink?'

Eddie introduced Jessica to the guv'nor of the pub and left her chatting to him while he sorted out the money he was owed. 'Won't be a sec, babe. Just going to see a man about a dog,' he said, winking at her.

Minutes later he returned with a big grin on his face.

Jessica nudged him, 'Did you get your money?' she whispered.

'Plus interest,' Eddie said laughing.

The Burnell Arms had a band playing and Jessica was happy to stay there. Ever since she'd met Ed, she'd gone off her food, so she didn't fancy a meal. The evening flowed nicely and Jess had a wonderful time. At half-eleven, Eddie turned to her.

'I think I should be getting you home now.'

'Oh, I don't want to go yet. Can't I stay at yours tonight?' Jessica asked.

Eddie shook his head. 'I promised your mum and dad that I'd have you home at a reasonable time. I know you often stay at mine, Jess, but that's when they think you're staying at your mate's. If you stay tonight, they'll know we're at it and I don't want them to get the wrong idea about me.'

Ed thanked the guv'nor, said his goodbyes and led Jess from the pub. She only lived a short distance away and as he pulled up near her house, he noticed her look of disappointment. Pulling her towards him, he kissed her softly.

. 'I'd love to wake up with you tomorrow, more than anything else in the world, but we need to do things properly. I know I haven't said this to you yet, but I'm gonna say it now. I love you, Jessica Smith, and that's why I want you to go home tonight. If we're gonna have a future together, we need your parents to be on our side.'

Jessica looked at him with moo-cow eyes. 'And I love you too. Please Ed, my mum wouldn't care if I stayed round yours and she'd smooth it over with my dad,' she pleaded.

Eddie shook his head. 'It's not your mum, Jess, I know she'd be OK. Look at things from your dad's point of view. He knows I'm thirty, he knows I've been married, he knows I've got kids. If you stay out tonight, he'll be worried sick and I don't want to fuck things up for us. Trust me, I'm a man and I know how they think.'

Unable to tear herself away, Jessica kissed him passionately. Aware of him getting all excited, she put her hand on his erection.

Laughing, he grabbed her hand and moved it away. 'Don't start all that, else you'll never get home. Seriously now, come on, be a good girl. I'll pick you up tomorrow, OK?'

Jessica opened the car door. 'Pick me up lunchtime if you like.'

Eddie shook his head. 'I've got a bit of business to attend to. I'll pick you up about six.'

'I love you,' Jess said.

Eddie winked. 'Sweet dreams and I'll see you tomorrow.'

THREE

Floating on air, Jessica let herself into the house. Thankfully, her dad was in bed, but her mum was still sitting up reading a book.

Joyce folded the page and urged Jess to sit next to her. 'I've been dying to know how your evening went. Oh, Jess, I thought he was lovely. Now, tell me everything from the start.'

Jessica's eyes shone. 'I've had such a wonderful evening, Mum. We didn't end up going to the pictures, we went to a pub in East Ham instead. Eddie's so popular, you know. Wherever we go, he has people hanging on his every word. And you'll never guess what, Mum?'

Joyce could barely contain her excitement. 'What? What's happened?'

Jessica giggled. 'He said the L word for the first time. He told me he's in love with me.'

Joyce clapped her hands. 'How did he say it? What were you talking about at the time? Did he say it in the pub?'

Jessica shook her head. 'It was right at the end of the evening. We were outside chatting in the car. I wanted to go back to his flat, but he said no. He said that he promised you and dad that he'd get me home early and then he just said it. "I love you, Jess," he said, and then he stared talking about our future together.'

Joyce clasped her daughter's hands. 'That's marvellous, darling. I'm so excited. I wish I'd seen his car. Why didn't he come round in it earlier?'

'His brother Ronny wanted to borrow it. Eddie's so kind, he said yes straight away.'

Joyce smiled. 'I've never been in a Mercedes. Do you think you and him could take me out for a ride in it one day?'

'Of course. I'll ask him tomorrow,' Jess replied.

'So what happens now? Do you think he might propose?' Joyce asked.

Jessica shrugged. 'Hopefully, soon he might. I'd definitely say yes if he did.'

Joyce studied her beautiful daughter. She was no longer a little girl. She was all grown up. Joyce held both of her hands. 'Let me give you some advice, darling. True love is extremely hard to find, I should know. So if you're lucky enough to have found it, make sure you hang on to it. I mean, Eddie's thirty, isn't he? And when a man's been married, he's obviously used to a sexual relationship. Don't let him get away, Jess, you do what you've got to do to keep him happy.'

Embarrassed, Jessica stood up. She was close to her mum, but wasn't used to discussing her sex life with her. 'I'm tired now, Mum, I'm gonna go to bed. I understand what you're saying and don't worry, I won't let him get away.'

As Jessica left the room, Joyce couldn't stop smiling. She couldn't wait to tell all of her friends at her dressmaking class. None of their daughters had captured a bloke half as good as Eddie, and she couldn't wait to brag about her daughter's rich, handsome boyfriend.

* * *

27

After a restless night, Eddie got up early and sorted out a meet with his father. Two o'clock at his aunt's house was the arrangement. His Auntie Joan lived locally in Whitechapel and she allowed them to hold all their urgent meetings upstairs in her house.

His Auntie Joan had all but brought him and his brothers up, and Eddie was still very close to her. His mum had died when he was five years old. Ed could just about picture her face and he remembered her giving him lots of cuddles. The only other memory he had was of her coughing continuously and spitting blood into a bucket. One day he'd gone off to school and when he returned, she was gone.

He was too young to understand what was happening at the time, but he found out years later that she had been taken to a sanatorium and had later died there. Apparently, she'd contracted tuberculosis, better known as TB, and it was that, and pneumonia, that had killed her.

Harry, his dad, had never remarried. His house was still a shrine to the woman he had lost and he spent hours tending her grave. He visited a woman called Sylvie and sometimes took her out, but he refused to get too close. 'Your mother was the kindest, most beautiful woman in the world. No other woman will ever hold a candle to her,' he repeatedly told Eddie.

Eddie looked at his watch. His stomach was rumbling and he needed a nice cooked breakfast to start his brain functioning properly. He opened Ronny's bedroom door.

'Wakey, wakey. You getting up today, or what?'

'What's the time?' Ronny mumbled.

'Ten o'clock. I've arranged a meet with dad for two. I wanna go to the café first, then we'd best pop our heads in the Flag, see if them bastards did any damage last night, before we meet the others.'

Ronny propped himself up and squinted at Eddie through one eye. 'Sorry if I was a bit out of order last night. Jess is a top girl and I really do want you to be happy.'

Eddie smiled. 'Forget it. Now get your fucking arse in gear, I'm starving.'

A full English fry-up was followed by the trip to their local. As Eddie walked in, he was relieved to see that the pub still looked intact. John, the guv'nor, was out, so he got the lowdown off Betsy, the barmaid.

'They never touched the bar area, but the sinks in the gents were pulled off the wall. Dirty, foul-mouthed bastards they were. You should have heard the things they were saying to Kim, the pretty new barmaid. She burst into tears in the end and I had to send her home.'

Eddie ordered himself and Ronny a drink. 'Did they cause agg with any of the regulars?' he asked.

Betsy shook her head. 'All the regulars left soon after they arrived. They were so bloody loud, no one could hear themselves think.'

Eddie told Betsy to keep the change and thanked her for the information. 'Tell John I'll pop back and see him tomorrow. And if anyone comes in asking for protection money, tell him not to pay it.'

'You don't think they'll come back, do you?' Betsy asked. 'Only, I'm in here on me own till tonight.'

'I doubt it. We'll have to pay 'em a little visit, let 'em know they're not welcome.'

Betsy smiled. She loved Eddie Mitchell: he was handsome, had a real presence about him and she wished she was twenty years younger.

Eddie and Ronny left the Flag and drove straight over to Whitechapel.

*   *   *

29

Auntie Joan let them in and gave them both a big hug. 'Your father, brothers and Uncle Reg are already upstairs. You go on up and I'll bring you up some tea and sandwiches.'

Eddie got straight down to business. His dad, Uncle Reg and brothers sat quietly as the story of the O'Haras unfolded. No one said a word until he'd finished, then Ronny was the first to speak.

'They're obviously trying it on on our turf again. I bet they go round all our boozers and start demanding protection money. I think we should go in the Chobham with shooters. Can you imagine their faces if the five of us walked in armed?'

Harry Mitchell looked at Ronny as though he'd just crawled out from under a stone. 'Shut up, you idiot. The Chobham's their fucking headquarters, they'll have so many witnesses backing 'em up, we'll be nicked within an hour.'

Ronny felt his face redden. His dad had a wonderful way of putting him down and treating him like an imbecile in front of the rest of the family. He never did that to Eddie. Whenever he came out with an idea, his old man listened intently.

'All right to come in, boys?'

Harry jumped up and answered the door to Joan.

'That plate is ham and the other one's salmon. I baked you some rock cakes and there's more downstairs if you want them.'

Harry smiled as he took the trays off Joan. When his beautiful wife had been so cruelly taken from him, her sister had taken over from where she'd left off. She'd cooked, cleaned, washed, ironed and even taken care of the boys for him. Harry had never forgotten her kindness and had seen her all right over the years. When her husband, Alf, had run off with another woman, Harry had had him kneecapped and paid up her mortgage for her. Alf was now confined to a wheelchair, lived alone and was unable to walk, let alone run, the fucking arsehole.

As Harry munched away on a ham sandwich, he came to a decision. He'd leave the boys out of this one and sort it out himself. Butch O'Hara had shaken hands with him and called a truce, which had now been broken. Therefore, it should be Butch that was made to pay.

Pouring himself a cup of sugary, strong tea, Harry sipped it in almost a ladylike fashion and then wiped his mouth with a serviette.

'Right, I've come to a decision,' he said.

As always, the table fell silent as the head of the family spoke. 'I don't want yous boys involved in this one. I had a deal with Butch and it'll be him that pays.'

Paulie was the first to speak. 'You can't do it alone, Dad. His sons are always with him, you'll need back-up.'

'You're not a teenager any more,' Ronny told his father.

Harry thumped his fist on the table. 'I'm fifty-five, not fucking ninety. Now, I want you all to take note of what I'm saying. I am sorting this one out alone and if any of yous starts your own war with Jimmy O'Hara or any of the others behind my back, you'll have me to answer to.'

No one argued. When Harry Mitchell gave out orders, he was always obeyed.

'How you gonna collar Butch on his own?' Eddie asked.

Harry smiled. 'Every Wednesday morning Butch travels alone up to Southhall horse market. It's his only day away from the boys. The horsebox he goes in isn't kept on the site, he keeps it in a lock-up around the corner. He leaves really early, about half-five and I'm gonna wait for him at the lock-up.'

31

Reg nodded. He loved the idea. 'What you gonna do? Frighten him or finish him off?'

Harry shrugged. 'I dunno. Butch is probably totally unaware that his boys have been performing on our territory. I might just shoot him in the foot, give him a little warning. Mind you, if we have any repercussions, I'll blow his fucking brains out.'

'Why don't you just blow his brains out anyway?' Ronny said, laughing.

Harry ignored his idiotic son. 'Oh, one more thing before we go. I'm gonna need a driver to come with me. You up for it, Eddie?'

'Sure, Dad. When do you wanna do it, this Wednesday coming?'

Harry pondered momentarily. 'I think we'll leave it till the following week. They might be waiting for repercussions and we want them to enjoy a nice little surprise.'

Ronny glanced at Paulie. Neither said anything, but both were thinking the same thing. At thirty-six, Paul was the oldest. Ronny was thirty-three, yet Eddie, the youngest, was the golden fucking boy.

Reg clocked Ronny's annoyance and looked away. He was Harry's younger brother and had always been in his shadow, yet it had never bothered him. He didn't mind Paulie, he was OK, but Ronny was a moron and Reg made a mental note to keep a close eye on him. For months, he'd noticed him becoming more and more jealous of Eddie and it wasn't on – they were brothers, for fuck's sake.

With the meeting over, everybody said their goodbyes and went their separate ways.

Joyce glanced at the clock and opened the oven door. She tested the knife in her fruit cake and, happy it was properly cooked, put it on the kitchen top to cool down. Eddie was due to pick her daughter up soon, and she'd baked it especially for him.

Sitting in his armchair, Stanley was unable to concentrate on *Hawaii Five-O*. Usually, he was glued to anything Steve McGarrett did, but today the only thing he could concentrate on was that smarmy bastard who would shortly be picking his daughter up.

Stanley hadn't been able to sleep properly the previous night and, when he had dozed off, he'd had nightmares about Harry Mitchell. He'd dreamt that Mitchell had taken out his eye instead of Roger Dodds'.

His nightmare had only come to an end when Joyce punched him in the side of the head. 'What you screaming out and fidgeting for? You silly old bastard,' she'd said.

Stan had ignored her and gone downstairs to make himself a cup of tea. He'd sat up the rest of the night, frightened to go back to sleep in case his nightmare returned.

Joyce heard her daughter coming down the stairs and yelled out to her to come into the kitchen.

'Well, how do I look?' Jessica asked.

Joyce stared at her. She was wearing a flowery top, white plastic boots and sexy yellow hotpants.

'You look sensational. Where did you get your shorts?' she asked.

Jess giggled. 'They're not called shorts, Mum, they're hotpants. They were only cheap, I got 'em down Petticoat Lane.'

'What time's Eddie picking you up? Where's he taking you tonight?' Joyce asked excitedly.

'He's picking me up at six, I'm not sure where we're going yet.'

Joyce smiled and pointed to the fruit cake. 'I made that for your Eddie. Are you gonna invite him in?'

33

'I wasn't planning to.'

Noticing her mum's disappointment, Jessica immediately changed her tune. 'I'm sure he'll have time to come in for a quick cup of tea,' she said.

Joyce urged Jessica to shut the kitchen door. Last night, she'd been so excited about her daughter's romance, she could barely sleep. She had thought of an idea and she really didn't want Stanley earwigging.

'What's the matter?' Jessica asked.

'You know what we were talking about last night? About you making sure you don't let go of Ed.'

Jessica nodded.

Moving nearer, Joyce continued. 'Why don't you trap him? You know, get pregnant on purpose. I mean, let's face it, Jess, blokes like him don't come along every day and I'm sure if you were carrying his child, he'd propose.'

Jessica looked at her mother in horror. She wanted Eddie to propose to her because he loved her, not because she had a bun in the oven. They'd done it twice without a rubber, but only because Ed had run out, and she had no intention of trapping him. She was about to tell her mum to mind her own bloody business when the doorbell rang.

'Quick, don't keep him waiting,' Joyce said.

'Don't you dare say anything about babies and stuff in front of him, Mum.'

Joyce pushed her towards the front door. 'Of course not, dear.'

Stanley felt himself flinch as Eddie walked towards him.

'Good evening, Mr Smith,' Eddie said, holding out his hand.

As Jessica stepped out from behind him, Stan glared

34

at her. 'Surely you're not going out like that? You've got no bloody clothes on.'

Jessica raised her eyebrows. She didn't know who she liked the least. Her domineering mother, who was always trying to run her life for her, or her old-fashioned father, who still thought she was twelve years old.

'It's the fashion, Dad. All the girls are wearing hotpants.'

'Well, I've never bloody well seen anyone wearing them.'

'That's probably because you spend half your life in the betting shop. No one's gonna be wearing them in there, are they?' Joyce shouted at him.

Desperate to get away from her warring parents, Jessica grabbed Eddie's arm. 'Come on, let's go,' she said.

Eddie let her lead him out of the living room. 'Nice to meet you both again,' he said politely.

'Hang on a minute,' Joyce shouted.

Seconds later she presented Eddie with an object wrapped in tin foil. 'That fruit cake you liked, I baked you one,' she said proudly.

Eddie pecked her on the cheek. 'You're a star, Joyce. I'll have that for me supper.'

Jessica felt relief wash over her as Eddie drove away from the house.

'What's up, babe?' he asked her.

Jessica sighed. 'Just parent trouble. They're always arguing and they make me feel like piggy in the middle. Both of them drive me mad and I don't know what to do about it.'

Eddie laughed. 'I know exactly what you can do about it.'

'What?' Jessica enquired.

Swinging the car onto a nearby kerb, Eddie got out,

35

walked round the other side and opened the passenger door. As he knelt on one knee, Jessica looked at him in amazement.

'What you doing?'

Eddie held both her hands and smiled. 'Jessica Smith, marry me?'

FOUR

Jessica immediately accepted her boyfriend's marriage proposal, but at Eddie's insistence, she said nothing to either of her parents.

'I'm a big believer in doing things properly, Jess. Keep schtum for now and next weekend I'll come round your house and ask for your parents' blessing. I'm a very traditional geezer at heart and I'm sure your dad would expect me to ask his permission.'

Jess loved Eddie's morals, but with her head in the clouds, she was desperate for the world to know of her good fortune. 'Can't I just tell my mum, Ed? It will be so hard keeping it from her and I know she won't say anything to my dad.'

Eddie shook his head. 'No, it's not right, Jess. We'll tell them together and then I'll take you shopping for a ring. I'll take you up Hatton Garden and you can pick whatever you want.'

How Jessica kept her mouth shut that week, she would never know. She didn't tell a soul, not even the girls at work. The following Saturday, she could barely contain her excitement and was out of bed before the birds had even started singing. She was unable to eat any breakfast, but made her parents boiled eggs, toast and tea and took it into their bedroom.

'What's all this in aid of?' her mother said, as she handed her the tray.

Jessica smiled. 'Eddie's coming round at twelve and I need you both to be here.'

Stanley sat up and eyed his daughter suspiciously. 'What's going on, Jessica?'

'Nothing untoward, Dad. Ed just wants to speak to you both, that's all.'

Hearing her brother moving about, Jessica swiftly left her parents' room and knocked on Raymond's door.

'Enter,' he shouted.

Jessica sat on his bed while he got himself ready. Raymond was a vain little sod and took longer to get his hair looking right than she did.

'What you up to today?' she asked him.

'I've got band practice, then I'm taking some bird out tonight.'

'Anyone I know?' Jessica asked him.

Raymond laughed and shook his head. He had a different girl on his arm every week and it was a standing joke between him and Jessica.

'What you up to then, sis?'

Jessica smiled. 'Eddie's coming round at twelve and then he's taking me shopping. I wanted you to meet him, Ray. Can't you hang about and say a quick hello to him, then go out after?'

Raymond checked his appearance in the full-length mirror. 'Sorry Jess, no can do. I'm meeting the boys at half-ten and they can't exactly practise without their drummer.'

Jessica stood up and gave her younger brother a hug. 'You have a good day and I want you to promise me that you'll make time to have a drink with me and Ed soon.'

Raymond wriggled out of her arms and checked his

shirt for creases. 'I promise. Why are you being all soppy and emotional?'

Jessica giggled. 'You'll find out later.'

As the clock struck twelve, Stanley sat fidgeting in his armchair. He'd arranged to meet his mate Jock in the pub at one and he was sick of this poxy Eddie messing up his Saturdays.

'I'll give him till half-twelve and if he ain't here, I'm off out,' he mumbled.

'You will do no such thing. You'll go out when I say you can go out,' Joyce told him.

Stan looked at the telly and said nothing. Ever since Jess had said that Eddie wanted to see them, his stomach had been in knots. Stan had a feeling that Mr Fucking Charming Bollocks wanted to take his daughter away on holiday and, if that was the case, he'd be far from happy about it.

Hearing a car engine, Joyce jumped out of her chair and lifted the curtain. She'd been bubbling with excitement all morning and was dying to know what Eddie needed to see them for. With a bit of luck he wanted to ask their permission to marry Jess.

'Here he is,' Joyce said, as the posh gold Mercedes pulled up.

Eddie picked up the bouquet and bottle of Chivas Regal he'd bought, and strolled up the path.

'How lovely to see you again, Joyce,' he said, handing her the flowers.

'Awww, you shouldn't have, they're beautiful. Let me put them in a vase.'

Eddie gave Jessica a lingering kiss and then followed her into the living room.

'Jess said you liked a drop of Scotch,' he said, handing Stan the bottle.

'Thanks,' Stan said ungratefully. If Eddie had turned up bearing solid gold bars, he still wouldn't like the bastard.

'Go and keep your mum company while I have a little chat with your dad,' Eddie told his girlfriend.

Jess gave his hand a good-luck squeeze and left the room.

Not one to go round the houses, Eddie came straight to the point. 'I have fallen head over heels for your Jessica, Mr Smith. She means the world to me and I would like to ask for her hand in marriage.'

Stanley felt every hair on his body stand up on end. Aware of his heart racing and his hands shaking, he urged Eddie to pour him a drink. Aware that Stan had turned a whiter shade of pale, Eddie was quite concerned.

'You don't look very well. Are you OK?' he asked, as he handed him a large Scotch.

Stanley downed the drink in one and immediately asked for a refill.

Desperate for an answer from the shivering wreck of a man, Eddie continued talking. 'Look, I know how you must feel and I know Jessica is still very young. But, I promise you, Mr Smith, you have my word that I will cherish and take good care of her.'

Unable to think of anything nice to say, Stanley grabbed the bottle of Chivas Regal and poured himself yet another.

'It's not up to me. Go and ask her mother,' Stanley muttered.

Eddie stood up and walked into the kitchen. 'Go and see your dad, Jess, I need to have a chat with your mum.'

Joyce smiled as he closed the kitchen door. 'Would you like some fruit cake?' she asked.

Eddie shook his head and cut straight to the chase. 'I am totally in love with your Jessica and I want to marry her. I've had a little chat with your husband and he said it's up to you, Joyce. I know she's very young, but I promise you with all my heart that I'll take good care of her.'

To say Joyce was over the moon was putting it mildly. Unable to stop herself, she flung her arms around Eddie's neck.

'I am so happy,' she sobbed. 'Welcome to the family, Eddie. My Jessica is a very lucky girl and I'd be proud to call you my son-in-law.'

Eddie smiled. 'I've got a bottle of champagne in the car. I'll bring it in and we can have a toast.'

Joyce sorted out her best crystal glasses and took four into the living room. She hugged Jessica. 'Congratulations, darling. Eddie's a wonderful man – you've bagged yourself a good one there.'

Noticing Stanley had a face like a smacked arse, Joyce kicked his leg. 'For Christ's sake cheer up, you miserable old bastard.'

Stanley said nothing as he was handed a glass of champagne.

Eddie kissed Jessica gently on the forehead. 'I'm taking Jess to Hatton Garden to choose a ring this afternoon. She can have the biggest diamond in the shop.'

Joyce couldn't wipe the smile off her face. The only rock Stan had ever bought her was a poxy old topaz. 'You'll have to pop back and show me your ring,' she said to Jess.

'I'll show you tomorrow. Now we're engaged to be married, you don't mind if I stay round Ed's tonight, do you, Mum? We want to go out for a meal to celebrate and we won't be back till late.'

Joyce nodded. 'That's fine by me, love.'

Stanley looked at his wife in disgust. His daughter

wasn't even married yet and Joyce was encouraging her to hawk her mutton.

'To my beautiful wife-to-be,' Eddie said, holding his glass aloft.

'To Jessica and Eddie,' Joycie crowed.

Stan looked at the clock. It was nearly half-past one and he was late to meet Jock. Desperate to get away from the man who had led his daughter astray, he stood up. 'I'm going out now.'

'You can't go out yet. We're in the middle of a celebration,' Joyce said angrily.

Eddie decided to stick up for his future father-in-law. 'It's fine, Joyce. To be honest, me and Jess need to make a move now ourselves. I'll drop you at the pub, Stan, if you like?'

Stanley shook his head. He'd rather crawl there on all fours than get inside Eddie's car.

Joyce tutted as her husband slunk away and then hugged both Jessica and Eddie. 'Have a nice evening and if you can't be good, be careful,' she giggled.

Feeling herself going red, Jessica dragged Eddie out of the front door. 'My mum is just so embarrassing at times,' she moaned to her fiancé.

Eddie waved at Joyce as they drove away. The old girl would jump in the river if he asked her to, but he'd have to work a bit harder if he was to win over the old man.

A few days after his engagement to Jessica, Eddie picked his father up at four o'clock in the morning. Butch wasn't expected to pick up the horsebox till around half-five, but his dad was keen to get there well before his intended victim.

Harry got into the car with a sports bag in his hand. 'What's in there?' Eddie asked him.

'Bolt-cutters. There's a yard bang opposite where Butch keeps the box. We'll cut the lock off and hide in there.'

'We're a bit early, ain't we?' Ed said.

'Do a right here, son. We're not going in your motor, we'll pick up the old Bedford van. It's still registered to some cunt in Luton, so worst ways we can burn it out if we need to.'

Eddie followed his father's directions and they swapped motors. Driving towards Stratford, Eddie told him about Jessica. 'I proposed to her at the weekend, Dad. I dunno when we'll get married yet, but I bought her a nice engagement ring. You'll have to meet her soon. She's a right little cracker and I know you'll like her.'

Harry patted his favourite son on the shoulder. 'I'm pleased for you, boy, I really am. I knew straight away that your mother was the one. She was a right little cracker as well.'

Thinking about his beautiful dead wife plunged Harry into silence and he didn't utter another word throughout the rest of the journey.

'Left here,' Harry said, snapping out of his trance. 'Pull up over there. That yard's the one we're gonna hide in, the one with all the graffiti.'

Checking that no one was about, Eddie opened the driver's door. 'What we gonna do if the people turn up and we're in their yard?'

Harry laughed. 'The yard belongs to Terry O'Donnell. He ain't used it for years and he owes me more than a few favours anyway.'

Taking the bolt-cutters out of the bag, Harry handed Eddie a pair of leather gloves and put on a pair himself. 'Put on the gloves and cut the chain, son. I've got another chain and lock in the bag to replace it with when we're done. I'd love to see Terry O'Donnell's face if he can't get in to his own yard. I'll send him the new key in the post.'

As Eddie opened the gate he came face to face with a massive rat. 'Fuck that! It frightened the fucking life out of me,' he said, as the rat scuttled away.

Harry laughed. 'Shut up, you big pansy.'

'What we gonna do with the van?' Eddie asked.

'Put it in here,' Harry said. 'I'll run across and, once I've shot the cunt, we can drive straight off.'

Eddie parked the van inside, then closed the gates. He stuck his hand through the large gap and loosely laid the broken chain back through the lock.

Harry sat down on an old tin drum. 'I had a drive down here earlier this week. There's no one about this time in the morning. As soon as we hear Butch pull up, I'll creep out and do him as soon as he opens his yard. When you hear the gun go off, start the van and pull out. Lock up the yard for us, then we're away.'

Eddie nodded. He was freezing his bollocks off and wished he'd put on warmer clothes.

The men sat in silence while they waited. Finally, at 5.23, they heard a diesel engine pull up outside. Harry peeped through the gate to check it was Butch. He waited until Butch opened the gates and went inside his yard, then he gently lifted the loose chain, crept out and followed him in.

Butch was just about to climb into his horsebox when he saw Harry Mitchell staring at him with a gun in his hand.

'What the fuck! What's going on, mush?'

Harry shook his head. 'I warned you, Butch, we had a deal. Your boys have taken a fucking liberty, yet again.'

Butch could feel himself shaking. 'What are me boys meant to have done?'

44

'Performed in the Flag the other night, they did. Smashed the bogs up, terrorised the bar staff. The Flag is our territory, you know it is, Butch. Your boys have no manners and I'm not putting up with it any more.'

'I didn't know, Harry. I'm sorry, I'll talk to 'em, I'll sort it.'

Harry smiled as he lifted the gun. 'It's a bit late for that. I warned you about all this once before.'

'Please, no, don't kill me,' Butch said, as he fell to the ground.

Harry moved deftly towards him. Butch had gone down before he'd even fucking shot him, the coward. Harry grabbed hold of the petrified man's right leg.

'No, please, no,' Butch begged.

Harry Mitchell ignored his pleas, pulled back the trigger and blasted him in the right foot. 'Take that as a warning, Butch. If I was you, I'd advise your family to move their caravans to a different fucking area.'

As blood poured from his foot, Butch was aware of shit running down his legs. He was in too much pain to speak any more; instead he just covered his head with his hands.

Harry walked away. 'Next time, I'll blow your brains out,' he said menacingly.

Eddie replaced the lock and jumped back in the van. 'Everything go OK?' he asked, as his father got into the passenger's side.

'All sorted, son. Now, I don't know about you, but I'm bloody well starving. Drop the van off, drive back to Canning Town and we'll have a nice little fry-up in Maureen's Café.'

FIVE

A month after announcing her engagement, Jessica sat nervously in the doctor's surgery, clutching her best friend's hand. Jessica's periods were usually as regular as clockwork; she could never remember it being one day late, let alone two weeks. Taking her friend Mary's advice, Jess had gone to see her doctor the previous week. The receptionist had given her a container for a urine sample, of which she was now awaiting the results.

Anxiously biting her nails, Jessica turned to her friend. 'What am I gonna do if I am? I mean, Eddie's already got two kids and he's never mentioned wanting any more. Say he finishes with me? He might call off the engagement and make me have an abortion.'

Mary put her arm around Jessica. 'You're being silly now. Eddie loves you, so why on earth would he treat you like that? I bet if you are pregnant, he'll be as pleased as Punch.'

About to reply, Jessica froze as her name was called. Mary accompanied her into the surgery and they sat down opposite Dr Hunter.

'I have the results of your test back, Jessica, and I can confirm that you are indeed pregnant.'

Jessica burst into tears. She and Eddie had only done it twice without a rubber.

'I'm too young to be a mum. I won't know what to do,' Jessica cried.

Mary hugged her and spoke to the doctor at the same time. 'I think it's a bit of a shock for Jess. Can we book her another appointment for next week?'

Dr Hunter nodded. In his profession he was used to this reaction. It's a shame these young girls never thought about the consequences before they opened their legs.

Mary thanked the doctor for his time and led Jessica outside. 'You wait here and get some fresh air while I book you another appointment,' she told her.

A trip to a nearby café proved to be a turning point in Jessica's anxiousness and, after three cups of tea, she even managed a smile.

'Me mum'll be pleased, I know that. She's always banging on about having grandchildren one day. As for me poor old dad, he'll probably drop dead with the shock of it all.'

Mary giggled. 'I wish I'd met a nice man like you have, I'd love to be in your position. When are you gonna tell him?'

Jessica took a bite of her bacon sandwich. 'I'm seeing Ed tonight, so I'll tell him then. Keep your fingers crossed, eh?'

Mary squeezed her hand. 'Everything'll be fine, I just know it will.'

Eddie counted the takings for the second time. Satisfied that they were spot-on, he placed the money in a carrier bag and stuffed it in his jacket pocket. Although his family owned salvage yards, most of their money came from pub protection. They tried not to hit on their own doorstep too much, and concentrated more on the surrounding areas. Everybody, including the O'Haras, thought that John, the

47

guv'nor in the Flag, paid them protection, but that wasn't the case. John was their mate, he looked after them and vice versa.

Eddie turned the radio on as he made himself a sandwich. He hated silence, it gave him the heebies. Hearing the croaky voice of Rod Stewart, he cranked up the volume. He loved that song, 'Maggie May'. It was all about a young boy having an affair with an older woman. Eddie thought back to his colourful past. He'd been in that position many a time in his youth, so much so that the song could have been written especially for him.

Smirking, Ed flopped onto the sofa and was just about to tuck into his doorstep special when the phone rang. 'Fucking nuisance,' he muttered, as he ran to the hallway to answer it.

'All right, Dad? What you up to?'

'I'm just leaving home. Have I got some news for you, Eddie, my boy. Meet me in the Flag, I'll be there in half an hour.'

Eddie could tell by his father's voice that whatever news he had was bloody good.

'Don't keep me waiting. Tell us now.'

Harry Mitchell laughed. 'No way. I need to see the expression on your face when I tell you. Be patient and move your arse.'

Eddie shook his head as he replaced the receiver. He was a funny bastard, his father, a proper fucking character.

Jessica had a bath, dried her hair and sat on the bed in her dressing gown. She was dreading telling her parents the news, but the quicker she told them the better. Her mum should be OK; it was her dad she was worried about. Jessica wasn't very good at lying.

48

'What's the matter with you?' her mum asked her earlier.

'Nothing,' Jessica lied. Her dad wasn't at home and she'd rather kill two birds with one stone than tell them separately.

Hearing the front door slam shut, Jessica chucked on some clothes and wandered downstairs.

'Any chance of a quick word with both of you?' she asked sheepishly.

Joyce and Stanley followed her into the living room.

'Sit down,' Jessica urged.

Stan said a silent prayer. Something was wrong and with a bit of luck Mr Fucking Charming Bollocks had kicked her into touch.

'What's up, love?' he asked hopefully.

Jessica felt too embarrassed to look them in the eye, so she focused on the carpet.

'Please don't have a go at me, but I found out today that I'm pregnant. I'm really sorry if I've let you both down.'

Joyce hugged her daughter. The timing wasn't perfect but, nevertheless, she was thrilled. She'd always fancied being a young grandma. She could barely wait to get dolled up and go out walking with the pram. As for babysitting, she would look after the child as much as Jess would allow her.

'I'm so pleased for you, darling. Now, don't you worry about being young and not being able to cope. Your old mum will teach you the ropes and I'll be there for you as much as possible. Perhaps Eddie will buy you a house nearby, so I'm always on hand to help out and babysit.'

Stanley sat paralysed in the armchair. He'd had so many high hopes for his beautiful daughter and now she was up the spout by that Mitchell bastard.

'Are you OK, Dad?' Jessica asked him.

Stan nodded and looked the other way. He didn't want her to see the tears in his eyes.

'What about the wedding? Will you bring it forward or get married after the baby's born?' Joyce asked.

Jessica shrugged. 'I'll speak to Eddie tonight. He doesn't even know that I'm pregnant yet. I don't really want a baby out of wedlock, so the sooner we tie the knot, the better. I'd rather do it before I start showing.'

Joyce nodded. She could understand where Jess was coming from. Walking down the aisle with a stomach like a rugby ball never looked good on anyone. She squeezed her daughter's hand.

'Whatever you and Eddie decide, me and your dad are right behind you, aren't we, Stanley?'

Stan said nothing. The quicker he got out of this bleeding nuthouse the better.

'Stanley, what do you think you're doing? Where you going?' Joyce shouted.

Ignoring his wife, Stan put on his checked cap and slammed the front door.

Eddie ordered another drink and glanced at his watch. His bloody father was late and he was doing buttons to know what had happened.

Five minutes later, a beaming Harry Mitchell strolled into the pub.

'Well, what's occurring?' Eddie asked him.

Ushering his son over to an empty corner of the pub, Harry sat opposite him. 'They've gone.'

Eddie shook his head, 'Who you on about? Who's fucking gone?'

Harry started laughing. 'The O'Haras. They've moved away, the whole lot of 'em. They've gone to Essex, by all accounts. Butch sent a message to me yesterday, via Ginger Mick. He told him to tell me that there won't be any repercussions and he wants an end to the feud for good. Ginger Mick said the old cunt was petrified and he can barely fucking walk. Yesterday they went – the site's completely fucking empty. Packed up their stuff and did a moonlight flit, apparently.'

Eddie couldn't stop smiling. He would never have to see Jimmy O'Hara's ugly boat race ever again.

'Bring us over a bottle of champagne, Betsy,' he ordered the barmaid.

Eddie shook his old man's hand. 'You know what this means, don't you? We can take over the Stratford boozers. I can't wait for us to bowl into the Chobham and demand money off that pikey-loving cunt of a guv'nor. I think we should stick the price up in there, charge him more than we charge anyone else.'

Harry laughed. 'My sentiments exactly. Apparently, they had seven boozers in Stratford on their payroll, all told. In the next couple of days we'll pay all of 'em a visit, get our foot in the door.'

Eddie sipped his drink. 'Are you sure that Ginger Mick can be trusted?'

Harry nodded. 'I've had him on me payroll since he was a young 'un. Safe as houses, he is. The O'Haras thought he was their Joey – what they didn't know was that I set it all up. We needed a spy in the camp, and Ginger Mick was perfect.'

Reg, Paulie and Ronny's arrival spelled the start of a glorified piss-up. Champagne corks went flying and there were pats on the back and handshakes all around.

'Come and join us, John,' Harry urged the guv'nor.

Ronny started the singalong and the rest of the lads joined in: 'When the inbred O'Haras go run, run, a-running

51

along, shoot the bastards, shoot the bastards, shoot, shoot, shoot the bastards.'

'What yous lot celebrating? Ain't won the bleedin' football pools, have yer?' Betsy asked, as she brought over yet another two bottles of champagne.

'We're celebrating being the kings of the East End,' Ronny shouted, grabbing her large backside.

'Keep yer dirty fucking hands to yerself, Ronny Mitchell,' Betsy said, laughing.

The raucous behaviour, jokes and songs continued for hours and, three sheets to the wind, Eddie completely lost track of time. 'Shit, I was meant to pick Jess up at seven,' he said, leaping out of his chair.

'Fuck her off, stay out with us tonight,' Ronny said.

'Yeah, let's go to a club and celebrate properly,' Paulie suggested.

Eddie shook his head. He was a gentleman and would never let Jess down at short notice. Realising he was in no fit state to drive, he asked John the guv'nor to call him a cab.

Five minutes later, he heard a bib outside and said his goodbyes.

'All of us will meet in here tomorrow at two o'clock. Then we can pay a nice friendly visit to the Chobham and the rest of them boozers in Stratford,' his father told him.

Eddie jumped into the cab and urged the driver to put his foot down.

Jessica, who had been standing looking out of the window for an hour, felt relief surge through her as Eddie got out of the cab. She ran to the front door.

'There you are.'

Eddie was full of apologies, 'I'm so sorry I'm late, babe. Something cropped up. It won't happen again, I promise.'

'I was so worried, I thought you'd had an accident or something,' Jessica said.

Eddie held her close and stroked her hair. 'I got stuck with some business, you know how it is.'

'Where's your car?' Jessica asked.

Eddie was saved from answering by Joyce's intervention.

'Would you like a beer, Eddie? Or a cup of tea and fruit cake?'

Eddie shook his head. 'The cab's waiting outside. I'm gonna take Jess out for a nice meal. Another time, eh, Joycie?'

Joyce could tell Eddie was a bit drunk, but boys would be boys. Her son Raymond was the same; he was always coming home tipsy.

Joyce winked at Jess and crossed two fingers on both hands. 'Good luck,' she mouthed, as they walked up the path.

Jessica sat in the restaurant and barely touched her food. 'Leave the chips if you like, but eat that fillet steak,' Eddie urged her.

'I'm not hungry,' Jessica said, as she slipped it onto his plate.

Having sobered up a bit, Eddie soon realised that Jess wasn't herself and obviously had something on her mind. He put down his knife and fork and took her hands in his.

'Come on, spit it out, what's a matter, babe? Are you having second thoughts about us getting married or something?'

Jessica shook her head. She just had to say it, there was no other way. 'I went to the doctor's today, Eddie. Please don't have a go at me, but I'm pregnant.'

Eddie's smile was that wide it almost lit up the restaurant. 'Are you sure? Have you had a proper test?'

Jessica nodded. 'The doctor gave me the results today. Look Ed, I'm so sorry. If you want me to get rid –'

Eddie leaned further across the table and kissed her on the lips. 'Get rid of it? Are you mad? Don't you get it, Jess? I love you and we can have as many babies as you want.'

Realising that he was telling the truth, Jessica smiled. 'What about the wedding, though? I'm not walking down the aisle with a bun in the oven, Ed. It will look awful, people will think I'm a tart.'

Eddie laughed. 'You ain't gotta walk down the aisle with a bun in the oven. Look, we'd have had trouble finding a vicar to marry us on the quick 'cause I've already been married. How about I book a register office? We can get married in the next couple of weeks if you want.'

Jessica's eyes shone. 'Really, Ed? Do you mean that?'

'Of course I do. Waiter, bring us over a bottle of champers,' Eddie said loudly.

Aware of all the other diners looking at him, Eddie smiled. He loved being the centre of attention, it was all part of his make-up.

He stood up and addressed the whole restaurant. 'You see this beautiful girl here,' he said, pointing at Jess.

'We, us two, are getting married and we're having a baby. Now, who fancies a glass of champagne to celebrate our happiness with us?'

'I'll have one,' said an old man with a bald head.

'We'll have a drink with you,' said a woman in a spotted dress.

Eddie ordered the waiter to get more bottles of champagne and share them between all the other diners. The restaurant was reasonably empty and, apart from themselves, there were only five other tables taken.

Jessica could feel herself blushing beetroot red. Eddie could be so bloody loud, especially when he'd been drinking.

'Nosy load of bastards. They were all looking at us,' he whispered to Jess.

Winking at her, Eddie carried on where he'd left off. 'Now come on, fucking stand up, I've just bought you all champagne.'

Well aware that he was probably a local villain, everybody leaped to attention. Eddie held his glass aloft.

'To Jessica, the most beautiful girl in the world,' he said.

Wary, but amused at the same time, everybody lifted their glasses.

'To Jessica,' they repeated after him.

Minutes later, Jessica's happiness partly disintegrated.

'I beg your pardon?' she said to Eddie. He was winding her up, he had to be.

'I said, I want you to pack your job up in the morning. Now we're getting married, things are different. I've got money – you don't need to work any more.'

Jessica looked at him in amazement. She liked her independence, enjoyed her little job and she had so many friends there.

'I'm not ready to give it up yet, Ed. I know when I've had the baby, I'll have to, but that's ages away yet.'

Eddie held her hands and gazed deep into her eyes. 'Look, if we're gonna get wed, you've got to get your priorities right. I mean what's more important, a poxy job in a shoe shop, or us and our baby's future? Marriage is all about give and take, Jess, and if you can't do this one little thing for me, then maybe you're not ready for such a big commitment.'

Jessica bit her lip. She had just found the man of her dreams and she couldn't lose him over something so trivial. She squeezed his hand.

'You're so right, Ed. I mean, I'd have to give it up in a few months anyway, so I might as well do it now. I'll ring them first thing tomorrow, to tell them that I'm leaving.'

Eddie smiled. 'That's my girl. You know it makes sense.'

Joyce and Stanley were watching a late-night film when Jessica arrived home. 'Did you have a nice evening? How did Eddie react to the news?' Joyce asked excitedly.

'Oh, Ed was thrilled. He said we can have as many babies as I want,' Jess said happily. 'And I'm giving my job up. I'm gonna ring the shop tomorrow to tell them I won't be coming back.'

Stanley looked at his daughter in astonishment. 'You can't give up your job. I thought you liked working in the shoe shop.'

Jessica shrugged. 'Eddie said that I don't need to work any more. He said he'll look after me and the baby from now on.'

Aware that her dad was anything but happy, Jessica looked away from him. 'I'll make us all a nice cup of tea,' she said, as she swiftly left the room.

Stanley glared at Joyce. 'She loves that bloody job. That bastard's trying to manipulate her already. It ain't right, Joycie. Next thing you know, he'll have her shut in a fucking cupboard. These villains have different principles to the likes of me and you. They keep their women under lock and key, and we've got to put a stop to it before it's too late.'

Joyce threw her husband a look of contempt. 'Don't you dare spoil our daughter's happiness. If Eddie wants to support Jess, then good for her. I wish I hadn't had to work when I was pregnant. Do you know how hard it was for me, dragging myself to that bloody office every day? I had no choice, we couldn't survive on your measly wages. You leave our Jess alone and keep your idiotic opinions to yourself, Stanley. Unlike me, she's found a rich man, a good 'un.'

About to answer his wife back, Stanley was stopped from doing so by Jessica's reappearance. 'Thanks, love,' he said, as she handed him his cuppa.

Jessica sat down next to her mum. She had one more bombshell to drop and she knew her dad wasn't going to be happy. 'Oh, by the way, Eddie and I have decided to get married in a couple of weeks' time. We're not gonna bother with a church do, we've decided on a register office.'

As the horror of the situation hit Stanley, he spilt half of the contents of his favourite mug over his leg. 'Bollocks!' he yelled, as the hot tea scalded him.

'Silly old goat,' Joyce whispered.

Jessica felt sorry for her dad. She knew it had always been his dream to one day walk her down the aisle. 'Are you OK, Dad?' she asked kindly.

Stanley said nothing as he dabbed his trousers with his handkerchief. Whatever he said would make no difference, so what was the bloody point? Both his wife and daughter thought the sun shone out of Eddie Mitchell's arse. With a sense of foreboding, Stanley said goodnight, left the room and trudged dejectedly up the stairs.

He was sure that the day would come when his wife and daughter would wish they had listened to him. Until that day came, Stanley had little choice other than to smile, be polite and keep schtum.

SIX

Joyce gasped in admiration as Jessica walked through the door.

'You look just like a model – so, so pretty. I am so proud of you, Jess, I really am.'

Not wanting her mother and father's arguments spoiling her big day, Jessica had opted to get ready over the road. Her friends, Ginny and Linda, lived next door to one another. Both worked as hairdressers and they had kindly offered to do her hair and make-up for free.

Noticing Jessica's hands shaking, her best friend, Mary, handed her a glass of wine. 'Your hair looks fabulous at the back. Whose idea was it to put those beads in it?'

Jessica smiled. 'It was Eddie's, actually. We saw a girl wearing white beads in her hair in a pub last week and Eddie said they'd look great for my wedding day. He likes me to wear my hair up.'

Jessica only had one set of grandparents still alive. Her dad's parents had both died in the last few years, but her mum's parents had recently retired to Norfolk. Her nan smiled at her. 'Beautiful dress, darling. Where did you get it from? Must have cost a fortune with that crochet and crystal trim.'

Jessica carefully sat down and took a sip of her wine. 'A shop in Knightsbridge. Eddie sent me there; his friend owns the place and I was allowed to choose whatever I wanted. Ed told me not to worry about the price, he wouldn't even let the man tell me how much it cost.'

Nanny Ivy pursed her lips. 'Sounds too good to be true, this Eddie,' she said curtly.

Joyce scowled at her mother. She saw very little of her parents, which suited Joyce just fine. They hadn't seen eye to eye for years and Joyce would never forgive her mum for forcing her to marry Stanley.

'No, he's not too good to be true, mother. He's a respectable gentleman, a lovely chap. In fact, he's the total opposite of what you made me end up with.'

Ivy knew when to shut up. There was nothing what-soever wrong with Stanley. Joyce had always had a high opinion of herself. Acted like Lady Dunabunk, she did, full of her own self-importance.

'Where is everybody?' Jessica asked.

Joyce looked at the clock and felt the first stirrings of annoyance. She'd been so wrapped up talking about the wedding, she'd forgotten Stanley had been due back ages ago.

'Christ knows where your father's got to. He was ready at ten o'clock this morning, had a bath and put his suit straight on, he did. Then he dragged your grandad and Raymond down the bookie's, said they'd only be half-hour. If he's in that pub, getting half-sozzled, I'll bleedin' well kill the bastard.'

Jessica felt her heart beating at double its usual pace. She was already nervous about the day ahead and the last thing she needed was her parents at one another's throats. Please God, not today, she prayed silently.

*   *   *

Stanley Smith stood in the betting shop and watched in dismay as trap six came stone bollock last.

'Stupid fucking mutt, wants putting down,' he cursed, as he made the short walk back to his local. 'Give us another three bitters, three whisky chasers, and a lager for Raymond,' he told Anna, the barmaid.

Anna smiled. 'You're going for it today, Stanley. Who's that older man you're with? And why are yous all dressed up?'

Not in the mood for polite conversation, Stanley mumbled the words, 'Father-in-law, going to a wedding,' and walked away.

Stanley was dreading the day ahead of him. The thought of handing his beautiful daughter over to a bastard like Eddie Mitchell filled him with hatred and anger.

'What's the time, Stan? Hadn't we better be getting back soon?' asked Bill, his father-in-law.

'Mum'll have her broom out if you're late,' Raymond joked.

'It's OK, we've got time to drink these,' Stan replied confidently.

Jock, Stan's best mate, necked his whisky chaser and smiled. 'Well, did you have any luck with that dog you had the tip on?'

Stanley shook his head. 'I think the bastard mutt's still running. My luck's fucked at the moment, in every way you could think of.'

Seconds later, Stanley's luck got even worse as he spotted an angry-looking Joyce stomping into the pub. 'Shit, tell her I've already left,' he said, as he threw himself under the table.

Knowing her husband's cowardly behaviour of old, Joyce crouched down and immediately found him. 'Stanley, get up from under that table and get your arse home this minute!' she screamed.

Aware of the whole of the pub laughing at him, Stanley crawled out like a naughty schoolboy.

'I'm sorry, Joycie. Me, Ray and Bill lost track of time. We were just gonna –'

Joyce lifted her umbrella and repeatedly whacked him on the backside. 'Home, Stanley, now, and I mean now.'

With Joyce and her brolly on his tail, Stanley ran out of the pub, twice as fast as the mutt he'd lost his money on.

Eddie stood in Barking register office and glanced at his watch.

'Don't worry, she will be here,' his brother Ronny assured him.

Eddie smiled. Paulie had been his best man at his first wedding to Bev, so he'd felt it only right to even things up by asking Ronny this time round.

Ronny had been thrilled to be asked. He'd hugged him, with tears in his eyes. 'I'd be honoured, bruv, fucking honoured.'

Eddie wiped the palms of his hands on his smart grey suit. 'Get someone to open that door, I'm sweating me cobs off in here,' he ordered Ronny.

'She's arrived. They're here,' somebody shouted.

Eddie took a deep breath as Jessica walked towards him. Smiling, he squeezed her hand. 'You look beautiful, really beautiful.'

The vows might have been short and sweet, but they were filled with emotion and spoken with meaning.

Eddie slipped the ring on Jessica's finger and kissed her tenderly. 'I love you, Mrs Mitchell,' he whispered.

*   *   *

With little time to organise the big event, Eddie had chosen a restaurant in Canning Town for a slap-up meal, followed by a knees-up back at his local pub. He'd booked a disco and had told John, the guv'nor, to serve free drinks all night. He hadn't invited too many people. Including Jessica's family and friends, there were about fifty at the wedding and meal, and another fifty or so invited to the reception at the boozer.

'I can't believe my best mate's married,' Mary said, smiling.

'You look so pretty, Jess,' Linda said.

'Beautiful,' Ginny agreed.

'Congratulations, darling,' Joyce said, hugging her daughter.

'I like Ed, he's a top bloke, sis,' Raymond said, kissing her.

Stanley felt his eyes water as he watched his daughter and Eddie gaze into one another's eyes. It would all end in tears, he just knew it would.

His mother-in-law felt the same way. 'I don't like him. Surely our Joyce must realise they're a family of villains? You've only got to look at them to see what they are.'

Stanley gave a defeated shrug. 'You know what Joycie's like, once she gets a bee in her bonnet. I never liked the flash bastard from day one, but as usual, my opinion counts for nothing in our house. I tried to tell Joycie, but she can't see the wood for the trees.'

Noticing her father's dismal expression, Jessica walked over and hugged him. 'I know you've got your doubts, Dad, but trust me, I love Eddie and I know what I'm doing.'

Stanley took a handkerchief out of his pocket and dabbed his eyes. 'I hope you're right, darling, for your sake I do.'

Covered in confetti, Jessica and Eddie posed for numerous photographs.

'Now all immediate family stand together,' the photographer shouted.

As the camera flashed, both families smiled – well, apart from Ivy and Stan, that was. Stanley flinched as he spotted Harry Mitchell glance his way. Please God, don't let him recognise me, he prayed.

Jessica felt nervous as she took her seat next to Eddie in the restaurant. Her own family were sitting at a different table and she'd have felt much more comfortable sitting with them.

She'd never met any of Ed's family, apart from Ronny and Paulie, until now. 'Where are Gary and Ricky? You said you'd bought them suits and they were coming.'

Eddie shook his head. 'Sore subject. They were meant to be here, but my cunt of an ex-wife had one of her tantrums and took 'em away on holiday. You wait till she gets home, I'll give her take my kids away without my permission.'

Not wanting to spoil his day, Eddie quickly changed the subject. 'This is my Auntie Joan that I told you about, who brought me up as a nipper, and this is my Auntie Violet, my dad's sister.'

'I'm very pleased to meet you both,' Jessica said shyly.

Auntie Joan patted the chair next to her. 'You sit next to me, my darling, and Ed can sit at the top of the table. Oh, look at her, Vi, ain't she pretty? Got the face of an angel, ain't she?'

'She's an absolute princess,' Violet replied.

As the two women showered her with compliments, Jessica felt her face redden. She wouldn't have felt so nervous if she could have had a proper drink, but obviously, she didn't want to make a show of herself in front of Eddie's relations.

Harry Mitchell smiled at her. 'You'll get used to our nutty family in time, honest you will. Now, where's your dad? I've been introduced to your mum, but I don't even know which one your father is.'

As Harry Mitchell strolled towards him, Stanley felt the colour drain from his skin. Memories of the past came flooding back and all he could picture was Roger Dodds covered in blood with his eye hanging out. Unable to swallow the lump of fillet steak in his mouth, Stanley began to make choking noises.

'For goodness' sake, Stanley, why do you always have to show me up?' Joyce yelled, as she punched him on the back.

As the meat flew out of his mouth and landed on Harry Mitchell's lapel, Stan felt his bowels loosen.

Raymond burst out laughing and, luckily for Stan, Harry Mitchell was in a jovial mood. 'Fucking hell, I've had a few bullets aimed at me in me time, but never a lump of meat,' he joked.

Jessica was mortified. 'Dad, this is Harry, Eddie's father.'

'Pleased to meet you,' Stanley mumbled, shaking his hand.

There was no recognition on Harry's face, and Stan breathed a sigh of relief.

'Christ, you're shivering. Shall I get them to turn the heating up?' Harry asked kindly.

Stanley shook his head. 'No, I'm fine thanks. I've got a bit of a chill, I think.'

Aware that her father was making a total penis of himself, Jessica quickly dragged Harry towards her brother. 'And this is Raymond, my younger brother.'

Raymond stood up and shook Harry Mitchell's hand. 'Nice to meet you, sir,' he said politely.

'I'm sure we'll all catch up again later in the pub,' Harry said, bemused by his new in-laws. The brother was a proper kid with a handshake like a man's. As for the father's limp hand, the less said the better. 'You can always tell a man's soul by his handshake,' his old mum used to tell him and Harry had learned over the years that she was spot on.

After everybody had finished their meals, champagne was poured freely all round. Harry Mitchell was the first to give a speech. He kept it short and sweet, but ended it by giving Jessica an envelope to open.

'My wedding present to both of you,' he said.

Jessica gasped as she looked inside. There were flight tickets and a stay in a five-star hotel in Italy. 'It's booked for next week. I've never flown before!' she yelled gleefully.

As the best man, Ronny was the next to stand up. He spoke about Ed as a kid and ending it by saying, 'Bev, my brother's ex-wife, was as thick as two short planks. She was ugly, a monster, and I'm sure that everyone will agree that this time Ed's got it right. Jessica is everything his first wife wasn't and I'm sure they'll be extremely happy together. Raise your glasses everybody. To Eddie and Jessica.'

Eddie locked eyes with his dad and Uncle Reg. All three shook their heads. Ronny had the brains and decorum of a fucking rat. Eddie quickly stood up, made a couple of jokes and glossed over his brother's comments. He ended his speech by handing Jess yet another envelope.

'You've made me so happy by becoming my wife, Jess. This is my present to you,' he told her.

Jess couldn't believe her eyes as she tore it open.

A few days ago they'd viewed a beautiful house not far from where her parents lived. Jess had fallen in love with it on sight. It was in a private road and was beauti-fully decorated.

'We can't afford it yet, Jess. Let's get the wedding out of the way and we'll find somewhere after we're married,' Eddie had told her.

Now she had the deeds and keys in her hand and could scarcely believe her luck. 'I can't believe it. Thank you, I love you so much,' she said, as she threw her arms around Eddie's neck.

Overcome by excitement, Jess lifted up the hem of her dress and ran over to her mum's table. 'Look, Mum, it's only ten minutes' walk from you. That's the house I told you about. There's a picture of it there.'

Eddie stood proudly behind his wife. 'I knew she wanted to live near you and what Jess wants, she will always get,' he told Joyce.

Joyce grabbed Eddie's face and planted a smacker on his forehead. 'I can pop round when you're at work and, when the baby arrives, I'll babysit whenever you want. I knew you'd make a great son-in-law the moment I saw you, Eddie. I can't thank you enough for buying her a house near her mum. Look, Stanley, isn't it wonderful?'

Stanley glanced at the piece of paper and nodded dumbly. As much as he hated Eddie, he was pleasantly surprised by this strange turn of events. Knowing Eddie's type, he'd have fully expected him to whisk Jessica miles away from him and Joycie.

'A young girl needs to be near her mum and dad. That's what families are all about,' Eddie said, smiling at Stan.

'Don't expect me to come round and change shitty nappies, will you, sis?' Raymond said laughing.

Eddie ruffled Raymond's hair. Jessica's little bro was a proper character. In fact, he reminded Ed of himself at sixteen. Eddie allowed himself a wry smile. Neither Jess nor Ray were fuck-all like their father, so surely at least one of them had to belong to the milkman.

With the speeches and surprises all over, Eddie started to organise cabs to get to the reception.

As Joyce went off to powder her nose, Ivy shifted herself next to Stan. 'I know I said this earlier, but I really don't like him, Stan. Whatever was my Joycie thinking of, encouraging Jess to get involved with the likes of him?'

Stanley shook his head. 'I've no idea, but I'm glad it ain't just me. I don't trust him, Ivy. He's got eyes like dead fish.'

Ivy shuddered. She'd noticed Eddie's cold, calculating stare from the moment she'd set eyes on him and the thought of her beautiful granddaughter sharing her life and bed with him sent shivers down her spine.

'She won't find happiness with him, Stanley. I've seen his sort before. He'll mould Jess into what he wants and, before she knows it, he'll suck the fucking life out of her.'

SEVEN

Seven years later – 1978

Aware of the commotion in the back of her car, Jessica turned down the radio. 'Will you two stop mucking about while Mummy's trying to drive? What are you doing in the back?'

'Frankie's took one of my new trainers and she's put it out the window,' Joey said, trying to grab his sister's arm.

As she stopped at a red light, Jessica glanced around. 'You'd better not have thrown his trainer out, Frankie. Now where is it?'

'I haven't, Mum,' her daughter said, showing her the proof.

'Give it back to Joey, now,' Jess ordered.

Giggling, Frankie gave the trainer back to its rightful owner.

Jessica sighed as she turned up the radio volume. Her children certainly drove her doolally at times, but she loved them more than life itself. She'd been horrified when the doctor had first told her that she was expecting twins.

'I'm only seventeen, I'll never cope,' she had cried to Eddie.

Eddie had put his strong arms around her and washed

away her fears. 'You'll be a natural, Jess. Remember, we're in this together. I'll help out as much as I can and your mum'll be brilliant, I know she will.'

As usual, Eddie was right and, once she had got over the initial shock, Jess had never looked back. She remembered the day she'd given birth as though it was yesterday. The pain was unbearable and, due to the size of the babies and her small frame, the doctors had given her an emergency caesarean.

'We think the babies could be in trouble,' they had said.

Eddie and her mum had both been by her side when she'd finally come round. 'Where are the babies? Are they OK?' were her first words.

Eddie had tears in his eyes as he gently lifted them out of their cots. 'We've got one of each, Jess. A boy and a girl.'

As rough and sore as she felt, Jess could barely believe her luck. The twins were a decent weight and absolutely perfect. To be blessed with one of each was a sheer gift from God.

Eddie and Jessica had spoken about baby names for months leading up to the birth. They hadn't known what they were having, so they had chosen two names for a boy and two for a girl.

Francesca was Jessica's choice. She thought it was the prettiest name she'd ever heard. Eddie chose Joseph. He wanted the name to be a tribute to his deceased grandfather. Their names were shortened within the first few years of their lives. Everybody referred to them as Frankie and Joey. They adored one another, and everything they did, they did together.

Jessica's thoughts were interrupted by her son.

'Mum, I think I'm gonna be sick.'

Unable to find her usual supply of sick bags, Jessica urged him to try and hold on for a minute. 'Open the window, Joey. I can't stop in the middle of the A13. Let me get round this corner and I'll –'

The sound of retching mixed with the smell of sick stopped Jess in mid-sentence.

'Urgh! Mum, open the roof.' Frankie said, holding her head out of the window.

Spotting a lay-by, Jessica pulled over to inspect the damage. It was everywhere – all over Joey, the seats and the bloody carpet. With nothing but a box of tissues, Jess did her best to clean up both her son and the car. She daren't tell Ed. He'd only recently bought her the red Mercedes convertible as a birthday present and he wouldn't be impressed to know it was now covered in spew.

'Make sure you've got a sick bag with you when you take Joey out,' Ed insisted.

Jessica had carried a couple originally, but Joey had already used them and, with a brain like a sieve, she had forgotten to replace them.

'Now, come on, don't cry,' Jessica said, wiping away her son's tears.

Poor little sod, it wasn't his fault that he was a terrible traveller. Frankie loved being in the car and was fine, but Joey, unfortunately, was the opposite.

Jessica put down the roof and continued her journey towards Tesco. Her parents and brother were coming over this evening and she had promised to cook them a slap-up meal. She couldn't wait to show her dad and brother around her new house. Her mum had already visited and had fallen head over heels with it, but her dad and brother hadn't yet seen the finished article.

'Oh, Jess, it looks like a mansion. It reminds me of

one of them posh houses in them American films your father watches.'

Jessica was thrilled with her new surroundings. The house was any woman's dream. Eddie had had it built from scratch by some pals of his. He'd bought the land, got planning permission and, even though it had taken ages to finish, it was well worth the wait. The area, in the country lanes of Rainham, Essex, was perfect for the kids.

Before they had moved, they'd still lived in Upney, near Jessica's parents, and Eddie had hated the area. 'It's a fucking shit-hole round here, Jess. Now the kids are nearing school age, we need to move somewhere nicer,' he had told her a couple of years back.

Jessica had been reluctant to move at first but, within a month, Eddie had persuaded her. Eddie had forbidden Jessica to see the new house until it was all finished, and when she had, she was gobsmacked. Set in an acre of ground, it had four bedrooms, two bathrooms, a big dining room, a luxury lounge and the most enormous, modern kitchen she had ever seen.

Jessica whooped with delight when she saw the garden. Eddie had made it into a playground for the kids. They had swings, slides, a trampoline, and he'd even had their own tree-house built for them.

'Well, what do you think?' he'd asked her.

'I absolutely love it. It's the nicest house I've ever seen in my life,' Jessica said, overwhelmed.

Eddie might be a rough diamond, but his good points definitely outweighed his bad. Jessica was sort of aware of how her husband earned his money, but she never asked any questions. Eddie had a dark side to him sometimes, especially when he drank Scotch. They were the times Jessica chose to forget. Many a time Ed's eyes would blacken and he'd lose his rag over the most trivial thing.

72

Jessica always forgave him. She loved him too much not to, but he did frighten her. He'd never hit her or anything like that, but there were occasions when she'd feared he would.

Overall though, Ed was a fantastic husband, a good dad and a wonderful provider. Jess had never wanted for anything since the day she'd met him and she had never seen him so much as glance at another woman. On the whole, their marriage was extremely happy and everyone had their faults, didn't they?'

'Mum, Mum, I need a wee-wee,' Joey said, snapping Jess out of her daydream.

Jessica quickly stopped the car. Her son had a weak bladder at the best of times.

'Go behind that bush over there,' she ordered.

Frankie laughed as her brother disappeared into the undergrowth. 'Joey is funny, isn't he, Mummy?'

Jessica ruffled her daughter's hair. Frankie and Joey might be twins, but in many ways they were chalk and cheese. They looked nothing like one another and their personalities were extremely different. Frankie had dark hair and was more like Eddie. She was a proper tomboy, a little daredevil, who would try anything once. Joey was the opposite. He had blond hair and was more like herself. He hated heights, was petrified of insects and cried every time he watched *Lassie*.

Eddie would get really annoyed with Joey sometimes. 'You're meant to be a boy. Stop acting like a fucking wimp,' he would shout at his son.

Jessica would comfort Joey, wipe away his tears, and then Eddie would have a go at her. 'You're to blame for the way he is. You mollycoddle the fucking kid. It's a hard life out there, Jess, and he needs to shape up before it's too late. Ricky and Gary were never like him, they were proper little boys. Joey acts like a sissy and if you don't knock it out of him, then I fucking will.'

Jessica smiled as her son got back into the car. 'You OK now, love?'

Joey nodded. 'Can me and Frankie have an ice cream from the shop, Mum?'

'No, because you won't eat your dinner,' Jessica said sternly.

'Please, Mum, we promise we will eat our dinner,' Frankie whinged.

Jessica could never say no to her kids and both of them knew it. 'OK, but don't tell your dad,' she said.

Frankie and Joey locked eyes. 'Thank you, Mummy,' they said, smiling at one another.

In the heart of London's East End, tempers were starting to fray. As Eddie Mitchell stared at the shivering wreck of a man, he felt nothing but contempt. 'What do you mean, you ain't got the fucking money? You know the rules,' he shouted menacingly.

'I'm really sorry. My car broke down and I had to get that repaired, then my fridge-freezer went wrong. I'll pay you next week, I promise I will,' the man pleaded.

Eddie turned to his two brothers. 'What do you reckon lads? Should we give him another week or cut the cunt's ear off?'

Ronny Mitchell gave a sadistic grin. 'I don't think we should chop off his ear. How 'bout we do his little finger instead?'

The shivering man fell onto his knees. 'Please don't hurt me. You know my wife is ill, she's disabled. I had to get the car fixed to take her to the hospital. If you hurt me she'll have no one to look after her.'

As Ronny licked his lips and pulled the knife out of his

pocket, Eddie ordered him and Paulie to wait in the car.
'But I thought you wanted us to do him?' Ronny argued.

'Just get in the fucking car, will you?' Eddie yelled.

Hearing the front door slam, Eddie helped the man up
and sat him on the sofa. 'The thing is, mate, I know that
you're lying to me. You never got no car fixed or brought
no fucking fridge-freezer. You spunked my money in the
pub and the bookie's, didn't you?'

'No, I never. I swear I –'

Annoyed at being lied to, Eddie stopped the man in
mid-sentence by grabbing him around his scrawny neck.
'Don't lie to me, you cunt, 'cause I'll kill you.'

The man started to sob. 'I'm sorry, I didn't mean to
spend it. It's so hard looking after my Elaine, a drink and
a bet is my only release.'

Eddie looked at the man with pure disgust. He knew
for a fact that he fucked off out every day and left his
poor disabled wife indoors to fend for herself. The
grapevine was a funny old thing and there wasn't much
went on that didn't reach his ears.

Eddie knelt down and moved his face inches away from
the man. 'Now listen to me and listen very carefully. I'll
waive the money you owe me, on one condition.'

'What? I'll do anything, I promise,' the man said.

'I want you to look after your wife properly. If I hear
that you've left her sitting in her own piss and shit for hours
while you're larging it in the pub or betting shop, I swear
I'll come back and personally fucking cut you to shreds.'

The man started to sob. 'Thank you Mr Mitchell. You
have my word.'

Over in Upney, Joycie Smith was busy showing her friends
the new machine that Eddie and Jessica had bought her
for her birthday.

75

Rita crouched down and stared at the object in question. 'What's it called again? And what does it do?'

'I've already told you twice. It's called a video recorder and you can record programmes off the telly and watch them at a later date.'

'But how can it do that?' Rita asked, bemused.

'You have to put a tape inside and pre-set it. I recorded *Corrie* the other night and I only watched it this morning.'

Hilda looked at her in awe. 'It's marvellous, ain't it? Bleedin' marvellous.'

Joyce went into her peacock mode. She could almost feel her feathers spreading out like a fan. 'It's modern technology, ain't it? Because Jessica and Eddie are so wealthy now, they know all about these things before anybody else does. You should see their new house – like a palace, it is.'

Hilda and Rita glanced at one another. They wouldn't upset Joycie for the world, but they'd already heard about Jessica's new house a thousand times before. So much so, the pair of them felt that they knew every tile, carpet and room inside out.

'Cooking a posh dinner tonight, my Jess is. All the family will be there. Me and Stan could have done without it, but Eddie adores us, insists that we come,' Joyce lied.

Bored as arseholes, Hilda furtively nudged her friend. Rita quickly clocked on and cleverly changed the subject.

'Where is your Stan? We haven't seen him for ages. My Arthur said he rarely goes down the bookie's any more.'

Joyce sighed. 'Out the back with them bleedin' pigeons of his. Thinks more of them birds than he does of me. Keeps talking about getting himself a new cock.'

Hilda and Rita roared with laughter. Eddie had bought Stanley his first racing pigeon a couple of years back and he'd been hooked from day one. Joyce had hated his new

76

hobby from the word go, but had put up with it because it was Eddie's idea.

'Dirty bastard things they are. Full of shit me garden is and I'm sure it's them that's killed me roses,' Joyce moaned.

Rita smiled politely. 'Well, I suppose it gives Stanley an interest. The only interest my Arthur's got is the pub and the horses,' she moaned.

'Maybe you're right. My Stanley don't even bother going to the pub that much any more,' Joyce said proudly, knowing full well that Rita's Arthur was a borderline alcoholic.

Glancing at the clock, Joyce realised the time was getting on. 'Please don't think I'm being rude, but I'm gonna have to start sprucing meself up in a minute. Jess's mansion is in the country and it takes us about half-hour to get there. She's expecting us at seven, so I'd best get me skates on.'

Rita and Hilda immediately stood up. Talk about outstaying your welcome, they both thought.

'Thanks for the tea and cake. See you soon, Joycie,' Hilda said.

Joyce did her queen wave at the door. 'Don't forget, anything you want to watch, come and see me and I'll record it for you.'

Slamming the front door, Joyce marched into the back garden. 'Stanley, stop cuddling your cock and get yourself bathed and changed.'

'Just give me ten minutes, dear, and I'll be with you,' Stanley said.

'No, Stanley. Put your cock away now, pronto.'

EIGHT

'So when is that cheeky old cunt gonna pay up then?' Ronny asked Eddie.

Eddie pulled into the pub car park. 'Next week. I'll go round and collect it myself,' he lied.

'Ain't you coming in for a quickie?' Paulie asked him.

Eddie shook his head. 'Got the in-laws coming round for dinner. I promised Jess I'd be home early.'

Eddie sighed as his two brothers walked away. He daren't tell Paulie and Ronny that he'd just wiped the geezer's debt. They wouldn't understand his reasons, they'd think he'd lost his marbles. It was only a monkey and Ed would rather ensure that the disabled wife was properly cared for than worry about a pittance.

Financially, Eddie was doing very nicely indeed and five hundred quid was no more than loose change to him. It hadn't always been plain sailing. When his dad had first retired and handed him the reins a few years back, he'd worked his plums off to get where he was now.

Becoming a loan shark had never entered Eddie's mind, but with the pub protection game becoming harder than ever, he'd sort of fallen into it by accident. A chance meeting with an old pal of his, who was coining it in, had put the idea in his head. Obviously, he'd consulted his father first. Although Harry had retired by then, Eddie still looked to him as head of the family and respected his wisdom.

Within months of becoming a loan shark, business was booming. They lent to any bastard they could. Businessmen, builders, milkmen, dustmen: as long as they could afford their weekly repayments and agreed to the hefty interest charges, they could borrow.

With the Mitchells' reputation, the majority of their clients paid up on time, and it was an easy life compared to smashing up boozers. There were the odd one or two who needed time to pay, or a couple of clever dicks who tried to knock them, but they always got their dough back eventually. A bullet lodged in the kneecap or the odd finger chopped off always seemed to do the trick and, like magic, their money would reappear within days. 'Abrafuckingcadabra,' Eddie would say, laughing his head off.

Both Paulie and Ronny had had their noses put out of joint when their father had retired and insisted on Eddie taking control. But their whingeing fell on deaf ears.

'I make the decisions in this fucking family and if I decide that Eddie's the man to take over, then that's how it's gonna be. If yous two don't like it, tough shit – you know what you can do,' their dad told them bluntly.

Eddie could sense the resentment, especially Ronny's, at the way things had turned out. Eddie was the baby of the family and should have been bottom of the pecking order. Now a couple of years on, all was forgiven. Eddie's loan-shark idea had turned up trumps and made him and his brothers very wealthy indeed. They still did a bit of pub protection here and there, but a lot of boozers had been bought by bigger breweries, so they just stuck with their remaining handful of privately owned ones. Uncle

79

Reg was still working with them but, due to health problems, was on the verge of retiring. His walking was giving him gyp, and he was waiting to see a specialist. The poor old sod could barely get about any more and he certainly didn't need the money, as he'd earned plenty over the years.

'Uncle Reg wants to pack it in, so I think we need to take someone else on,' Eddie had told his brothers only yesterday.

'We don't need anybody else. The three of us is more than enough,' Ronny insisted.

Eddie disagreed. They needed a bit of young blood and he had just the right person in mind. All Ronny was worried about was his wallet. He was a greedy bastard and wouldn't want to share out any of his profits. Ronny had recently bought a house and moved in with Sharon, and all he did was brag about paying cash for it.

The Mitchell family still owned the salvage yard in Dagenham, but Harry had now sold off all the others. He'd made a handsome bit of dough on a couple of them. He'd flogged two to property developers and had come out with well over a million in profit.

Eddie put his foot down as he hit the A13. He'd recently treated himself to a Porsche 911 and loved the fact that its turbo engine left every other car on the road standing. He turned off at Barking and headed towards his old address. When he and Jessica had moved out, he'd allowed his ex, Beverley, and his two boys to move in. Gary and Ricky were now fourteen and twelve and had both been expelled from two schools in Canning Town, where they'd previously been living. Neither were particularly bad lads, but it had hit them hard when Eddie had left home. Without a man around they were forever getting into scrapes and fights, and trouble seemed to follow them.

Beverley had been an awkward bitch to deal with when Eddie had first remarried. She had stopped the boys going to the wedding, and many a time she had cancelled arrangements when Ed was supposed to be having them for the weekend.

Eddie had wanted to kill her with his bare hands on many occasions, but in the end he'd done the sensible thing and hit her where it hurt. 'I've got a right to see my boys every weekend and take 'em away in the summer. You'll not get another penny out of me, Bev, until you agree to my terms,' he'd told her.

It had almost killed him knowing that his kids were going without, but he had to be cruel to be kind. Bev held out for two months, then one day turned up in the Flag begging for money and forgiveness. Eddie had had regular contact with his boys ever since. He kept to his word and always saw Bev all right. Most of the money he gave her, she spunked on alcohol and takeaways. She'd only been eight stone when he'd first met her and now she weighed eighteen.

Eddie pulled up outside his old house. He always picked the boys up on a Friday and took them back home on the Sunday. They were doing much better at school since they'd moved to Barking and they loved spending their weekends at his new house.

'You got all your stuff? Where's your mother?' Eddie asked them.

'She's drunk. She's been drinking cider all day and she's asleep on the sofa,' Ricky said, giggling.

Eddie ordered the boys to go and sit in the car. Annoyed, he marched in the house and woke Beverley up.

'Whaddya want?' she asked, bleary-eyed.

'There's your money,' Eddie said, throwing an envelope at her. 'Look at the state of yourself, Bev. No wonder them boys have got problems, seeing you like this every day.'

Beverley sat up. 'I do my best. Anyway, what do you care? All you're bothered about is the wonderful fucking Jessica and your twins.'

Eddie shook his head. 'I wouldn't be letting you live here rent free if I weren't fucking bothered. Drop the bitter act, Bev, it don't suit you, love, and take my advice – sort yourself out before it's too late.'

Beverley burst into tears. She knew she'd let herself go and didn't need Ed to tell her. 'Go on, fuck off home to your other family and leave me alone!' she screamed.

Eddie stormed out and slammed the front door. There was no reasoning with Bev when she was pissed, so he might as well save his breath.

'Can we go in the swimming pool when we get there, Dad?' Gary asked.

'Not tonight, son. We've got guests coming over for dinner, but you can muck about in there all day tomorrow, if you want.'

Eddie smiled as he listened to the boys gabble away in the back. Since he'd married Jess he'd turned into a proper family man. He loved nothing more than spending his weekends with his beautiful wife and children. Over seven years they'd been married now, and he'd never so much as looked at another woman in that time. Marrying Jessica was one of the best decisions Ed had ever made and he worshipped the ground that she walked on. Like any other couple, they had their rows. Eddie knew he could be a Victorian bastard at times and, overall, Jessica suffered him well.

'Look, Dad. That house you always tell us to look at has got a sold sign up.'

Wondering if Gary had got it wrong, Ed swung the

Porsche around and drove back to be nosy. 'Fuck me, you're right son,' he said mystified.

The house in question was a beauty and, unlike his own, had needed nothing doing to it at all. Eddie had tried to buy the place himself. He had viewed it, but the price was way over the top. The owner lived abroad and wanted well over a quarter of a million for it. Ed had tried to barter with him, but the geezer was having none of it. The house had much more ground than the one Eddie had bought, at least another couple of acres.

Eddie turned the car back round and sped towards home. That house had been on the market for a couple of years and he was desperate to make a few phone calls, see if he could find out who had finally landed it.

'What are you doing, Stanley? You've done a left, ain't you meant to have done a right back there?'

Stanley glared at his wife. The only thing she had ever driven in her life was him – bloody mad. 'I do know where I'm going, dear. I have been here before, remember?'

Recognising certain landmarks, Joyce guessed that for once, her husband was right. 'Miserable old goat,' she mouthed to Raymond, who was sitting quietly in the back.

Raymond ignored his mum and stared out of the open window. His parents drove him crazy and he'd taught himself to switch off from them. He felt a bit sorry for his dad sometimes. His mum ruled his old man's life, but it was his own fault, as he should have put his foot down years ago. Raymond rested his head against the seat. The evening sun and cool breeze felt lovely against his skin. He shut his eyes, deep in thought.

Eddie had rung him earlier at the scrapyard. He'd told him to make sure he definitely came tonight, as he wanted to have a chat with him about work.

'Don't worry, you ain't done nothing wrong. What I've got to say is all good,' Eddie assured him.

Raymond had been employed by Eddie since he was eighteen years old and he'd always worked bloody hard. He had left school at sixteen with medium qualifications and high hopes of getting a record deal with his band. It hadn't happened and, with his dreams shattered, Raymond had given up his music career and taken on a job as a trainee butcher. From the word go, he hated the job. The smell was disgusting, the sawdust they put on the floor got down his throat and the sight of dead animals turned his guts. Listening to his complaints one day, Eddie had offered him a lifeline.

'I need someone to work in the salvage yard. I'll give you the address – go down there first thing Monday morning and ask for Pete. I'll tell him to expect you.'

Raymond had started work there that day and had never looked back since. He no longer resembled a skinny little rock star. The physical nature of the job had given him muscles he had never known existed. His mother had been embarrassing him lately whenever her friends came round.

'Look at my Raymond. Six foot tall and built like a brick shithouse, ain't he?' she'd say proudly. 'Nothing like his father.'

'Left here and then left again, Stanley,' Joyce yelled, making Raymond jump out of his skin.

Annoyed at yet again being told what to do, Stanley drove the Cortina along his daughter's drive at speed and then slammed his foot on the brake. Seeing Joyce's head nearly hit the dashboard, he chuckled as he got out.

'You silly old bastard, you've nearly bloody killed me. I bet I've got whiplash now because of you.'

Holding the door open for his wife, Stanley winked at

84

Raymond. 'I'm so sorry, dear. It's these new shoes you bought me, my foot must have slipped.'

As Frankie and Joey ran out to greet their nan, Joyce's whiplash was forgotten.

'Hello, my babies. Give your nanna a big kiss.'

Joey clung to one of her hands and Frankie the other. 'Have you brought us any presents, Nanny?' Frankie asked bluntly.

'Yep, but you can't have them till after your dinner.'

Playfully scolding her daughter, Jessica welcomed her family. 'So lovely to see you all. Cheekier by the day, my Frankie's getting. Take no notice of her,' she laughed.

Once inside the house, Joyce took it upon herself to give her husband and son the grand tour. Both of them had seen the house before, but not in its finished state. 'Look at the downstairs bathroom – marble them tiles are. Handsome, aren't they?'

Barely giving them a chance to look, Joyce dragged Stanley and Raymond into the lounge. 'Look at that chandelier, Stanley. Ain't it beautiful, Raymond? Cost an absolute fortune that did. Pure crystal, it is – ain't it, Jess?'

Hearing her husband come down from upstairs, Jessica quickly changed the subject. 'We're in the lounge. Can you get everybody a drink, Ed?'

Eddie beamed as he kissed Joyce and shook hands with both Stanley and Raymond.

'Sorry, I was on the phone, I didn't know you'd all arrived. Now, what can I get you?'

'I'll just have a lager, Ed,' Raymond said immediately.

'Can I have a sherry?' Joyce asked, with a silly giggle.

Eddie smiled at Stanley. 'I've got a nice twenty-year-old Scotch for me and you to crack open, Stan.'

'Lovely,' Stanley said, rubbing his hands together.

'You don't want that, Stanley. Scotch is too strong for you. Why don't you just have a beer?' Joyce piped up.

'He'll be fine having a drop of Scotch, Joyce. Jessica's made up the guest room for yer. Stan ain't gotta drive, has he?' Ed said, sticking up for him.

Not wanting to behave like an old dragon in front of Eddie, Joyce forced a smile. 'Go on then, but take it easy, Stanley. I don't want you getting drunk and showing me up, like you have in the past.'

'Can I sit on your lap, Grandad?' Joey asked him.

Stanley smiled as his grandson plonked himself on his lap. He loved the twins and prided himself on being a good grandad. He'd often taken them out for days with Joyce. They'd go for picnics, trips to the zoo and he'd teach them how to fly his pigeons.

It was just after the twins were born that Stanley had decided to make an effort with Eddie. Joyce had dragged him up the hospital and, as soon as he'd first laid eyes on Frankie and Joey, he'd gone all gooey, into grandad mode. Not wanting to miss out on their childhood, he'd had little choice other than to be polite to their father. It was hard at first, but over the years, he'd sort of got used to it.

As much as Stanley hated to admit it, Eddie did have some good points. He always stuck up for Stan when Joyce put her two penn'orth in, he'd given Raymond a half-decent job and he spent every weekend with Jessica and the children.

'Cheers, Stan,' Eddie said, handing him his Scotch.

Stanley thanked Eddie and watched him walk away. He could never go as far as to say he actually liked him or trusted him, but he'd learned to make the best out of a bad situation. Eddie was OK, in a very-small-dose kind of way.

Eddie lifted up Frankie and swung her around above his head. 'You ain't heard who's bought that big white house, have you, Jess?' he asked.

'Put me down, Daddy,' Frankie said giggling.

Jessica smiled at him. 'What, that massive place down the road here?'

'Yeah, that's the one. I've just made a few phone calls, but no one knows who's got it.'

Hearing a commotion out the back, Jessica stood up. 'I'll ask down the school, see if anyone knows. Ed, you'd better go out in the garden. Gary and Ricky are fully clothed in that swimming pool, they're fighting with one another, I think.'

Stanley and Joyce both looked at one another in horror. They didn't agree on much in life, but the one thing they both thought was what uncontrollable, rude little toerags Eddie's eldest sons were.

'I'm just gonna check on the meat,' Jessica said brightly.

Joyce stood up and looked out the back. 'I didn't know them little bastards were gonna be here,' she said to Stan.

Frankie smiled. 'What is a bastard, Nanny?'

Stanley stood up and picked up his granddaughter. 'Basket, Frankie. Nanny said she didn't know Mummy had a basket here.'

Hearing the voices of Gary and Ricky, Stanley handed Frankie to Joyce. 'I dunno about you Joycie, but I most certainly need another drink.'

Joyce smiled with rare affection at her husband. 'Me too, and make it a large one, Stanley.'

NINE

Eddie carved up the roast beef, while his wife brought in the side dishes.

'I'll just serve up a little plate for Frankie and Joey and the rest of yous can help yourselves,' Jessica said.

Making sure everybody had enough meat on their plates, Eddie opened a couple of bottles of wine. 'Who wants red and who wants white?' he asked.

'I'll have red, but just a small one,' Joyce giggled. She'd already had three glasses of sherry and was feeling a little bit tipsy.

'Can me and Gary have a drop of wine, Dad?' Ricky asked innocently.

Still annoyed with his sons for arsing about in the swimming pool when he'd blatantly told them not to, Eddie glared at his middle son. 'No, you can't, and don't be so bloody cheeky.'

Ricky scowled and nudged his brother. 'Mum lets us have a drink indoors, don't she, Gary?'

'Well, I'm not your mother and you're not indoors now. You're in my house and you abide by my rules. As for your mother letting you drink alcohol, I'll be having a little word with her about that. Now, shut up the pair of you and eat your fucking dinner.'

Desperate to change the subject, Jessica picked up one of the dishes. 'More roast potatoes anyone?' she asked.

'I'll have some, sis,' Raymond said, grinning.

Joyce pointed towards Stanley. 'Your father will have a couple more as well,' she told Jess.

As the potatoes were put on his plate, Stanley looked up in amazement. He had obviously spoken without him moving his mouth.

Joey slid off his chair. 'Don't want no more, Mummy.'

Jessica looked at his plate. He'd barely touched a morsel. She knew she shouldn't have let him eat that ice cream he'd pleaded for earlier.

'Try and eat some more, darling, see if you can eat as much as your sister.'

Joey shook his head. 'I don't feel well, I got tummy-ache,' he lied.

Eddie shook his head as his youngest son left the table. All of his kids were good eaters, bar Joey, who was a finicky little waif. 'He'll be ill, that kid, if he don't start eating more. You wanna get him up the doctor's, find out what's wrong with him,' Eddie told Jess.

Jessica shrugged. 'He's OK, he's just fussy, that's all. He wasn't well earlier, maybe that's why.'

Frankie smiled as she took her brother's Yorkshire pudding off his plate. 'Joey was sick all over Mummy's new car,' she said, giggling.

Eddie looked at Jess in horror. 'He weren't, was he?'

Jessica stood up and began to clear the dinner plates. 'It wasn't his fault, Ed. I forgot to put some bags in there for him. The poor little sod can't help being travel sick.'

Eddie wanted to say plenty, but instead said nothing. A fortune he'd paid for that Mercedes convertible and already it must smell like a fucking hospital ward.

'Who wants dessert? I've got Black Forest gateau or fresh strawberries and ice cream,' Jessica asked gaily.

'I'll have some strawberries, love,' Stanley replied.

Joyce snatched the empty dish out of his hand. 'No, he won't. Fruit gives him terrible wind and I've got to sleep next to him tonight,' she told Jess.

Eddie burst out laughing. How poor old Stanley put up with Joyce, he would never know. He stood up. 'Come on Stan, I'll take you outside and show you me new car. We can go for a quick spin in it if you like?'

Stanley grinned. He'd always been a Ford man himself, believed in buying the best of British, but he wouldn't say no to a ride in that Porsche. Apart from his pigeons and horse racing, cars were his only other real passion. He leaped up from the dining table. 'I'm ready when you are, Ed.'

'You coming with us, Ray?' Eddie asked.

'No, Uncle Raymond. We want you to see Milky the Cow,' Frankie said, with her hands on her hips.

'Please don't go, Uncle Raymond,' Joey begged.

With two pairs of pleading eyes desperate for his company, Raymond decided to stay put.

'We'll have that chat when I get back,' Eddie told him.

Stanley followed Eddie out of the front door. 'What were the kids on about? Have you got a cow out the back?'.

Eddie started to laugh. Stan didn't have a clue, bless his cotton socks. 'No, course not. They're talking about their new toys – Milky, the Marvellous Milking Cow. Drove me mad for 'em, they did. All the toy shops had sold out and I spent a whole day driving around looking for 'em. I got two in the end, had to drive all the way to Southend to pick the bastard things up. The things you do for kids, eh?'

90

Stanley said nothing. Eddie was a good dad, a good husband, but there was still something very sinister about him that Stan couldn't put his finger on.

Hearing the front door slam, Joyce and Jessica grinned at one another. No words were needed, but both of them were absolutely thrilled that Stanley and Eddie had got over their little differences and become friends.

'Is it OK if me and Ricky go out the back and play football? We won't go near the swimming pool, I promise.'

Jessica ruffled Gary's hair. 'Of course you can. Mind the flowerbeds, though.'

Joyce helped Jessica take the dirty dishes into the kitchen. 'I'll wash up for you, love,' Joyce insisted.

Jessica giggled. 'There's no need, Mum, I've got a dishwasher.'

Joyce looked at the metal machine with interest. She'd heard about dishwashers, but had never seen one up close before. 'You sure it cleans them properly, Jess? I mean, it ain't like human hands, is it?'

'Of course it cleans them properly. Now, if you wanna make yourself useful, Mum, pour us both another drink.'

Frankie poked her head around the kitchen door. 'Grandma, where's our presents? It's after dinner now.'

Topping up her glass with sherry, Joyce followed Frankie into the living room. She delved into her big black shopping bag. 'Here we go. You've got a jamboree bag each and me and Grandad clubbed together and bought you both a new toy.'

'What is it? Can we have it now?' the twins asked excitedly.

'Have the jamboree bag now and as soon as Grandad gets back, you can have your toys.'

'Oh, I want mine now,' Frankie said, sulking.

'Do as Nanny says,' Jessica shouted sternly.

Joey was a polite kid, but her daughter could be a stroppy little cow at times.

Ten minutes later, an ashen-faced Stanley walked back into the house, alone. 'Jesus Christ, drove like a lunatic, he did. Nearly killed us on that bend down the road there. I think I'm gonna bring me dinner up,' he moaned.

Raymond got himself a lager and poured his shell-shocked father a large Scotch. 'Eddie always drives fast. Get that down your neck, you'll be fine,' he told his dad.

As Stanley ran to the toilet and retched, Eddie was still sat in the car, laughing. Watching Stanley leap out looking like death warmed up and then stagger up the drive was one of the funniest things he'd ever seen. He knew deep down that Stanley only suffered him for the sake of the kids and driving like a maniac was payback time. Picturing Stan's face when he'd hit that bend, Eddie had to hold his bollocks to stop himself pissing on the seat. With his hand still clutched around his privates, Eddie walked towards the house. Unable to keep a straight face, he tried to think of something else.

'Dad feels ill – did you have to drive like a nutcase? He's just brought all his dinner up,' Jessica said angrily.

'Gotta go a loo,' Eddie said, running upstairs.

Locking the bathroom door, Eddie put his hand over his mouth. Stanley spewing his guts up had tipped him over the edge and, instead of just having the giggles, he was now on the verge of hysterics.

'Can we have our toys now?' Frankie asked impatiently.

'Grandad will give them to you,' Joyce said, handing them to her husband as he walked back into the room. Poor Stanley looked so ill, she wanted to lighten him up a bit. Remembering that he'd earlier jolted the car and nearly broken her neck, she quickly snatched them back from him.

'Nanny chose them so, on second thoughts, Nanny should give them to you,' she told the twins.

Having managed finally to compose himself, Eddie nodded to Raymond to follow him outside. 'Do you wanna cigar?' he asked him.

Raymond shook his head. 'No thanks, I'll have a fag.'

Staring at Raymond, Eddie put both hands on his shoulders and spoke in earnest. 'When I first gave you a job, Ray, I sort of did it for Jessica's sake. You were just a kid, her little brother, and I must admit, although I liked you, I had me doubts. Over the years you've proved me wrong. You've been honest, loyal, a real top-class employee. The thing is, Raymond, you're not a boy any more, you're now a man and that is why I want to offer you a handshake, a proper in.'

Raymond nodded. He'd learned to understand Eddie's lingo over the years and he knew exactly where the conversation was going.

Eddie smiled at him. 'My Uncle Reg is on the verge of retiring. We need another pair of hands and I want you to join the family properly. You're gonna be working with me, Paulie and Ronny. You're no fool, you know the set-up. What's your opinion on that?'

Unbeknown to Eddie, Raymond had been waiting for this moment for a long time. Unable to control his emotions, he grabbed the big man and hugged him.

'I'm honoured, Eddie, and I promise you faithfully that I will do you proud.'

Laughing, Eddie pushed him away and squared up to him. 'You'd better do me proud,' he said, as he lunged into a bit of play-fighting.

Gently pushing Raymond away, Eddie put his serious head on, once more. 'You won't be a gofer. You'll have a three-month trial, then you'll be on virtually the same cut as Paulie and Ronny are.'

Raymond could scarcely believe his luck. He'd prayed

for this day to happen and now it finally had. He could move out of his parents', buy his own property. If he played his cards right, the world could be his oyster. 'Thanks, Eddie. I'll do whatever you ask of me and I truly mean that.'

Eddie nodded. 'Good lad. Now, a few ground rules. You don't say a word to anyone about anything we do. Birds, mates, family – not a soul. If anyone asks, you're a debt collector.'

Raymond nodded. He understood perfectly.

Deep in thought, Eddie tilted his head. 'I think it's probably for the best that I lend you some dough and you get your own place. If any shit hits the fan, you don't want your parents involved, do you?'

'I've been wanting to leave home for ages anyway. I think the world of me mum and dad, but they do me head in,' Raymond said frankly.

'First thing on Monday, Ray, I'm gonna take you out, rent you somewhere and get you kitted out as well. Remember one golden rule: a man is always judged on what he wears. You've always got to look the part, wear good clobber. We'll go up Savile Row and get you a couple of suits from there.'

'Daddy, what are you doing out here? I want you to see my new toy.'

Eddie picked up Frankie and held her in his left arm. He held his right out to Raymond. 'Welcome to the family, son.'

After a couple more Scotches, Stanley's stomach had settled and he was now on the floor playing with the twins.

'What you got, then? What's Nanny and Grandad brought you?' Eddie said, kneeling down.

'I've got a Madame Alexander doll, and Joey's got a Tonka truck,' Frankie said proudly.

Eddie admired their gifts and, noticing Gary and Ricky sitting alone, he stood up and walked towards them. 'You all right, boys?'

'I'm OK,' Gary said.

'Me too,' said Ricky.

Eddie sat in between them and put an arm around each of them. He'd had the hump earlier when he couldn't find out who had brought the poxy house he'd wanted and he shouldn't have taken it out on them for having a dip. 'Sorry for shouting at you earlier. Listen, I'll do you a deal. Go and pour your old dad a drink and you can both have a can of lager.'

Gary smiled. 'Can we really?'

'Just the one, mind. Now move your arses, 'cause Daddy's thirsty.'

Eddie felt a pang of guilt as they ran excitedly from the room. They must feel left out sometimes with all the attention showered upon the twins. The poor little sods didn't have much of a home life and they were good kids at heart.

'Christ, you must have poured half the bottle in there,' Ed said to Gary, as he was handed a full glass of Scotch.

Urging the boys to sit down next to him, he told them about his plans for the following weekend. 'Grandad Harry is organising a surprise party for your Uncle Reg to celebrate his retirement, so we're going to that on Friday, and you know Pat Murphy who owns that old converted farmhouse not far from here?'

Ricky looked bemused, but Gary nodded. 'Is that the man you took us to see, he used to be a boxer?'

'Yep, that's the one. Well, every year he has this big bank-holiday party, where he invites all his family, all his mates and the neighbours. Well, as we're neighbours now, we've got an invite. I've never been before, but it's meant to be the bollocks. He has everything there, rides for the kids, a boxing ring, there's a barbecue, a disco. It's next Sunday, so do yous boys fancy it?'

'Yeah. Can I have a go at the boxing?' Gary asked.

'Me too. I wanna box as well,' Ricky said.

Eddie gently banged their heads together. 'Only if you behave yourselves in between.'

'We will, we promise,' they both said.

Gary and Ricky both loved boxing. Eddie had sent them up to Peacock Gym in Canning Town at quite a young age and they were both good little prospects, according to their trainer.

Hyped up, Gary and Ricky went out the back to practise their sparring.

'What party's that, then?' Jessica asked, sitting down next to Eddie.

'Pat Murphy's. The kids will love it. He has clowns, all sorts of entertainment for them, it'll give you a chance to meet some of the other wives as well. Next Sunday, it is.'

Jessica squeezed his hand. He was such a softie, her Ed. A real family man. 'It sounds wonderful. Roll on next week,' she said, kissing him gently.

'Mum, Dad, Joey won't give me my new doll back,' Frankie whinged.

Seeing his son cradle the doll, Eddie bent down and snatched it away from him. 'The Tonka truck's yours. Boys don't play with dolls, Joey.'

Lip trembling, Joey looked at his father. 'Sorry, Daddy.'

Eddie put on some music and the rest of the evening swam by.

'Do you want my body, am I really sexy?' Joyce sang, getting all Rod Stewart's lyrics wrong.

Aware that she was pointing at him, Stanley turned his back. 'Don't start all that, Joycie, will yer?'

Not used to drinking large amounts of alcohol, Joyce felt her legs go from under her. 'Oh dear, I think I'm drunk,' she said, as she clung on to the sofa for dear life.

'Are you OK, Mum?' Jessica said, helping her up.

'Yes, dear. Actually, I feel wonderful.'

Embarrassed, as he'd never witnessed either of his parents so pissed before, Raymond jumped into action. 'I think we should all call it a night now and get some shut-eye. Give me a hand, Dad, to help Mum up the stairs.'

Used to being told what to do, Stanley jumped to order. 'Goodnight all,' he yawned.

Eddie winked at Raymond. 'I hope the sofa's comfortable enough for ya. I'll put the kids to bed and we'll speak again in the morning,' he said.

The twins were crashed out on the floor, so Jessica lifted up Joey and Eddie grabbed Frankie. 'Where's Gary and Ricky?' she asked.

Eddie laughed. 'I told 'em they could have one can of lager and I'm sure the little bastards had about three. I had to help them into bed about an hour ago. I put 'em in Joey's room.'

Jessica giggled. It had been their first proper get-together in their new home and she had loved every single minute of it.

Whether it was due to the amount of sherry she'd drunk, Joyce wasn't sure, but for the first time in years, she felt amorous. 'Stanley, wake up,' she said, poking her husband in the ribs.

Receiving no response, she moved her hand around a bit. 'Stanley,' she said seductively.

Aware of a hand around his cobblers, Stanley jumped up like a bush kangaroo. 'What the fuck! What are you doing, woman? Have you gone mad?'

Jessica just happened to be passing the guest room as her father bolted out in his Y-fronts.

'Whatever's the matter?' she asked, noticing his shocked expression.

Stanley held his hand over his parcel. 'It's your mother – she's having a funny turn.'

'What, is she ill?' Jessica said, panicking.

'No, not that kind of funny turn,' Stanley said, embarrassed.

Realising what had happened, Eddie grabbed Jessica and dragged her into their bedroom. Hysterical, he could barely speak for laughing.

'Your mother's after a bunk-up.'

'Oh, don't say that,' Jessica said, mortified.

Hearing raised voices, Jessica poked her head around the bedroom door.

'I mean it, Joycie, if you touch me again in that way, I'll go and sleep downstairs in the armchair,' she heard her father say.

Hand over her mouth, Jessica stood in stupefied shock. 'I can't believe it,' she said to Eddie.

Unable to stop laughing, Eddie grabbed her and threw her onto the bed. 'You are so naive, Jessica Mitchell, and do you know what? I fucking well love you for it.'

TEN

After dropping his two boys home early on Sunday evening, Eddie shot up to the Flag for a prearranged meet with his dad, brothers and uncle.

As he explained that he'd offered Raymond a place in the family firm, Ronny flew into one of his tantrums. 'He's a fucking outsider. How do you know he ain't a grass? He could rob us blind for all you know,' he screamed at Eddie.

Harry Mitchell did his best to defuse the situation. He took Ronny outside the pub and, knowing the best way to handle his son, spoke to him gently and respectfully.

'Look, Ronny, I know you've got your doubts about Ed taking on someone new, but he knows what he's doing. Raymond's no stranger to us. He's been working for Eddie on the scrap for years and seeing as he's Jessica's brother, he's got family ties with us, ain't he?'

'But I don't wanna share my cut of the profits. The fact is, Dad, we don't need anybody else, especially a fucking kid,' Ronny argued.

Harry put an arm around his shoulder. 'Look, Raymond's only on trial at first. Chances are, he might not be what Eddie's looking for and it won't work out anyway. If you're concerned about him being young and wet behind the ears, have a word with Eddie, get him to set up a task, see if Raymond's cut out for our line of work.'

The fact that his dad was taking him seriously for once was enough to make Ronny calm down. 'Maybe you're right, Dad. Testing the cunt out ain't such a bad idea. There's a couple of people been fucking around with us lately. That big skinhead geezer, Mad Dave, owes us a lot of wedge and ain't breaking his neck to pay it back. How about if the wonderful Raymond pays him a visit? Mad Dave's about six foot three. He's a massive bastard, with arms like tree trunks. Let's see how the dear little apprentice pits his wits against him, eh?'

Harry led his son back inside the pub. 'Don't rub Eddie up the wrong way now. Just put your idea forward sensibly,' he urged Ronny.

Eddie sat in silence as he listened to Ronny's plan.

'I think it's a great idea,' Paulie said immediately.

Reg glanced at Eddie and shrugged. 'I suppose even if the kid gets a pasting, it'll show us what he's made of.'

Eddie shook his head. 'For fuck's sake, Raymond's only twenty-three – can't we test him out on someone else? Making him confront Mad Dave on his tod is like slinging him into a cage of starved lions.'

Looking at his dad for support, Eddie was surprised when, for once, he didn't receive any.

'I was thrown in at the deep end when I was a lad. Never did me any harm,' Harry said honestly.

Aware that he was alone in fighting Raymond's corner, Eddie had no choice other than to agree to the ridiculous idea.

'Fine, it that's what everyone wants, then I'll sort it,' he said.

*   *   *

100

Unaware of the big task he had coming his way, Raymond was up a 5 a.m. the following Monday morning.

'Christ, what's up with you? Shit the bed or something?' Stanley asked, as his son plonked himself down opposite him.

'I'm just really excited, Dad. Starting me new job today, ain't I? Couldn't sleep last night at all, so I thought I'd get up and pester you before you went to work.'

Stanley offered his son a piece of toast. 'What's this job all about then? I know you said you're going to be debt collecting, but what sort of people are you going to be dealing with?'

'I don't know yet. Eddie's picking me up at nine. He's taking me out to buy me some good clothes. He says I have to look the part for this kind of job.'

Suddenly losing his appetite, Stanley threw his toast in the bin and turned away from his overly enthusiastic son. He didn't like the sound of this new job, not one little bit and he feared for the safety of Raymond.

Stanley buttoned his shirt up and put on his uniform jacket. He sat down opposite Raymond and shook his hand. 'Good luck, son. I hope it all goes well for you, but will you promise me one thing?'

'What's that, Dad?'

'Promise me if the job turns out to be dangerous in any way, you'll walk away and look for something else.'

Raymond nodded. His father was such an old stick-in-the-mud, but he meant well. 'I promise, Dad,' he said untruthfully.

Whether the job was dangerous or not, Raymond had no intention of walking away from it. He had been waiting for an opportunity like this all his life, and he would do literally anything to impress Eddie and secure his place in the family firm.

'Goodbye son, see you tonight,' Stanley shouted.

Raymond sighed as his father shut the front door. How he could sit on that stinking bus every day, being abused by schoolchildren, Ray would never know. It was watching the old man come home moaning about his job every night that had given Raymond the determination to make something of his own life. He loved his dad dearly, but would rather die than end up like him.

'Morning, darling. I'm so excited for you. Now, let your old mum cook you a nice bit of egg and bacon. You need to keep your strength up if you're gonna be working with Eddie and his brothers.'

Raymond shook his head. 'Thanks, Mum, but I've already eaten. I haven't had a bath yet, so I'd best go and get meself ready.'

Joyce smiled as he bolted upstairs. Her Raymond working with Eddie and his brothers had made her the proudest mother in the universe and she couldn't wait to tell her friends. Hilda and Rita would be so jealous. Both their sons had crappy jobs and not much to show for their lives. Raymond had always been far too intelligent to end up like them.

Eddie picked Raymond up at nine on the dot. 'I've found you a flat. It belongs to a mate of mine who's doing a bit of bird. It's fully furnished and he only wants a score a week rent. I'll take you there now, it's in Dagenham, and it's only ten minutes away from me and Jess.'

Eddie said very little as Raymond walked around the flat and studied the joint. It was very basic, but clean and certainly liveable.

'Whaddya think?' Eddie asked, once Ray had looked in every room.

'Yeah, it's OK. Beats listening to me parents argue,' Raymond said bluntly.

102

'Once you find your feet, you can get yourself some-where better. It'll do you until then, though. Get your stuff packed up tonight and I'll pick you up in the morning and help you move in,' Eddie told him.

Raymond looked at Eddie in amazement. He hadn't expected things to move this quickly; he thought he'd be moving in a month or so. He hadn't even told his parents that he was leaving home yet. 'It's a bit quick, ain't it, Ed? Can't I move in in a couple of weeks? It'll give me more time to sort stuff out.'

Eddie shook his head. 'If you're gonna be working with me, you definitely need your own space. Too many eyes, too many questions, Raymond.'

Raymond nodded. He could hardly argue with Eddie, could he now? He forced a smile. 'Tomorrow it is, then.'

The next step was Savile Row, where Eddie forked out on two suits, four shirts, three ties and a pair of black leather shoes. Eddie had known the guy who owned the tailor's shop for years.

'Seeing as my family are your best customers, how quick can you get one of them suits altered for me?' he asked.

'It'll be done by tomorrow afternoon, Mr Mitchell,' came the owner's reply.

'There's nothing like people showing you a bit of respect, Raymond. One day that will be you, son,' Eddie said, as he guided him towards a posh restaurant.

With the menu written in French, Raymond urged Eddie to order for the both of them.

'And bring over a bottle of your finest champagne as well,' Eddie told the waiter.

Sipping the bubbly, Eddie and Raymond chatted about Jessica and the kids until their food arrived.

Raymond, who was by now starving, bolted his down within minutes. 'Nice bit of grub, ain't it, Ed?'

Eddie laughed. 'It's OK, I've had better.'

Already loving his new life, Raymond gladly accepted the offer of another bottle of champagne.

Clearing his throat, Eddie decided it was time to drop the bombshell. In detail, he explained the conversation he'd had with his family and the task Raymond had been given.

'So where do I find this Mad Dave?' Raymond asked immediately.

'He owns a two-bob car lot on an industrial estate in Leyton. He's in a right remote spot at the back of it. There's a young bird works for him, calls herself his secretary, but really he's shafting her behind his old woman's back. I can't remember the bird's name, but she's about eighteen, a single mum and she leaves at three to pick her kid up from school. Mad Dave ain't got many friends – horrible cunt he is – so chances are, once she's gone, he'll definitely be on his Jack Jones.'

'How much does he owe you?' Raymond asked calmly.

Eddie was pleased, but also quite taken aback by the kid's attitude. He seemed keen to pass the task and Ed hoped that it wasn't just the champagne talking.

'Eight grand he's fucked me over for. He brought a load of hooky motors off of me. He owed ten altogether, but he paid back two, then he came out with some cock and bull about the Old Bill nicking the cars off him. It's a load of old bollocks, I know it is, but he's been fobbing me off ever since. I try and be fair with people, Ray, but I'll be honest with you, if I still hadn't got me dough by the end of this month, I was gonna do the cunt meself.'

'Can I take something with me to use if I need to?' Raymond asked.

'I'll give you something to carry. I've got a cosh, a baseball bat – you can take whatever you want. Anyway, you ain't gotta worry. Me and the boys will sit just outside the gate. Any agg, we'll be there like a shot, mate.'

Raymond smiled. He'd never suffered from having a nervous disposition and he wasn't about to get one now. He needed this job and he would do whatever he had to, to prove his worth. 'I've got me own tool, I'll use that, and thanks anyway, but I'm sure I won't need any help.'

Eddie was stunned by the boy's coolness. 'Be warned, Ray, Mad Dave's a big old lump. A wanker he is, but a pushover he ain't.'

Smiling, Raymond topped up both of their glasses. 'To me and Mad Dave. May the best man win, eh?'

Two days later, all Savile Rowed up, Raymond sat in the back of a white transit van alongside Eddie, Ronny and Paulie. Uncle Reg had donned his check cap and pipe, and had offered his services to drive.

'I wore this just in case we were seen. I look like some OAP on a jolly boys' outing, no one's gonna clock us with me driving,' he laughed.

'So you're ready to play with the big boys are you, Ray?' Ronny asked sarcastically.

Raymond could tell immediately that Ronny didn't want him in the firm and was determined to prove him wrong. 'More than ready,' he answered politely.

'Next on your right, Reg. You know where it is, don't you? Straight down the bottom of that road.'

'Don't worry, I know I've semi-retired meself, but I ain't fucking senile yet,' Reg said jokingly.

Ronny nudged Paulie as they pulled up outside Mad Dave's appalling-looking car site. 'I'd love to be a fly on the wall, wouldn't you?' he whispered.

Paulie ignored him. Whatever the end result, this kid had bigger bollocks than most.

'What tool did you bring?' Eddie asked, as he opened the back door.

From nowhere, Raymond pulled out the biggest butcher's knife Eddie had ever seen. 'Fucking hell. Where did you get that from?'

'I used to be a butcher, didn't I? And I know exactly how to use it. Now, are you sure his bird's gone home?'

Eddie urged Reg to poke his head around the gate.

'She drives a light-blue Ford Fiesta and parks it just on the right as you go in.'

Within seconds, Reg hobbled back, giving the thumbs up.

Ronny sat quietly as Raymond stepped out of the van and strolled into the car lot like he owned the place. *Flash little cunt, I hope he comes unstuck,* he thought to himself.

With the knife tucked firmly down the inside of his jacket, Raymond spotted the Portakabin and marched straight in.

Mad Dave was sat on a black leather chair. He had his feet on a wooden desk, a beer in one hand and a copy of the *Sun* newspaper in the other. 'Can I help you?' he said, without properly looking up.

'Yes, you can. I work for Eddie Mitchell and I'm here on his behalf to collect the eight thousand pound that you owe him.'

Mad Dave took a large gulp of beer, burped, then threw his head back with laughter. 'You're 'aving a giraffe, ain't yer, mate? So you're telling me that that mug Eddie Mitchell has sunk so low in his fuckin' business empire that's he's sent some teenage kid round to threaten me?'

Raymond grinned. 'I'm not a teenage kid and I'm not threatening you. I'm just asking for the dosh that you owe.'

Mad Dave cracked open another beer and downed it

within seconds. 'Do yourself a favour, kid, and fuck off home,' he told Raymond.

As Mad Dave stood up, Raymond felt a slight twinge of fear. The geezer was fucking ginormous. 'I don't want no aggro, just pay me the money and I'll leave,' Raymond urged him.

Laughing hysterically, Mad Dave walked towards Raymond and lifted him by his new shirt and tie. 'Go away, you silly little boy,' he said, as he dragged him towards the Portakabin door.

As fast as a greyhound chasing a hare, Raymond pulled the knife out and shoved it straight through Mad Dave's guts.

As he hit the floor, Mad Dave's eyes rolled straight into the back of his head. Raymond bent down to check on him; he had seen enough dead animals to know when someone was brown bread. Desperate not to get the man's blood on his new suit, Raymond knelt to one side as he searched through Mad Dave's pockets. He'd spotted the safe when he first came in and it was one of them cheapies that wasn't coded by numbers. Finding a massive bunch of keys, Raymond walked towards the safe and tried numerous ways to unlock it. 'Come on,' he said, as he turned key after key.

Finally, Ray felt the lock turn. He quickly grabbed all the money from inside, pocketed it, and washed the blood off his hands in the sink. Spotting a tea towel, he wiped the safe, the desk and the door. He hadn't touched anywhere else, he was sure he hadn't. Washing the blood off the knife, he put it back inside his jacket. His new suit was ruined. He'd caught his pocket with the knife and ripped it, and not only that, it was also sprayed with blood.

With the tea towel firmly attached to his hand, Raymond opened the cabin door. He then ran for his bloody life.

Waiting for Raymond to return was the longest wait of Eddie's life. Ronny hadn't helped with his stupid comments and jokes. Willing the kid to come through for him, Eddie smiled as he saw him running towards the van.

'Drive, quick, go,' Raymond said, as he leaped into the back.

Paulie and Ronny were stunned to see splashes of blood on Ray's suit. He didn't have a mark on him, so it couldn't be his.

'Are you OK? What happened?' Eddie asked nervously.

Raymond was aware of his arms shaking as he put his hand in his pocket and pulled out bundles of £20 notes wrapped up in elastic bands. 'There's ten bundles there. I should imagine there's a grand in each,' he managed to stutter.

Ronny couldn't believe his eyes. 'What the fuck? What did you do? Whose blood is it?'

Raymond put his head in his hands. 'I had to kill him, I had no choice.'

Uncle Reg nearly took the van straight up the kerb. He'd seen some newcomers over the years, but none like this kid. 'Don't worry, son. We'll get rid of the knife and your clothes and clean you up round mine.'

Seeing the shocked expression on the faces of his brothers, Eddie burst out laughing. 'I think Raymond's passed his little task, don't you boys?' he asked sarcastically.

Paulie immediately held his hand out to Raymond. 'Well done, mate. Welcome to the family.'

Ronny had no choice other than to do the same. 'I can't believe you killed the cunt. How did it happen?' he asked in awe.

Having by now composed himself a bit, Raymond repeated what had happened in full. 'I knew he was dead immediately. Remember, I know by the eyes, I used to chop up dead animals, didn't I?'

Thrilled by the way Raymond had come through for him, Eddie grabbed him in a playful headlock. 'Well you certainly chopped up a big animal back there, didn't you, eh?'

Uncle Reg lived in Bow, and within the hour, Raymond was as good as new. A bath had scrubbed the blood away, the knife was long gone and all his clothes, including his socks, pants and shoes, had been burnt to cinders. As he sat on the armchair wearing Uncle Reg's clothes, Raymond was enjoying being the centre of attention.

'You can't go out like that. You look like fucking Alf Garnett,' Paulie chuckled, as he handed the hero a large Scotch.

'Thank God you moved into your new flat. Can you imagine your mother's and father's faces if you came home from work looking like that?' Eddie said, ruffling his hair.

Raymond smiled. He had already got over the shock of what he'd done, but the adrenalin was like a drug and he felt high with all the excitement. His parents had been shell-shocked yesterday when he'd moved most of his stuff out.

'What will you eat? Who's gonna cook for you and wash and iron your clothes?' his mother had said.

'He's moving out to become a proper villain. He'll be locked up for murder before you know it,' he'd heard his father shout.

Raymond smiled to himself. If he had the choice of killing people and making loads of money or killing his own soul by driving around in a bus, then he'd definitely choose option A.

As Ronny counted the money, the Scotch flowed around the room. 'There was two grand in each bundle, there's twenty grand here, not ten,' Ronny shouted out.

109

Eddie filled Raymond's glass right up to the very top. 'I think you should come and stay with me and Jess for a few days, just in case the Old Bill come sniffing around.'

Raymond agreed immediately. He'd already been given an alibi and he knew exactly what to say. Auntie Joan was covering for him and she had already been briefed to say that he'd been round at hers.

A knock on the front door spelled the arrival of Harry Mitchell. Hearing the story in full, Harry shook Raymond's hand and hugged Eddie. 'I told you throwing him in at the deep end was the right thing to do,' he told his son.

Eddie laughed. 'So you're taking all the credit for our new addition, are you? I don't think so, Dad – in your dreams, mate.'

As the jokes and drinks flowed, Eddie stood up and ssshed everyone. 'Let's have a toast to our wonderful new family member.' He smiled at Raymond. 'I'm gonna change your name for you, boyo. Raymond don't really suit you, it sounds too wank. From now on, after your performance today, you are officially called Raymondo.'

Raymond laughed as all the men stood up. 'To Raymondo,' everybody said, toasting him.

Raymond's smile lit up the room. He may not have made it as a rock star, but life was all down to fate, and he had certainly made it now.

ELEVEN

Jessica did her best to avoid attending Uncle Reg's surprise party, but Ed was having none of it.

'Why don't you just go with the boys and Raymond, Ed? I've got a bit of a headache and if we've got that party on Sunday, I'll be shattered.'

Eddie poured himself a Scotch. Jess pissed him off at times. For years, he'd fallen over backwards to entertain her family, yet when it came to his, it was an effort for Jess to give them the time of day.

Knocking his drink back in one, Ed glared at her. 'You can be such a selfish fucker at times. You've gotta come. All my family are gonna be there, and it ain't gonna look good if I turn up without you. Not only that, I want the kids to be there. My dad, aunts and brothers ain't seen 'em for fuck knows how long.'

'But I don't really know your family that well, and I won't know anyone else there. It's all right for you, Ed, you'll be stood up the bar with the boys all night, while I'm sat alone like a lemon,' Jess argued.

About to lose his rag, Ed stopped himself. 'I'll tell you what, why don't you ring your mum and dad and invite them. That way, you ain't sitting on your Jacks. Give us the phone, I'll ring 'em for you.'

Knowing when she was beaten, Jess reluctantly passed Ed the telephone. She'd never felt comfortable around Eddie's family. Ed always seemed to get drunk when they had a get-together and Jessica dreaded these odd occasions.

'Sorted,' Ed said, as he handed Jess the phone.

'What did Mum say? Is my dad coming as well?' Jessica asked.

Eddie laughed. 'Your mother nearly had a heart attack with the excitement of it all. Your dad's popped out, but your mum said he'll do as he's told. Right, you'd better get your arse in gear, I told me dad we'd be there at seven.'

About to walk out of the room, Jess saw Eddie pour himself a refill. 'Ed, promise me you won't get drunk tonight?'

Eddie shook his head in annoyance. 'Jess, you're me wife, not me keeper. Do yourself a favour, go and get ready and stop treating me like a fucking moron.'

Harry Mitchell had sworn everybody to secrecy. He didn't want Reg to clock on, so, instead of holding the party in the Flag, he'd booked the hall in the Marquis of Salisbury. He'd told Reg he was taking him out for a quiet meal with the boys.

'I don't want no fucking circus,' Reg warned him.

'You're not fucking getting one. What do you think I'm gonna do? Throw you a big party?' Harry lied.

Family and friends had been told to arrive at the Marquis at seven, half an hour before Reg was due there.

'For fuck's sake, cheer up a bit. You look like you're going to a funeral,' Ed hissed, as Jess got out of the cab.

Annoyed with his wife's demeanour, Eddie ushered Gary and Ricky inside and left Jess to deal with the twins.

'There you are. I wondered where you'd got to,' Joyce said, as she spotted her daughter.

112

'I've had the day from hell. Ed's been in a bad mood and the kids have driven me mad,' Jess moaned.

'Mum, can I have some crisps?' Frankie asked in a whining voice.

'You can have some when Daddy comes back from the bar. Now go and sit next to Grandad.'

'Mum, Mum,' Joey said, tugging her arm.

'What's the matter?' Jess asked, as she noticed Joey was crying.

'I think I've peed my pants.'

Ed reappeared at precisely the wrong moment. 'What's up?' he asked, handing Jess her drink.

'Nothing. I'm just going to take Joey to the toilet.'

'I'll take him. It's about time he started using the gents,' Eddie said, grabbing his son's hand.

'No. He thinks he's had a little accident, Ed. Leave it to me and I'll sort him out.'

Eddie looked at his son in disgust. 'What's the matter with you? You're not a baby, you're six years old. Why don't you ask if you wanna go to the fucking toilet?'

Jessica picked up her sobbing son. 'Don't shout at him, Ed. He can't help it.'

'He's a fucking embarrassment,' Eddie hissed, as he headed back to the bar.

Stanley glanced at Joyce as Eddie walked away. Neither of them had heard the conversation, but both of them got the gist that their son-in-law wasn't happy.

'I don't trust him as far as I can throw him, Joycie.'

'Stanley, just drink your drink and shut your cakehole,' Joyce ordered.

Uncle Reg arrived at quarter to eight.

'Surprise!' everyone shouted, as he shuffled in, embarrassed.

113

'Fuck you, Harry. You know how I hate anything like this.'

Sylvie, Harry's lady friend, had spent the morning decorating the hall with balloons, banners and old photographs of Reg.

'Oh, for fuck's sake,' Reg said as he clocked an enlarged image of himself as a spotty-faced teenager wearing an old army helmet.

Ed stood up the bar with Raymond, Ronny and Paulie. All four of them were in the mood for a party and were knocking the Scotch back like it was going out of style.

'Where's Jess?' Ronny enquired.

'Dunno, probably mollycoddling the fucking kids, as usual,' Ed replied arrogantly.

Seeing Gary and Ricky nick someone's beer, Eddie smiled. They were boys to be proud of. Not once had they ever shown him up by pissing themselves in public.

Stanley was frozen to his chair as he spotted Harry Mitchell strolling towards him with a bottle in his hand.

'Joyce, Stanley, lovely to see you again. And how are my beautiful grandchildren?' Harry said, patting the twins on the head.

Noticing Stanley flinch, Harry held up the bottle and smiled. 'Champagne, anyone?'

'Yes, please. I do like a drop of champers,' Joyce said, in a silly posh voice.

Harry poured her a glass and then turned to Stanley. 'And would you like a drop of the finest, Stanley?'

'No, not for me,' Stanley said, as he bolted to the toilet.

Frankie and Joey nudged one another as the strange man sat next to them.

114

'This is your grandad, Harry. Say "hello, Grandad Harry,"' Joyce said in a stupid, childlike voice.

Frankie giggled. She'd been in a naughty mood all day. 'My brother has peed his pants,' she said proudly.

'No, I didn't,' Joey shouted.

'Stop it, Frankie. She's only joking,' Joyce awkwardly informed Harry.

'No, I'm not. Joey always wets himself.'

As Joey burst into tears, Joyce burst into false laughter. 'Kids, eh? Say the funniest things don't they, Harry?'

Not sure what planet Joyce or his grandchildren were on, Harry stood up. 'Excuse me, Joycie. I have to answer a call of nature.'

'Bye Harry, lovely to see you again,' Joyce yelled, as he walked away.

Seeing Stanley hovering nervously by the doorway, Harry pretended not to notice him. He knew full well why Stanley was shit-scared of him. Harry never forgot the face of a victim or their friends, and he knew Stanley was the geezer who had been in the pub with Roger Dodds on the evening he'd unfortunately taken his eye out. Harry had recognised Stanley on the night of Eddie's wedding. He'd had him checked out afterwards, just to confirm that his mind was as sharp as ever. Harry smiled. The look on Stanley's face when he'd waved the champagne bottle towards him was a picture of pure fucking fear.

Auntie Joan and Auntie Vi were in their element. Harry had booked a duo, one singing and one on the piano, that were playing every war song that Joan and Vi had sung down the shelters.

Gee, it's great after bein' out late
Walkin' my baby back home

Arm in arm over meadow and farm
Walkin' my baby back home.

Eddie interrupted Joan and Vi's sing-song by plonking himself in the middle of them. 'How's my two favourite aunties?' he asked cheekily.

'Oi, go and get your bleedin' own,' Vi said, as he nicked a sausage roll off her plate.

Joan squeezed his hand. 'It's a wonderful evening, Eddie. Thoroughly enjoying ourselves, me and Vi are. Mustard this duo, ain't they?'

'Bit old hat for me. I prefer The Who or a bit of Rod Stewart meself,' Ed joked.

'Your mother loved all these songs, Eddie. There was no telly in them days, and we'd sit round your mum's coal fire singing these songs. Kept us amused, they did, especially when the sirens went off and we were stuck down them bloody shelters for hours on end,' Joan told him.

Eddie was overcome by emotion. 'I wish I could remember more about me mum. I can picture her face, but that's about it.'

Vi smiled at him. 'She was a kind, wonderful woman. Had a heart of gold, didn't she, Joan?'

Joan nodded. 'Give you her last ha'penny, she would. She was one of life's gentle souls.'

Aware that his eyes were starting to well up, Eddie stood up.

'Where's the little 'uns? We've seen Gary and Ricky, but we ain't seen the twins yet, have we, Vi?' Joan said.

'I'll tell Jess to bring 'em over in a minute,' Ed said, as he walked away.

Bowling over to the table where his wife was sitting, Ed could see no sign of her. 'Where's Jess?' he asked Stanley.

116

Stanley shrugged. 'Joyce has took the kids to the toilet, but I've no idea where Jess is.'

Eddie's eyes scanned the hall. He wasn't happy with Jessica's behaviour tonight. How could she not take the twins over to say hello to his two old aunts? She was out of fucking order.

Unable to see hide nor hair of Jess, Eddie walked back to the bar.

'What's up?' Paulie asked him.

'Nothing,' Eddie said, as he urged the barman to leave a bottle of Scotch on the counter.

Spotting Raymond chatting up a bird, Ed walked over to him. 'Where's Jess? You seen her?'

Raymond shrugged. 'She was sitting with me mum and dad. Don't worry, she won't go far without the twins. I'm gonna make a move now, Ed. This is Jane and we're going back to mine.'

As the singer took a toilet break, Ed smiled when his dad leaped on the stage and began one of his infamous speeches.

'Everyone knows why we're here tonight. We're celebrating the retirement of the oldest swinger in town. Reg, where are you? Now, I might be his brother, but I ain't giving you no old flannel. He was a horrible fucker when he was a kid. At six years old he . . .'

As Ed spotted Jess all cosied up with some good-looking geezer, he lost track of his father's speech. Fuming, Ed marched towards her, grabbed her arm, and pulled her away. 'Whaddya think you're fucking doing?'

Jessica looked at Eddie in horror. 'I beg your pardon. Are you drunk, Eddie? Don't embarrass me, please.'

Eddie sneered at the bloke. 'Who's that cunt?' he asked Jess.

'Lee Jones. You remember my old schoolfriend, Mary?

Well, Lee's her older brother. Please don't start, Ed. We're catching up on old times, that's all.'

'I am not a happy man, Jess. My aunt Joan and aunt Vi are sitting on that table near the door. You ain't said hello or fuck all to 'em. Asking me if the twins are here, they were. I want you to take the kids over to 'em, now, before I lose my temper with yer.'

'I'll take them over in a minute. Please don't show me up in front of Lee, Ed. I'd hate any bad stories to get back to Mary.'

Ed sneered. 'Fuck Lee and fuck Mary. I'm your husband and you'll do as I say.'

As Ed stormed back to the bar, Jess made her excuses to Lee and went off to find the twins. Sometimes her husband's temper was like a ticking time bomb and she would hate to create a scene.

'Who was that geezer Jess was all over? Got bored of you already, has she?' Ronny joked.

Eddie pushed Ronny up against the wall. 'Shut it, else I'll punch your fucking lights out.'

Ronny was taken aback. 'I'm only mucking about, Ed. I didn't mean it, honest I didn't.'

'What's going on?' Harry asked, pulling Eddie away.

'Nothing, Dad. It's him, he's off his fucking head,' Ronny said, feeling brave now his father had appeared.

Harry had a quiet word with Eddie. 'Look son, I don't know what's bugging you, but leave it tonight, eh? This is your Uncle Reg's party and I want him to have a good time.'

Eddie nodded. 'I'm fine, Dad. Ronny just needs to learn when to shut it, that's all.'

'Come on, twins. Say goodbye to Auntie Vi and Auntie Joan,' Jessica said, searching for her husband out of the corner of her eye. As she dragged the twins away, she clocked him. Ed was standing at the bar only yards away from Lee and his friends.

Jessica hadn't seen Lee Jones for years and was surprised to see him at Reg's party. Apparently, he was best friends with Ed's Uncle Albert's son, and he'd invited him. Jessica's heart was in her mouth as she sat back down with her parents. Unbeknown to Eddie, Lee had been her first love. She'd met him through his sister, Mary, and she'd had a crush on him for well over a year before he'd finally noticed she existed. They'd dated for two years on and off and Jess had lost her virginity to him. The relationship had ended when Jess had left school. It had run its course and both she and Lee amicably decided to go their separate ways.

Aware that Lee was talking about Jessica, Eddie edged towards him. Albert's son, John, had his back to Ed, otherwise he'd have warned Lee to shut up.

'Jess was always good-looking when we were kids, but she's a fucking stunner now. What a shame she's married. I wonder if she's up for a bit on the side? I'd give me right arm to fuck her again. You never know, she might even dump her husband for me,' Lee joked.

Like a madman, Eddie lunged towards Lee. 'That's my wife you're talking about. I'll kill you, you fucking cunt!' Ed shouted, as he rammed Lee's face repeatedly against the wooden bar post.

As Jessica screamed and ran towards the bar, Stanley felt the colour drain from his face.

'Stop it, Daddy, stop it,' Frankie cried, as she followed her mum from the table.

'Do something, Stanley,' Joyce shouted, as she tried to comfort Joey. Her grandson was trembling and had crawled under the chair.

119

It was Harry and Reg who managed to drag Eddie outside. His victim's face was smashed beyond recognition and somebody had already called for an ambulance.

Pushing his son against the wall, Harry glared at him. 'What the fuck was that all about?' he asked Ed.

Reg went back inside. He hated big parties at the best of times and had never wanted one in the first place. Now he had to somehow get to Lee and bribe him, to make sure he didn't involve the police.

'Why did you do it, Eddie? Why?' Jessica sobbed, as she ran over to her husband.

Using all of his strength, Ed pushed his old man flying and grabbed Jessica around the throat. 'What are you, some slag? How many other men have you fucking well slept with?' he roared, as he tightened his grip and slammed her head against the brick wall.

'I'm sorry, Ed. Stop it, please, you're hurting me,' Jess pleaded.

Harry grabbed Ed around the neck from behind. 'That's enough. Now get back inside.'

As Ed stormed off, Harry put a comforting arm around Jessica's shoulder. 'Are you OK, love?'

Jessica burst into tears. 'Ed frightens me when he drinks that Scotch. It turns him into a monster.'

Harry sat Jessica down on a nearby wall. He handed her his handkerchief and told her to dry her eyes. 'You leave Ed to me, I'll have a word with him. Is your head OK? You're not hurt, are you?'

Jessica shook her head. 'I love him so much, Harry. What am I gonna do?'

Squeezing her hand, Harry smiled. 'And my Ed loves you very much. I know he's a wild card at times, but he worships the ground you walk on, Jess. Tonight was just a one-off, he'd never intentionally hurt you, I know he wouldn't.'

For the first time ever, Jessica saw Harry Mitchell in a different light. She'd never had much to do with him in the past. Feeling guilty for all the years she'd tried to keep Harry away from the twins, she turned to face him. 'Why don't you come over for dinner one day, Harry? I'll cook us a nice roast and you can bring Sylvie with you.'

Harry winked at her. 'That sounds perfect.'

Stanley resembled a startled deer as he saw Harry clock him. He'd been rooted to the spot for the past five minutes and could barely believe what he'd witnessed. He'd seen Eddie with his hands around Jessica's throat, and was about to react before Harry had stepped in.

'Have a chat with your dad and I'll speak to Ed,' Harry said, walking away.

'Are you OK? He didn't hit you, did he?' Stanley asked.

Jessica stood up. 'No, he didn't. I'm fine, Dad, honest I am. It's cold out here, let's go back inside.'

'What's going on?' Joyce asked, as Stanley and Jessica sat down at the table.

As Jess hugged the twins, Stanley moved next to his wife. 'Thanks to you, our daughter's married to a fucking lunatic. As I walked outside, Ed had his hands around Jessica's throat and was trying to strangle her.'

'Why? What's she done wrong? Didn't you try and stop him, Stanley?'

'His father dragged him off of her. Anyway, what was I meant to do? They're villains, Joycie. They probably carry guns with them. They ain't gonna take no notice of a little man like me, are they?'

Lee had been carted off in the ambulance and had been told in no uncertain terms to say that he'd fallen down the stairs that led up to the hall, or else.

121

Eddie had now calmed down a bit. His dad had given him a good talking to and he was back at the bar having a drink with his brothers.

Most of the guests, including Auntie Joan and Auntie Vi, hadn't batted an eyelid when Ed had kicked off. Most family get-togethers ended up in a ruckus of some kind, and once you'd seen one poor bastard beaten to pulp, you'd seen them all.

Vi and Joan had been dancing to 'I've Got a Lovely Bunch of Coconuts', when the fight had erupted.

'Eddie's smashing some bloke's head against the bar,' Vi had said casually.

Joan carried on singing without even bothering to look round. She'd brought the boys up, and knew full well what cloth they were cut from.

Pissed off with Ronny and Paulie bombarding him with questions about Lee, Ed walked over to his dad. 'Can I have a quiet word?'

Harry excused himself from Sylvie and followed his son outside. 'I'm sorry for pushing you, Dad. I just lost it, you know how it is.'

Harry put a wise arm around his son's shoulder. 'Take my advice, Ed, talk to Jess and tell her you're sorry. Good women are hard to find and you'll be a fool to yourself if you lose her. I know I'm sort of courting Sylvie, but she'll never replace your mother, no one can.'

Ed nodded. He had no intention of taking his dad's advice, he was far too clever for that. Give women an inch and they take a mile. 'Thanks for the guidance,' he said, walking away.

'Oh, and by the way, Ed.'

Eddie turned around.

'If you ever push me like that again, I swear I'll knock your fucking block off.'

Eddie nodded, took a deep breath and strolled over to the table where Jess was sitting. 'Come outside, we need to have a little chat,' he told her.

'I've ordered a cab, Jessica wants to go home,' Stanley said curtly to Eddie.

'Cancel it. Jessica's going nowhere without me,' Eddie said, glaring at Stanley.

Stanley looked down at his feet. He knew when to shut up.

The twins were both asleep now, and Ed stroked their hair. 'We need to talk, Jess,' he said firmly.

As Jessica followed Eddie outside, Stanley turned to Joyce. 'If our Jess forgives him for tonight, she wants her bleedin' head tested.'

Joyce said nothing. For the first time ever, she had her doubts about Eddie. Trying to strangle Jessica was not something she had ever thought Ed would do.

'This is all your fault, Joycie, encouraging her to get involved with the likes of him. I tried to tell you but, as always, you wouldn't listen.'

Joyce stared at her husband. He was beginning to get on her nerves. He was forever blaming her for Jess getting involved with Eddie, and Joyce had had enough of it. 'Just shut up, Stanley. Jessica chose her own husband, it was nothing to do with me. All I did was support her choice, like any good mother should. I know Eddie was out of order tonight, but every couple has their arguments. Look at me and you, we don't stop arguing. The trouble with you, Stanley, is you never liked Eddie from day one. Ever since our Jess brought him home, you've been waiting for something like this to happen, just so you can say, "I told you so".'

123

Defeated, Stanley shook his head. 'It will all end in tragedy and tears, dear. You mark my words.'

Eddie lit a fag and leaned against the wall. 'You should have told me, Jess. If I'd known Lee was your ex, if you'd have said something, I wouldn't have lost it. How do you think I felt? Here I am at me uncle's retirement party and there's some geezer standing at the bar bragging about fucking me wife.'

Standing on tiptoe, Jessica cupped her husband's handsome face and gently kissed him. 'I'm sorry, Eddie. I can't believe Lee stood at the bar saying those things. We were only young when we dated, and he was a nice, quiet boy. He was my best friend Mary's brother.'

Eddie stared at the floor. 'It's ruined my night, Jess. I mean how would you like it, if some bird was giving it large about shagging me?'

With the memory of her husband trying to throttle her totally erased from her mind, Jessica apologised once again. 'I'll never keep anything from you again, Ed. I'm really sorry. Can't we go back and enjoy the rest of the party and forget all about it? I promise there'll be no more secrets.'

Ed shrugged then nodded. 'As long as you ain't got no more skeletons locked in the closet, I'm willing to forget about tonight.'

Jessica felt relief as she hugged him. 'I love you,' she whispered.

Eddie held her tight. 'Oh, and one more thing. I don't want you to have any more contact with that Mary.'

Jessica agreed. She rarely spoke to Mary now anyway. Eddie's feelings were far more important to her than those of some old schoolfriend.

The perfect gentleman, Ed held the door open for Jessica. As she walked through, Eddie smirked. The best form of defence was attack and, as usual, Ed had turned the situation around to his advantage.

TWELVE

As Eddie Mitchell ended the phone call, he could barely wipe the grin off his face. His father had just rung him and, in undercover lingo, let him know that the Old Bill were officially treating Mad Dave's murder as a bungled burglary and were looking for two young black males who had been seen loitering around that area the previous week.

Desperate to tell Raymond the good news in person, rather than via the phone, Eddie picked up his car keys. Ray had been at it all weekend with the tart he'd met at Reg's party, and had only just got rid of her.

'Finish getting the kids ready, Jess. I'm just popping out for a bit, I'll be back in about half-hour.'

'Where are you going?' Jessica called, as he slammed the front door.

Flustered because she was running late and was not even ready herself, Jessica marched Joey and Frankie downstairs and ordered Gary and Ricky to keep an eye on them for her. 'I won't be long. I just want to have a quick shower and get changed. Make sure they don't go out in the garden. They're ready for the party and I don't want them to get covered in mud.'

'Where's me Dad?' Gary asked.

Jessica shook her head. 'How should I know? You know what your father's like, comes and goes as he pleases.'

'Can I come upstairs with you, Mummy?' Joey whined.

'No, stay down here with your sister. Mummy won't be long, be a good boy and Gary and Ricky will play a game with you.'

'Please, Mum,' Joey screamed, clinging on to her legs.

Dragging him up by his arm, Jessica smacked him gently on his bottom. 'Do as I say, or Daddy won't let you go to the party.'

Desperate for twenty minutes to herself, Jessica left her son bawling his eyes out and went upstairs to make herself glamorous. The argument between herself and Eddie was now well and truly forgotten. Jess had a big bump on the back of her head where Ed had thrown her against the wall, but she hadn't told him that he'd hurt her. After the Lee episode, she was just thankful he'd forgiven her.

Sipping the coffee Raymond had just made him, Eddie pulled a face and spat the contents of his mouth back into the mug.

'Fucking hell, that's rancid. I think the milk's gone off.'

Raymond ignored his complaint. He was more interested in hearing about the Old Bill's findings than worrying about poxy milk.

'Right, tell me from the beginning what your dad said.'

Eddie explained the conversation in full. 'So, it looks like we're all off the hook. The filth always hated Mad Dave, he led 'em a merry dance for years, so they're not gonna pursue his death with five-star treatment.'

Raymond felt a surge of relief flow through his body. He'd been getting jumpy last night and hadn't slept too well. At least with the new information, he could now relax a bit. 'How does your old man know all this?' he asked Eddie.

Eddie smiled. 'The old man's had a couple of coppers on his payroll for years. One's a bent sergeant. The dodgy cunt demands a serious backhander for his info. It's worth it in the long run, though, we'll never get nicked with him on our side. He's tipped us off a few times in the past, when the filth were on our cases. An insider of that quality is worth his weight in gold.'

Raymond nodded in agreement. 'What you up to today, Ed? Is it all right if I come round to see Jess and the kids?'

Raymond loved having his new flat and independence, but he hated being alone for too long. That's why he'd let Jane, the bird he'd met, stay for two nights.

'We're going to a party down the road from me. This geezer has a big do every year. Pat Murphy his name is, he's an ex-boxer. Go and get yourself ready, Ray, and you can come with us. Jess won't mind, she'd love you to come,' Eddie told him.

Raymond didn't need asking twice. He was so used to his mum and dad constantly shouting at one another, he couldn't get used to the silence. 'I'll just run a quick bath. I'll be fifteen minutes, tops.'

Eddie laughed at his eagerness. 'Best you move your arse then, 'cause I told Jess I'd only be half an hour. Leave the door open, so you can give me the full lowdown on that little floozy you tugged.'

Jessica tried on a few outfits. She opted for her white linen trousers, red patent platform boots and a patterned vest top. She had originally chosen to wear her new dress, but had decided to keep it casual, as she had no idea what the other women would be wearing. Jess put a

128

cardigan, a pair of denim hotpants and a pair of flip-flops in her bag. She might get changed later on and, if she wanted to dance, she could take her boots off and wear her flatties.

'I'm home, babe,' she heard Eddie shout.

Unable to walk properly in her new chunky footwear, Jessica held on to the stair rail for dear life as she plodded down the stairs.

'Fucking hell, sis! You look like Wonder Woman in them.'

Surprised, but pleased to see her brother, Jessica playfully punched him. 'This is all the rage, Ray. You wouldn't know about women's fashion if it smacked you over the head, so I'd keep quiet if I was you,' she joked.

'Ed said I could come to the party with you. You don't mind, do you?'

Jessica smiled. 'Not at all. The twins will be thrilled.'

With Frankie in one arm and Joey in the other, Eddie walked towards Jessica. 'You look fabulous, but you don't need all that make-up on,' he said, pecking her on the lips.

Jessica wiped off her eye shadow. 'I didn't know what to wear. It's so warm today, I was going to wear my hotpants, but I don't know what the other women will be wearing and I'd hate to turn up looking tarty.'

Eddie smiled. 'You could never look like a tart, Jess. We ready to make tracks then?'

Both Jessica and Raymond nodded.

'Gary, Ricky, move your arses. You've got one minute or I'm leaving you here,' Ed shouted.

Patrick Murphy was a big, flash, loud Irishman who loved nothing more than being the centre of attention. He'd been holding his legendary bank-holiday parties for over ten years now and every year he tried to push the boat out a couple of yards more. Over the years, Patrick had fathered six children by three different women. Like many a good man, he adored his own, but wasn't that keen on anybody else's. This year, to rectify his own little problem, he'd fenced off a great big part of the field just for the kids. He'd hired fairground rides, swings and slides. He'd even booked Bob the balloon man and a clown from Corringham to keep the little bastards occupied and well away from the adults.

Eddie had chosen to drive his Porsche to the party. He had no intention of driving it home drunk, but was determined to show off his wealth. Jess had urged him to get a cab, but he'd flatly refused. She was a woman and she didn't understand the method in a man's madness.

With the whole family unable to fit in the Porsche, Jessica had also brought her Merc. 'We'll get a cab home later and pick the cars up tomorrow,' Ed told her.

Parking on the packed field, Eddie suddenly wished he had got that cab after all. 'Jesus wept! Look at the motors here. Look at that Roller – I wonder who that belongs to?'

'I dunno, but the guests here are all obviously minted. Look at that green Bentley, Ed. Ain't it a beauty?' Ray said.

Annoyed that his motor paled into insignificance, Eddie quickly leaped out and urged Ray, Gary and Ricky to do the same. 'Come on, Jess has just parked up and I'm gagging for a drink.'

Walking towards the gates of the house, Eddie was surprised to see a big bloke in a suit vetting people.

'Names?' the guy asked bluntly.

Eddie gave him his name and explained who Raymond was.

'In you go,' the geezer told him.

'Eddie! Great to see you,' Pat Murphy said, shaking his hand.

Eddie introduced his family and gratefully accepted the glasses of champagne that a waiter appeared with.

'We're gonna get a hot dog, Dad,' Gary said, dragging Ricky away.

'Mummy, can I go and see the clown?' Frankie screamed.

'I wanna balloon. Get me a balloon,' Joey said, tugging Jessica's arm.

Patrick smiled at the two spoilt brats. 'Do you want to come with me? Uncle Patrick has booked childminders to look after you and keep you amused. We've got games, toys, even fairground rides – safe ones, of course.'

'Yes! Can we go Mummy, please?' Frankie screamed.

Jessica looked at her husband for guidance. 'I'm not sure, Ed. Shouldn't they stay with us for a bit?'

Joey burst into tears and threw himself onto the ground. 'I want a balloon and I want one now,' he sobbed.

Embarrassed by his son's behaviour, Eddie yanked him up by one arm. 'I'll give you more than a balloon in a minute, Joey. Stop behaving like a baby and act your fucking age.'

'I'll go over the play-area bit with 'em, if you want,' Raymond offered.

'No, you won't. As Pat says, they'll be fine. It's time they were let off the harness. If we didn't pamper them so much, they wouldn't make a show of us in public every time we took 'em out. I'm sick of 'em whingeing and crying every time they don't get their own way and I ain't putting up with it no more,' Eddie said, glaring at his wife.

Jessica looked away. Once Eddie got a bee in his bonnet, there was no point arguing with him. She knew he was having a dig at her, but she couldn't help the way she was. She hated letting the twins out of her sight. The week they'd started school was the worst week of her life. She'd drop them off, drive straight home and sob her heart out until it was time to pick them up again.

'Go on, then. Uncle Patrick will show you the play area. Enjoy yourselves,' she said, as the twins skipped happily away.

Sensing Jessica's awkwardness, Raymond put an arm around her shoulder. 'If we stand over there by that bar, we can keep more of an eye on 'em,' he said.

Jessica nodded gratefully.

Seeing that Eddie was already surrounded by a fan club, Raymond tapped his arm. 'Me and Jess are gonna stand by that table next to the bar.'

'No probs. I'll be over in a bit,' Eddie replied.

Spotting Frankie and Joey joyfully running around hitting one another with plastic hammers, Jessica relaxed and took in the rest of her surroundings. There were two makeshift bars, about half a dozen waiters walking about with trays and right in the centre was the biggest barbecue that Jessica had ever seen.

Aware that his sister was clocking the grub, Raymond pointed towards the conservatory. 'They've got tons more food in there. There's sandwiches, seafood, everything. I saw it as we walked past. Are you hungry? Shall I get you something?'

Jessica shook her head. 'I'll have something later. What's that man doing with them boxes? And what's that big square thing over there?'

Raymond craned his neck. 'I think the geezer carrying the boxes is the DJ. He's probably setting his stuff up for later and I think that's the boxing ring over the back. From what Eddie was telling me, I think all the lads lark about in it later on.'

Noticing a crowd of women sitting together, Jessica

had a look to see what they were wearing. 'Good job I never wore my denim hotpants. No one is very dressed up. In fact, I feel silly in these boots now, I'm gonna put my flip-flops on.'

Raymond laughed as Jessica frantically tried to tug her boots off. Women were funny creatures. Blokes didn't give a shit what they were wearing – well, apart from Eddie, that was. He insisted on buying the best of everything.

Seeing Gary and Ricky bound towards her, Jessica asked them a favour. 'Don't tell your dad I asked you, but will you check on the twins for me? They're in that play area that's sectioned off.'

Gary and Ricky did as they were asked and were back within minutes. 'They're having a great time. Frankie is hitting the clown with a big plastic hammer and Joey's skipping about with some other little boy,' Gary told Jess.

'We told them where you're standing, so they know where to find you,' Ricky said to Raymond.

Seeing Eddie walk towards her with another couple, Jessica smiled at him.

'This is Dougie, an old pal of mine from way back and this is his girlfriend, Vicki,' said Eddie. 'Dougie, Vicki, this is Jessica, my wife, and my brother-in-law, Raymondo.'

As the men shook hands, Jessica grinned shyly at Vicki. Dougie looked well into his forties, but his girlfriend only looked about the same age as herself. Jessica liked her immediately. Vicki was very pretty with long dark hair, a warm smile and was a very trendy dresser.

As the waiter came up, both girls reached for the bubbly. 'I love your shoes – where did you get them from?' Jessica asked.

'Dougie bought them for me. He got them up the West End,' Vicki replied.

133

Overhearing their conversation, Eddie noticed that Jess had put on an old pair of flip-flops. He gently pulled her to one side. 'Put your boots back on, babe, I don't like you in them flip-flops. They make you look like a cleaner.'

Feeling a bit embarrassed, Jessica smiled at Vicki. 'Men, eh?' she muttered as she quickly did as Ed had asked.

Vicki did her best to put her at ease. 'Dougie's the same. He always tells me what to wear. Wow, them red boots are just fabulous.'

Eddie grinned. 'See,' he said nudging Jess. 'Your husband knows best.'

Jessica nodded and turned back to Vicki. 'So, are you and Dougie local? I take it you live together.'

Vicki nodded. 'Your husband was telling us where you live. We're about five minutes away. You'll have to come round one day. We can have lunch while the men are at work.'

'I'd love to,' Jessica replied, thrilled.

Ever since Jess had married Eddie, she'd lost touch with virtually all of her friends. She'd still heard from Mary, but Ed had even put a stop to that now. Eddie hated her going out of a night. Ginny had rung her recently and invited her out for a meal to celebrate their friend Linda's birthday. Eddie had made it perfectly clear that he didn't want her to go. 'Only old slappers go on girls' nights out when they're married with kids,' he told her. Jess didn't bother to argue. What was the point when she always came out second best?

'I won't be a sec. I'm just going to check on the kids,' Jess told Vicki.

'Where you off to?' Ed asked her.

'To make sure the twins are OK,' Jess replied.

Eddie sighed and turned back to Dougie and Raymond.

'What about that pikey that's bought that big house near you? He's fucking cakeo, he is,' Dougie said.

'What pikey? You talking about the big white gaff near the bend?' Ed asked.

'Yeah, that's the one. I don't know his name, someone pointed him out to me earlier. He's here at the party, pulled up outside in a Roller, he's a mate of Patrick's, apparently.'

Eddie felt his blood start to boil. He'd despised travellers ever since he was a teenager and he certainly didn't want them living near him. The O'Haras were the main cause of his hatred and, even though he hadn't seen them for years, he still hated Jimmy with a passion. Annoyed, Eddie snatched a couple more glasses off the waiter's tray and handed one to Dougie.

'I ain't fucking happy about a pikey living near me. You know what thieving bastards they are, I'll have to fucking nail everything down. See if you can spot the cunt and show me who he is.'

Dougie craned his neck and shook his head. 'Maybe he didn't stay long. I can't see him now.'

Raymond laughed at Eddie's annoyance. 'Whoever it is, if he's brought a house the size of that white one and is swanning about in a Rolls-Royce, I doubt you'll need to worry about him nicking your plant pots, Ed.'

Luckily for Raymond, Eddie saw the funny side and laughed. Maybe he was overreacting a bit. The feud with the O'Haras was now in the past, and it was wrong to tar every other traveller with the same brush.

Jessica returned with not only the twins, but two other little boys in tow as well.

'Fuck me, we only had two kids when they went in there,' Eddie joked.

Jessica smiled. 'They wanted you and Uncle Raymond to meet their new friends.'

135

Seeing Frankie holding hands with a little boy, Eddie smiled. Seeing that Joey was also holding hands with a little boy, Eddie knocked his arm away. 'Frankie can hold hands with boys. You can only hold hands with girls, Joey. Do you understand?'

'Yes, Daddy,' Joey said meekly.

Jessica felt sorry for her son. 'Don't have a go at him. He's only six, and at that age they hold hands with girls and boys,' she said to Eddie.

Feeling guilty, Eddie ruffled Joey's hair. 'What's your mate's name then?'

'Michael,' Joey mumbled.

Eddie smiled at Frankie. 'And what's your friend's name?'

Holding hands with the object of her affection, Frankie put her other hand on her hip. 'He's not my friend, Daddy, he's my boyfriend and his name is Jed.'

Eddie bent down and shook hands with both kids. 'Pleased to meet you Michael, pleased to meet you Jed,' he said, laughing.

'Can I take Frankie to play in the woods?'

'Cheeky little bugger,' Eddie said to Raymond and Dougie. 'No, you bloody well can't,' Eddie told him laughing.

'Yes, I can,' Jed said, pecking Frankie on the cheek.

Eddie couldn't believe the front of the kid. He wasn't even used to grown men answering him back, let alone an ankle-biter. Grabbing hold of Frankie, Eddie hoisted her into his arms. 'Off you go now, Jed. Go and find your own mum and dad.'

Jed shook his head. 'I wanna stay here with Frankie.'

'Please, Daddy, let me go and play in the woods with Jed,' Frankie cried.

Getting more annoyed by the second, Eddie handed his daughter over to Jessica and knelt back down to face the brat. 'Listen Jed, I'll tell you once more, go away, else I'll go and find your father and get him to drag you away.'

Jed stared into Eddie's eyes. 'No, you won't. My daddy knows you, he don't like you. He won't do as you tell him.'

Suddenly, an awful feeling washed over Eddie. Surely not? It couldn't be, could it?

Eddie felt his mouth go dry as he asked the question. 'Who is your father, Jed?'

Jed smiled. 'My dad is Jimmy O'Hara.'

THIRTEEN

Realising that Eddie was anything but happy, Jed decided it was time for him to jog on.

'Bye Frankie,' he shouted as he ran away.

Petrified, little Michael bolted as well. Absolutely seething, Eddie vented his anger towards his six-year-old daughter. 'If I ever find out you've been playing in them woods with a gyppo, I'll break your fucking legs, Frankie.'

Sobbing, Frankie clung to her mum. She was far too young to understand what she had done so wrong. 'I'm sorry, Daddy,' she whispered.

Not used to seeing his sister so upset, Joey started to sob too. Jessica was furious. 'Pull yourself together, Ed. Your daughter's only six years old, for God's sake.'

Desperate to try and smooth things over, Raymond grabbed Eddie's arm. 'Come on, me and you will go and get another round of drinks,' he told him.

Still shell-shocked, Eddie allowed himself to be led away.

Embarrassed by her husband's behaviour, Jessica apologised profusely to Dougie and Vicki. 'I'm so sorry about that. Eddie's such a great dad usually, I don't know what's come over him.'

With both twins still sobbing and clamouring for her

attention, Jessica did her best to placate them. 'Now, come on, stop all that crying. Daddy didn't mean what he said, he just got angry, that's all. He is silly at times your daddy, isn't he?'

Holding one another's hands, Frankie and Joey nodded simultaneously.

Looking into their innocent little eyes, Jessica felt like crying herself. Picking on her was one thing, starting on the kids was another. Aware that Eddie was on his way back from the bar, she quickly pulled herself together. 'Shall Mummy take you to get an ice cream from that van over there?'

The word ice cream usually managed to stop the tears and Jessica was relieved as, once again, it worked wonders.

'Can I have a ninety-nine?' Frankie asked brightly.

'I want a screwball, Mummy,' Joey grinned.

As Eddie reappeared he tried to wrap his arms around her, Jessica scowled and walked away with the twins. Watching Jessica walk away, Eddie stood chatting to Raymond and Dougie. He wasn't really concentrating on the conversation – he couldn't. The party was pretty packed now and Ed had no idea where O'Hara was, but he couldn't get him out of his mind.

He'd never set eyes on any of the O'Haras since the day they'd moved off the site in Stratford. He'd heard rumours over the years that Jimmy was doing well for himself in the scrap game. He also heard that he'd originally moved to Basildon and then, more recently, to Kent. Finishing his Scotch, Eddie headed back to the bar to get himself another.

O'Hara being at the party was bad enough, but the fact that the cunt was swanning about in a Roller and had bought the fucking house that he'd wanted was far too much for him to swallow.

'All right, Dad? Can you get me and Ricky a beer?'

Eddie smiled at his eldest two boys. ''Course I can. What you been doing?'

Gary grinned. 'We've been sparring in the ring. I met this boy, Billy O'Hara. Same age as me, he is, and he thinks he's the bollocks. He wants to fight me later and I'll beat him, Dad, I just know I will.'

Eddie handed the boys their drinks. 'I need you to beat that boy, Gary. I know his father and I hate him. Now, don't let me down, son.'

Gary smiled confidently. 'I won't. I'll let you know when we're ready to fight and you can come and watch me,' he said, dragging Ricky away.

About to walk away from the bar, Eddie came face to face with his very worst nightmare.

'How you doing, mush?' Jimmy O'Hara asked him.

Not wanting to mug himself off, Eddie kept his voice calm. 'Fine. And you?'

Jimmy smiled. 'I'm cushti. Actually, I'm glad we bumped into one another. I dunno if you've heard, but I think we're about to become neighbours. Bought the place down the road to you, I have. I'm moving in this week.'

'So I hear,' Eddie said brightly. He was desperate to sound normal and hide the jealousy in his voice.

Jimmy O'Hara tilted his head to one side. 'Look, mush, I know we've been through a lot of shit in the past, but we've both moved on now, so can we call it quits?'

As Jimmy held out his right hand, Eddie had little option but to shake it. 'Suits me. I've got a family now, I don't want no grief,' Eddie replied.

Jimmy smiled. 'Same here. I'm putting a mobile home next to me new gaff, so me mum and dad can live there. Three chavvies I've got now, all boys. Actually, I think me youngest, Jed, has got a crush on your daughter. You never know, we might have a wedding on our hands, Eddie boy.'

Eddie made an effort to smile. If O'Hara thought for one minute that his beautiful daughter would ever be jumping over a broomstick, pissing in a bucket and eating a wedding banquet of baked hedgehog in clay, he could fucking think again.

'I best be getting these drinks back now, the lads'll be wondering where I've gone. I'll see you around, Jimmy.'

As Eddie walked away, Jimmy O'Hara smirked. The scar he'd given him was a pure work of art. He could sense that Eddie Mitchell was thoroughly pissed off with him buying the house and that pleased him immensely. Jimmy O'Hara wasn't as forgiving as he portrayed himself. As if he was ever going to forget his father being shot in the foot. His old man was a shadow of his former self and had walked with a limp ever since.

He and his brothers had all sworn to their father that they would let bygones be bygones. They had promised to forget about their feud with the Mitchells, once and for all. Knowing his dinlo brothers, they probably had forgotten about it. Jimmy didn't see much of them now. Ever since he'd given up the pub protection racket, he kept well away.

Opting to go legal was the best decision Jimmy had ever made. The month he'd spent in hospital after Eddie had beaten him to a pulp had given him food for thought. Jimmy had always been the brains of the family since he was a nipper, and he was now the proud owner of fifteen scrapyards in Kent and Essex. Millions he'd made, fucking millions, and he made sure his wife, chavvies and parents were all well provided for.

Ordering a round of drinks, Jimmy nodded to Eddie as he walked back past him. He would never break his

141

promise to his dad while Butch was still alive. Jimmy grinned as he marched across the field. He would bide his time, play Mr Nice Guy and then, one day, when the time was right, he'd make Eddie Mitchell wish that he'd never been born.

'Please Mummy, can we go and play on the rides?' Joey asked.

'We'll be good, we won't be naughty,' Frankie added.

Jessica looked at Eddie with pleading eyes. 'Let them go and play, Ed. They'll only be bored standing here with us.'

Eddie shook his head. He was drunk now, very drunk. 'Fuck me, you've changed your tune. You didn't want to let them out of your sight a few hours ago. They ain't going nowhere, they're staying put.'

Seeing the twins faces crumple, Jessica stood her ground. 'If you won't let them go and play, I'm taking them home, Ed. It's too hot for them sitting here and I'm not gonna let them watch you drink yourself into a stupor again. They were petrified when you kicked off the other night. It's not fair on them, they're only babies.'

Furious at being spoken to like shit in front of Dougie and Raymond, Eddie grabbed Jessica by the arm and dragged her towards the bar.

'Ed, stop it, you're hurting me!' Jessica cried.

Dougie had had enough of Eddie's drunken behaviour by now. 'I've just spotted a pal of mine over by the entrance. Tell Eddie I'll see him later on,' Dougie told Raymond as he dragged Vicki away.

Raymond nodded. He could see that his sister was upset and he didn't know what to do for the best. His dad had told him about the row at Reg's party, but getting involved in other people's maritals just wasn't his scene.

142

'Can we go home now, Uncle Raymond?' Joey pleaded.

Raymond glanced back towards the bar. Seeing Eddie shouting at Jessica, he decided he had no choice but to step in. Blood was thicker than water, after all. 'Stay there, don't move,' he ordered the twins.

Running towards his sister, he pushed himself in between her and Eddie. 'For fuck's sake, can yous two stop arguing? You're upsetting the kids and everybody's looking at you. It's embarrassing.'

'Eddie's drunk, Ray. All I want to do is go home,' Jessica wept.

'I've told you, you're my missus and you'll go home when I say you can,' Eddie said nastily.

Raymond put a protective arm around his sister. 'Come on, Jess, let's go and stand over by the disco. The kids can have a dance and we can watch 'em.'

Eddie sneered as his wife and brother-in-law walked away. He knew deep down that he was in the wrong. As a rule, he was a good drinker, he could hold his own with the best of them. But on the odd occasion when he hammered the Scotch, he knew he turned into an arrogant arsehole.

'There is nothing worse than seeing a grown man drunk and acting like a fucking idiot. Watch your booze intake, Eddie, 'cause when you're steaming, that's exactly what you turn into,' his father had told him only recently.

Eddie ordered himself another large Scotch. He had every right to get pissed after the shock he'd had today. Jessica wouldn't understand. For years he'd only had to look in the mirror and see his scar to be reminded of Jimmy O'Hara.

'Dad, Dad. Quick, the boxing's about to start,' Gary said, tugging at his sleeve.

Putting his arm around his eldest, Eddie swaggered

over to the ring with him. 'Beat that O'Hara kid and I'll give you a score, Gary.'

'What about me?' Ricky asked.

'You win your bout and I'll give you a score as well,' Eddie said laughing.

'Are you OK?' Vicki asked, as she sat down on the grass next to Jessica.

Jessica nodded. 'Eddie's never usually like that, so please don't think badly of him, will you?'

Vicki squeezed her hand. 'I don't. I have to put up with a lot with my Dougie sometimes, believe me.'

Jessica smiled. 'Aren't you and Dougie going to get married or have children?'

A sudden look of sadness washed over Vicki. 'Dougie's ex-wife died of leukaemia and I think he still loves her. He don't wanna get married again, he says no one can ever take her place. He reckons he wants more kids, but I don't know if he's just bluffing. It's hard sometimes, Jess, I feel like I'm second best to a ghost.'

Noticing tears in Vicki's eyes, Jessica hugged her new friend. 'We're a right pair we are, aren't we?'

Their conversation was ended by an excited Frankie. 'Look Mummy, Joey's dancing.'

Jessica stood up to get a better look at her son. The DJ was playing the Village People's 'YMCA' and Joey stood in a circle full of adults. He was waving his arms and copying the funny dance they were doing.

Vicki linked arms with Jessica. 'Ah, look. He's just so gorgeous, both of your kids are. You're really lucky, Jess. I'd give my right arm for two kids like yours.'

Jessica smiled proudly. Everybody said how gorgeous her twins were and they were right, of course.

* * *

144

Eddie's heart thumped with adrenalin as Gary stepped into the ring. He could see Jimmy O'Hara standing opposite and he just prayed that the training his son had been given at the Peacock Gym would pay off.

'Go on, Gary, I'm banking on you, son,' he yelled, as the fight started.

'Jab, jab, Gary. Hit him with your right,' Raymond urged.

As Gary swung a right hook and the O'Hara boy hit the canvas, Eddie and Raymond leaped up and down.

Not only was Patrick Murphy the referee, he also ran a book on these special occasions, and both Eddie and Raymond had stuck a oner on Gary to win. 'He's a good little boxer,' Patrick told Eddie, as he handed over their winnings.

Eddie smiled as Jimmy O'Hara approached him. 'Got a good right hook, won fair and square your boy. How old's your other one? My second one down, Marky, is thirteen.'

'My Ricky's twelve, but he can handle himself all right.'

'Get him in the ring, then,' O'Hara demanded.

Eddie and Gary placed another oner bet each and watched as Ricky put on a pair of gloves. 'Hit him hard, son, as hard as you fucking can,' Eddie urged him.

'He's a lot taller than me,' Ricky said vulunerably.

'The bigger they are, the harder they fall,' Eddie told him.

'Go on, Ricky, you can do it,' Gary yelled as the bout began.

Desperate to make his dad proud of him, Ricky flew out of his corner. Within a minute he had knocked the O'Hara boy down.

'Marky's fine, let him carry on,' Jimmy O'Hara shouted.

Patrick Murphy waved his hands to signal the end of

145

the fight. 'And the winner is Ricky Mitchell,' he shouted, holding Ricky's right arm aloft.

Jimmy O'Hara was pissed off. He'd had £200 each on his boys and they'd both let him down. 'Why did you stop it? He slipped over,' he moaned to Pat Murphy.

Patrick shrugged. 'You know the rules, Jimmy. He never slipped, he was put down. One knock down, fight over. They're only kids, remember.'

Seeing the smarmy expression on Eddie Mitchell's face, Jimmy walked towards him. 'Let's put the little 'uns in there, then. How old's your youngest?'

'My Joey's six, but his mother won't be letting him get in there,' Eddie chuckled.

Jimmy tried to goad him, 'Does your wife wear the trousers, then? Five he is, my Jed. Come on, let the chavvies have a go. What are you? A man or a mouse?'

Eddie shrugged. Jed might only be five, but he certainly wasn't a wimp like Joey was. As it wasn't in his nature to back down, Eddie went off to find his youngest.

Seeing Jessica sitting with Vicki, he walked over to them. 'Where's Joey?'

Jessica smiled and pointed to the makeshift dancefloor. Eddie's blood boiled as he spotted his son. He looked a right pansy dancing in a circle with six little girls.

'He's coming with me. I've organised a little boxing match for him,' Eddie told Jessica bluntly.

Jess looked at her husband in horror. 'What do you mean? A boxing match?'

'He's going in the ring with that little Jed. They're only having a spar up, it's nothing dangerous,' Eddie said reassuringly.

'No, he is not,' Jessica said immediately. 'He's six years old, Eddie.'

Ignoring her, Eddie marched towards Joey and dragged him out of the circle.

'Leave him alone!' Jessica screamed, chasing after her husband.

'Daddy, no, leave Joey alone,' Frankie cried.

Vicki caught Jess by the arm and cuddled her. 'Leave it, Jess. You won't win. Men like ours, they don't listen, love.'

'Please, Daddy. I don't want to box, I want to dance,' Joey sobbed.

Picking up his son, Eddie marched him towards the boxing ring. 'Stop crying else I'll wallop you. Now, all you've got to do is get in that ring and land a few punches. Just hit him as hard as you can, Joey. You're older than him, you'll be fine.'

'I don't want to, Daddy,' Joey said, trying to wriggle out of his father's arms.

Eddie slapped his son gently around the face. 'Like it or not, you're doing it. Dancing is for girls, boxing's for boys. Now get in that ring and make your dad proud of you.'

Jessica was hysterical as her son was lifted into the ring. 'Do something, Raymond, please,' she screamed.

Grabbing hold of her and Frankie, Raymond hugged them both. 'It'll be fine, Jess. I can't do nothing, you know what Ed's like. Just face me and don't look. It'll be over within seconds.'

Joey shook like a leaf as the boy stared at him. 'Hit him, Joey, hit him!' Eddie screamed.

'I can't. I don't want to,' Joey sobbed, as Jed lunged towards him.

As the punch landed on Joey's chin, he hit the deck with an almighty thud.

Seeing Patrick Murphy wave his hands, Jimmy O'Hara

jumped into the ring and lifted Jed up in triumph. He'd had £500 on his youngest, so at least he was no longer out of pocket.

Eddie dashed into the ring to tend to Joey.

'Is he OK? I'm a first-aider,' he heard someone say.

'He doesn't look OK,' somebody else shouted.

Jessica pushed Raymond away and took in the pandemonium. Hysterical, she ran towards her son. 'Joey, Joey, Joey!' she cried.

Seeing her son's limp body, Jessica screamed louder than she had ever screamed before.

FOURTEEN

'I've just examined Joey. He's absolutely fine, you can take him home now,' the doctor told Jessica.

Relieved, Jessica repeatedly thanked the doctor and hugged her mum. 'Ring Dad and get him to come and pick us up,' she told Joyce.

Joey had come round five minutes after he'd been knocked out cold. Petrified that he might have concussion or suffered permanent brain damage, Jessica had brought him to casualty. He'd been kept in overnight as a precaution and Jess was thankful that her prayers had been answered and he was OK.

She had used Patrick's phone to call her parents, who had been brilliant. Stanley had taken the hysterical Frankie home with him, while Joyce had stayed with Jessica and Joey at the hospital all night.

Eddie had turned up at the hospital late the previous night, but Jess had immediately sent him packing. 'Get away from me and my children,' she screamed.

'Please, Jess, let me see Joey. I'll make it up to him, I'll make it up to you and Frankie as well. Nothing like this will ever happen again, I promise,' Ed pleaded.

Jessica was having none of it. She had seen a side to her husband over the last couple of days that she'd never seen before. A nasty, vicious, drunken side, and she would never forgive him for what he had done to Joey. 'Just go, Ed. If you don't I shall scream blue murder and tell the nurses and doctors what really happened,' she told him.

With tears in his eyes, Ed walked away. Jess knew he felt terribly guilty – she could see it in his eyes – but she could never excuse what he had done.

She had told them in casualty that Joey had fallen off a swing. She could hardly tell them the truth, could she? Their faces would be a picture if she told them her husband had forced their six-year-old son to participate in a boxing match. She'd have social services knocking on her door if the doctors found out the truth..

'Hello, Mummy. Are we going home now? I want to play with Milky the Cow.' Joey said chirpily.

Jessica scooped her son into her arms. 'We're going to stay with Nanny and Grandad for a few days,' she told him.

Joey looked perplexed. 'But I haven't got any toys at Nanny and Grandad's house. Can't we go to our house, Mummy?'

Jessica stroked his thick blond hair. The innocence of his eyes tugged at her heart strings and she felt a tear run down her cheek. 'Frankie's round at Grandad's. You want to see your sister, don't you? And what about the pigeons? Grandad will take you out and you can help him fly them.'

Joey could tell that his mum was upset, but he wasn't sure why. 'OK,' he said, smiling.

'Hello, darling, how's Nanny's little soldier?' Joyce said, as Jessica walked towards her with Joey in her arms.

'I'm hungry, Nan. Can I have some chips?'

Joyce kissed Joey on the forehead. 'As soon as we get home, Nanny will cook you whatever you want.'

*   *   *

150

As soon as Raymond opened his front door, Eddie walked inside and sat on the sofa with his head in his hands. He hadn't slept a wink and he was consumed with guilt and an aching heart. Ed knew he'd been bang out of order. Seeing O'Hara had made his blood boil. Overcome by jealousy, he'd got paralytic and the rest was history.

'I know Joey's all right. I rang up the hospital this morning. What am I gonna do, Ray? Say I've lost Jess? She might leave me and take the kids with her.'

Raymond shrugged. This was an awkward situation for him, and his loyalty really lay with his sister. Seeing tears in Eddie's eyes, he decided not to rub salt in his wounds. He obviously knew what he'd done was wrong, so there was no bloody point in making it worse for him.

'I dunno what you're gonna do, Ed. Is Joey still in hospital or have they let him out?'

'The nurse I spoke to said that he was OK and he'd be discharged this morning. I can't see Jess coming home, though. Your mum's up there with her and I reckon she'll take the kids round to hers.'

Raymond nodded. He'd shot up the hospital last night and spoken to Jessica and his mum, and he knew she wasn't planning on going home. 'Do you wanna drink? You're shaking,' Raymond said to Eddie.

Ed shook his head. 'It's drink that's fucking caused all this. If I hadn't been so pissed, none of it would have happened.'

Raymond opened a can of lager and sat down opposite Eddie. 'I really don't know what to say, Ed. The only advice I can give you is to let me sister calm down a bit. I wouldn't go round me mum's just yet. I mean, Jess has got to come home at some point, she's got no clean clothes for herself or the kids with her, has she? And what about school? She won't want the twins having too much time off, will she?'

Eddie stood up. 'I'm gonna go home and wait there in case she comes back. I might try and ring her at your mum's, see if she'll talk to me. I'll do anything to get her to forgive me, Ray. I love her, she's my life and without her I'm nothing.'

'Joey,' Frankie cried, throwing her arms around her brother's neck.

Stanley hugged Jessica. He'd always known that one day that bastard she'd married would show his true colours and he just hoped that his daughter had the courage to leave him now.

'I'm gonna have a lie-down on the sofa,' Jessica said.

'Let Mummy have a rest. Nanny's going to cook some of her special crinkled chips,' Joyce said, leading the kids into the kitchen.

Stanley sat in his armchair. He needed to have a chat with Jessica in private. 'You've got to leave him, Jess. I mean, if he's done what he's done to his son, it proves that he's capable of anything. It's not like it's a one-off. He nearly strangled you the other night, love. The man's a fucking monster.'

Jessica looked down at her hands and said nothing. Punishing her husband was one thing; leaving him was another.

Her dad carried on talking. 'You've got to put the kids first, Jess, and if their safety is at risk, you've no option but to leave him.'

Jessica felt her eyes welling up. 'I need to make this decision myself, Dad. I'll stay here for a few days, get me head straight and then I'll decide what to do.'

Stanley shook his head. 'If you stay with Eddie, you're

152

a fool, Jess. He's obviously an animal and you'd be far better off without him in your life.'

Pleased that the twins had run back into the room and ended such an awkward conversation, Jessica went outside to talk to her mum. 'Dad reckons Eddie's dangerous. He said I've got no choice other than to leave him.'

'Don't take no notice of that silly old bastard. What does he know, eh? Look, what Eddie did this weekend was wrong, very wrong, but you can't just walk away from an otherwise happy marriage because of two stupid mistakes. You said yourself, he was drunk both times. Lay the law down to him. The ball's in your court, Jess. Tell him you'll only come home if he promises not to drink Scotch in front of you and the kids any more.'

Jessica sighed. She had so much on her mind, she felt as if her head was about to burst. 'I really don't know what came over him, Mum. He's usually such a good husband and father, and I've never seen him as drunk as he was yesterday. There was some bloke at the party that he's had this feud with over the years. Eddie hates this O'Hara fella. I think he was the one that scarred his face and I just don't think Eddie could handle seeing him again.'

Joyce smiled. 'There's your answer, then. It was a one-off, Jess. Play hard to get, make him sweat for a few days before you go back home, but you must go back, dear. Look at your lovely house, you don't want to lose that and your nice lifestyle, do you now?'

Jessica nodded. The house and her lifestyle were the last of her bloody problems, but sometimes it was easier just to agree with her mum than to argue her point.

Eddie paced up and down the living-room carpet. He was desperate to speak to Jessica, but too nervous to ring her.

153

Debating whether to call his dad and ask for advice, he decided against it. His dad had got the pox of him the other night, so how could he admit he'd now allowed his six-year-old son to be knocked out cold?

Furious with himself, Eddie punched the wall. He was probably the laughing stock of Rainham. Gossip tended to travel at a hundred miles an hour in the circles he mixed in. Noticing one of Jessica's sweatshirts lying on the chair, Eddie picked it up and held it to his nose. As he took in her scent, he felt a comfort within.

'Forgive me, Jess. I love you so much,' he whispered.

Looking around the house he'd been so proud to have built, Ed decided that he now hated it. Without Jessica's constant chattering and the twins' happy laughter, it wasn't homely at all. He'd dropped Gary and Ricky home earlier and the silence was killing him. Desperate to make things right again, Eddie picked up his car keys. A phone call wasn't the answer. He needed to see his beautiful wife face to face, tell her how sorry he was. Even if he had to go down on his bended knee to get her back, so be it.

Jessica was upstairs freshening up when she heard the doorbell go.

'Mummy, Daddy's here,' Frankie shouted.

Feeling her body go rigid, Jessica stood rooted to the spot. She wasn't ready to face him yet – she couldn't.

'You're not going to answer the door, are you?' Stanley said to Joyce.

'Of course I'm going to answer it. You stay there, and mind your own business. I'll speak to Eddie in the kitchen.'

Joyce ushered the twins out of the room. 'Frankie, Joey, go upstairs with Mummy. Nanny needs to have a little chat with your dad.'

'Is Daddy angry with me because I lost at boxing?' Joey asked innocently.

Joyce stroked his head. 'Of course not, darling. Just go upstairs until Nanny calls you, then you can come down and say hello to your dad.'

As Joyce opened the front door, Eddie was standing there holding a massive bouquet. 'I am so sorry for what happened, Joyce. Where's Jess? I desperately need to talk to her.'

Joyce led him into the kitchen. 'She's very upset, Ed. I don't know if she's ready to have it out with you yet. Let me make us a brew and then I'll go upstairs and try and persuade her to talk to you.'

Eddie sat on a stool. 'I ain't slept all night. How's Joey? I take it he's here?'

Joyce nodded. 'The twins are both upstairs. Joey seems OK now, he's just eaten a big plate of chips, bless him.'

Eddie put his head in his hands. 'I feel so guilty, Joyce. I'll make it up to Joey, I promise I will. If Jess can find it in her heart to forgive me, I'll book us all a holiday. We can spend some proper time together as a family, it will do us all good.'

Joyce handed him his cup of tea.

'What do you want?' she asked, as Stanley peered around the door.

Ignoring Eddie, Stanley walked in. 'The pigeons need feeding,' he said curtly.

As Stanley shut the back door, Joyce locked it. The crafty old sod had only come out to be nosy. She smiled at Eddie. 'Stands out there for hours with his cock in his hand,' she joked.

Eddie did his best to force a smile. He wasn't in the mood for jokes, no matter how funny they were.

'Go upstairs and speak to Jess for me, Joyce. Ask her if I can go up and talk to her.'

Jessica was sitting on the bed with the twins either side of her.

'Are you angry with Daddy?' Frankie asked her.

'Can we go and see him now?' Joey pleaded.

Joyce opened the bedroom door. 'Ed wants to talk to you, Jess. I'll take the kids downstairs and send him up, shall I?'

Jessica shook her head. 'I don't want to see him, Mum. I'm not ready to go through all this yet.'

Joyce put her hands on her hips. 'Look dear, he's your husband, you have to talk to him and there's no time like the present.'

Jessica sighed. 'OK, but let the twins stay here for a minute. I'll send them down when he comes up. I'm not leaving them on their own with him.'

Joyce nodded and left the room.

'Go up, Eddie. She's in her old bedroom.'

Eddie felt his heart rate quicken as he carried the flowers up the stairs. He took a deep breath and walked into the room.

'Daddy!' Frankie and Joey exclaimed.

'Hello, kids. Can Daddy have a cuddle?' he said, with tears in his eyes.

Hugging them both tightly, Eddie crouched down and kissed them. 'You go downstairs and see your nan for a minute,' he told them.

They both nodded. 'Will you come and see Grandad's pigeons with me?' Joey asked him.

'Another time, son,' Eddie said, wiping his eyes on his sleeve.

As the twins left the room, Eddie handed the flowers to Jess. 'Peace offering,' he said.

Without looking at them, Jessica put them on the floor. 'It's gonna take a bit more than a bunch of flowers, Eddie.'

156

Eddie knelt down in front of her and tried to take her hands in his, but Jessica quickly snatched hers away.

'Jess, I'm so sorry for what happened. I was bang out of order and I promise you faithfully that nothing like that will ever happen again. Please, Jess, look at me. You and the twins mean the world to me, just give me another chance, let me make it up to you.'

Aware that Ed was crying, Jessica averted her eyes. If she looked at him she'd melt and she was desperate not to thaw that easily. 'What you did to Lee the other night was bad enough, but what you did to your own son was despicable, Eddie. How am I ever meant to trust you again? How can I live with a man who I'm frightened to leave alone with his own children?'

'Don't say that, please don't say that. You make me sound like a monster, Jess. I love my kids, you know I do. I made a mistake, one stupid mistake, that's all. Just give me another chance. I'll do anything you say, anything,' Eddie begged.

Jessica shook her head. 'It's not that easy, Eddie. I thought Joey was dead, I really did. How do you think that made me feel?'

'I'm sorry babe, I really am. Let's go home, we can talk indoors,' Eddie pleaded.

Jessica stood up and opened the bedroom door. 'I want you to leave now, Eddie. I need to think things through, decide what I want to do. I need you to bring some clothes here for me and the kids. Bring their school bags as well and Milky the Cow and some other toys.'

Shell-shocked, Eddie stood up. 'How much stuff shall I bring? Do you think you'll be back home by next weekend?'

Jessica kept her cool. She was damned if she was going to make this easy for him.

'Who says I'm coming home at all? I've got a massive bump on my head and my son nearly died. The way that I feel at this moment, Eddie, I never want to see you or that bloody house ever again.'

FIFTEEN

Many visits, phone calls and apologies later, Jessica agreed to go out alone for a meal with Eddie to discuss their future.

Her mother had done her head in and just wouldn't let sleeping dogs lie. 'You can't keep messing your husband around, Jess. Two mistakes he's made and even though they were big mistakes, you can't keep punishing the man forever. There'll be women out there who will be waiting in the wings as we speak. I'd make things right with him, if I was you, before it's too late and some little dolly bird gets her claws into him.'

Not wanting the kids to see her going out with their father, Jessica had asked her dad to take them to the pictures. 'I don't want Frankie and Joey to see Ed. They're missing him and it might upset them. He's picking me up at seven, so don't bring them back until at least half past,' she told her father.

'Don't worry, I'll take them for a pizza after the film, but I'll tell you something, if you get back with that arsehole, you want your bloody head tested,' her dad said bluntly.

Jessica ignored his comments. It had been just over a week now since she'd moved back in with her parents and between them they'd driven her up the bloody wall. She did appreciate them both caring, but they wouldn't leave the subject of her marriage alone and the fact that their opinions differed so much made it all the worse.

Sighing, Jessica fished through her temporary wardrobe. She had very little to choose from because most of her clothes were still in Rainham. Not wanting Eddie to think she'd made too much of an effort, she decided to wear her faded jeans. Matched with her red bag, T-shirt and stilettos, she could still look nice without going over the top.

Pleased with her overall appearance, Jessica carefully applied her mascara and lipgloss. Knowing that Eddie hated her wearing too much make-up, she deliberately added some blusher and eyeliner. Sod him, Ed wouldn't have the guts to say anything about her appearance tonight, the bastard would be far too busy grovelling.

Jessica felt slightly apprehensive as she walked down the stairs. She had already decided where she wanted her future to lie, but there was a lot that needed ironing out first.

As Jessica walked into the kitchen, Joyce looked at her in horror. 'Christ, you could have made more of an effort. I thought you was going out for a nice meal. You can't sit in a posh restaurant in those old-looking denim jeans. You look like a bloody workman.'

'Mum, please don't start, I'm not in the mood. I feel a bundle of nerves as it is. Is there any of that wine left in the fridge?'

Joyce tutted as she poured her daughter a small glass. Every night this week Jessica had insisted on having some wine with her evening meal and Joyce was beginning to think she was turning into an alcoholic.

'Don't drink too much while you're out with Eddie tonight. You need a clear head on you – you don't want to act like an old lush. Men hate to see their women drunk, especially men like Eddie.'

Jessica snatched the glass and stomped out of the kitchen. The quicker she got out of this lunatic asylum, the better.

Eddie sat upstairs in his Auntie Joan's house. His father had called an urgent meeting and Ed knew by the look on his face that whatever news he had was good news.

'I heard what happened at the party last week, Gavin Smith told me. How's Joey? Recovered, has he?' Ronny said, laughing.

'Joey! What's a matter with the boy?' Harry Mitchell asked.

Eddie shot his brother a look of pure hatred. His dad knew nothing about what had gone on at the party and if anyone was going to tell him, he'd rather do it himself. 'I'll tell you later, Dad. Tell us your news first,' Eddie said, embarrassed.

Ronny was such a loudmouth prick. Now he knew, there was little point in hiding the truth from anyone else.

As Auntie Joan tapped on the door, Eddie jumped up to let her in. 'There's chicken and beef in the sandwiches. Now, are you sure you don't want me to make you a nice brew, Harry?'

Smiling, Harry shook his head. 'We've good news today, Joanie, so we'll be having a little celebratory tipple instead,' he told her.

Joan nodded and shut the door. The men had important business to discuss and they didn't need her hanging about like a mother hen.

Harry opened a bottle of expensive Scotch and urged Paulie to do the honours. Sipping his own, he smiled at Raymond. 'Well, Raymondo, I have some very good news

161

that is of particular interest to you. The police yesterday arrested a lad in connection with the murder of Mad Dave. I've since heard they've formally charged him. They'd been looking for two black boys who were already well known to them. One of them is called Rowan, I don't know his surname, but they found his fingerprints in the Portakabin. Apparently, Mad Dave reported a burglary down his yard a few weeks back, so chances are it was this Rowan kid and his mate, who are well-known thieves. I suppose the Old Bill have found the kids' prints and surmised it was him that came back and killed him. What a fucking result, eh? Leaves the rest of us in the clear.'

Raymond lifted his glass. 'To Rowan,' he chirped.

'To Rowan,' everybody else said, laughing.

Looking at his watch, Eddie realised it was gone half-six. 'Listen, I'm sorry to have to leave so quickly, but I've gotta be somewhere.'

'You ain't even drunk your drink yet, at least have that first,' Paulie told Eddie.

Eddie stood up. Fuck the drink – the last thing he needed was to turn up round Jessica's mum's smelling like a brewery.

'She's got you right where she wants you, that old woman of yours,' Ronny goaded.

Eddie chose not to rise to the bait. 'I'll catch up properly with you all next week or something.'

'What was you gonna tell us about Joey?' Harry enquired.

Shaking his head, Eddie walked towards the door. 'I'll give you a ring tomorrow, Dad, and don't listen to what anybody else says. Ronny's heard what happened through the rumour mill. At least if you hear it from me, you know it's kosher.'

Harry Mitchell nodded. 'Take care, son.'

* * *

Jessica was annoyed as she lifted back the curtain and peered out of the upstairs window. Eddie was already a quarter of an hour late and if he didn't arrive before the kids got back, she would tell him to go and take a running jump. Furious with herself for having agreed to go out with her husband in the first place, Jessica lay down on the bed. Her mum's voice quickly made her stand up again.

'Jess, Eddie's here, love.'

Glancing in the mirror, Jessica ran down the stairs. 'I won't be late, Mum, and don't forget, if the kids ask, I'm out with Mary.'

'Aren't you going to invite him in?' asked a disappointed Joyce.

'No, I'm not,' Jessica said, as she opened the front door.

Eddie smiled as he saw his stunning wife walk towards him. 'I'd better say a quick hello to your mum,' he said.

'No, let's just go,' Jessica told him.

The conversation in the car was awkward, but polite.

'I haven't booked us anywhere yet. I thought I'd let you decide where you wanted to eat. How do you fancy that nice Italian we took me dad to on his birthday that time?' Eddie asked.

Jessica nodded. 'That'll do fine. I liked it there, the food was lovely.'

The restaurant was about ten minutes' drive away and, as Eddie led Jessica inside, he was relieved to find that it wasn't too busy. He pulled the waiter to one side. 'Can we have a table right at the back, we need a bit of privacy,' he told him.

Jessica chose a seafood dish and Eddie opted for the mouth-watering lasagne.

As the waiter topped their glasses up with wine, Eddie

leaned across the table and held Jessica's hand. 'I've missed you and the twins so much,' he told her.

Jessica nodded and averted her eyes. Eddie still gave her butterflies after all these years and the way that her heart was pounding reminded her of when they'd first got together. 'I have missed you too, Ed, but after what happened, if we do make another go of it, there have to be some changes.'

Relieved that she was softening towards him, Eddie smiled at her. 'Your wish is my command, Jess. I'll do whatever it takes to get you back. What is it you want me to do?'

Jessica took a deep breath. 'Firstly, I want you to apologise to the people from the party. I think we should both pop round to see Pat Murphy and Dougie and Vicki. You were so loud and argumentative, Ed, you upset everyone. We've only just moved into the area and I don't want people to think we're the dregs of society. Just tell them you was drunk and how awful you feel about forcing Joey into that boxing ring.'

Eddie nodded. 'I'll do it. I'll go and apologise first thing tomorrow.'

Jessica paused, before carrying on. 'I want to come with you. I don't want the women down the school making snide comments about us, so I want to show that we're united as a couple. Another thing I want you to do is knock at that O'Hara bloke's and shake his hand to show there's no bad feelings. We only live down the road from him, Ed, and I really don't want any aggravation. I can't live my life looking over my shoulder and if you and him have got this feud going on, it's not safe for me and the kids to live there.'

Eddie looked away from her. Apologising to Pat and Doug was one thing, making things all right with that cunt O'Hara was another. He turned back to Jess. 'The feud between my family and the O'Haras has been going on for years, Jess. It's complicated – you wouldn't understand.'

Jessica stood her ground. 'What's more important, Ed? Jimmy O'Hara, or me and the children? I'm not coming home until you do as I say, and if you don't, then I'm leaving you for good.'

Knowing his wife meant business, Eddie nodded once again. He hated the thought of swallowing his pride, but the thought of life without Jess was far worse. 'OK, I'll do it,' he said.

'I'm coming with you. I want us to go to the O'Haras' together. I don't want his wife and family to think that there's any ill feeling. I'll probably bump into the woman at some point and I don't want any awkwardness.'

Having little choice, Eddie reluctantly agreed. 'Is that it? When are you moving back – tomorrow?' he asked Jessica.

'I haven't finished yet. There's more,' Jessica told him, much to his dismay. 'I don't want you to stop drinking because I know you're usually fine, but I want you to promise me that you'll never get drunk like that in front of me and the children again. It's the Scotch, Eddie, it doesn't agree with you. You are a horrible drunk and I can't live like that. I also want you to lay off Joey. You're always picking on him because he's not as rough and ready as Gary and Ricky. He is what he is, Ed, and I love him for that and so should you. You favour Frankie and it shows. It's not fair, Ed, Joey's a little darling and he loves you very much.'

Eddie was shocked by his wife's comments. 'I don't favour Frankie, I love Joey just as much. With boys, Jess, it's a father's job to toughen 'em up a bit. My dad brought me and my brothers up that way and I did the same with Gary and Ricky. I mean, you want him to be able to stick up for himself, don't you? We don't want him getting picked on at school, do we?'

Jessica bit back. 'I just want you to leave him alone, Ed, you're always on his case. You go mad if he picks up one of Frankie's dolls or does something that you don't consider boyish. He's six years old, for God's sake. Gary and Ricky never had twin sisters – if they had, they'd have probably played with their toys as well.'

Eddie shrugged. In his eyes, he hadn't been doing anything untoward. All he'd been trying to do was teach the boy right from wrong. 'I'll promise I'll never get drunk like that again, and yes, I'll let Joey grow up in his own time. But Jess, don't ever say that I love any of my other kids more than him, 'cause it's untrue. You've hurt me saying that; he's my son and I'd fucking die for him.'

Realising that Eddie looked a bit choked up, Jessica felt awful. She wanted to say something about how he'd grabbed her round the neck and hurt her head, but perhaps this wasn't the right time. Maybe she had been too harsh on him, too brutal. 'So, when shall the kids and I move back home, then?' she said, squeezing his big, lifeless hand.

With tears in his eyes, Eddie managed a smile. Jess and the twins were coming home where they belonged and nothing else really mattered. 'How about tonight? It's only eight o'clock. Shall we bolt our dinner down, then go and pick the twins up?'

Jessica nodded. 'I'd like that very much.'

Because they were on their school holidays, Joey and Frankie were allowed to stay up later than usual. As the

166

front door opened, they ran to greet their mum and were surprised, but also delighted, to see their dad.

'Cuddles, Daddy, cuddles,' Frankie demanded.

Joyce poked her head around the door and beamed at the happy family atmosphere.

Eddie put Frankie down and held his arms out to Joey. 'Come and have a cuddle with your dad, eh?' he urged him.

Joey ran into his arms. 'Do you still love me, Daddy?' he asked solemnly.

Eddie held his son tighter than ever before. 'I love you more than you'll ever know, Joey,' he said, stroking his head.

Jessica ushered her mum back into the lounge and had a brief word with both of her parents. 'Mum, Dad, thanks ever so much for letting me and the kids stay here. You've been brilliant, both of yous have.'

Joyce hugged her. 'Everything sorted, love? You going back home?'

Jessica nodded. She was desperate to get back to her big house and taste her home comforts once more.

Stanley sat stony-faced staring at the telly. He had nothing to say, nothing at all.

'You don't mind if we shoot off now, do you, Mum? Our clothes and the kids' toys we can pick up tomorrow.'

Joyce smiled as Eddie walked into the room with a twin in each arm.

'I'll pack all your stuff up for you in the morning. Yous get yourselves home,' Joyce urged them.

Eddie grinned. 'I wouldn't mind a cup of tea first, Joycie. You make the best brew I've ever tasted, and I'm parched.'

Thrilled by her son-in-law's compliment, Joyce jumped up and almost ran to the kitchen.

Unable to take any more of Eddie's old bollocks, Stanley stormed out of the room.

'You OK, Dad? Where are you going?' Jessica shouted after him.

'To feed the pigeons. Take care, love,' Stanley shouted, as he slammed the kitchen door.

Relieved to be alone, Stanley spoke quietly to his birds. Ernie and Ethel were his pride and joy. They might only be pigeons, but they listened to him, they understood, and that was more than he could say about his family.

'It will all end in tears, Ernie. You mark my words, Ethel, that Eddie's no good. Jess'll never be happy with him,' he told them.

'Coo-coo, coo, coo-coo,' the pigeons replied.

Stanley felt a tear roll down his cheek. Even his pigeons could see through Eddie's charade. If only his family could do the same.

SIXTEEN

Much to Eddie's dismay, Jessica insisted that the twins sleep in the king-size bed with her, and he sleep in the spare room.

'Please let's share a bed, Jess. I've missed your warmth, I need a cuddle,' Eddie pleaded.

Jessica shook her head. By the time they'd got home, both the twins were out for the count and they had had to carry them up the stairs. 'It's only for tonight, Ed. I don't want them waking up wondering where they are. Anyway, they've both had a bit of a tummy bug. I want them next to me, so I know they're all right.'

The following morning the twins were both full of beans. 'Can we go and play outside?' Frankie asked excitedly.

'You can play in the garden later. Firstly, you've both got to have a bath and then Daddy's gonna take us all out for lunch,' Jessica told them.

Frankie stuck her bottom lip out. 'I don't want to go out for lunch, Mummy. I want to have a picnic in the tree house.'

Jessica smiled. Trying to keep the kids from getting dirty in the garden could be a real pain sometimes, but she was glad to be back home. 'How about if we go to that pub that's got the big play area?' Jessica asked hopefully.

Joey and Frankie jumped up and down on the bed. They liked the pub with the play area, there were lots of other children there. 'Can we go now, Mummy?' Joey pleaded.

Jessica lifted them both off the bed. 'Bath first and then we can go,' she laughed.

Hearing Jess and the kids banging about, Eddie got up himself. 'Good morning, sexy,' he said, hugging his wife.

His touch felt good and Jessica returned the compliment. 'I've told the kids we'll take them to that Beefeater that's got the big play area. Get yourself ready, Ed, and we can stop on the way and deliver our apologies.'

'Can't we do that tomorrow? We can't take the kids with us, can we?'

Annoyed that he was trying to go back on his word, Jessica pulled away from him. 'Don't start breaking promises, Ed. We said we were gonna do it today and we will. The kids'll be fine – we'll only be a minute and they can sit in the car.'

Knowing he was still on a trial run, Eddie unwillingly agreed. He was dreading being marched up to people's houses like a naughty schoolboy. Him – Eddie Mitchell? Talk about making him look a cunt but, unfortunately, he didn't have much choice. He wanted his life with Jess to get back to normal and if a few apologies allowed that to happen, it was worth it.

An hour later, Eddie stood at Pat Murphy's front door and rang the musical bell. Hearing it play, 'When Irish Eyes are Smiling', Eddie couldn't help but laugh.

'Trust Patrick! Fuck knows where he got that from,' he said to Jessica.

Patrick immediately opened the door. 'My auntie who

lives in Limerick got hold of it for me. Good, isn't it?' he said chuckling.

Eddie held out his right hand. 'Patrick, I've just popped round to apologise for my drunken behaviour at your party. I was well sloshed and I probably upset a few people other than my wife.'

Patrick Murphy laughed loudly. 'Bejesus, Eddie, you were fine. I've had a lot worse than you here over the years, that I have, for sure.'

Spotting the twins waving at him from the car, Patrick nodded towards them. 'How's your son now?'

Eddie smiled at Jessica and squeezed her hand. 'He's absolutely fine. No thanks to his dad though, eh, babe?'

Jessica nodded. 'Well, we'd best be going now, Patrick, and once again, we're sorry for spoiling your party.'

Patrick waved them goodbye. 'I'll see you both soon,' he shouted.

The next stop was Dougie and Vicki's house. 'Hello yous two,' Vicki said, as she opened the front door.

'Is Dougie about?' Eddie asked her.

'He's in his office. Spends half his life in there, he does. Come in, I'll tell him you're here.'

Jessica gesticulated to the twins to tell them that they would only be a minute. 'Stay in the car, you're not to get out,' she shouted.

As Eddie stood apologising to an unfazed Doug, Vicki and Jessica swapped phone numbers. 'How about you and Doug come over to ours for dinner next week?' Jessica asked her.

'We'd love to, wouldn't we, Doug?' Vicki replied.

Dougie smiled. 'I've told Ed, the party's long forgotten. Christ, if I had a pound for every time I've got pissed and made a prick of meself, I'd be a very rich man, and yes, dinner sounds great,' he added.

Jessica and Eddie said their goodbyes and left. Driving towards Jimmy O'Hara's house, Eddie felt his stomach start to churn. Two down and one to go and this was the bastard he was dreading.

Pulling onto O'Hara's drive, Eddie was surprised to see that the beautiful grounds of the house he'd once been so keen to buy now resembled a shit-hole. There were two big, tatty mobile homes either side of the house, six lurchers, three Jack Russells and dog shit everywhere. There were a load of horses standing behind a wire fence and there was even a fucking goat staring at him.

'Typical fucking pikeys,' Eddie muttered as he got out of the car.

'Can we go and see the horses?' Frankie squealed with delight.

'Can we stroke them? Joey asked.

With dogs leaping up at him from all angles, Eddie did his best to stay calm. 'Yous two stay in that car and don't move,' he ordered the twins.

'Please, Daddy, let us see the horses,' Frankie whinged.

'No, Frankie, and I mean no. Do you wanna stay in the car with the kids, Jess? There's more animals running around than there is in a fucking circus.'

Jessica opened the car door. She needed to know that Eddie had said the right things to Mr O'Hara. 'I'm coming with you,' she insisted.

With a Jack Russell trying to shag his right leg, Eddie made his way towards the house. Seeing a miniature tractor drive past, he took little notice. Goats, horses, dogs, tractors – they all seemed to blend in with the territory.

With a heavy heart, he knocked on Jimmy O'Hara's front door.

Frankie looked in amazement as the tractor stopped

by the car and Jed, whom she'd met at the party, leaped off it.

'Frankie!' he exclaimed. He opened the door of the car and urged her to move over.

Unusually for Frankie, she came over all shy. 'Do you live here?' she mumbled, averting her eyes from the grinning Jed.

Joey could feel his heart pumping though his T-shirt. This was the boy who had hit him in the boxing ring and he was petrified of a repeat performance.

Aware of Joey's anxiety, Jed held his hand out to him. 'I'm really sorry for hitting you so hard. I didn't mean to hurt you. I had to do it, else my dad would have beat me.'

'Shake his hand then, like Daddy does,' Frankie urged her brother.

Joey did as he was told and sat quietly as Jed spoke to Frankie.

'Come for a ride on my tractor,' Jed urged her.

Frankie shook her head. 'My dad said I had to stay in the car. He'll tell me off if I get out.'

Jed laughed. 'You're a scaredy cat. Go on admit it, you're frit to death. You think I can't drive, but I can. I can even drive my dad's car – I can, honest I can,' Jed bragged.

Jimmy O'Hara smiled as he locked eyes with Eddie Mitchell. 'Well, well, well, this is a nice surprise,' he said, with a hint of sarcasm.

Embarrassed that the Jack Russell was still trying to mount him, Eddie gently pushed it away.

Jimmy O'Hara laughed as he picked the dog up. 'His name's Rocky; I named him after me cousin. He likes you, look. Got his cory out, for you, he has.'

Eddie ignored Jimmy's crude comment and held out his right hand. 'My wife and I were just passing and we thought it could be a good idea to stop by, just to say no hard feelings about last week. As you said at the party, we're neighbours now and all of us want a quiet life.'

Jimmy shook Eddie's hand and nodded towards his car. 'My little Jed's chatting up your daughter again. Ain't stopped talking about her since that party last week. I'd definitely say we're gonna be in-laws one day,' Jimmy said, chuckling.

Eddie glanced at the car in horror. 'We'd best be going now. Come on, Jess,' he urged.

'I appreciate you dropping by, Eddie. Goodbye, Mrs Mitchell,' Jimmy said, as he shut the front door.

'Who was that?' his wife Alice asked.

'Eddie dinlo fucking Mitchell,' Jimmy said, laughing his head off.

Breaking into a run, Eddie reached the car before Jess. 'What are you doing in there?' he shouted at Frankie.

'Nothing, Daddy. You said we wasn't allowed to get out of the car, so Jed got in to talk to us.'

'We're going now, so time for you to get out, boy,' Eddie told Jed.

Grinning from ear to ear, Jed leaned towards Frankie and pecked her full on the lips. 'I'm your boyfriend now, Frankie, and I'll come and see you soon,' he yelled, as he climbed back on his tractor.

Eddie waited for Jess to get in. Furious, he started the engine and put his foot down.

'Frankie's got a boyfriend, Frankie's got a boyfriend,' Joey sang to his sister.

Frankie felt herself go all weird again. 'No, I haven't,' she said shyly.

'Yes, you have and you kissed him,' Joey giggled.

174

Annoyed that some old dodderer was driving too slow, Eddie held his hand on the hooter and cursed as he over-took him.

'You stay away from that boy, Frankie, do you hear me?' Eddie demanded.

Aware that Jed was the boy who had knocked Joey down in the boxing ring, Jessica was more worried about her son. 'Are you OK, Joey? Did that boy frighten you, love?'

Joey shook his head. 'He said sorry, Mummy. He said that his dad made him hit me.'

'Sounds a bit like you, dear,' Jessica said, nudging her husband.

Eddie drove in stony silence. Shaking hands with Jimmy O'Hara had made him feel physically sick, and as for that cheeky fucking kid of his, he'd kill that little bastard if he ever came anywhere near his daughter again.

Seeing the expression on Eddie's face, Jessica guessed today had been hard for him. 'Thanks Ed, for doing that for me,' she said, stroking his arm.

'Are we going to the pub now, Daddy?' Joey asked.

Still in a foul mood, Eddie tried his hardest not to show it. 'Yep, we're going there now, son,' he replied, as cheer-fully as he could.

An hour and a couple of pints later, Ed had finally calmed himself down. Sitting opposite Jessica on a wooden bench in the beer garden, he gently held her hand. 'This is what life's all about, eh? Me, you and the kids,' he said, nodding towards the twins, who were playing happily on the apparatus.

Jessica smiled as Frankie waved at her.

'Watch me, Mummy,' she yelled as she hurtled down the big slide.

Jessica turned her attention back to her husband. 'I know

we've had our ups and downs recently, but I do love you, Eddie Mitchell.'

Eddie winked at her. 'Does that mean we're gonna sleep in the same bed tonight and you're gonna let me have my wicked way with you?'

Jessica felt her cheeks redden. Even after all these years, Eddie still had the ability to make her blush. 'Yes, we will sleep in the same bed tonight and, if you behave yourself, I just might let you have your wicked way with me,' she told him shyly.

Their intimate moment was ended by a screaming Joey. Standing at the top of a climbing frame, he was bawling his eyes out.

'What's the matter?' Jessica asked, walking towards him.

Frankie giggled as she took stock of the situation. 'Joey's too scared to come down, Mummy,' she said, as she ran over to her dad.

Knowing her son didn't like heights, Jessica urged him to hold the metal rail and walk backwards. 'Just come down the way you went up, Joey,' she urged him.

'I can't, Mummy. I can't get down,' Joey sobbed.

Aware that some other children were laughing as him, Jessica had little option but to go up herself and carry Joey back down. 'It's all right, Mummy's here now. Come on, stop crying, there's a good boy.'

'Isn't Joey a crybaby, Daddy?' Frankie said laughing.

Eddie was embarrassed. There were other parents looking over at him and he was thankful that nobody knew him in this boozer.

Jessica walked towards him with Joey in her arms. 'I'm gonna take him to the toilet and sort him out. He's had a little accident. Give us your car keys, Ed, I've got a spare set of clothes for him in the boot.'

'What do you mean accident? Has he hurt himself?' Eddie asked, bemused.

'Don't tell no one, Mummy,' Joey begged his mother.

'He's wet himself,' Jessica mouthed to Eddie.

Annoyed, Eddie slung her his car keys. His youngest son was a total fucking embarrassment. That Jed might be a little bastard, but at least he was a kid for his father to be proud of. Joey was a total tart and showed himself and his family up wherever he went.

'I'm going on the swing now, Daddy,' Frankie said, as she climbed off his knee.

Eddie sipped his beer and watched his daughter swing higher than any of the other kids. At least Frankie had a bit of spirit about her; Joey had fucking none whatsoever. Seeing his wife and son walk towards him, Eddie forced a smile. He couldn't have a go at Joey or say anything about him, as he'd promised Jessica he wouldn't.

'Panic over. What shall we do, Ed? Shall we order some food now? The kids both want burger and chips.'

Eddie stood up. 'Keep an eye on Frankie. She's over there with some little boy, he keeps following her around,' he told Jessica, as he headed to the bar.

The little boy in question was quite taken with Frankie and had been trying to attract her attention for the last ten minutes. 'My name's Luke. What's yours?' he asked her.

'Not telling you,' Frankie shouted at him.

'Why not? I've told you my name,' Luke said, trying to hold her hand.

Frankie snatched her hand away. Placing her hands on her hips, she scowled at her stalker. 'Go away and leave me alone.'

As Eddie walked back from the bar, he saw Frankie clump the boy. Putting the drinks on the table, he went over to rescue the poor little sod, who was now sprawled on the ground crying.

'I'm really sorry,' he told the boy's shocked parents.

Eddie lifted his daughter up and carried her back to the table. 'It's naughty to punch people. Why did you punch him, Frankie?'

'Because he wanted to be my boyfriend. I don't like him, Daddy. I want Jed to be my boyfriend.'

Tilting his daughter's chin towards him, Eddie stared at her coldly. 'Listen to me, Frankie, I'm only ever saying this once. If you ever, ever mention Jed's name again, I'm gonna wash your mouth out with soap and water. Do you understand what I'm saying to you?'

Shocked by her father's attitude, Frankie felt her eyes fill up with tears. She flung her arms around his neck and sobbed.

'I'm sorry, Daddy. I won't say Jed any more.'

Wiping her tears away, Eddie smiled at her. 'You promise me, Frankie?'

Thrilled that her father was no longer angry with her, Frankie smiled at him. 'Yes, Daddy, I promise.'

SEVENTEEN

Nine years later – 1987

Glancing at his watch, Eddie picked up his bunch of keys. 'I'm gonna make a move now, love. I've gotta go up north today to speak to some arsehole that's knocked me. I might be really late back, so don't wait up.'

Jessica brushed a bit of fluff off her husband's collar and hugged him tightly. 'Be careful, Eddie. I love you,' she told him.

As the front door slammed, Jessica resumed her housework duties. Eddie had always tried to convince her to let him hire a cleaner, but she was having none of it. 'I like doing the housework myself, Ed. Anyway, I don't want a stranger poking around in my home. Vicki and Doug had to sack their cleaner, she was thieving off of them. We're OK as we are,' Jessica insisted.

Happy with the cleanliness of her kitchen, Jessica decided she had done more than enough to earn herself a brew and a biscuit. Dunking the chocolate digestive into her cup, she savoured its flavour and her thoughts returned to her husband. Eddie's job worried the life out of her sometimes. She knew he was still loan-sharking and even though he'd done very well out it, she wished he could find a profession that was less dangerous.

Over the years, Eddie's business had grown, but the

risks had grown with it. Ronny had been shot and was now confined to a wheelchair. He'd been blasted through the lower back and the doctors had since – unsuccessfully – carried out three operations to try to repair his spine.

The one thing that did please Jessica was that Gary and Ricky were now both working with their father. Twenty-three and twenty-one respectively, Gary and Ricky were into bodybuilding and Jessica worried a lot less knowing that they were with Eddie.

Paulie and Raymond were still in the firm, so there were five of them in all. The accident had made Ronny very miserable and bitter and, according to Eddie, he now spent his days drowning his sorrows in numerous pubs. The last time Jessica had seen Ronny was when she had been to visit him in hospital with Eddie. He had been really nasty towards her and she had run from the ward, crying.

'Take no notice. He's one bitter and twisted cunt. He's always been jealous of our relationship,' Eddie said soothingly.

Even though Ronny spoke to Eddie like shit, Eddie still included him in the family business and looked after him financially. Ronny still lived with Sharon, and Eddie did all he could for her sake.

Neither Jess nor the twins had a great deal to do with any of Eddie's family. In Jessica's heart, she knew what they were and she had never felt particularly comfortable or wanted the twins around them. Eddie wasn't like his brothers. He was the odd one out, the good guy. Eddie's family rarely bothered to come to their house in Rainham and that suited Jessica down to the ground. The odd cup of tea and a sandwich around Auntie Joan's or an occasional meal out with Harry was the only contact she and the kids really had with them now.

'All right, Mum? What's for breakfast?'

Snapping out of her daydream, Jessica began fussing around her daughter. 'Look at your uniform – your skirt's all dirty. You can't wear that, Frankie. Go upstairs and change it.'

Frankie tutted and snatched at the dishcloth. Her skirt only had a tiny mark on it and it was easily wiped off.

'There, done. Now instead of getting on my case, do you think you can make me some breakfast? I'll have a fry-up, if that's OK.'

Jessica put the frying pan on and buttered some bread. 'Go and ask Joey if he wants one, too,' she ordered Frankie.

With a stomp of her feet and a flick of her hair, Frankie marched out of the kitchen. Jessica sighed and shook her head. The twins were her life, she adored them, but they were fifteen going on fifty. Frankie, in particular, drove her up the wall. She was her father's daughter all right, she was Eddie to a tee.

People who had never met the twins before always assumed that Frankie was older than Joey. They didn't even look like twins. Frankie was voluptuous, with dark hair and tanned skin like her father. Joey was as skinny as a beanpole, with blond hair and pale skin like herself. Their personalities were also very different. Frankie was hot-headed and impulsive, while Joey was laid-back and comical.

Frankie had always been Eddie's favourite out of the two and still was. Both fiery, they argued constantly, but adored one another at the same time. Joey's relationship with his father was more complex. They had nothing in common whatsoever, and although their conversations tended to be polite, they were also stilted.

'Joey just wants toast,' Frankie said, plonking herself down at the kitchen table.

181

Jessica pricked the sausage to make sure it was done properly, then dished up her daughter's breakfast.

'Morning, Mum,' Joey said, kissing her on the cheek.

'Toast won't fill you up. Why don't you let me make you a nice bacon sandwich?' Jessica asked him.

Joey sat opposite his sister. 'Toast is fine, Mum. What you up to today? You off out anywhere nice?'

Jessica smiled. Unlike Frankie, Joey was always so interested in her life. 'Yes, I am going out. Vicki's coming round and we're going clothes shopping together. We're gonna pop in and have lunch with Nan and Grandad on the way back.'

'Mum, see if you can get me a pair of bleached jeans with rips in them. Don't get me rubbish ones though, get a decent make. I'm bursting out of a size eight now, so you'd better get me a ten,' Frankie told her.

'OK, darling, I know the ones you mean. What about you, Joey, do you need anything?'

Joey smiled. 'I could do with some new trainers. Get me Nike, Mum, the ones with the light-blue tick down the side.'

Seeing time was getting on, Jessica urged the kids to finish their breakfast. Living in the lanes meant they needed a lift to and from school and she didn't want them to be late again. 'Come on, hurry up. You've got your exams soon and you don't want to fail them,' Jessica said sternly.

Frankie and Joey smirked at one another as they followed their mum out to the car. Little did she know, neither of them had any intention of spending their day studying for their exams. Joey and Frankie hated school and going through the school gates wasn't on their agenda.

Driving up the M1, Eddie was deep in thought. Ronny had just rung him, shouting and bawling and, for the second time that week, Ed had bitten his tongue.

No one, including Eddie, knew exactly what had happened to Ronny. Ed had apparently been owed a lot of money by a Scottish geezer called Jake Souness. 'I'm gonna fucking blow his brains out,' Ronny had drunkenly bragged one day.

Eddie had told his brother to stay away from Jake. 'Leave it to me. Souness is no fucking mug – he's heavy material. I'll have a word with Dad. He'll know how to play it,' Ed warned him.

As silly as arseholes, Ronny had ignored Eddie's advice and gone to see Jake Souness alone. He had been found half dead two days later and had no recollection of what had actually happened. All he had said was that Jake had poured neat bottles of vodka down his throat, forcing him to drink it. 'I don't remember anything after that. My next memory is waking up, being in agony and not being able to walk,' Ronny said.

Harry Mitchell had come out of retirement to get revenge for his son. He had tortured Jake Souness for three days and, when Jake's body could take no more, he had chopped his head off while he was still alive.

Eddie had been with his father that day and Jake Souness's screams would live with him forever.

'Take the next junction, Ed,' Raymond said, snapping Ed out of his daydream.

Eddie was heading towards a gypsy camp on the outskirts of Birmingham. Dickie Pearce had taken the right piss out of him. Fifteen grand, Eddie had lent him and the cunt had done a runner with it. Finding Dickie Pearce hadn't been easy. Eddie would never have lent him the cash in the first place if he had known he had links with the travelling community. Eddie thought Dickie was just your average guy, and he'd been shocked to find out that the piss-taking bastard was, in fact, a plastic pikey.

'Answer that,' Eddie ordered Raymond as his phone rang.

'It's your dad. Says it's urgent,' Raymond told him.

Knowing that he had his shooter in the Land Cruiser with him, Eddie swung into a lay-by. The Vodafone he owned weighed a ton, it was hard to hold while driving and he could do without causing an accident, today of all days.

'I'm driving. What is it, Dad?' he asked impatiently.

Listening to what his father had to say, Eddie's mood lifted like magic. 'No. When? How?' he asked joyfully.

As Eddie ended the phone call, he turned around in his seat and smiled at Paulie, Gary and Ricky.

Raymond nudged him. 'Come on, don't keep us in suspense. What's happened?'

'Dad's just heard that Butch O'Hara's brown bread. He ain't sure how he croaked it, but someone he knows said it was a heart attack. Apparently Jimmy's gonna set fire to his trailer with the body inside.'

'Why ain't they gonna have a proper funeral for him? Didn't they like him?' Ricky asked bewildered.

Eddie laughed. 'They like a bit of DIY, the old pikeys. I think it's custom for 'em to burn the dead in their own homes. Strange bastards, they are, I've always said that.'

Eddie whistled as he continued his journey. Lady Luck hadn't been very kind to Jimmy over the years, and every time he received yet another kick in the bollocks it pleased Eddie immensely.

Even though they lived near one another, Eddie saw very little of Jimmy. His wife, Alice, had left him years ago. Apparently, she had walked into one of his salvage yards and had caught her beloved Jimmy having his cock sucked by some little dolly bird.

Alice was a typical feisty travelling lass and, by all

184

accounts, had gone mental. Rumour had it, she had gone home and, on Jimmy's return, she had clumped him over the head with a claw hammer. The following day, Alice had packed her bags, shoved the kids in the car and left him for good.

Eddie was overjoyed by Jimmy's little mishap and dined out on it for months afterwards.

Jimmy was never the same man after Alice left him. Without his wife and kids by his side, he let his businesses slip, sold his Roller, and became a bit of a recluse.

Eddie grinned as he turned off the M1. Jimmy's mum had died a couple of years back and, now the old man had popped his clogs, he had no one living on his acres of land bar himself.

Eddie stifled a snigger. At least he had his dogs and horses. Maybe the fucking goat was still alive and that could keep poor Jimmy company on his big piece of land.

Frankie put her last fifty pence into the fruit machine. 'Poxy thing,' she said, kicking the base of it.

Joey laughed as she walked towards the table. 'Why do you waste your money on those things? I've told you before, gambling's for mugs,' he said as she sat down.

Spending their days in the café in Dagenham with a group of their friends was a regular pastime for Frankie and Joey. The café was owned by the sister of one of their best mates and she always allowed them to hang out there. Sometimes they went to school, but most days they couldn't face it. They would wave to their mum as she dropped them off and as soon as she drove away, they would cross the road and catch the bus to Dagenham.

Neither Joey nor Frankie were fans of their school uniform, so they always carried a spare set of clothes with them. They would get changed upstairs on the bus, then would change back into their school uniform on the return journey.

Neither of their parents were aware of what they got up to. Both the twins smoked and drank and sometimes they would stand on the corner totally wasted, waiting for their mum to pick them up. They were always careful, though, and only stuck to vodka, as it had no smell. Their mum would go apeshit if she knew, and their dad would probably rip their heads off.

Writing sick notes had become second nature to both of them. Joey wrote Frankie's, copying his mum's handwriting, and Frankie returned the favour for Joey, copying her dad's.

'What's the time?' Frankie asked her brother.

'Half-one,' Joey replied.

'I'm bored sitting here. Let's go to the park and drink our vodka, eh?'

Joey shrugged and turned to their friends. All of them were partial to a tipple, but Frankie was an absolute nightmare. Joey stood up and urged the others to do the same.

'Come on, Alkie Annie wants her daily fix,' he joked.

Laughing, the six good mates left the café together.

Stanley smiled as his daughter tucked into her ham-salad sandwich. She was a breath of fresh air, his Jessica, and even now, at thirty-three, she was still as beautiful as ever.

'So, how are your pigeons, Stanley? Are you still racing them?' Vicki enquired.

Stanley loved nothing more than discussing his birds and launched into a full account of their day-to-day activities. He liked Jessica's friend and was pleased that his daughter had someone local to turn to if she ever needed her help.

Stanley still didn't like or trust Eddie. His son, Raymond,

had turned into a clone of the man and he was extremely bitter about it. Stanley had little option but to play happy families. He loved his daughter and grandchildren so, all in all, Eddie had him by the bollocks.

When Jessica had left Eddie that time, Stanley had stuck to his guns. He hadn't spoken to Eddie for nine months, nor visited the house. He had eventually given in. He had missed Jess and the twins terribly and Joyce's constant moaning had forced him to change his mind. Since then, a happy medium had been met. He was polite to Eddie for the sake of his family, though inwardly he still hated him.

'We're gonna have to go now. I've gotta pick the kids up in an hour,' Jessica informed her parents.

Joyce stood up and cuddled her daughter. 'So will we see you before Christmas?'

'Of course, it's weeks away,' Jessica said smiling. 'I'll pop over next week. You and Dad will stay for a few days at Christmas, won't you? If you come over Christmas Eve in the afternoon, you can go home the day after Boxing Day.'

Joyce looked at Stanley. 'It all depends if Jock's around to feed the pigeons. If not, we can still stay, but I'll have to pop back to see to them every day,' Stanley said.

Joyce raised her eyebrows. 'Stanley's cock will be the death of me.'

Roaring with laughter, Jessica and Vicki left the house.

Eddie drove past the gypsy site and hid the Land Cruiser as best as he could down the end of a dirt track. It was two weeks since he'd found out where Dickie Pearce was actually living and he'd had him watched ever since.

Unfortunately for Eddie, he had no chance of getting his money back. Dickie had a gambling problem and was up to his eyeballs in debt. Eddie wasn't overly bothered

187

about the dosh. He was cakeo and fifteen grand was peanuts to him. What Eddie was annoyed about was the fucking liberty Pearcey had taken. No one messed with the Mitchells, and Eddie couldn't be seen to be lapsing in his old age. Dickie had bragged to a lot of people that he'd knocked Eddie for the dough and, because of that, Ed had no option but to take the silly man out.

'It's gone six o'clock. What time did you say he was due?' Paulie asked.

Eddie knew that Dickie had been making ends meet by selling flowers from the roadside. He also knew that he drove a white Escort van down this road at approximately six o'clock every evening.

'He'll be here any minute,' Eddie told his brother.

'Can't you turn on the engine so we can have some heating? I'm freezing me bollocks off here,' Paulie moaned.

Eddie glared at him. Paulie had turned into Ronny, he was sure he had.

'Shall I put the music on as well? We can dance and have a party, then everyone will know we're here, you soppy cunt.'

Paulie quickly shut up. Ever since Ronny had left the firm and Eddie's boys had joined, he'd felt like a complete fucking outsider.

'Right, there's headlights coming our way,' Eddie said, starting the engine.

'It's him, I'm sure it's a white van,' Raymond told him.

Making sure no one else was about, Eddie crawled along the road. Nearing the van, he switched on his beam. Seeing a startled-looking Dickie put his hands over his face, Eddie pulled up alongside him. Dickie immediately spotted the gun.

'Drive down the end of the dirt track, then open the door and get out,' Eddie ordered him.

Dickie did as Eddie asked. Petrified, he squealed like a pig as he fell to his knees. 'Please don't shoot me. I'm sorry Eddie, I'll pay you back, I promise I will. I've got kids and a grandkid – you can't shoot me, you can't.'

Eddie got out of the Land Cruiser. He put his big foot on top of Dickie's head and pulled back the catch.

'Pull the car forward,' he urged Raymond. He'd only just bought his new Toyota Land Cruiser and he didn't want it covered in some scumbag's blood.

'Kids, grandkids! Shame you didn't think of them before you knocked me, you mug,' Eddie said, smiling at Dickie Pearce's fright.

Lifting Dickie's chin up with his boot, Eddie winked at him. 'Bye-bye Dickie,' he said, as he casually pulled the trigger.

Eddie got into the passenger seat. 'Do us a favour, Ray, find a McDonald's or something. I'm fucking starving.'

'Frankie! Joey! Your dinner's ready,' Jessica shouted up the stairs.

'We're not hungry yet. We'll warm it up later,' Frankie shouted back.

Jessica sighed and covered the plates with cling film. She had gone to a lot of trouble to cook for them and now they were too busy to eat. Not wanting to eat alone, Jessica covered her own up. She hated eating alone, always had done.

Bored, Jessica poured herself a glass of wine. The twins worried her at times. She knew they were working hard for their exams, but she didn't want them overdoing it. Whenever she picked them up from school lately, they seemed so knackered. They barely spoke on the way home because they were so worn out.

189

'We're going upstairs to do our homework,' they would say as soon as they got through the front door.

'But you've only just left school. You must have a break. Can't you do it later?' she would ask them.

'You don't understand, Mum. The school gives us tons of homework and if we don't do it, we'll get in big trouble,' Frankie told her.

A couple of times Jessica had gone upstairs to try to help them do their homework, but they'd both been fast asleep.

As she sipped her wine, Jessica made a decision. She would go to that school tomorrow and have a quiet word with the headmaster. She wouldn't tell Frankie and Joey her plans. They were typical teenagers and they'd get all embarrassed. She wouldn't even tell Eddie, he'd say she was being a drama queen. Jessica smiled as she topped up her glass. She was a good mum and good mums were protective of their brood. Joey and Frankie were only fifteen and they shouldn't be working like Trojans, bless them.

EIGHTEEN

'Good morning sleepyhead.'

Jessica opened her eyes and smiled. She had slept like a log and wasn't even aware that Eddie had been lying beside her. 'What time did you get in? I didn't hear you come to bed,' she asked him.

'I got back about two, but I sat up for an hour. I was watching all the news programmes. That fire at King's Cross station was fucking terrible, wasn't it?' Eddie said.

Jessica propped herself up on one elbow. 'Mum rang and said something about a fire. To be honest, Vicki came round last night and we had a few glasses of wine. Doug was away on business, so she didn't leave till twelve. We sat in the kitchen playing tapes. I was gonna put the telly on, but by the time she left, I forgot all about it. What happened then? Did anybody get hurt?'

Eddie sighed and kissed Jessica on the forehead. His wife rarely watched or listened to the news and she didn't have a clue about current affairs. In fact, half the country could collapse in an earthquake and Jessica wouldn't be any the wiser.

'The escalator went up in flames. It was just after rush hour, so a lot of people got caught up in it. I think the death toll is about twenty-seven or something. They reckon it might turn out to be more, though, there are still a lot of people classed as critical.'

Jessica's eyes filled with tears. 'Oh Ed, that's awful! I feel so sorry for the poor people that died. How must their families feel, knowing they've been burned alive?'

Eddie held her tightly. 'Don't upset yourself, Jess. These things happen.'

Jessica wiped her eyes and changed the subject. 'How did you get on up north? Did you find that man and get your money back?'

Eddie nodded. 'Yeah, all sorted.'

'Did he pay you straight away?' Jessica asked.

Eddie smiled as he thought of Dickie with his brains blown out. 'Oh yeah, he paid all right,' he said.

Feeling himself getting hard, Eddie nibbled Jessica's earlobe. 'Stop it, Eddie. I've got to take the kids to school. What time is it?' Jessica said giggling.

'Sod the kids. Look what you've done to me,' Eddie told her, as he placed her hand on his erection.

Unable to resist her handsome husband, Jessica urged him to enter her. Arching her body, she gasped as he sped up his rhythm.

As Eddie orgasmed and rolled onto his back, Jessica sat up and stroked the hairs on his chest. 'What do you want for breakfast?' she asked him.

Eddie smiled at his beautiful wife. He had never been a selfish lover and unless Jessica was satisfied, then neither was he. 'I want you,' he said, as he moved down the bed and pleasured her with his tongue.

Aware of the animal-like noises coming out of her parents' bedroom, Frankie got out of bed and crept next door to wake Joey.

'What time is it?' her brother mumbled.

Frankie pulled the quilt from over his head. 'Forget the time. Mother and Father are at it again. They're just so embarrassing. When I hear 'em making them noises, it puts me off me breakfast.'

Joey smiled and sat up. 'They are married, Frankie – they're entitled to have a bunk-up, you know.'

Frankie pulled a face. 'I'm never gonna have sex after listening to them two. No wonder I'm still a virgin, they've put me off for life.'

Joey couldn't help but laugh. She could be a funny girl, his sister, at times. 'You'll have sex when the time's right. You just ain't met the right person yet, that's all.'

Frankie playfully punched his arm. 'Hark at you, the expert. You've never been out with a girl for more than a couple of weeks.'

'So?' Joey answered.

'So, how come you're so knowledgeable? Both Leanne and Sarah said you never slept with them. So, who have you slept with, then?'

Joey laughed as he forcefully but playfully removed Frankie from his bedroom. 'That's for me to know and you to find out,' he told her.

Jessica stood over the cooker with a smile on her face. 'Do you want mushrooms and beans?'

'I'll have whatever you're offering,' Eddie replied suggestively.

Jessica giggled. 'So what are you up to today? Will you be home late tonight?'

Eddie shook his head. 'I've got a few people to visit, all local, and I'll probably poke me head in the Flag and see if Ronny's in there. I won't be late, I'll be home before teatime. What about you? You doing anything?'

Debating whether to tell him she was worried about

the twins and was off to see the headmaster, Jess heard Frankie and Joey's footsteps and decided to keep quiet. 'I've not planned anything, although I might pop into Romford and get some more Christmas presents.'

'What's a matter with you? Too old to give your dad a kiss now, are you?' Eddie asked Frankie.

Frankie politely kissed him then, screwing up her face, smiled at her brother.

'You didn't kiss him on the lips, did you? You don't know where his tongue's been,' Joey whispered in Frankie's ear.

Frankie punched Joey and laughed.

Eddie finished his breakfast and put the plate in the dishwasher. 'I'm off now, babe,' he said to Jess.

'See you later, kids. I'm back early tonight. Shall we all go out for a Chinese or shall I order a takeaway?'

Frankie nudged Joey. They'd already decided not to attend school today and they didn't want to drink vodka all afternoon, then have to sit in a restaurant with their parents. 'We've got tons of homework, Dad. Me and Frankie would prefer a takeaway,' Joey replied.

Eddie put on his jacket. 'I'll see you all later, then. Pick what you want off the menu and I'll order it as soon as I get home,' he said.

Jessica fed the twins, tidied up the kitchen, then went upstairs to get changed. Usually, she drove the children to school in a tracksuit or jeans, but she couldn't do that today. How could she expect the headmaster to take her seriously if she looked like a tramp?

'What you all done up for?' Frankie asked, as she came down the stairs.

Feeling flustered, Jessica searched for her handbag. 'I'm going Christmas shopping after I've dropped yous two off,' she lied.

*   *   *

194

Due to heavy traffic, the journey to the school took about twenty minutes.

'Bye, Mum,' the twins said, as they slammed the car door.

Jessica waved and drove away. She'd already hatched her plan. She would park a couple of streets away, then drive back once they were inside their classroom.

Half an hour later, Jessica made her way into the school gates. She had been to the headmaster's office a couple of years ago, when Joey had been taken ill and, as luck would have it, she remembered where it was.

'Can I help you?' asked a stuffy-looking woman sitting at a typewriter.

'I'd like to speak to the headmaster about my children,' Jessica stated.

'And who shall I say wants to speak to him?'

'Mrs Mitchell. I'm Francesca and Joseph's mother.'

The woman smirked. 'Take a seat. I'll let Mr Redknapp know that you're waiting.'

Jessica sat nervously tapping her fingers. She wasn't very good at confrontation and she was beginning to wish that she hadn't come alone. Eddie was much more businesslike than she was, he would have known exactly what to say.

'Mr Redknapp's ready for you to go in now,' the woman told her.

As Jessica walked in, the headmaster smiled. 'Please sit down, Mrs Mitchell,' he said.

'I've come to see you because I'm very worried about Joseph and Francesca,' Jessica rambled.

The headmaster nodded. 'I'm very pleased you have come to see me. In fact, I was going to contact you next week. We at the school are also very worried about Joseph and Francesca. They seem to be catching one illness after another and it's seriously affecting their schoolwork.'

Jessica looked at the headmaster in amazement. 'What illness? They're not ill. I've come to talk to you about the amount of homework they've been given. I don't understand, what do you mean?'

Picking up his phone, Mr Redknapp pressed a button. 'Margaret, could you bring in the Mitchells' file with the children's letters, please?'

Jessica was bemused. 'What's going on? Why have the twins been telling you they're ill?'

Mr Redknapp smiled. Parents could be so naive at times, especially mothers. 'Thank you, Margaret,' he said, as his secretary left the office.

Throwing the letters onto the desk, Mr Redknapp urged Jessica to take a look at them. 'Is that your or your husband's handwriting, Mrs Mitchell?'

Jessica recognised the writing immediately. It belonged to Joey and Frankie. Reading the letters, she felt herself go cold. 'How long has this been going on?' she asked Mr Redknapp.

'About eight months. I'm surprised no one mentioned it to you at the parents' evening.'

'I never came to the last one. The kids told me that ten of the teachers had the flu and parents' evening had been cancelled.'

The headmaster sighed. 'Joseph and Francesca obviously have very inventive imaginations, don't you think?'

Jessica wished the ground would open up and swallow her. 'Where are they? Can you go and get them out of their classroom for me?'

The headmaster chuckled. 'I'm afraid they're not here today, Mrs Mitchell. In fact, we've only seen them twice in the last three weeks.'

'But I dropped them off at the gates this morning.

I drop them off here every morning and I pick them up in the afternoon.'

Mr Redknapp shrugged. 'Well, I'm afraid your children have been pulling the wool over everybody's eyes. Maybe you can have a word with your husband, Mrs Mitchell. With their exams coming up, the situation needs to be sorted as soon as possible.'

Seething and red-faced, Jessica stood up. 'Thank you for telling me, Mr Redknapp. I will speak to my husband and I can assure you that both Francesca and Joseph will be attending on a regular basis in future. It is my duty as a mother to march them into their classrooms if I have to.'

Mr Redknapp nodded. 'I'll leave the problem in your more than capable hands, then, Mrs Mitchell.'

Unaware that their mother was talking to their headmaster about them, Frankie and Joey were having a little tipple. 'Give us a swig of yours, Joey. Mine's all gone,' Frankie demanded.

Joey handed her the vodka bottle. 'You're such a greedy cow, Frankie. Don't drink it all, give us it back,' he said, snatching at it.

Frankie giggled and let out a burp. 'You're such an old woman, Joey. Make yourself useful and light me a fag.'

Glancing at his watch, Joey jumped off the park bench. 'Shit, it's half-past two. Come on, Frankie, let's run to the bus stop, else Mum'll be waiting for us.'

Frankie laughed and gently pushed him. 'I'll race you. Last one to the bus stop is a retard.'

Not wanting to upset Eddie at work, Jessica decided not to call him on his mobile, and, instead, wait for him to get home. Unable to concentrate on any Christmas shopping, Jessica went home and got stuck into the housework. To say she was furious was an understatement. The twins had taken her for a complete and utter fool and they needed to be punished. She wondered where they were spending their days and what they were doing. Maybe they were walking the streets or sitting round at a friend's house, or maybe they were up to worse.

Feeling as though she no longer knew them, Jessica picked Frankie and Joey up from school at their usual time. As hard as it was, she decided not to let them know she'd cottoned on. Eddie was a much better disciplinarian than she was and he would know exactly how to handle the situation. Filled with fury, Jessica did her best to act normal. 'How was your day?' she asked.

'Oh, the usual, Mum,' Joey replied.

'I got top marks in maths today,' Frankie added.

Jessica felt like screaming. Part of her wanted to stop the car and swing for the devious little toe rags, but somehow she managed to stop herself.

'We're going upstairs to do our homework,' Frankie said as soon as they got indoors.

Jessica was glad. Keeping her temper was difficult and the further out of her sight the pair of them were, the better.

Eddie arrived home at half-past five. 'Hello, darling, I'm starving. Shall I order the grub? Have the kids picked out what they want?' he asked Jessica.

'You'd better sit down,' Jessica told him.

Explaining the story in full, Jessica expected Eddie to go ballistic and was surprised when he didn't.

'I'll go up and speak to 'em. They've got to be punished. I think we should ground them till the New Year. What do you think?' Eddie said calmly.

Jessica was flummoxed. 'Is that all you've got to say? Aren't you even annoyed with them?'

Not wanting to cause an argument, Eddie held Jessica in his arms. 'Of course I'm annoyed and I'll let them know that. But the thing is, Jess, kids will be kids. I used to bunk off school, me brothers did it too. Gary and Ricky were the same – it's what kids do, ain't it?'

Jessica shook her head. 'I never did it. I was too frightened to do anything like that, I was worried I'd get caught.'

Eddie laughed. 'You wasn't a Mitchell though, was you?'

Eddie went upstairs and spoke to the kids, calmly, but firmly. 'Now, I want to know where you've been hanging out. And what you've been doing. And don't lie to me, because I will find out the truth.'

Frankie nudged Joey. 'We've been changing out of our school uniform and going to the café in Dagenham,' Joey mumbled.

'And sometimes we sit in the park,' Frankie added.

'Well, from now on you're going to school every day. And you're both grounded until New Year,' Eddie told them. He was sure they were telling the truth. He could see it in their eyes.

'Oh, but Dad. What about our Christmas disco?' Frankie whinged.

Eddie winked at her. 'You should have thought of that before you played hookey. Now, get your devious little arses downstairs. I'm starving and I wanna order some dinner.'

Jessica wasn't quite as forgiving as her husband and she ignored the twins as they sat down to eat.

'Would you like some more rice, Mum?' Frankie asked her.

'No, eat it yourself,' Jessica replied angrily.

At nine o'clock the twins both yawned. 'We're going to bed now,' they said.

They knew they had got off lightly and they didn't want to push their luck.

Once her deceitful offspring were out of her sight, Jessica began to relax a bit. 'Shall we have another glass of wine?' she asked Eddie.

Eddie stood up to fetch another bottle and was interrupted by the phone ringing. 'All right, Doug? How's tricks?'

'OK, mate. I want you and Jess to come round for dinner on Saturday night. It's Vicki's birthday and I've got a surprise planned for her. She'll definitely want your Jess to be there, I know that,' Dougie said.

'Yeah, that's fine. What time do you want us round?' Eddie enquired.

'About eight.'

'So, what you got planned then?' Eddie asked, intrigued.

Dougie lowered his voice. 'I'm gonna propose and, as long as she says yes, I've booked a holiday for us to go on next week. It's in the Caribbean, I've arranged for us to get married out there. I'm not gonna tell her till we get there. I thought I'd be spontaneous and shock her, for once.'

Eddie laughed. 'You're a fucking boy, you are.'

''Ere, talking of shocks, you heard about Jimmy O'Hara?' Dougie asked.

'I know the old man popped his clogs,' Eddie replied.

'Yeah, that's right, and Jimmy's got back with his old woman. Moved back in yesterday, Alice did, with his youngest kid, Jed.'

'Fuck me, that's a turn-up for the books. You can tell me more on Saturday,' Eddie said, gutted that Alice had forgiven the bastard.

Eddie ended the call, poured the wine and snuggled up next to his wife.

'Put the news on, Ed. I still haven't seen anything about that fire,' Jessica said.

As Ed switched channels, he was shocked to see a picture of Dickie Pearce flash up on the screen.

'A man has been found dead in a gangland-style shooting in Birmingham. Fifty-one-year-old Richard Pearce, a father of two, was found in the early hours of this morning. Police are appealing for witnesses.'

'Poor man. How awful for his children,' Jessica said sadly.

Eddie felt like bursting out laughing, but instead put on his most solemn voice. 'I don't know what this world's coming to, Jess – my life, I don't!'

NINETEEN

As Christmas approached, Jessica was like a dog with two tails. The festive season was her favourite time of year and she always went to town with it.

'You're a fucking girl, you are,' Ed had told her only last week, as she'd arrived home with yet more lights and decorations.

Jessica sighed. When the kids were young, they had got into the Christmas spirit with her. Now they were fifteen, they had no interest in it whatsoever. They didn't even want presents any more, they just wanted money. Frankie and Joey had both been spoilt and were more interested in receiving rather than giving and Jessica blamed herself for that. Ever since they were toddlers, she had always given them anything they asked for, and now she was older and wiser, she wished she had been stricter with them.

'Right, I'm off now, babe. Are you sure you don't fancy coming with me?'

Jessica shook her head. Eddie was going to visit his family to drop their presents off and she'd managed to wangle her way out of going with him. 'Honestly, Ed, I would have loved to have come, but I've got far too much to do. Mum and Dad are coming at three and I haven't even tidied the guest room yet. I've got to cook that big lump of ham, vac, polish, prepare dinner and –'

Ed stopped her mid-sentence. 'OK, I get the message. You do what you've got to do and I'll see you when I get back. I'll probably pop in the Flag for a Christmas tipple with me dad and brothers this afternoon, but I won't be late home.'

Jessica hugged him. 'Don't rush back. You enjoy yourself, I'm sure I can manage to entertain Mum, Dad and the kids without you.'

Eddie kissed her on the forehead. 'Oh, you've just reminded me, the kids want to go out tonight. It's only round a mate's house. It's OK with me if it's OK with you.'

Jessica was dubious. 'I'm not sure, Ed. I want to have a drink tonight and I'm not drinking and driving. Anyway, I'm not sure I trust them any more.'

Eddie disagreed. 'They'll be fine. I'll give 'em the money to get a cab. They've been stuck in for nearly six weeks, Jess, we can't keep 'em locked up forever. We'll tell 'em they've got to be back by eleven.'

Reluctantly, Jessica agreed. Ever since her trip to the school, Frankie and Joey had attended regularly and worked very hard. She had been in touch with Mr Redknapp, their headmaster, and he had organised a homework rota to enable them to catch up for their exams. They were still way behind their classmates, but Jessica couldn't fault their efforts. They'd worked tirelessly most evenings, so a little break might do them good.

The roads weren't as busy as Eddie expected them to be and it didn't take him long to get to his aunt's house.

'How's my favourite nephew? Come inside and warm yourself up by the fire. Bleedin' taters out there, ain't it?

203

I've made you a nice bread pudding – it's just cooling down,' Auntie Joan said, thrilled to see him.

Eddie made himself comfortable. 'What you doing tomorrow? You off to your friend's, as usual?'

Auntie Joan spent every Christmas and Boxing Day at her friend Ada's house. 'Yep, Ada's son is picking me up this evening. I've got me little case packed. What about you? Have you and Jess got a house full this year?'

'Not really, no. Jessica's parents are coming to stay and that's about it. Gary and Ricky have sodded off to Tenerife and Raymondo is spending Christmas Day round his new girlfriend's house. We'll probably have a house full Boxing Day. Our friends Dougie and Vicki are coming over. They're the ones that I told you about, the ones that have just got married abroad and I think Raymondo is bringing his posh bit of skirt round to meet us.'

Auntie Joan laughed. 'I'll go and pour you a nice cuppa. The bread pudding should be cool enough to cut now.'

Eddie smiled as she handed him a plate and put his tea on the table.

'What's your dad and brothers doing?' Joan asked him.

'Dad's going round to Paulie's for dinner and I'm not sure, but I think Ronny and Sharon are going as well. Reg is going round Uncle Albert's, I know that. You're always welcome to come over to mine, Auntie Joan. I know I'm wasting me breath, 'cause I've asked you a thousand times, but the offer's always there. I can pick you up Boxing Day and drop you back home whenever.'

Auntie Joan shook her head. 'It's nice of you to ask, love, but you know how set in me ways I am. I like me East London, I don't do Essex, I'm afraid.'

Eddie smiled. When they made his aunt, they broke the bloody mould.

'There is something you can do for me though, boy.

You remember old Molly? Lives in the flat over the back here. Molly Jenkins – little woman with grey hair, walks with a limp.'

Eddie nodded. 'I know who you mean.'

'Well, I'm really worried about her. Michael, her son, is a bastard to her. Got a drink and drug problem he has, and he keeps turning up at her door asking for money. Poor old Molly only lives on a pension and she's petrified of him. Twice he's clumped her now and it's not on, Eddie. He drinks in the Grave Maurice, always in there, he is. He'll definitely be in there now. Somebody needs to have a little chat with him, if you know what I mean.'

Eddie knew exactly what she meant. 'Leave it with me,' he told her.

An hour later, Eddie stood up. Fishing in his jacket pocket, he pulled out an envelope and handed it to Auntie Joan. 'I want you to treat yourself to something nice, Auntie,' he told her.

Embarrassed, Joan flapped her arms about. 'I don't want your bleedin' money. What do I need money for at my age?'

Eddie chuckled. They had this same argument every Christmas. 'Please don't insult me. If you don't want it, give it to the fucking dogs' home or something.'

Auntie Joan hugged him. 'Me old winter coat's going home a bit, maybe I'll treat meself to a new one,' she told him.

Wishing her a happy Christmas, Eddie jumped into his Land Cruiser and headed towards the pub. The Grave Maurice was literally minutes away on Whitechapel Road. Eddie had no idea who Michael Jenkins was, but he knew Alan, the landlord.

'Eddie! What a lovely surprise,' Alan said, shaking his hand.

205

Eddie accepted his offer of a drink and sat down on a bar stool next to him.

'What can I do for you, son?' Alan asked him.

'I'm looking for a Michael Jenkins. He drinks in here, apparently.'

Alan nodded towards a scruffy-looking geezer who was standing alone at the opposite end of the bar. 'Local pisshead, he is.'

Eddie nodded. Shame it wasn't his own fucking money he was getting pissed on, he thought, anger rising inside him. He turned back to Alan. 'His mother's a mate of my Auntie Joan. Apparently, the lovely Michael has been knocking her about for his beer money. She's seventy-odd, his poor old mum, Al. He needs a little wake-up call, don't you think?'

Alan nodded. 'Be my guest, Eddie. I don't like the bloke and he's a fuckin' nuisance in here at times.'

Eddie finished his drink. 'Thanks, Al. I'll take him outside and speak to him. Take care, mate, and have a nice Christmas.'

Michael Jenkins didn't like the look of the man who approached him and he certainly didn't fancy going outside with him.

'Do as I say, else I'll break your fucking legs,' Eddie whispered in his ear.

'I can't go anywhere, I've gotta meet me mate in a minute,' Michael pleaded.

Eddie's eyes clouded over. 'If you don't walk outside now and get in the Land Cruiser, I swear I will come back with a gun and blow your fucking brains out.'

Like a lamb being led to the slaughter, Michael Jenkins did as he was told.

Eddie started the engine. 'Where are you taking me? What am I supposed to have done?' Michael said nervously.

Eddie said nothing. He knew of a dead-end turning a few streets away that was always deserted. Reaching his destination, Eddie opened both doors. 'Get out,' he ordered Michael.

Petrified, Michael started to flinch. 'What am I meant to have done? You've got the wrong person. I swear it's not me. You're Eddie Mitchell, aren't you?'

Eddie dragged Michael into the alleyway. Pulling a knife out of his pocket, he pointed it at him. 'You are one piece of fucking shit. And if I ever find out you've laid one finger on your mother again, I will personally fucking kill you. You leave her be, you keep away from her. Do you get my meaning, cunt?'

'I promise I won't go near her again. She offered me money, she gave it to me,' Michael said sobbing.

Despite his odd fib to Jessica, Eddie hated liars. Unable to control his temper, he threw Michael to the floor and stood on his wrist. 'You lying fucking scumbag,' he said, as he positioned the knife on his thumb. Hacking away, Ed realised that the job wasn't complete and the thumb was hanging on by a thread of skin. Determined to chop the bastard thing off, he brought the knife down once again.

Eddie kicked the thumb down the alleyway. Smiling, he left Michael screaming and wriggling and walked back to his motor. 'You say one word or mention my name to anyone, then I'll come back and chop your cock off,' he shouted to his victim.

Reversing out of the dead end, Eddie rang his dad. Reg, Ronny and Paulie were all in the Flag with him and Ed was pleased, as it meant he could kill four birds with one stone.

Turning on the radio, Eddie smirked as he heard the song being played. 'Little Lies' by Fleetwood Mac was very appropriate for poor Michael. Eddie smiled as he thought of what he'd just done to him. Years ago when he was a little boy, his dad used to take him to the fish-monger's. Eddie was obsessed with the live eels wriggling about in the big bowls of water and he loved watching the man chop them up alive. Eddie grinned. That's what Michael Jenkins' thumb had reminded him of today, a live fucking eel. Laughing out loud, Eddie put his foot on the accelerator and sped off.

'Joey, Frankie, your nan and grandad are here,' Jessica shouted up the stairs.

Thrilled that their mother had agreed to them going out later, the twins bounded down stairs with smiles on their faces. Staying in every night doing tons of home-work had been soul-destroying for them, so much so that they'd climbed out of the window last week and gone out for the evening. It had nearly all ended in tears, as Joey had struggled to climb back up, lost his balance and fallen backwards onto the drive. Frankie had had to creep down-stairs and let him in at the front door. It was a miracle he was just bruised and not badly injured. It was also a miracle that their parents hadn't heard the commotion.

Joyce and Stanley made a real fuss of the twins. 'What you done to your face? You've got a big bruise. You ain't been fighting, have you?' Joyce asked Joey.

'No, I fell out of bed, Nan.' Joey told her sincerely. He'd got the bruise when he'd fallen off the roof.

Frankie backed him up. 'It's true, Nan. He went to bed one night and woke up like that the next morning. I can vouch for him, honest I can.'

Frankie glanced at her brother and he winked at her.

'How's school? You must have your exams soon.' Stanley asked both of them.

208

Jessica shot the twins a look. She'd warned them not to tell their nan and grandad about the fiasco at the school.

'We've been working really hard, Grandad. We take our exams very seriously,' Frankie said cheekily.

Jessica felt her lip curl. She could swing for that girl sometimes, she really could.

Eddie tutted as Paulie brought over another drink. He already had three lined up on the table and was struggling to get through them. 'What you trying to do – get me pissed? I've already had about six. I can't drink all of them, I've got the motor outside,' he joked.

Ronny was in a quiet mood. He hated being stuck in a wheelchair and he couldn't stand other people being happy. No one knew what his life was like. Being treated like a cripple made him feel so inferior that sometimes he wished he was dead.

'Looking forward to Christmas around Paulie's?' Eddie asked him cheerfully.

'Yeah, can't wait. I'm gonna dress up as fucking Santa and slide down the chimney while singing "Rudolph the Red-Nosed Reindeer",' Ronny answered sarcastically.

Eddie glanced at Sharon. She had just turned up to take Ronny home and Eddie felt truly sorry for her. Years ago, he'd never been a massive fan of his brother's bird, but just lately his heart went out to her. Most women would have run a mile after Ronny's accident, but Sharon had stuck by him through thick and thin. Ronny showed her no love at all, he spoke to her like shit and Eddie didn't know how she put up with him. It wasn't as though they had kids or anything to keep her there.

'Come up the bar; let me get you a drink, Sharon,' Eddie said.

'Yeah, go on. Fuck off with him, I dunno why you

turned up so early – I ain't going nowhere yet,' Ronny said nastily.

With tears in her eyes, Sharon followed Eddie up to the bar.

'What do you want, love?' Eddie asked her.

Sharon shrugged. 'I'll just have an orange juice, please.'

Eddie smiled at her. 'Why don't you have something stronger? Have a glass of wine or something. One won't hurt you.'

Sharon shook her head. 'Living with Ronny has put me off drink for life.'

Eddie shouted up an orange juice and handed it to her. 'Listen, if you ever need any outside help, just let me know. I can pay for a carer or someone who will give you a break.'

Sharon felt her eyes well up again. She wasn't used to kindness. 'I can manage all right. I just wish he was more grateful and didn't drink so much. When he's drunk, he says the most terrible things to me.'

Eddie nodded sympathetically. 'My offer will always be there for you, Sharon. You know my number. If things get too much for you, then ring me.'

Sharon smiled sadly. 'Thanks Ed, I will.'

'What's for dinner, love?' Stanley asked his daughter.

'I've done a nice cold-meat buffet with crusty bread, pickles, jacket potatoes, cheese and coleslaw. I thought it best that we don't overeat tonight – we don't want to spoil ourselves for tomorrow, do we?'

Joyce agreed. 'Any chance of another glass of Baileys, dear?'

'We're going out now, Mum,' Frankie said, as she walked into the room all dolled up in a denim miniskirt.

Jessica looked at her in astonishment. 'It's only ten to

six – your dad's not even back yet. Why are you all dressed up? You're only going round your friend's house, aren't you?'

Joey stepped out from behind his sister. He was also dressed smartly. 'We've gotta make an effort, Mum. All our school friends are going to be there. We can't look like tramps at Christmas,' he said.

'Whose house are you going to? Are their parents going to be there?'

Frankie spoke earnestly. 'We're going round Joey's friend David's house. And I'm not going to lie to you, Mum, his parents are going out for a meal, but David said they'll be back by ten o'clock.'

Jessica nodded. She had met David a couple of times and he was a pleasant enough boy. At least Frankie had been honest with her about his parents going out for the evening, so maybe she'd learned her lesson.

'How are you getting there?' she asked the twins.

'Cab. We've already ordered it. It's double fare after six; that's why we're going out early,' Frankie answered.

Hearing a toot outside, Jessica smiled at them. 'Go on, off you go. Have a good time and no getting drunk.'

'We won't, Mum, I promise,' Frankie said, nudging her brother.

'And don't forget to be back by eleven,' Jessica shouted out.

As Frankie slammed the door, Joey smiled. 'Do you think she believed us?'

Frankie giggled. 'Course she did. Especially when I said that David's parents weren't gonna be at home. I saw the gleam in her eye at my honesty.'

Joey laughed. 'You're such a cow at times, Frankie.'

Frankie and Joey got into the minicab.

'Where are you going?' the driver asked.

Frankie laughed. It was Christmas, the season of good-will and it was about time her brother knew that she was aware of his interesting little secret.

'We're gonna be ending up at the Angel pub in the village. But can you go to Cherry Tree Lane first?' Joey said.

'Are we picking someone up?' the driver asked.

Frankie smiled. 'Yes, my brother's boyfriend.'

TWENTY

Astonished that his sister knew his secret, Joey urged her to shut the fuck up. He didn't want the cab driver knowing his business; he couldn't take that risk.

'Change of plan, mate. Drop us at the Cherry Tree lights. We've gotta get some fags and stuff, we'll walk from there,' Joey told the driver.

'So, you're not going to the Angel now?' the bewildered cabbie asked.

Joey shook his head. 'Nah, we're not, mate.'

'That'll be three-eighty,' the cabbie said, giving Joey a strange look and the once-over.

Joey handed him a fiver and told him to keep the change. 'I haven't really got a boyfriend, mate. My sister has a lot of mental issues and tends to blurt out these things,' he said, as he shoved Frankie out of the cab.

Seeing the driver's bemused expression, Frankie couldn't stop laughing. 'Your face was a picture, Joey. I bet he goes back to his office and tells his colleagues he's just picked up a shit-stabber and a nutcase.'

Joey didn't share her warped sense of humour. He lit up two fags and handed her one. 'How do you know?' he asked bluntly.

Frankie took a long drag and blew the smoke in his

face. 'I've known for ages, you idiot. Don't you remember that time around Simon's house? You and David were upstairs going through his record collection and I sneaked up. I saw you leap apart from one another. It was obvious you'd been kissing!'

Joey didn't know whether to laugh or cry. He felt awkward that Frankie knew, but was also relieved that she did. 'Does anybody else know? You won't say anything to Mum and Dad, will you?' he asked her.

Frankie threw him a sarcastic look. 'Of course, I'm gonna tell 'em tomorrow. I'll wait till we're eating our Christmas dinner and hold a sausage on me fork while screaming out "Joey likes willies," shall I?'

Joey laughed. He trusted Frankie and knew she wouldn't dob him in it.

'Have you, you know, done anything with him?' Frankie pried.

Joey smirked. 'Well, sort of.'

Frankie was perplexed. 'Like what?'

'I'll tell you all about it another time. Now come on, we'll be late. I'll race you to David's house. Last one there's a plonker.'

Jessica waited for Eddie to arrive home, and then brought out the buffet. 'Mum, Dad, help yourselves,' she urged.

Eddie pecked his little homemaker on the cheek. 'What time did the kids go out?'

'Just before six. They didn't want to pay double fare. How was your day, love?'

Eddie smiled. Best he didn't mention that he'd chopped someone's thumb off. 'It was good. I went to see me Auntie Joan, then popped in the Flag to have a drink with the rest of the family.'

'Did you see your dad?' Jessica asked.

214

'Yeah. He looked tired, the old man. Said he's had some agg with a few kids knocking on the door late at night. Reckons they're potential burglars, knocking to see if there's anyone at home. The silly little bastards obviously don't know who me father is, do they? If they set one foot inside his property, me dad'll fucking kill 'em,' Eddie replied, laughing.

The buffet was beautifully presented and went down a treat.

'That's me done. Bleeding handsome, love,' Joyce said, rubbing her stomach.

'Can I get you anything else, Dad?' Jessica asked, picking up her father's empty plate.

'I'm absolutely bloated. I could manage another Scotch though,' Stanley said cheekily.

Joyce pursed her lips. 'You've had four already, Stanley. Can't you have a cup of tea instead?'

'Whatever you say, dear,' Stanley said calmly.

'Do you want a cuppa as well, Mum?' Jessica asked.

'Oh, no! I'll have a Baileys, love.'

Eddie and Jessica looked at one another and burst out laughing. Joyce couldn't understand why they were laughing at her. 'What's the matter?' she asked annoyed.

Eddie handed his father-in-law a Scotch. 'Thanks, Eddie,' Stanley said gratefully.

Joyce took the glass of Baileys from Eddie and downed it in one. She scowled at Stanley. Her husband was one greedy bastard at times, he really was.

'Bye, Mrs Hughton, bye, Mr Hughton. Have a lovely Christmas,' Joey shouted to David's parents as they left the house.

Frankie laughed at his politeness. 'I'll leave you and lover boy to it,' she said, as she skipped on ahead.

215

David looked at Joey in amazement. 'You ain't told her, have you?' he asked horrified.

Joey shook his head. 'She knew. She's known for ages, apparently. Do you remember that time we were round at Simon's and we thought she'd caught us? Well, she did.'

David was much more macho than Joey and was desperate to keep his confusion over his sexuality a secret. 'Well, that's fucking great, Joey. She won't say nothing, will she? I mean, I am captain of the football team. Can you imagine what the lads would say?'

'She's my twin – of course she ain't gonna fucking say anything,' Joey told him.

As Frankie strolled on ahead, the two lads walked in silence. David's attitude annoyed Joey at times. Joey wasn't ashamed of fancying boys, and if it wasn't for his father finding out and probably burying him alive, he'd have shouted if from the rooftops. David was the opposite. He'd always claimed that he was straight. He was adamant that he was just experimenting and, one day, would marry and have children.

Joey had no intention of following in his so-called boyfriend's footsteps. He'd known from a very early age that he only liked boys, and was 100% positive that he was gay. He'd been out with a couple of girls, but kissing them had turned his stomach over.

'Sorry if I snapped at you. Are you OK, Joey?' David asked him.

Joey nodded. 'Let's catch up with Frankie, eh?'

As Eddie left the room to make a few phone calls, Jessica switched on the television. Her mum and dad were both having forty winks and the house seemed so quiet all of a sudden. Flicking through the channels, Jessica spotted a programme where a mother was holding a newborn baby. 'Aah,' Jessica murmured as she realised that the baby looked just like Joey had when he was born. Sighing, Jessica switched channels. The twins were all grown up now. They didn't need her any more and she didn't want to depress herself.

'What's up? You look sad,' Eddie said, as he sat down next to her.

Forcing herself to stop being sentimental, Jessica smiled. 'Nothing's wrong. I'm fine.'

Hours later, Joey grabbed his sister's arm. 'Frankie, hurry up, the cab'll be waiting outside.'

Frankie was tipsy and in no rush to leave the pub. 'Tell the cab to go away and come back after twelve. Mum and Dad'll be all right; they'll probably be pissed by now anyway.'

Joey shook his head. His sister could be such a pain in the arse sometimes. 'Look, if we're late, Mother'll probably ground us again. You might be willing to take that chance, but I bloody well ain't. Sod not being allowed out on New Year's Eve. I wanna celebrate the start of 1988 in style.'

Seeing Joey getting annoyed, Frankie poked her tongue out at him. 'OK, you win. I'm coming. Just let me say goodbye to the girls.'

'Where's David?' Frankie asked, as she walked outside. 'He's staying for a bit. He ain't gotta be home till after twelve,' Joey said.

Frankie laughed. 'No kisses for you tonight then, dear.'

'Just shut up and get in the car, will you?' Joey told her sternly.

As the front door slammed, Jessica nudged Eddie and smiled. 'They're bang on time. It's one minute to eleven, bless 'em,' she said.

Frankie bounded into the lounge. 'As it's Christmas, can me and Joey have a proper drink, Mum?' she asked boldly.

Jessica looked at Eddie. 'I don't see why not,' he said.

'We'll both have a vodka and Coke then,' Frankie said, sitting in between her grandparents.

Joey sat down next to his mum. 'How was your evening, love? Did you have a nice time with David?' she asked.

Frankie laughed. 'He always has a nice time with David, don't you, Joey?'

Joey scowled at his sister and quickly changed the subject.

Tanked up on Baileys, Joyce was in a playful mood. 'Why don't we have a little game? Who fancies playing *Give Us a Clue*?' she asked.

Eddie laughed. 'You mean charades, Joyce?'

'Whatever.' Joyce laughed. 'Never been the same, that programme, since Michael Aspel left and Parky took over.'

'Who's going first?' Jessica enquired.

Joyce leaped up and waved her hands.

'TV, two syllables,' Joey said.

Crossing her legs, Joyce urged her family to guess the first syllable.

'You look like you're busting for a piss, the way you're standing, Joycie,' Eddie said, taking the mickey.

Joyce turned to Stanley.

'Knees? Legs?' he asked.

Unable to control her annoyance, Joyce let rip at him. 'Didn't you notice me crossing me legs? It's *Crossroads*, you silly old bastard,' she said, flopping down in the armchair.

Eddie stood up to take his turn.

'Film, two words. The something,' Jessica said.

'*The Godfather*,' Frankie shouted correctly.

'Clever girl,' Stanley said, impressed.

Frankie smiled. 'That was easy, it's Dad's favourite film.'

'Sounds about right,' Stanley mumbled, as he nodded politely.

Already bored with Christmas, Joey stood up. 'I'm really tired. I'm gonna go to bed, if that's OK.'

Frankie nodded. 'Me too,' she said, finishing her drink.

'Do you want waking up early to open your presents?' Jessica asked them.

'Leave it out, Mum. We asked for just money; we're fifteen, not five,' Frankie replied, laughing.

Seeing Eddie yawn, Jessica smiled. 'Shall we finish this game tomorrow and go to bed now?' she said.

Eddie nodded. 'Are yous two staying up for a bit?' he asked his in-laws.

Joyce stood up. 'No, we've had enough as well. Come on, Stanley, leave that drink, you've had enough. Come on, chop-chop.'

Having little alternative, Stanley left the glass of Scotch and followed his wife up the stairs.

Jessica felt glum as she pulled the quilt over herself. She had been in a funny mood all night, and was struggling to snap out of it. Eddie got undressed and snuggled up next to her. Planting kisses on the back of her neck, he asked her what was wrong.

'I'm fine, honest I am,' Jessica insisted.

'No, you're not. We've been married for a long time, Jess, and I know when something's wrong.'

Jessica turned to face him. 'You're gonna think I'm ever so silly if I tell you.'

Eddie leaned over her and moved her fringe out of her eyes. 'Tell me, I promise I won't think you're silly.'

Jessica struggled for the right words. 'It's just that now

the kids are older, it doesn't really feel like Christmas any more. I've noticed it this year more than any other. They'll soon be leaving school and it's as though they don't need me, Ed. I feel like I've been made redundant all of a sudden.'

Eddie saw a tear roll down her cheek and held her close. 'Ssh, don't cry, Jess,' he whispered.

He didn't really know what to say to her. He was glad the kids were nearly off their hands, but he tried to put himself in her shoes. From the time they were babies, Jess had been stuck indoors, nurturing them. He'd always been out working and, although he hated admitting it, he'd barely noticed them growing up. Eddie had always been an impulsive bastard and tonight was no exception. It broke his heart to see his wife look so sad. He loved her so much, he would literally do anything in his power to make her happy.

'Let's have another baby,' he said to her.

Jessica turned over and looked at him with an incredulous expression. 'What? We can't – I'm thirty-three and you're forty-six.'

Eddie laughed. 'So? Me dick still works, don't it?'

Jessica shook her head. 'Oh, we can't, Ed. What will me mum and dad say? And the twins would be horrified.'

Smiling, Eddie straddled her and refused to move until she agreed. 'Fuck your parents and fuck the kids. This is all about me and you, Jess. It's our future, no one else's.'

'Are you really serious or are you just winding me up?' Jessica asked him.

'I'm as serious as the day I asked you to marry me. Come on, Jess, let's go for it, eh?'

Jessica thought over his suggestion. She'd thought her nappy-changing days were well and truly finished and she hadn't expected this bombshell to be dropped on her.

'We'll have to talk about it properly, weigh up the pros and cons,' she said.

Eddie smiled. Unlike him, Jess was sensible. 'Go on, say yes, you know you want to. Just think about that pitter-patter of tiny feet.'

Jessica grinned. It would be lovely to have a focus and be needed once more.

Knowing how she hated being tickled, Eddie did exactly that. 'Go on, let's be devils. You know I've got super-sperm, don't ya? Well, this time next year, we could have a cot in that corner and it could be our baby's first Christmas.'

Laughing hysterically, tears ran down Jessica's face as she begged him to stop tickling her.

'Say yes and I'll stop,' Eddie told her.

'Yes,' Jessica yelled. 'Yes, yes, yes!'

TWENTY-ONE

On Christmas morning, Jessica woke early with a big smile on her face. Desperate to check that her husband had meant what he'd said the previous evening, she gently prodded him until he opened his eyes.

'What time is it?' Eddie mumbled.

'It's half-past six. You did mean what you said last night, didn't you? It wasn't the drink talking, was it?'

Eddie smiled at her. 'Of course I meant it. Why don't we have a little practice now. No time like the present, eh?'

Jessica giggled as Eddie leaped on top of her. 'Be quiet, Ed. I don't want me mum and dad to hear us.'

'Well, in that case, I'll make as much fucking noise as possible,' Eddie told her laughing.

Unable to put up with Joyce's snoring any longer, Stanley decided to get up and have a shower. At home, he and his wife slept in separate bedrooms. When they stayed at Jessica's, they were forced to share, unfortunately.

Not wanting to wake Joyce up, Stanley decided to tiptoe towards the en-suite bathroom in the dark. Seconds later, he caught his leg on the chair and fell flat on his face.

Joyce woke with a fright and switched on the light.

'What are you doing, you senile old goat?' she screeched at him.

Stanley stood up. 'And a happy Christmas to you too, dear,' he said, slamming the bathroom door.

After making love to his wife, Eddie had a quick shower and went downstairs to make breakfast. Smoked salmon and scrambled eggs washed down with a glass of champagne was a Christmas-morning ritual. The festive season was the one time of the year when Eddie mucked in with the cooking to give his long-suffering wife a break.

'Morning, Stanley. Do you fancy some smoked salmon and scrambled eggs?' he asked.

Stanley pulled a face. 'Makes me feel ill, that bleedin' salmon. Ain't got any bacon, have you?'

Eddie smiled as his father-in-law shuffled into the living room. Poor old Stanley had never been high up in the class stakes, bless him.

The twins ambled downstairs as the rest of the household were eating. 'Where's ours?' Frankie said, annoyed that no one had called them.

Eddie chuckled. 'Go and make something yourself, you lazy pair of sods.'

Jessica put on the Christmas CD and began to sort through the many presents under the tree.

'Do we have to listen to this rubbish, Mum? Can't we put on some house music or something?' Frankie complained.

'No, this is staying on,' Jessica said, grinning at Eddie. Jess was so excited about their baby plans, she couldn't stop thinking about it. It was the best Christmas present Eddie could have given her.

As all the gifts were being opened, Eddie studied his son. Joey was nothing like Gary and Ricky at all. Dressed

223

in bleached jeans with a pink jumper, he looked and acted like a poof. Even the way he opened his gifts was done in a feminine way; he kept squealing like a fucking girl. Eddie sighed. Thank Christ Joey had brought a couple of girlfriends home earlier this year. Eddie was relieved that his son was actually into birds, as over the years he'd had his doubts. Can you imagine? Eddie Mitchell's son, the poof: he'd never have lived that one down.

'This is for you, Dad. It's from me and Joey,' Frankie yelled, handing him a present.

'Sorry, angel, I was in a dream world there,' Ed said, as he unwrapped the Pringle jumper. 'Thanks, kids,' Eddie said, handing his wife a small velvet box.

Jessica opened it and squealed with delight. 'Oh, Ed, it's beautiful,' she said, as she studied the diamond ring.

Joyce snatched it from her and showed it to Stanley. 'Look, dear, a diamond ring. Better than them poxy slippers you bought me, don't you think?'

With all the giving and receiving over, Eddie stood up. 'I'm just gonna give my family a ring, then I'll pour us some more drinks.'

Busy putting the wrapping paper into black bin liners, Jessica looked up. 'Ring Ray for us, Ed, and bring the phone in here so Mum and Dad can talk to him.'

Eddie rang his dad first, but got no answer. He than rang Paulie. 'Is the old man there yet?' he asked his brother.

'Nah. If he ain't at home, then he's probably over Mum's grave or on his way,' Paulie told him.

About to ring Raymond, Eddie was thrilled when the phone rang and it was Gary and Ricky in Tenerife. 'Merry Christmas, Dad. Gary's pissed already,' Ricky said, laughing.

Eddie chuckled. 'How you getting on? What's the weather like?'

'It's fucking well hot, Dad. The apartment is the nuts and there's plenty of crumpet out here. We're gonna spend today on the beach with two little sorts we met yesterday,' Ricky told him.

Gary snatched the phone from his younger brother. 'I ain't pissed, Dad, take no notice of him. He was well gone last night, you know what a lightweight he is.'

'Where you having your Christmas dinner? Have you booked anywhere?' Eddie asked Gary.

'Nah. We ain't gonna bother. It's too hot for a roast, so we'll have a barbecue on the beach instead. Listen, Dad, the pips are going, we'll call you in a couple of days. Have a good one and give our love to –'

Eddie smiled as the money ran out. Gary and Ricky were obviously having a whale of a time, the lucky bastards.

Punching in Raymond's mobile number, Eddie could tell that he was already at his girlfriend's house. 'What you talking all posh for, you wanker?' he ribbed him.

'I'm not. Don't start all that tomorrow when we come over,' Raymond whispered.

Eddie chuckled as he took the phone into the living room. Polly, Raymondo's new bird, was a posh bit of stuff, by all accounts, and came from an extremely wealthy family.

'The prodigal son,' Eddie said, handing the phone to Joyce.

'Hello, Raymond. Are you having a nice time, love? What's their house like?'

'Yep, I'm having a lovely time thanks, Mum,' Raymond replied, ignoring her second question.

'What's the house like?' Joyce prompted him once again.

'Yes, happy Christmas, Mum. Can I say hello to Dad and Jess now?' Raymond asked.

Disappointed she hadn't got any more out of him, Joyce handed the phone to Stanley. 'He obviously can't talk properly; her parents must be in the room,' she said to Jessica.

'Looking forward to seeing you tomorrow, son,' Stanley said, handing the phone to Jessica.

Jessica wished Ray happy Christmas and asked what time he would be arriving the following day.

'About four o'clock, sis, if that's all right? Polly's dad wants us to go for a quick drink in his local before we leave.'

'That's fine. Well, give our love to Polly and her family and tell her we'll look forward to meeting her tomorrow.'

Jessica smiled as she ended the call. 'He sounds so loved-up for the first time in his life,' she said.

'What did he say, then? Did he say what the house was like?' Joyce said, getting more agitated by the minute with the lack of information she was receiving. All Raymond had told her was that Polly's parents were well off and lived in Chelsea. Joyce couldn't wait to meet them. If their daughter was getting serious with her son, then she had every right to check out the in-laws.

The rest of the morning and early afternoon passed pleasantly and at half-past two, Jessica ordered Eddie to start carving the turkey, ham and beef.

'Frankie, can you give me a hand with the vegetables?' she asked her daughter.

'Can't Nan help you?' Frankie whinged.

Joyce stood up and Joey ordered her to sit back down. 'You're a guest, Nan. I'll help Mum,' he said, glaring at Frankie. She was a lazy cow, his sister, and she only got away with it because she was his dad's favourite.

The dinner looked delicious and, as Jessica brought in the stuffing balls, cauliflower cheese and sausages rolled

226

in bacon, she urged everybody to tuck in. 'Help your-selves. I'm just gonna make a drop more gravy,' she said, as the phone rang.

'Leave that or give it to me and I'll tell whoever it is to fuck off,' Eddie shouted out.

Jessica answered it and was surprised to hear Paulie's voice on the other end. 'Jess, is Eddie there?' he asked her.

'We're just eating our dinner. Can he call you back, Paulie?'

'No, it's urgent, Jess, I need to speak to him now,' Paulie replied.

Sighing, Jessica took the phone into the dining room. She had no time for either of Eddie's brothers; they were both arrogant bastards. 'It's Paulie. He says it's urgent,' she said, handing the phone to Eddie.

Cursing, Eddie put down his knife and fork. Snatching the phone, he stormed out of the room. 'This had better be important. What's the fucking problem?' he asked his brother.

'No one knows where Dad is. He was meant to be here hours ago and he ain't showed. I've rung Reg and he ain't heard a dickie bird from him. I wondered if he'd rung you.'

Eddie felt his pulse quicken. His dad was Mr Reliable and he instinctively knew that something was wrong. 'He ain't rung me. Maybe he's still over at Mum's grave. What time was he due at yours? Have you been round to the house?'

'He said he'd be here by twelve. I sent Sharon round there at two, but she said there was no answer. I've rung the Flag, but he's not in there. I ain't got a key to his house. Joan's got one, but she's away.'

'I've got a key,' Eddie said immediately. 'I'll leave now. Can you meet me there?'

'Course. Shall I bring Ronny as well?'

'No, just bring yourself. I'll be about twenty minutes, if I put me foot down.'

Replacing the receiver, Eddie noticed that his hands were unsteady. 'Please God don't make him have had a stroke or heart attack or something,' he mumbled to himself.

Poking his head around the dining-room door, Eddie urged Jessica to come outside.

'Whatever's the matter?' she asked concerned.

'It's me dad. He ain't turned up round Paulie's for dinner. It ain't like him. I reckon he might have had an accident or a funny turn indoors. I've got a spare key, I'm gonna shoot round, make sure he's OK.'

Jessica nodded understandingly. 'I'll warm your dinner up for you when you get back. Will you be OK? Do you want me to come with you?'

Eddie shook his head. 'I've got me mobile. I'll call you when I've found out what's happened.'

Jessica was worried as she heard Ed's Land Cruiser zoom away. Eddie was very close to his dad and it would be awful for him if he'd fallen seriously ill on Christmas day.

'What's up?' her mother asked, as she walked back in the room.

'Nothing. Ed's just had to pop out for a bit.' Jessica said awkwardly. She didn't want to spoil everybody's day and there might be no reason to panic yet.

Frankie glared at her mother. 'Well, you must know where Dad's gone. It must be important or he wouldn't have left his dinner.'

Jessica pushed her plate away. Suddenly, she didn't feel hungry any more. 'He's popped round your grandad's. Apparently, Grandad was meant to go to your Uncle Paulie's for dinner, but he never turned up.'

Frankie shrugged. 'Knowing Grandad, he's probably out on the lash with his mates and Dad's had a wasted journey,' she said.

With Eddie's unexpected absence, the mood at the dinner table became sombre. 'Do you want some more meat or potatoes, Dad?' Jessica asked, trying to keep things normal.

'No thanks, love,' Stanley replied.

'I'll have some,' Frankie said.

'Have you got any more sausages in the kitchen, Mum?' Joey asked.

With only Frankie and Joey still eating, Jessica began to clear the plates away. 'Who wants Christmas pudding and who wants banoffee pie?' she asked brightly.

'Why don't we wait till Eddie gets back, dear?' her mother said soothingly.

Joey and Frankie nudged one another. 'I'm bored. Shall we get pissed?' Frankie whispered.

Joey replied with a wink.

Paulie was already waiting outside his dad's house when Eddie pulled up. 'I've knocked again and rung the bell,' he told Eddie.

With a heart that felt like lead, Eddie fumbled for the key in his pocket .

'Dad! Dad!' he shouted, as he opened the front door. His legs were like jelly.

'Fuck! No!' Paulie whispered as they walked into the lounge. The place had been ransacked.

There was no sign of their father, so Eddie ran up the stairs. 'Dad!' he screamed. 'Dad!'

Walking into his father's bedroom, the first thing Eddie saw was splattered blood. 'No, fucking God, no!' he screamed, as he cradled his battered father.

Hearing his brother's screams, Paulie galloped up the stairs. 'Oh no! Tell me he's alive, Eddie. Please tell me he's still alive.'

Tears running down his face, Eddie could barely bring himself to speak. 'Who's done this to you, Dad? Who's done this?' he cried.

Taking a closer look, Paulie saw that his father's head was pummelled to a pulp. 'I'll call the police, I'll ring an ambulance,' he shouted.

Kneeling in his father's blood, Eddie cradled his father's face in his hands and sobbed. 'It's too late. We're too fucking late. He's dead, Paulie, Dad's dead!'

TWENTY-TWO

Paulie made the 999 call. Within seconds of the Old Bill arriving, Eddie washed his father's blood off his hands and his shock turned to fury. He couldn't show himself up in front of these mugs – it wasn't an option. 'When I find out who's responsible for this, I'll torture the cunt for so long, he'll wish he'd never been born,' he said to his brother.

Approached by a DS, Eddie distractedly shook his hand.

'I know this has been an awful shock for you, but are you able to answer a few questions for us, Mr Mitchell?' asked the copper.

Still in a trance, Paulie poured two large brandies, handed one to Eddie and urged him to do all the talking. Eddie explained exactly what had happened. 'So when me dad never turned up for dinner, me and Paulie came round to check on him, and that's how we found him.'

The DS nodded sympathetically. 'Can you think of anyone who might have a grudge against your dad? Maybe someone he's recently had an argument or some kind of falling-out with?'

Eddie shrugged his shoulders. His father had probably upset hundreds of people over the years, but he could hardly tell the filth that, could he?

'What about them young kids dad was having grief with? You know, the kids he was talking about on Christmas Eve?' Paulie said, remembering the conversation in the pub.

Eddie repeated the story, and then told the copper that he'd had enough. 'Me head's all over the place. I've just found me father with his brains hanging out, for fuck's sake. Any other questions are gonna have to wait.'

Topping up his brandy, Eddie dragged Paulie out into the garden. 'I bet the O'Haras have got something to do with this. Seems funny it's happened just after Butch died.'

Paulie shook his head. 'It's too unprofessional for them. They'd have just shot Dad through the head; they wouldn't have bothered to ransack the place.'

Eddie shrugged. 'I wouldn't put anything past them pikey scumbags. How do you know they ain't just made it look like a burglary to cover it up?'

Paulie handed his brother a cigarette. 'You're barking up the wrong tree, Ed. I mean, Dad told us about them kids he'd had grief with and, if you want my opinion, it looks like the work of young 'uns.'

Eddie disagreed. 'Dad might have been knocking on, but he was still as strong as an ox. He'd have killed a couple of kids with his bare hands. This is the work of men, strong men, you mark my words.'

'Excuse me, Mr Mitchell.'

Eddie dobbed out his fag and walked towards the DS.

'We're going to do some house-to-house enquiries. In such a residential area, we're sure somebody must have seen or heard something.'

Eddie nodded and looked at Paulie. Fuck the police: he would be doing his own house-to-house enquiries. 'Me and you had better start making some phone calls. You ring Ronny, then Uncle Albert and get hold of Reg. I'll ring Raymond and I'll have to try and contact Gary and Ricky, somehow. Don't let anyone tell Auntie Joan, Paulie. The shock'll fucking kill her. I'll wait till she gets back from her friend's and go and tell her in person. Don't let anyone tell Sylvie either. She was courting the old man for years, and it's only right that I tell her meself. It's what Dad would have wanted.'

Paulie nodded. His dad was barely cold and already he felt like a spare part. Eddie gave out the orders and, like a mug, he just obeyed.

Jessica was frantic. She had been constantly trying to call her husband's mobile for the past three hours and was still unable to get hold of him.

'Try not to worry too much, Mum. Dad's battery is always flat – they don't last very long on them mobiles, you know,' Joey said soothingly.

Stanley and Joyce glanced at one another. Christmas was absolutely ruined and they didn't know what to do or say.

'Why don't I warm up some mince pies and pour everyone a drink?' Frankie said helpfully.

Jessica looked at her in amazement. She was surprised her lazy daughter even knew how to use the oven. 'Go on then, love,' she told her. Until they knew what had happened, they had to try and carry on as normal.

The shrill of the phone diminished any hope of normality. 'Eddie, where are you? What's happened? I've been so worried,' Jessica asked frantically.

Her husband's reply knocked her for six. Feeling the colour drain from her face, she clung on to the armchair to stop herself from falling.

'Listen Jess, I've got to go. The police want to speak to me again. I'll call you back as soon as I can,' Eddie told her.

Unable to breathe properly, Jessica felt her legs buckle underneath her. Joyce and Stanley leaped off the sofa and rushed to her aid. 'Go and get your mum some water, Joey,' Stanley shouted.

'What's the matter, Mum? What's happened to Dad?' Frankie asked.

Managing to sit up, Jessica sipped from the glass that her mother was holding.

'Don't just stand there, Stanley! She's in shock, go and get her some brandy,' Joyce bellowed.

Not able to cope with all the dramatics, Joey burst into tears.

Desperate to pull herself together for the sake of her children, Jessica downed the brandy in one. 'It's OK. Dad's OK,' she told the twins.

'What's happened, Mum?' Frankie asked fearfully.

Urging her father to top her glass up, Jessica took a deep breath. 'It's G-g-grandad, he's been m-m-murdered,' she stammered.

Relieved that it wasn't their father, the twins breathed a sigh of relief.

Raymond walked towards Eddie and grabbed him in a bear hug.

'You didn't have to come straight over, Ray. I bet your girlfriend weren't too pleased,' Eddie said to him.

'Her parents didn't look too happy, but Polly was OK. Now, tell me everything from the start. I loved your old man, Ed, I can't fucking believe this has happened.'

With tears in his eyes, Eddie repeated the story. 'He was bludgeoned to fuck, Ray. Paulie thought he'd been done with a hammer, but I'm sure it was a baseball bat. I could see the marks engraved on his face.'

Again, Raymond hugged Eddie. What could he say?

No one would know what to say in a situation like this, there were just no words of comfort.

Pulling away, Raymond looked him in the eye. 'Who do you think's responsible?'

Eddie shook his head. 'I really don't know. It's a novice's job, but my guess would be that Jimmy O'Hara ordered it. I swear, Ray, if I find out it's him, I'll skin the pikey cunt alive. My poor dad. Gutted I am, Ray, fucking heartbroken.'

Raymond nodded. 'If it is O'Hara, I'll help you get revenge, Ed.'

Seeing Ronny hurtling towards him like a paraplegic Speedy Gonzales, Eddie sighed. 'Talk to this cunt for me, Ray. He's pissed out of his brains, been spouting all sorts in front of the filth, he has. I can't be doing with him right now, I really can't.'

Leaving Raymond with his brother, Eddie walked over to his Uncle Reg. 'Is Albert not with you?' he asked him.

Reggie shook his head. Albert was his and Harry's younger brother. Albert was a nice enough geezer, but had never been involved in the family firm and instead had spent his life working as a greengrocer. 'He wanted to come, but I told him to wait at home. You know our Albert, he's about as useful as a one-legged fucking donkey in situations like these.'

Eddie nodded. He was desperate to get home to Jessica. He needed her arms around him and her soothing voice telling him everything was going to be OK. Seeing Ronny was now annoying the life out of the neighbours, Eddie walked back over to Raymond. 'Why don't you, Paulie and Reg come back to mine? There's no point us standing here, is there? We can't do anything, can we?'

Raymond agreed and pointed to a house across the street. 'The old boy opposite, Mr Miller, wants a word with you.'

235

Eddie strolled across the road and knocked on the door. He hadn't seen old Cyril Miller for years and was surprised by how frail he had become. He used to be a hefty lump, but had lost so much weight that he was virtually unrecognisable.

'Sorry to hear about your dad, son, he was a good neighbour. The Old Bill knocked earlier and I told 'em what I saw. There was three lads out here last night, about ten o'clock it were, 'cause I was watching the news. They were kicking up a din, I saw your old man come out, have a go at 'em. He chased 'em and they ran off down the road. I didn't see their faces, but they looked like young 'uns – I'd say about thirteen, at a guess.'

Eddie shook Cyril's hand. 'Get a pen and take down my phone number. If you remember anything else or see 'em round here again, call me, not the police.'

Cyril nodded and went into the hallway to fetch a pen and paper. Thanking him, Eddie walked towards Paulie and told him the plan. 'It's depressing me, standing here – let's go to mine,' he told him.

Paulie nodded. 'Ronny'll have to come as well, though. We can't pack him off on his own if we're all going back to yours.'

Full of reluctance, Eddie agreed.

Jessica took the phone call and hugged the twins. 'Dad's on his way home. Raymond's with him and Uncle Ronny and Paulie are coming back as well.'

Choking on his glass of whisky, Stanley thumped his chest and put the glass on the table. He felt as if he was in *The Godfather* movie and part of him expected to see Marlon Brando walk through the door with his colourful son-in-law.

'What's the matter with you? You need to see a doctor

about that continuous choking of yours,' Joyce told him.

Stanley nodded. This was the worst Christmas he'd ever had and, with Eddie's family on their way, it was about to deteriorate even more.

'Is it OK if me and Joey have another drink, Mum?' Frankie asked. Joey and herself had been drinking with the adults all day.

Jessica nodded. Her children's alcohol consumption was the least of her problems at this particular moment in time.

Hearing the scrunch of gravel outside, Jessica ran to the front door. She wasn't overly pleased that Ronny and Paulie were coming back, but what could she say at such a terrible time?

'Come in, you must be freezing. Make yourselves at home,' she said awkwardly to Eddie's brothers.

Frankie ran to the front door and threw her arms around her father. Eddie kissed her and then locked eyes with his beautiful wife. She was the only one who could console him. 'Go and pour the lads a drink, Frankie. I need to talk to Mum alone for a minute.'

Eddie walked upstairs and nodded towards Jessica to follow him. He took off his coat, sat on the marital bed and put his head in his hands. Everything seemed like a bad dream and he wished it was just that. Jessica crept into the room.

'Oh, Eddie, I'm so sorry about your dad. It's awful – what a terrible thing to happen to him. He was such a nice man.'

Eddie stood up and held her tight. Jessica was his rock and he needed her more now than ever. 'You didn't mind me bringing the boys back, did you?' he whispered.

'Of course not. Don't be so silly,' Jessica replied.

Eddie stroked her long blonde hair and found comfort as he took in the scent of her coconut shampoo. 'I really love you, Jess. Me dad's death won't change anything. We'll still try for that little baby, everything will be OK, I promise you.'

Jessica's eyes welled up. 'The baby can wait Eddie, but I'll tell you something now – if it's a boy, we'll call him Harry as a tribute.'

'Do you mean that?' Eddie asked.

'Yes, I do,' Jessica said adamantly.

Downstairs, Joyce was rather enjoying all the drama. Unfortunately, Stanley wasn't.

'I think we should go to bed soon, dear, give the family some space,' he whispered to his wife.

Joyce had no intention of going anywhere. She was upset over what had happened to Harry Mitchell, but would dine out on the excitement for weeks. Being part of a notorious gangster's family suited Joyce down to the ground. She didn't even bother to read her Mills & Boon books any more. 'So did you say it was a baseball bat or a hammer, Ronny?' she asked again.

Extremely drunk, Ronny spilt his guts. 'It was a baseball bat. The lifestyle we lead, I suppose something like this was always bound to happen,' he bragged.

Desperate to get his grandchildren away from the wheelchair psycho, Stanley ordered them to follow him into the kitchen. This was no conversation for such young ears. 'Take no notice of Uncle Ronny. He's very drunk and talking nonsense,' he told them.

Frankie and Joey were unfazed. They had known what their family was for years. Insisting that they were fine, they got rid of Stanley and went outside for a sneaky smoke.

'I bet it'll be a big funeral,' Frankie said to Joey.

Joey nodded. 'Be every villain for miles there. I wonder if it'll be televised.'

Frankie laughed. Her brother did love the camera. 'It won't be on telly. Grandad weren't Al Capone, you know.'

Joey hugged his sister. 'I dunno about you, Frankie, but I need to get out of this house tomorrow. I wish I could meet a boy I liked. David's started to bore me now.'

Frankie slipped her arm into his. 'Let's get New Year out the way and then I'll take you to a gay club. We look old enough to get in and you'll find a decent bloke there.'

Joey squeezed her hand. 'I'm so glad you know, Frankie. You're the only one I can really talk to.'

Frankie smiled. She often wound Joey up – she always had – but she loved her brother more than anyone. 'Are you upset about Grandad Harry?' she asked him.

Joey shrugged. 'I suppose so. He was our grandad, but we never really saw him, did we? I'd be much more upset if it was Grandad Stanley.'

'Me too. Grandad Harry never seemed like a proper grandad. I don't remember him hugging us or playing games with us, or anything, do you?'

Joey shook his head. 'He was sort of invisible in our lives, so I doubt I'll really miss him.'

'So why did you do your dramatics and burst out crying earlier, then?' Frankie teased.

'I didn't know what was going on. I thought something had happened to Dad and I hated seeing Mum so upset,' Joey told her.

'Joey, Frankie. What you doing? You'll catch pneumonia out there,' Jessica shouted.

'Best we look upset again now for Mum and Dad's sake,' Jessica told her brother.

Joey smiled. 'I can burst out crying again if you want. It's probably a gay thing – you wouldn't understand.'

Giggling at their own wit, the twins raced one another back to the house.

TWENTY-THREE

The TV crews and reporters started to arrive on Boxing Day morning and this infuriated Eddie. His father might have been a notorious villain, but he had always tried to keep Jessica and the kids out of the spotlight. 'If them parasites think they're camping outside my gates, they've got another fucking thing coming,' he yelled.

'Any chance of a lager or something?' Ronny asked bluntly.

Eddie looked at his brother in disgust. Ronny had been that pissed last night, he'd slept in his wheelchair and shit himself. Now, at nine o'clock in the morning, he wanted to start all over again. Throwing Ronny a look that could kill, Eddie dragged Paulie out to the kitchen. 'I'm gonna have to get Ronny out of the house. I had to wipe the cunt's arse this morning while you were asleep. Take him home, do whatever you like with him, as long as he's out of my face. He's a fucking arsehole, spouting his mouth off like there's no tomorrow and it ain't fair on Jess and the kids.'

Paulie nodded. 'I'll take him home now. I dunno how we're gonna get past the press though, they're mob-handed out there.'

Eddie shrugged. 'Just drive your car at the cunts, they'll

soon move out the way. Make sure Ronny keeps his trap shut. Take Reg with you, he can sit in the back with Ronny and keep him under control.'

Stanley got showered and sat watching his wife put her slap on. 'I really think we should go home this morning, dear. Maybe we can take Frankie and Joey back with us for a couple of days. They shouldn't be in this environment, it's not right. I always knew our Jess shouldn't have got involved with Eddie. Something like this was always bound to happen, and say there's repercussions? I'm worried for Jess' and the twins' safety, I really am.'

Zipping up her make-up bag, Joyce turned to her husband. 'It wasn't a gangland-style killing. You do over-react, Stanley. Harry was burgled by the sound of it, by yobs who then murdered him. I don't want to go home. We've got to stay here; our daughter needs us.'

'Well, I need to pop home to check on the pigeons. I know Jock's looking after them, but I need to make sure they're OK.'

'Can't you bloody well ring him?' Joyce asked, annoyed.

'You know the way I feel about me hen and me cock, dear. I need to see Ethel and Ernie with me own eyes. I won't be long, I just need to put me mind at rest.'

Joyce smirked at her husband's turn of phrase. She hadn't seen his actual cock for years, thank God.

Slightly hungover, Joey opened his sister's bedroom door. 'Frankie, wake up. There's loads of cars and people at the bottom of our drive.'

Yawning, Frankie wandered over to the window to see what the fuss was all about. 'I think it's the press. They've got cameras and that, I think.'

242

Joey squealed with delight. 'Quick, get dressed, we'll go out there. You never know, we might get our pictures on the front page of one of the nationals tomorrow.'

Frankie smiled at her brother's excitement. He'd always loved a bit of drama and having his picture taken. 'I'll be ready in half-hour,' she giggled.

Eddie slammed the front door and breathed a huge sigh of relief. His brothers and uncle had just left and he was glad to see the back of them.

'Why don't you let me make you some breakfast, Ed? You need to eat, love,' Jessica told him.

Eddie shook his head. All he kept seeing was his poor old dad with his brains hanging out, and he didn't fancy a morsel. 'I'm gonna try the hotel again, see if I can get hold of the boys.'

He had tried to ring Gary and Ricky the previous evening, but had not been able to track them down. The receptionist had promised to get an urgent message to them, asking them to call home, but so far, Eddie had heard nothing.

Eddie dialled the number. Not in a good mood, he found his patience running out within seconds. 'Ain't you got someone there that can speak fucking English, mate?' he shouted. As Eddie was passed to someone else, he immediately slammed the phone down. 'They ain't been back to the hotel all night, Jess. I dunno how I'm gonna get hold of them. They're the ones I need here, not Paulie and fucking Ronny.'

Jessica put her arms around her husband's waist and laid her head on his muscular shoulder. 'The boys will probably ring later. Everything will be OK, Ed. Please let me make you a sandwich and a coffee. I'm so worried about you.'

243

Eddie held her close to him. 'Go on then, make me a bacon sarnie and I'll eat it just because I love you so much.'

The doorbell made Eddie nearly jump out of his skin. Peeping through the glass to check it wasn't another reporter, he was relieved to see Dougie and Vicki standing there.

'I'm so sorry, mate, I've only just heard,' Dougie told Eddie.

Eddie sent Vicki into the kitchen to see Jessica and ushered Dougie into his office. 'I will find out who murdered me dad and I'll treat them to the most painful death possible. I can't do anything at the moment; the Old Bill are coming round later to take a statement. I'm gonna wait till the boys get back from Tenerife, let it die down a bit and then I'll start me own investigation. I'd put money on it that Jimmy O'Hara was involved in some way, shape or form.'

'When did the police say your dad was murdered?' Dougie asked.

'They ain't said yet, but he was as dead as a dodo when I got there. He was freezing cold he was, looked like he'd been dead for hours. It was awful, Doug, really awful. At least if someone had shot him in the head, the poor cunt wouldn't have suffered. He must have had a terrible death and I swear I'll get revenge for him, if it's the last thing I ever do.'

'Mickey Finley rang me and told me what had happened. He said Harry's house had been burgled and there was no sign it was gangland.'

Eddie shook his head. 'I reckon some cunt's made it look that way on purpose. There'd been some kids hanging around the area outside me old man's house. He told me on Christmas Eve, said they were being a fucking nuisance. I reckon it was a set-up, my life, I do.'

244

Dougie shrugged. 'Jimmy O'Hara's back with his old woman now. Apparently, he had a big bash at his gaff on Christmas Eve that lasted late into the early hours. Patrick Murphy told me. He went round there, by all accounts, so it couldn't have been Jimmy.'

Eddie felt deflated. O'Hara had been his only suspect. 'I'll find out who it was, Doug, don't worry about that. I can't get dad's face out of my mind. Half of his brains were hanging out over the carpet, I was smothered in me own father's blood. Can you imagine how that feels? Dougie, can you?'

Dougie hugged his pal. 'The truth will raise its ugly head. It always does, Ed.'

Frankie and Joey put on their most solemn expressions as they came face to face with their mother. 'How are you, Mum, and how's Dad?' Joey asked sympathetically.

'I'm OK, but your dad's devastated,' Jessica said sadly.

'Can we go out for a while, Mum? It's doing mine and Joey's heads in, all this. We'd like to spend some time with our friends, chill out a bit,' Frankie said.

Jessica didn't know what to say. She didn't want the twins' Christmas to be any worse than it already was, but she was worried about the hordes of press outside. 'I don't know if you can leave the house. Your dad's in his office with Dougie, I'll ask him when he comes out. Go and see Nan and Grandad for a minute – they're sitting in the lounge on their own.'

Vicki smiled as Frankie and Joey wandered off obediently. 'They're such good kids, they really are. Actually, I know this isn't the right time, but I've gotta tell you. I'm pregnant, Jess, I did the test yesterday.'

Thrilled for her friend, Jessica forgot about her own problems and embraced her. 'I am so pleased for you,

245

Vicki, I really am. I'll let you into a little secret as well. Chances are we might be new mums together. Eddie and I have decided to try for another baby.'

Vicki squeezed her friend's hand. 'That's wonderful. We can go shopping for baby clothes together and our kids can be best friends.'

Jessica nodded. 'I'm just so worried about Ed, Vick. Finding his dad murdered like that must have been such a shock for him. I can't imagine how he must feel.'

Vicki nodded sympathetically. 'Was you close to Harry? You never saw him that much, did you?'

Jessica shrugged. 'When me and Ed first got together, I saw him a fair bit. He used to come round sometimes when the kids were young, but once we moved to Essex, the visits sort of dwindled. I wasn't really close to him but, at the end of the day, I loved him because he was Eddie's dad. I preferred him to Eddie's brothers and uncles, I never liked them very much and still don't. I do remember once, though, when Harry was very kind to me. It was at Reg's retirement do. Me and Ed had had a massive row and Harry calmed things down. I returned the favour by inviting him and Sylvie round for dinner. They came the once, but after that I didn't see Harry for yonks.'

Seeing her husband and Dougie walk into the kitchen, Jessica quickly changed the subject. 'The twins want to go out to see their friends, Ed. I think it will do them good to get out of the house, don't you?'

Eddie nodded. He had been so wrapped up in his father's death, he hadn't given Frankie and Joey much thought. 'Me and Dougie are gonna pop out to see a few people, so I'll drop 'em off on the way. You'll be OK here with your Mum, Dad and Vicki, won't you? If the Old Bill turn up, just fuck 'em off till later. If Gary and Ricky ring, tell 'em to get the first flight home.'

246

Jessica was worried. She knew how hot-headed Eddie could be and she didn't want him doing anything stupid. 'Where are you going? You won't be long, will you?'

Eddie shook his head. 'Couple of hours, tops. Gonna go for a couple of pints with Dougie and Pat Murphy.'

Relieved that he was only going to the pub, Jessica called Frankie and Joey. 'Your dad's going out and he's gonna drop you off at your friend's,' she told them.

Frankie and Joey glanced at one another. Friend's my arse – they were going straight to the pub.

Opening the front door, Eddie spotted a geezer in a bush with a camera. Furious, he lost his rag and chased him. 'Get off my land, you cunt. I told you earlier, this is private fucking property. You step one foot in here again and I'll chop your fucking bollocks off.'

'I just want to ask you a few questions, Mr Mitchell. Is it true that –'

Picking the paparazzo up by the throat, Eddie snatched his camera from him and jumped up and down on it. The petrified man fell to the floor and curled himself up in a ball. 'Please don't hurt me – I'm sorry,' he pleaded.

Dougie grabbed hold of Eddie. There were flashbulbs going nineteen to the dozen and his pal wasn't doing himself any favours. 'Get back indoors, kids. Come on, Ed, leave it – he's not worth it,' Dougie urged.

Hearing the commotion outside, Jessica let out a scream. Stanley tried to comfort his daughter. 'Ssh, Jess, it's all finished now, love. Eddie's coming back inside,' he told her.

'Good for Eddie. They want locking up, them press,' Joyce said boldly.

Dougie dragged Eddie into the house and told Jessica to pour him a strong drink. 'He don't need all this shit with them knobs out there,' he said, sticking up for his friend.

247

Stanley put on his jacket. 'I'll drop the kids off at their mate's. I've got to go home to see to me pigeons,' he offered.

Jessica nodded. The further away from all this upset the children were, the better.

'I will come with you, after all. I could do with a bit of fresh air,' Joyce told her husband. She had suddenly realised how wonderful it would be if her photo appeared in a newspaper. Her friends were already in awe of her underworld connections and they would be so, so jealous if they opened their newspaper tomorrow and saw her face smiling back at them.

'Come on, then,' Stanley said angrily. He knew his wife better than she knew herself and he guessed her intentions were not entirely honourable.

Joyce gave a royal wave as the electronic gates opened. On their father's orders, Joey and Frankie hid their faces under a blanket in the back of the car.

'Stop waving at them, you stupid old bat,' Stanley screamed.

'Just shut up and drive,' Joyce replied, still waving.

Relieved that they weren't being followed, Stanley told the twins to uncover themselves. He felt so sorry for his grandchildren. 'Where do you want me to drop you?' he asked sympathetically.

'In the town centre, by the clocktower, Grandad,' Frankie replied.

'What one of your friends lives by the clocktower?' Stanley pried.

'Stacey,' Frankie said, nudging her brother.

Five minutes later, Stanley put his indicator on and stopped the car. 'Now are you sure you're going to be all right? Me and Nanny will watch you go into your friend's house,' said a concerned Stanley.

'We're fine, Grandad. Stacey's mum owns that pub across the road. It's called the Angel.

'Stacey and her family live upstairs,' Joey lied.

Stanley watched the twins walk into the pub. Worried sick, he turned to Joyce. 'Them kids won't grow up to be normal, not in an environment like that, they won't.'

'Jessica and Eddie are wonderful parents. Them kids have never wanted for a thing in their lives,' Joyce said angrily.

Stanley scowled at his superficial wife. 'A bit of normality wouldn't go amiss for them. Everything's about money with you, isn't it, Joycie? What do you know about parenting anyway? You was the one that encouraged your own daughter to take up with a villian in the first place.'

Joyce was shocked by the change in Stanley's attitude. 'Turn the car around and drop me back at Jessica's, immediately. How dare you talk to me like that, Stanley? How dare you?'

Furious, Stanley swung the car around. 'I'm trying to make you see sense. Something bad will happen to our Jess or them kids. I can feel it in me bones, Joycie, on my life I can. One day you'll be sorry you never listened to me.'

TWENTY-FOUR

1988

Eddie knotted his black tie and glanced at himself in the mirror. Greasing his hair back with Brylcreem, he put on a pair of dark sunglasses to enhance his image. Today was his father's funeral, God rest his soul. The police had kept hold of Harry's body for six weeks and they would have kept it longer, had Eddie not intervened. He'd threatened to blow the whistle on a couple of his dad's old acquaintances just to get things moving.

'You want us to catch your father's killer, don't you?' the bent DS asked Eddie sarcastically. The bent DS was nothing to do with Harry's case and wasn't keen to intervene.

Unable to function properly while his father was lying on a cold slab in the mortuary, Eddie gave it to him. 'If you don't get my dad's body released by next week, I will personally ensure that the shit hits the fan. I know every dodgy deal my father did with you and your pals and I'm sure it would make interesting reading for the Chief of Police. The mugs leading the hunt are no nearer to finding his killers now than they were the day he died. Useless cunts, the lot of them. Just release me dad's body so he can get the send-off he deserves and then I'll find the killer me fucking self.'

The threat worked wonders and the following day Eddie received a phone call allowing him to organise the funeral. The six weeks since Harry had been murdered had been the hardest in Eddie's life. Many a night he'd woken up in a cold sweat as a nightmare had brought it all back to him. The images of his father's battered face and body seemed to torture him every time he closed his eyes.

Ed had finally got hold of Gary and Ricky the day after Boxing Day. They had flown home within twenty-four hours and, along with Raymond, had been a great support to him ever since.

With the Old Bill about as much use as a chocolate fucking teapot, Eddie had started his own line of investigation. He, Ray and the boys had spoken to every underworld connection they knew, but nobody had heard so much as a whisper.

Frustrated, Eddie had turned his attention towards his dad's neighbours. The young lads that had been harassing his father had been spotted by all of them and Eddie managed to get a description. The problem was, seeing as they'd always worn their hoods up, the description was rather vague.

The one thing that did prick Eddie's ears was something that Iris next door had said. Annoyed with the boys making a racket outside, she had confronted them and chased them with her rolling pin. 'They were laughing at me, Eddie, taking the right piss, they were. The one that spoke to me – called me a silly old cow and told me to fuck off – wasn't a Cockney. He had an accent, a strange accent. I couldn't say where it was from, but his voice had a country lilt to it.

From day one, Eddie was positive that the O'Haras were behind his dad's untimely death and Iris's bit of info only confirmed his belief. Jimmy O'Hara and his motley crew all originated from the Cambridgeshire area and their accents were just how Iris had described. With no actual proof, all Eddie could do was sit back and bide his time. He was positive that the young boys had been sent to his father's as a ploy. He was also sure that somebody much bigger and stronger had committed the actual murder.

The police had told Eddie the reason why none of the neighbours had heard his father's screams. The coroner said Harry had been gagged at the time of his death, which had occurred between midnight and 2 a.m. on the morning of Christmas Day. His official report stated that Harry had eleven serious injuries, among which were a broken jaw, bones and a fractured skull. A baseball bat had been used on Harry's head and the rest of his body had been kicked around like a football. With so many injuries, the actual cause of death wasn't properly identified. The coroner had said he was 90% certain that Harry had died of head injuries, but couldn't be absolutely positive. The only thing everybody could be sure about was that Harry Mitchell had died in one of the worst ways imaginable.

Picturing Jimmy O'Hara and his cronies gloating, Eddie smashed his fist against the bedroom wall. O'Hara had held a party round his on Christmas Eve to give himself an alibi, Eddie was certain of that. He obviously hadn't committed the murder himself, but he must have organised it.

Seeing Jessica walk into the room, Ed tried to pull himself together. 'Are you OK, love? What have you done to your hand?' she asked, noticing his knuckles were bleeding.

'I caught it in the drawer,' Eddie lied.

Jessica stood on tiptoes and put her slender arms around his shoulders. 'Me and the kids are ready. Shall we make a move now?'

Eddie nodded. He just wanted the day to be over.

Joyce stood in Harry Mitchell's front garden. The flowers and tributes that kept arriving completely took her breath away. A keen gardener, she had never seen so many flowers. Hundreds and hundreds there were, and she had just seen another enormous arrangement arrive that spelled out the word LEGEND. Aware of a photographer standing over the road, Joyce patted her hair into place. Ever since she had got her picture on page seven of the *Sun* newspaper, she had felt like a local celebrity. People were still stopping her in the street now and the article had appeared six weeks beforehand.

As more and more people arrived to pay their respects, Stanley became increasingly uncomfortable. Most of them were obviously well-known villains and he felt like a spare prick at a wedding. Noticing Roy Shaw, the notorious prize-fighting champion, looking his way, Stanley quickly averted his eyes. He didn't feel at ease around these people and he couldn't wait to get home to his pigeons.

As the horse-drawn hearse arrived carrying Harry's body, all the neighbours came out of their houses. The street was heaving with mourners and it was more like a carnival than a funeral.

Eddie got into the first car. He was joined by Paulie, Ronny, Reg, Albert, Auntie Joan, Auntie Vi and his dad's distraught long-term lady-friend, Sylvie. Gary and Ricky got into the second car with Jessica, the twins, Raymond, Joyce and Stanley. The other cars were filled with more distant relations.

253

The funeral was to take place at East London Cemetery in nearby Plaistow. Harry had purchased his own plot years before, insisting he wanted to be laid to rest next to his beautiful wife.

Frankie nudged Joey as the procession made its way through the crowded streets. Hundreds of people had made the effort. Some were waving banners and flags, but most were bowing their heads as a mark of respect. Jessica pointed a flag out to the twins. 'Look at that. "Harry Mitchell, simply the best", it says. Your grandad was very popular, wasn't he?'

'Shame we never saw him,' Joey whispered to Frankie.

Stanley felt his face redden as the TV crews pointed a camera in his direction. He could just imagine all his old pals down the bus depot watching the news tonight and seeing him on there. Thank God I took early retirement, Stanley thought. He was embarrassed to be a part of such a family.

'Will you stop fucking waving,' Stanley shouted at Joyce, who was milking it. Her outfit looked awful. She had a massive black-netted hat on her head and Stanley thought she looked like a fucking witch. The only thing she was lacking was a broomstick.

Due to the horrific circumstances surrounding Harry's death, the service itself was a very solemn affair. The vicar who presided over the proceedings was an old pal of the Mitchells. He had married Harry and his wife many moons ago.

Eddie stood up to say a few words, but was too choked up to go through with it. Seeing Ronny race towards him in his wheelchair, Eddie handed him the piece of paper.

'My Dad was the best and, I swear on God's life, we'll get revenge for you, Dad. Whoever did this to you, we'll do a hundred times worse to them,' Ronny slurred, ignoring what was written down in front of him.

Eddie cringed. Trust Ronny to be pissed and say something like that in the house of God. Frantically waving his hands, Eddie urged the organist to play the song that he had chosen. Harry's all-time favourite was the old war time classic, 'Heart of My Heart'.

'When I pop me clogs, I want that played at me funeral. It was me and your mother's favourite song, Eddie,' his dad had told him.

Lots of tears flowed as everybody joined in with the words.

> When we were kids on the corner of the street,
> We were rough and ready guys,
> But oh, how we could harmonise!

Feeling his eyes well up, Eddie did his best to hold back the tears. Every villain in London was here and he was desperate not to make a tit of himself in front of the world's finest. Pulling himself together, Eddie joined in with the singing:

> I know a tear would glisten,
> If once more I could listen,
> To the gang that sang
> 'Heart of My Heart'.

As the chapel began to empty, Jessica squeezed Eddie's hand. 'It was a lovely send-off. Your dad would have been proud,' she told him.

Eddie stood by the graveside, amazed by the number of people in attendance. There had been hundreds unable to fit inside the chapel and they had listened outside to the service on a loudspeaker. Eddie stood between Sylvie and Auntie Joan. Both women were beside themselves and he had to nigh-on physically support them.

As his father's body was finally laid to rest, Eddie breathed a sigh of relief. 'God bless, Dad,' he whispered, as he threw earth on top of the coffin.

Desperate to be seen as an important member of the family, Joyce grabbed Eddie's arm. 'Come and look at the beautiful flowers,' she insisted.

Eddie let her drag him away and listened as she rattled on about who had sent what. 'Look at that beauty that says BIG H; Freddie Foreman sent that. I love the LEGEND one, don't you? That's from the Krays. Look at that boxing glove, Ed, it's massive, ain't it?'

'Who sent that?' Eddie asked, completely disinterested.

'Er, I can't remember. Here we go: the card says Jimmy O'Hara and family.'

Eddie felt the blood in his veins run cold, 'Give us that fucking card,' he yelled.

Wondering what she had done so wrong, Joyce nervously handed it to him. Eddie stared at it. 'To Eddie and family. Our thoughts are with you at this sad time. Jimmy O'Hara and family.'

Eddie was livid. He left Joyce standing with her mouth open and stomped over to his brothers. 'The cheeky pikey cunt, he's taking the fucking piss out of us,' he yelled.

Raymond ran over and tried to calm him down. 'Don't say nothing here, Ed. If Jimmy's done it to wind you up, you don't want him to think he's succeeded. There's too many eyes and ears around. Just forget about it for now and we'll discuss it tomorrow.'

Eddie brushed Raymond's arm away. 'Let's get away from here. Tell the undertakers we're ready. I need a fucking drink.'

As Jessica ran over to see what their father was upset about, the twins nudged one another. 'I think our family is really weird, don't you?' Joey whispered.

Frankie burst out laughing. 'I wouldn't say they're weird, but they're definitely not normal.'

Joey smiled as he saw Auntie Joan, Auntie Vi and another lady heading their way.

'Look at yous two. Ain't you all grown up, and such handsome kids. Look Sylvie, these are Harry's grandchildren. This is Frankie, who's a ringer for her father, and doesn't Joey look like his mother?' Vi said.

Sylvie shook hands with the twins. 'We have met before, but it was years ago and I'd never have recognised you now.'

Frankie and Joey both kissed her politely.

'Kids, come on, we're going!' Eddie yelled.

'Goodbye Sylvie, bye Auntie Joan, bye Auntie Vi. Are you all coming back to the pub?' Joey asked.

'No, lovey. It's been a long day. Me, Vi and Sylvie are gonna toast your grandad indoors. We're going back to mine for a drink,' Joan told him.

Joey linked arms with his sister and led her back to where the cars were parked.

'Dad didn't look too happy, did he?'

Frankie giggled. 'I shouldn't fucking think so. He has just buried his father who happened to be brutally murdered in his own bed.'

'I didn't mean that – you know what I meant,' Joey said, annoyed.

Frankie laughed. 'Come on, I'll race you. Last one back buys the fags later.'

Eddie had no other option than to book the Flag for the wake. His father had spent so many hours of his life in there, he would have come back and haunted Eddie if it had been held anywhere else. Obviously there was a free bar, but the size of the pub was a problem. With so many mourners, there weren't enough staff behind the bar or enough room for people to stand comfortably. Eddie made a quick phone call and organised another free bar in the Ordnance Arms, which was also an old haunt of his dad's. People could make their own mind up where they wanted to go. If they weren't happy being squashed like sardines in a tin, they could have a drink in Harry's memory down the road.

Jessica stood in the corner of the pub with Vicki. Dougie was up at the bar with the men. Neither Vicki nor Jessica were annoyed that their husbands had deserted them. On this type of occasion the men always clubbed together and the women were left to their own devices.

'Where are the twins? Can you see them? I have to keep my eye on them, as they do like a drink, you know,' Jessica said to her friend.

Vicki craned her neck. 'I can't see them, but I'm sure they're fine. How old are they now? Nearly sixteen, aren't they? I was drinking in pubs at their age, weren't you? I wouldn't worry about them too much.'

Jessica nodded. The twins were a bit too streetwise for her liking and she couldn't help but worry about them.

Eddie stood up at the bar with all the old school.

'Can I have a quick word with you, Eddie?' Patrick Murphy asked him.

Eddie followed the big Irishman outside the pub and they found a quiet spot. 'Please don't think I'm sticking my nose in your business, Eddie, but I'm telling you now, your father's murder had nothing to do with the O'Haras. I was round at Jimmy's on Christmas Eve. His sons were there, his brothers, his cousins. I didn't leave there till three in the morning. I know this must be awful for you, Ed, but you've gotta look somewhere else for your answers. You know as well as I do that when Alice left Jimmy, he lost his swagger. I know you've had a feud with him in the past, but he's a changed man now. He don't want any grief, especially now Alice has agreed to give him another chance.'

Eddie put his thinking cap on. Maybe the stress of what had happened to his father had caused him to bark up the wrong tree. If the whole of the O'Hara clan were at Jimmy's, then maybe, just maybe, it wasn't them. Rubbing his tired eyes, Eddie looked at Patrick for answers. 'Apart from the O'Haras, I can't think who else had a massive grudge against my dad. I mean, if someone would have blasted his brains out, I could have dealt with it, understood it. But battering the life out of him – who would do a thing like that? It ain't exactly our style, is it?'

Patrick handed Eddie a cigar. 'No, it's not the work of people like us, Eddie. This is what I'm trying to tell you. I know Jimmy's a traveller, but he's a family man and, like us, he has rules. I know your old man shot his, but if he wanted revenge, he would have returned it the same way. Can you honestly see him ransacking your dad's house and torturing him? Jimmy ain't a bad geezer deep down and that ain't his style. He has standards, for fuck's sake.'

Eddie accepted a light and urged Patrick to go back inside. 'Shout me up a large Scotch. I just need five minutes to meself,' he told him.

Patrick nodded. 'Promise me you'll think about what I've said, Eddie. I'm friendly with both you and Jimmy and I'd hate to see your feud reignited for no reason. You've got to think of your wife, Eddie, your children. Do you really want to put them in danger?' If you start

259

a war, how do you know your family won't be caught up in the crossfire? You've got to let sleeping dogs lie on this one, Ed. Jimmy O'Hara never killed your father.'

Eddie watched the big man walk away. Patrick Murphy was no man's fool and deep down, Eddie knew that what he was saying made sense. Waiting for the police to release his dad's body had made his brain go all wonky. It couldn't have been Jimmy O'Hara, it wasn't his style and he had a cast-iron alibi.

As Jessica walked towards him, Eddie smiled at her.

'Are you OK? I was worried about you. Why are you out here on your own?'

Eddie held his arms out and hugged his wife tightly. Jessica was his life and he'd never do anything to endanger the welfare of her and the kids, not in a million years.

TWENTY-FIVE

In the weeks that followed Harry's funeral, Eddie got himself back into his usual routine.

As he and the police had drawn a blank on the identity of his father's killer, Eddie had little option other than to throw himself into his work. Since Christmas, he had let things slip, but he was determined not to fuck up the Mitchell reputation his dad had fought so hard to create in the first place.

The nightmares of what had happened still haunted Eddie. Many a night, he would get up about 3 or 4 a.m. and sit downstairs drinking endless cups of tea. Jessica had been a real star. She was very supportive and, if he was having a black day, she was gentle and understanding.

'For fuck's sake, Dad. Three times I've asked you the same question and you still ain't answered me.'

'Sorry, Rick, I was miles away, son. What were you saying?'

Ricky stood up. 'Forget it. It's my round. Same again?'

Eddie nodded. It was his forty-seventh birthday today. Jessica was at home preparing for a dinner party for him. It would be the first time they'd entertained at home since his dad's untimely death.

Gary and Ricky had declined the invitation of a quiet

night in. 'We're going to a rave up town, Dad, but we'll take you out for a beer in the day,' they'd told him.

Eddie hadn't minded. They were only in their early twenties and he had been exactly the same himself at their age.

Ricky handed his brother and father their drinks.

'What exactly is all this rave shit you keep on about?' he asked his sons.

Gary laughed. 'If you ain't heard of raves, Dad, then you must be getting old.'

'They're a new thing out. Word has it, they're gonna sweep the country this summer. The music's blinding, Dad. They play house music. Everyone gets out of their nuts and they go on all night long,' Ricky added.

'You two ain't fucking taking drugs, are you?' Eddie asked.

Gary shook his head. 'We just get pissed and pull all the birds, Dad,' he lied.

Neither Gary nor Ricky were really into drugs, but ecstasy tablets were a new thing out, and they liked to drop an occasional one. They liked the ones called American burgers. They were proper happy pills and you could dance all night on them. These raves went on for hours and without something in your system to keep you going, you'd be as out of place as a pig in a synagogue.

'So, who's coming round yours tonight?' Ricky asked his father.

'Raymondo's bringing Polly, his bit of posh, round. We ain't met her yet. He was bringing her round Boxing Day but, obviously, when Grandad was found dead, he didn't. Vicki and Dougie are coming and I've also invited Patrick Murphy and his old woman.'

'Well, I hope you have a good night, Dad. How are the twins? Will they be there?' Gary asked.

Eddie smiled. 'They're OK. They didn't wanna sit in with their old dad, either, so they're pissing off out. Jess worries when they go to these parties and stuff, but they're nearly sixteen and all their friends are allowed to go and come home late. I always give 'em cab money to get themselves home, mind. I've told them the day I find out they've been pocketing the money and walking home is the day I put me foot down.'

As their dad went to the toilet, Ricky turned to Gary. 'Shall we give him the present now?'

Gary took the black velvet box out of his pocket. The lads had clubbed together and brought their father a new watch. It was a Rolex and had cost them a fucking fortune.

'Happy birthday, Dad. That's from the two of us,' Gary said, as Eddie returned to the table.

Eddie was choked as he opened the box. 'Fucking hell! It's beautiful, but you shouldn't have spent that kind of dough. A shirt would have done me. I'd rather see yous spend your money on yourselves.'

'You've always been a great dad to us and this is the first year we've been in a position to buy you something decent,' Gary insisted.

Eddie took his old watch off and put the new one on. 'I love it,' he said truthfully.

Ricky glanced at his brother. 'We're gonna have to go in a minute, Gal. We promised Mum we'd be there by three.'

'How is your mother?' Eddie asked.

Gary sighed. 'She ain't been well, Dad. The doctor's told her she'll be dead in two years if she don't knock the drink on the head. She's so thin now and her skin looks kind of yellow.'

Eddie shook his head sadly. 'I know me and your mother were never Romeo and Juliet, but I'm sorry to

263

hear that. Go on, yous get going, and tell your mum, if she needs money or anything, she knows where I am.'

Gary and Ricky said their goodbyes and left. Eddie ordered himself another drink and sat at the table alone. He'd met his sons in a pub in Aveley where no one knew him. It was nice to have a quiet bevvy and be anonymous for once. Glancing at his new watch, Eddie smiled. Gary and Ricky had always been thoughtful and generous. From the age of five upwards, they'd made or bought him nice presents. Frankie and Joey were the opposite. The twins had been given far too much from an early age and they'd grown up in their own little world. They rarely remembered his or Jessica's birthdays and, even though they received plenty of pocket money, they never bothered spending it on anyone other than themselves.

Deep in thought, Eddie didn't notice the man walk towards him.

'Eddie, how are you, mush? I was sorry to hear about your father. Our families might never have been muckers, but your old man didn't deserve to die like that. This is Alice, my wife. Can I get you a drink?'

Looking at Jimmy O'Hara's outstretched hand, Eddie didn't know whether to break it or shake it. Not wanting to make a scene, he did neither. 'I can't stop. My Jess is expecting me back. We're having people round for dinner later,' he said abruptly.

As Eddie stood up, Jimmy nodded to Alice to make herself scarce. 'Go and get the drinks,' he ordered.

Alone with Eddie, Jimmy faced up to him. 'I know you probably think your old boy's death was something to do with me, but it weren't. Life's too short to hold grudges and if I was gonna retaliate for your father shooting mine, I'd have done it in an honourable way. At one point, I was desperate to get my revenge, but

I'm not fiery like I used to be, Eddie. Losing my Alice gave me the kick in the bollocks I needed. My family come first now and I don't want no feud with anyone. I would never jeopardise losing Alice and my kids again, ever.'

Eddie stared into Jimmy's eyes. He was quite an expert on reading people by their behaviour and expressions and he came to the conclusion that O'Hara was either telling the truth or was a fucking top-drawer liar. More confused than ever about his father's death, Eddie said his good-byes and left the pub.

Later that evening, Jessica smiled as Eddie launched into yet another one of his anecdotes. She'd been worried that tonight might be too much for him but, thankfully, she had been wrong. Eddie was on top form and she was relieved he was back to his old self.

'There's plenty more to eat in the kitchen. Is anyone still hungry?' she asked.

With everyone telling her they were full to the brim, Jessica started to clear the table. She had chosen an Italian menu for the dinner party and the food had gone down a treat.

Eddie poured his friends another drink. He was a bit unsure about Polly, Raymond's bird. The girl was pleasant enough, but spoke with a plum in her chops.

'No more for me, thanks, Eddie. Three is my limit,' Polly told him firmly.

With everybody sorted, Eddie took a glass of wine out to Jessica in the kitchen. 'She's a funny one, Raymondo's bird, ain't she?'

Jessica smiled. 'I wouldn't put her with our Raymond in a million years, but as long as she makes him happy, that's all that matters.'

'Do you reckon he's fucking her? I can't imagine her in the sack, can you? Oh, Raymond, please hurry up and shoot your load, the butler will be here soon,' Eddie said, mimicking Polly's posh tones.

'Sssh, they might hear you,' Jessica scolded him.

Eddie could be such a piss-taker at times and she didn't want him upsetting the wonderful evening they were having. Eddie tilted her chin and kissed her. 'I think we should up our baby-making sessions from this week onwards – what do you say?'

Jessica sighed. Tonight, she was more worried about the two she'd given birth to than about creating another. 'I don't like Frankie and Joey being allowed to stay out round their friends' houses. It worries me sick. I mean, we don't even really know the parents.'

Frankie and Joey had gone to a sixteenth birthday party. The party was miles away, in Fulham, and Jessica had been dead against them going from the start.

'But Mum, Dionne, was my best friend throughout most of my school years. It's not her fault that her parents have moved to Fulham. I'm not going on my own, am I? I've got Joey to take care of me. Her mum said we can stay in the guest room and she's going to call you to confirm,' Frankie whinged.

Jessica discussed it with Eddie and, in the end, they had decided to let the twins go. She hadn't been able to get hold of Dionne's mum, but had spoken to her older sister, who had confirmed the arrangements.

'Shall I give them a call? Make sure they got there all right,' Jessica asked Eddie.

She had insisted that they take their father's mobile phone so she could contact them to put her mind at rest.

Eddie shook his head. 'They're nearly sixteen, Jess. We

266

need to learn to trust them, not check up on them all the time. They're good kids: they'll be fine, trust me.'

Joey and Frankie stood near the bar. The gay club was an eye-opener for both of them and they were overwhelmed by the atmosphere. The Dionne story had been a cover-up and their friend, Paige, had done a wonderful job pretending to be Dionne's sister.

'He's nice. Look, the tall one with the blond hair who's looking over.'

Joey shook his head. 'Nah, he ain't my type.'

Frankie smiled. She had promised Joey months ago that she would come to a gay club with him and this was their first visit. She could sense her brother's excitement; he was like a kid in a sweet shop, bless him.

'Talk to me Joey, quick. I've got some meaty lesbian making eyes at me.'

Joey slung his arm around Frankie's shoulder and ordered another drink. 'Maybe you're really into a bit of pussy. I mean, you don't seem to get very far with boys, do you, Frankie?' he said, winding her up.

Frankie glared at him. 'Fuck you, I'm not into women. I'm just fussy. I mean, look at the boys around our way, the ones that have asked me out. Would you fancy them?'

Joey shook his head. He had finished with David a while back and, apart from him, there'd been no one else local to catch his eye. In a way, he could understand Frankie's dilemma. 'What type of bloke do you actually want?' he asked his sister.

Frankie shrugged. 'We've been brought up with a certain lifestyle, Joey, so I'm hardly liable to date some mug. I want a bloke that's gonna make me laugh, treat me like a princess, like Dad always has. To be honest,

I suppose I'm looking for someone who is a bit like Dad. You've always been closer to Mum, but I ain't.'

Joey laughed. 'So you're looking for a scar-faced, top-class villain. That should be easy – why don't I just place an ad in the local paper for you?'

As usual, Frankie appreciated her brother's wit. The pair of them had realised at an early age what sort of family they were part of, and often had a joke about it.

'Joey, you've pulled again and this one is nice. He's that gorgeous, if it turns out he ain't a woofta, then I'll have him. Look, standing over there, to your left.'

Looking around, Joey spotted the bloke who was staring his way. The guy was older than him, probably well into his twenties. 'Wow,' Joey mumbled, as he felt his stomach lurch.

Mr Gorgeous was well over six feet. He was wearing light stonewashed jeans and a tight-fitting white T-shirt. He had a perfect body, face and physique and was an absolute out-and-out sort. Aware of Mr Gorgeous smiling at him, Joey turned away. He felt like a fox startled by headlights. 'He's a lot older than me. I dunno,' he said dubiously.

Frankie burst out laughing. 'He's fucking amazing, what is wrong with you? Please don't tell me you've dragged me all the way here and now you're shit-scared to go for it.'

Glancing back at the mystery bloke, Joey quickly looked away. 'Go and get us another drink – and get me a double,' he ordered his sister.

Waving her money at the barman, Frankie couldn't stop smiling. Her brother was such a funny bastard at times.

'All right? My name's Lisa. First time here, is it?' asked a hefty woman with a skinhead.

Frankie nodded. 'I'm here because of my brother. He's gay, not me.'

The woman smiled. The newcomers all said that. In denial, the lot of them. 'Let me buy the drinks,' the skin-head bird said.

Frankie refused. 'Thanks, but no thanks,' she said curtly.

The woman smiled at her. 'It's not unusual to be curious. You're only young and sometimes it takes a while to come to terms with what you was born to be.'

Frankie snatched the drinks off the barman. 'I am not a fucking dyke, so will you sod off and pester someone else,' she said angrily.

Realising that his sister wasn't happy about something, Joey went to her rescue. 'Is everything OK? What's the matter?'

The shaven-haired woman scowled at him. 'Your sister's got issues, love,' she said, walking away.

As Frankie repeated the conversation, Joey couldn't stop laughing. 'Don't laugh – it ain't fucking funny. She thought I was a lesbo,' Frankie said, fuming.

Too busy winding Frankie up, Joey didn't notice Mr Gorgeous walking his way.

'Hi, my name's Dominic. Can I buy you a drink?'

Her brother's startled expression amused Frankie immensely. 'His name's Joey and, yes, he'll have a large vodka and orange. I'm Frankie, his twin sister, by the way.'

Dominic shook Frankie's hand and smiled. 'And what would you like?' he asked.

'I'd just like my brother to meet someone as handsome as you and get himself laid,' Frankie replied, grinning at Joey.

Joey was horrified. Frankie could be such a cow at times. 'Take no notice. My sister can't help having a mouth like a sewer,' he said awkwardly.

Dominic squeezed Joey's arm. 'Your sister can shout up the drinks. Come and dance with me,' he said.

Joey was petrified as he followed Dominic onto the dancefloor. His silly liaison with David was nothing compared to the way this guy made him feel. Dominic was a man, not some confused schoolboy.

Chatting to a transvestite at the bar, Frankie watched her brother with interest. He and Dominic had been dancing for over ten minutes now and were getting on like a house on fire.

As the DJ changed the tempo, Dominic took Joey in his arms. 'Are you OK?' he asked gently.

Joey nodded. Truthfully, he felt anything but OK. His heart was beating like a drum, his palms were sweaty and he was talking rubbish. 'I think I'm a little bit nervous. I've never done anything like this before,' he admitted.

Dominic smiled at him. This boy was so different from any of the others he had ever met. He was innocent and gorgeous. Aware that Dominic had an erection, Joey didn't know whether to laugh or cry.

Conscious of Joey's predicament, Dominic brushed his lips against his. He smiled and spoke softly. 'Relax Joey. I'll be gentle with you, I promise.'

TWENTY-SIX

Joey and Dominic's relationship developed quickly and, within a few weeks of meeting, both of them were head over heels in love. The situation was awkward. Dominic lived near the Angel in Islington. He had a demanding job working as a money broker in the city. Joey was studying for his GCSEs and finding time to see one another regularly was virtually impossible.

On a healthy wage, Dominic had his own property, a two-bedroom flat. He kept begging Joey to stay over, but Joey had only been able to do so twice.

Dominic had a very manly voice, so Joey had given him his home telephone number and had told his parents that he and Frankie had met a new mate. Desperate not to arouse suspicion, he told Dominic to ask for either him or his sister if his dad or mum answered the phone.

'Oi, oi! So how was last night, then, lover boy?'

Joey smiled as his sister entered his room and sat on the edge of his bed. He had spent the previous night at Dominic's and told his parents he was staying at David's to revise for his exams. 'It was wonderful,' Joey said, beaming.

'Well, give us the gory details, then.'

Joey ordered Frankie to shut the bedroom door. He had stayed around Dominic's once before, but his nerves had got the better of him. Last night, he had actually done it and had enjoyed every second. 'It was fantastic, Frankie. Dom's got a body to die for and his willy is absolutely enormous.'

Inquisitive by nature, Frankie was desperate for more detail. 'So, what exactly happened then? I mean it ain't like a girl and a boy, is it?'

Joey felt his cheeks redden. 'What are you like, you nosy cow? I'm not discussing the ins and outs – it's private.'

Frankie laughed at Joey's embarrassment. 'Go on, tell me more. Did you go all the way this time?'

'Yes, and that's all I'm telling you, so don't bother asking me no more questions.'

Joey being gay didn't bother Frankie one iota. She enjoyed winding him up, but was also genuinely pleased that he had met someone he liked. She had always got on better with boys than girls and would have hated Joey to have gone out with some bimbo she hated. That would have made her extremely jealous.

'So, did you come?' Frankie asked, desperate to know more. They had always had such a close, open relationship. Joey told her everything and vice versa.

'Yes, of course. Now, can we shut up about it now, 'cause Mum's calling us.'

Jessica smiled as the twins bounded down the stairs. 'What are you laughing at?' she asked Frankie.

'Nothing important. Joey was just telling me about the biology homework he was doing last night.'

Jessica tutted. 'You wasn't being rude, Joey, was you?'

'Of course not, Mum,' Joey replied, kicking his smirking sister under the table.

'I wanted to talk to yous about your birthday. You're

272

sixteen soon and Dad and I asked you ages ago what you wanted to do. Have either of you decided yet?'

Joey nudged Frankie. Their parents had wanted to throw a big party at home and invite all of their friends. The twins were totally against the idea. There was no way Joey could chance inviting Dominic, and Frankie reckoned it would be as boring as hell. There was a new place where everyone was going called the Berwick Manor. It had started a rave night on a Friday and the twins were desperate to go there.

Frankie smiled at her mum. 'We have thought about it and we've decided we want to go out with our friends on the Friday, which is our actual birthday, then maybe have a smaller party here with you, Dad, Nan, Grandad and the rest of the family on the Saturday.'

Jessica found it hard to hide her disappointment. 'Why don't you want the big party for all of your friends? Dad could have done a barbecue and all your mates could have brought their costumes and had a swim.'

Frankie decided to be truthful. 'Our friends like drinking, not swimming, Mum. They'll laugh at us if they come here and only get offered soft drinks. We can still have a barbecue – we can do that on the Saturday with the family.'

Defeated, Jessica shrugged. She didn't mind the twins having the odd drink or two, but she wasn't about to let their friends do the same. Say one of them got drunk and was ill, how would she explain that to their parents? It would make her and Eddie look awful and tarnish their responsible reputation. 'OK, I'll let your dad know,' Jessica said miserably. The twins were at an age now where they wanted to do their own thing.

'Where is Dad?' Frankie asked. He never worked weekends and was usually glued to her mother's side.

273

'He's popped out to see a mechanic. There's a problem with the Land Cruiser and he wants to get it repaired. I should imagine he'll be home soon – he's already been gone ages,' Jessica said.

Aware that his mum was upset about the birthday party, Joey stood up and hugged her. 'Frankie and I aren't doing anything today. How about when Dad gets back, we all go out for something to eat? Frankie and I will treat you and Dad for once. Because we've been so busy doing homework, we've saved loads of pocket money.'

Jessica smiled. 'That would be lovely, Joey.'

Eddie Mitchell sat in the car park of the Robin Hood pub in Dagenham. He was looking for a geezer called Tommy Trott. Trottsy, as he was better known, was out of Canning Town and had borrowed five grand from Eddie six months ago. He had paid back the first three instalments, then had disappeared off the face of the earth.

Eddie had received a phone call only yesterday, telling him that the cheeky bastard had resurfaced in Dagenham and was larging it in the Robin Hood. Usually Eddie dealt with the mugs who tried to knock him alone, but Trottsy had annoyed him more than most, so he'd brought Raymond with him. Eddie had known Trottsy for years and had helped him out on many occasions in his younger days. That's why Trottsy's deception was that much worse.

Raymond looked at his watch. 'What time did this geezer say Trottsy normally gets here?'

Eddie tapped his fingers on the steering wheel in annoyance. Twelve o'clock was the information he had received and it was now quarter to one. 'He'd better hurry up. I told Jess I wouldn't be long, she thinks I'm getting the car fixed. Twelve, I was told. We'll give it another half-hour and if there's still no sign of him, we'll have another bash tomorrow.'

'I can't make tomorrow, Ed. Polly's dad has a boat and we're all going sailing,' Raymond said awkwardly.

Eddie nodded. He was a good boss and didn't expect any of the lads to work at weekends, unless it was unavoidable, of course. 'Don't worry, Gary and Ricky will have to get their lazy arses out of bed or, worst ways, I'll bring Paulie with me. So, how's things going with Polly? It sounds serious.'

Raymond smiled. He was a deep person at times and didn't like to give much away, especially when it came to relationships and stuff. His mum was brain damage and Eddie was a piss-taker, so he always kept his cards close to his chest. 'It's going all right. She's a nice girl,' was all he said.

About to pry some more, Eddie was stopped by the appearance of Trottsy walking towards them. 'Here he is, the low-life cunt, just crossing the road. Go and grab him, Ray, put your arm around his shoulder and lead him over here. There's tons of traffic about, so be careful. Any probs, show him the gun under your jacket.'

Raymond had never met Tommy Trott before. 'Is that him? The geezer in the denim jacket?' he asked.

'Yeah, go on, quick as you like,' Eddie replied.

Whistling as he walked, Tommy Trott crossed the busy road and stopped to spark up a Rothmans. He didn't see Raymond approach him – he was too busy trying to shield his lighter from the gusty wind.

'Who are you? What the fuck do you want?' he yelled, as Raymond grabbed hold of him.

'Shut the fuck up and walk with me. A mate of mine wants a little word with you,' Raymond said calmly.

'I ain't going nowhere. I'm –'

The gun being thrust into his ribs stopped Tommy in mid sentence. Immediately, he realised that Eddie Mitchell must be involved.

'I'm gonna pay Eddie back, I've just been a bit short. I lost me job, I was paying him up until then,' Tommy whinged.

'Shut up and tell him yourself,' Raymond said coldly.

As Raymond and Tommy walked towards the motor, Eddie smiled as he switched on the ignition. Trottsy's face was a picture of panic, the fucking moron.

Longbridge Road was far too busy at this time of day for Eddie to do the business, so he ordered Raymond to put his prey in the back and sit beside him.

'Long time no see, Tommy boy,' he said sarcastically.

'Ed, I'm so sorry, I lost me job. I'll get your money. Next week I'll pay you, I promise,' Tommy pleaded.

Ignoring his pleas, Eddie did a left out of the pub car park. He knew a quiet little spot, a couple of miles away. Ever since his father's cruel death, Eddie had found that his violent streak had worsened. He had always enjoyed a bit of rough and tumble and an odd finger or thumb dismembered, but finding his father the way he did had made him more brutal than ever.

Eddie drove down to the bottom of a road that led only to high-grass wasteland and turned off the engine. Relieved that there wasn't anyone in sight, Eddie opened the driver's door. 'Get out,' he ordered the shivering wreck previously known as big, bold Tommy Trott.

'I will pay you back, Eddie. Please don't hurt me,' Trottsy begged.

Eddie laughed as his expensive black leather shoe repeatedly made contact with Trottsy's head. As Tommy's front teeth flew onto a nearby rock, the blood running down his throat hampered his speech.

'Please, Eddie, please! I'm sorry,' he slurred in pain. Realising that Eddie was losing the plot, Raymond tried to drag him away. 'Come on, Ed, you've made your point. Give him a chance to pay up,' Ray shouted.

'Made me point, made me fucking point! I've known this cunt for years. Taken the right piss out of me, he has. Fuck the money, I want him dead.'

Hearing a dog bark, Raymond grabbed Eddie and shook him. 'There's someone coming. Let's go, come on. Think of Jess, for fuck's sake.'

The mention of his wife's name and a Rottweiler bounding towards him was enough to snap Eddie out of his violent trance. Tommy Trott's face was barely recognisable as Eddie aimed a farewell kick at it. 'Next week I want my money or you're dead, you cunt,' he spat.

Raymond bundled Eddie into the passenger side of the Land Cruiser. Both men had clocked that the Rottweiler was sniffing around Trottsy, licking his wounds. 'Buster, Buster!' its owner was yelling in the distance.

Raymond jumped into the driver's seat and did a speedy three-point turn. Putting his foot down, he pulled away just as the dog's owner came into full view. 'That was close. You don't think Trottsy will say ought, do you?'

Eddie smirked. 'What do you think? The mug's jaw is smashed to smithereens. Would you say ought? I bet he can't even speak for a month.'

Raymond headed towards his new house. He had recently purchased a property in Gidea Park, Romford. Meeting Polly had prompted him to move out of his previous address. Polly had class and he wanted to show her that he had it, too. 'We'll go to my house. You're covered in claret, you can't go home like that. You can borrow something of mine, it'll save Jess having kittens.'

Having now calmed down, Eddie couldn't stop laughing.

'Did you see that fucking Rotty? I'm sure it swallowed Trotty's teeth. It was sniffing at them and then I saw them disappear. They were lying on that big bit of rock beside him.'

Eddie's laugh was infectious and Raymond quickly joined in. 'The funniest bit was when the dog was licking his face and then had a shit not two yards from his head.'

Eddie had been too focused on his victim to see the dog have a dump. 'How fucking funny is that? Top dog! I must invest in a Rottweiler, Raymondo, I really must.'

'Ring Dad again, Mum. Me and Joey are starving,' Frankie whinged.

Jessica tried her husband's mobile for the umpteenth time. 'It's still switched off,' she said worriedly.

Bored out of her brains, Frankie urged Joey to follow her upstairs. 'We're going to listen to some music, Mum.'

'Give us a shout when Dad gets home,' Joey shouted out.

Frankie put the radio on. House music was a new thing out and she and Joey loved listening to the local pirate radio stations that were playing it.

Frankie shut her bedroom door. 'Thanks, Joey. Now we're stuck going out with Mum and Dad tonight and, if that ain't bad enough, you've said we'll pay for it.'

Joey shrugged. 'I felt sorry for Mum. You could have explained about the party in a kinder way.'

'Well, what was I meant to say? You know as well as I do that she would have embarrassed us. Can you imagine our friends drinking lemonade, playing pass the parcel and eating jelly and fucking ice cream? Well, no, neither can I. I explained it the best way I could. You always leave it to me, Joey, so best you do it in future.'

Joey sighed. He had always been the coward out of

278

the two of them and left Frankie to it. 'Sorry, sis,' he said kindly. He and Frankie rarely argued, and on the odd occasions they did, they were friends again within the hour.

Frankie hugged him. 'I wish Dad would hurry up, I'm ravenous.'

Joey smiled. 'Me too.'

By the time Eddie arrived home, Jessica was a bag of nerves. 'Where have you been? I was so worried!' she exclaimed, breathing a sigh of relief.

'Sorry, babe. The car needed a new part and the mechanic had trouble getting it. I should have called, but me battery on me mobile went dead and I couldn't find a phone box that worked,' Eddie hated lying to her, but on odd occasions like these, he had little choice.

'Why are you wearing different clothes? You had your grey trousers on and your white shirt earlier.'

Eddie smiled at his wife's bemused expression. She was so naive and he fucking loved her for it. 'I had to help the mechanic fix the bastard motor. The boy that normally works with him phoned in sick. Covered in oil, I was. Raymondo popped down to keep me company, so I went back to his to get changed. You know how I hate being dirty.'

Jessica smiled. 'You'll never guess what. The kids are taking us out for a meal tonight and they're paying for it.'

Eddie laughed. 'Well, that's a first. Are they fucking ill? Or are they hiding a terrible secret?'

A couple of hours later, Eddie was sitting in a restaurant with his wife and kids. 'Ain't this nice? Me, you and the twins,' he said, squeezing his wife's hand.

Jessica smiled. 'It's lovely.'

The waiter approached the table. 'Are we all ready to order?' he asked.

Ever the gentleman, Eddie urged Jessica and the kids to order first.

'And you, sir?' the waiter asked.

Usually, Eddie liked his steak medium rare. Thinking of the state he had made of Trottsy's face earlier, he smiled. 'I'll have a T-bone. I want it cooked rare, and bring us over a bottle of your finest champagne, please.'

Jessica and the kids all turned their noses up as Eddie's steak arrived.

'That looks like a live animal, Dad,' Frankie complained.

'Your plate's smothered in blood,' Joey moaned.

'You don't normally have your steak like that, dear,' Jessica commented.

Eddie savoured the taste as the steak mixed with blood slipped down his throat. Now he knew just how that Rottweiler had felt earlier.

TWENTY-SEVEN

On the morning of the twins' sixteenth birthday, Eddie was up at the crack of dawn.

'Where you going? You promised you weren't working today,' Jessica said sleepily.

'I'm not. I've gotta go out and pick up a surprise for the twins,' Eddie replied.

Jessica sat up with a bolt. 'But they wanted money and I've already got them a load of surprises to open.'

Eddie put on his tracksuit. 'I won't be long, probably about an hour or so. I'll have a shower and shave when I get back. What time are your parents coming?'

Jessica was bemused. 'They're not coming till tomorrow, about one. What have you got to pick up for the kids?'

Eddie laughed. 'That's for me to know and you to find out.'

Jessica was annoyed as he ran down the stairs and slammed the front door. She hated being kept in the dark and she hoped he wasn't bringing home something impractical. He had a devious glint in his eye and that was never a good sign with Eddie.

Jessica had a quick shower, then woke the twins up. 'Come on, birthday boy and girl. I haven't allowed you to have a day off school so you can lie in bed all day.'

'Oh, leave off, Mum, I'm tired,' Frankie moaned.

Joey jumped out of bed. Filled with excitement, he ran into his sister's room and leaped on top of her. 'Come on, Frankie, let's go and open our presents,' he pleaded.

'Drop dead, Joey,' Frankie mumbled.

Knowing how his sister hated being tickled, Joey did just that. 'Come on, sweet sixteen and never been kissed. Get your miserable arse out of bed, you boring cow.'

Fully awake by now, a defeated Frankie got up.

Tutting, Jessica went downstairs to cook the twins a nice birthday fry-up. The way they spoke to one another was beyond belief at times, but she knew they didn't really mean what they said. They had inherited their father's warped sense of humour, unfortunately.

Frankie plonked herself down at the kitchen table. 'Where's Dad?'

'Gone to pick up your birthday surprise and don't ask me what it is, because I haven't a clue,' Jessica told her.

'Can't we open our presents before breakfast?' Joey pleaded with his mum.

'No, Joey, wait till your dad gets back. He'll be upset if you open them and he's not here. Now, do you both want a sausage as well as some bacon?'

Frankie threw her brother a sardonic look. 'Let Joey have mine, Mum, he likes a nice juicy sausage.'

Joey aimed a sly kick Frankie's way. 'Bitch,' he whispered.

Eddie smiled as the two new additions to the family sat quivering on Raymond's lap.

'Fucking hell, Ed, slow down, will you? One's just pissed all over me.'

Eddie dropped his speed. Raymondo had a nice wet patch on the leg of his trousers.

'What time is Polly coming? Is she staying with you tonight or arriving tomorrow?' Eddie said, struggling to contain his laughter.

'I'm picking her up early tomorrow morning. She's working today,' Raymond replied, annoyed that his £100 trousers were covered in slash. He was dreading tomorrow. Eddie and Jessica had already met Polly, but his mother and father hadn't.

'Be warned, my mother's absolute brain damage. If she starts asking you loads of questions, don't feel you have to answer them. Me dad's OK, but him and me mother don't stop arguing,' he had warned Polly on the phone the previous night.

Eddie read Raymond's thoughts and smiled. 'I bet Joycie will have a field day. She's been dying to interrogate Polly ever since you first mentioned her.'

'I don't need reminding, Ed. Ouch! That little fucker just bit me,' Raymond exclaimed.

Chuckling, Eddie put his foot down and sped towards home.

'Dad's been gone ages. Can't we just open a few presents, Mum?' Joey begged.

'At least let us open one,' Frankie whinged.

Hearing her husband's tyres scrunch against the gravel outside, Jessica was relieved. The twins hadn't stopped moaning since the moment they had opened their eyes. 'He's here now. Go out and see what he's got for you,' she told them.

Jessica wiped the kitchen top down and, hearing whoops of delight, went outside to see what all the fuss was about. 'What the hell?' she said, as she spotted their presents bounding towards her.

Eddie smiled at her. He hadn't asked Jessica's

permission, as he knew she would say no. 'The kids have always wanted a dog. Ain't they gorgeous?' he said anxiously.

Jessica glared at her husband and her brother. She kept her house spotless and didn't want it any other way.

'Nothing to do with me,' Raymond declared.

She walked towards Eddie. 'You should have asked me first. What breed are they? They won't get big, will they?'

Eddie slung his arm around Jessica's shoulder. 'Ahh, look. The kids love 'em. It is their sixteenth, ain't it? They'll look after 'em, walk 'em and that.'

Jessica repeated her previous question.

'They're Rottweiler puppies. They don't grow that big,' Eddie lied.

Desperate to get the smell of the dog's piss off his new trousers, Raymond went into the house to clean himself up. Eddie could be an impulsive bastard at times and he could tell his sister wasn't amused.

'Look, Mum, isn't he cute?' Frankie said, lifting one of the dogs up.

'Can I have this one, Frankie? That one's mental like you, this one's the quiet one, like me,' Joey asked, his eyes shining. When he was little, he'd hated dogs, been petrified of them. These were adorable, though.

Jessica clocked the twins' elation. How could she say no? She could hardly tell them they couldn't keep the pups now that they'd seen them. Frankie and Joey would be heartbroken and she would feel like the Wicked Witch of the West.

Aware that Jessica was mellowing, Eddie told the kids to let their mother hold the puppies.

'Aren't they meant to be dangerous, Rottweilers? I mean, say I get pregnant. We can't have them around a newborn,' Jessica whispered to Eddie.

'They'll be fine. I'll train 'em up as guard dogs. Since me dad died, I worry about you and the kids being alone in the house. They'll be protection for you when I'm at work,' Eddie assured her.

'Yeah, but what about the baby?' Jessica whispered again.

'We'll worry about that when the time comes. I can build a kennel outside,' Eddie replied.

'Do you wanna hold them, Mum?' Joey asked.

Not wanting to be a spoilsport, Jessica had little choice. Peering down at the two little funny faces, she smiled as they both licked her hands. 'Aw, they are sweet. What are you going to call them?' she asked the twins.

'What about calling one Buster? That's a good name for a dog,' Eddie spouted.

'I like Bruno,' Frankie said immediately.

'I don't mind mine being called Buster, Dad. You did buy them for us,' Joey said gratefully.

Eddie ruffled his son's hair. 'That's sorted then. Let me have a shower and some breakfast and then we'll take a drive down to the pet shop. We'll buy them a bed and some toys. I've brought 'em some food already.'

Jessica smiled at the twins. 'Bring Buster and Bruno inside and you can open your other presents,' she said.

The rest of the day passed by in a happy bubble. The twins were thrilled with the acid-washed denims Jessica had brought them and excitedly pocketed the £200 each that was in their cards. Frankie and Joey had begged their dad for mobile phones and couldn't believe their luck when they received one each.

Jessica cooked spaghetti bolognese for dinner, the twins' favourite. By teatime, Buster and Bruno were flaked out in their doggy beds, looking pleased with their new surroundings.

At six o'clock, Frankie elbowed Joey. They were meant to be going out at eight and needed to get their arses in gear. 'Mum, Dad. Is it OK if we stay round our friend's tonight? We told you we're going to the pub in Rainham, didn't we? Well, Stacey said we can go back to hers and stay there after,' Frankie asked politely.

'No, you're lucky you're allowed to go to the pub. You can come home at twelve,' Jessica said sternly.

Frankie poked Joey. 'But, Mum, we are sixteen now. Dad has already charged our mobile phones and we'll carry them with us,' Joey said, doing his bit for once. He had arranged to meet Dominic later and, along with Frankie, they were going to a rave, then planned to stay in a nearby hotel.

'Say something, Eddie. They've only just got them dogs and already they want to leave us to look after them.'

Eddie shrugged. He would never let Frankie stay out all night alone, but Joey wasn't exactly a wild one, and he knew he would look after his sister. 'If you stay out, I want you back here by eight in the morning. I also want you to ring home when you're in safely from the pub. I know everyone around this area and if I find out either of you were drunk, you're grounded,' Eddie told them.

As the twins skipped happily upstairs to get ready, Jessica turned to her husband. 'We don't even know this Stacey's parents. The kids could be up to all sorts for all we know,' she said.

'Look, they're leaving school in a couple of months and then they'll be working, Jess. They can fucking leave home the age they are now, if they want. We can't wrap 'em in cotton wool – we've gotta give 'em some leeway. I mean, they ain't bad kids, are they? I know we caught 'em out playing hookey that time, but other than that, they've never given us major reasons not to trust 'em.'

As Buster and Bruno walked towards her, Jessica picked their little bodies up and sat them on her lap. 'I know you're right, Ed. I just worry about them, that's all.'

Eddie laid her head on his shoulder. 'Frankie and Joey will cause us no problems. They ain't the type – trust me!'

Joey and Frankie met Dominic in the Albion pub in Rainham.

'A couple of Frankie's friends will be here soon, so we must be discreet,' Joey warned his boyfriend.

Dominic nodded understandingly. He knew Joey didn't want anyone to know about their relationship. Joey hadn't told him an awful lot about his father, but the few bits he had told him were enough to make him wary, and Dom guessed this was the reason why Joey insisted that they keep things secret. The more people that knew, the better chance of his dad finding out.

'Happy birthday to you, Your arse smells of poo,' sang Frankie's friends.

Frankie giggled as she hugged Stacey, Demi and Paige. She didn't have that many girl mates, but these three were a bit tomboyish, like herself. Along with David and Wesley, the girls were the crowd that she and Joey had bunked off school with and they had all known one another for years.

'Where's David and Wesley?' Paige enquired.

'Wesley's meant to be coming, but David can't make it,' Frankie said, glancing at her brother. The relationship between Joey and David had never repaired itself since their couple of fumbles. David didn't even come out any more if Frankie and Joey were going to be there.

'Who's that? He's a sort. How old is he?' Demi whispered to Frankie.

287

Realising Demi was pointing at Dominic, Frankie laughed. 'His name is Dominic, he's twenty-six and I'm positive he ain't got a girlfriend.'

Stacey, Paige and Demi all had their tongues hanging out. 'Where do you know him from? Does he live round here?' Stacey asked.

'He lives in north London. He's a mate of Joey's. Now, shall we get drunk?' Frankie said, trying to change the subject.

With the vodka and pineapple going down nicely, the girls talked excitedly about the night ahead. This rave lark was new to all of them and they couldn't wait to try the experience.

'Do you think we're dressed right?' Demi asked.

Frankie shrugged. 'Dunno. Joey's mate, Dom, said he's been to one up his way. He said it's casual, everyone wears jeans and trainers and stuff.'

Joey smiled as Dominic bent over to pick some money up he'd dropped. He only had to look at the muscles in Dominic's buttocks to experience a feeling of butterflies. 'So, did you book the hotel?' he asked him.

Dominic nodded. 'There's nothing decent around here, so I got us into a little B&B. There's no bar, but I dropped me stuff off there and stocked the room up with drink. I booked two rooms, one for us and one for your sister and her mates. I asked for single beds, obviously. Don't worry, it won't look suspicious.'

Joey smiled. He had been on double vodkas and already felt merry. 'Fuck it – come to me family barbie tomorrow. I'll get Frankie to invite her mates as well. If there's a crowd of us there, no one will bat an eyelid.'

Dominic was unsure. Joey's father sounded a bit too heavy for his liking. 'I dunno, say someone says something, Joey?'

Checking none of the girls were watching, Joey squeezed Dominic's hand. 'There's only me, you, and Frankie that knows. No one's gonna say anything. Come on, please say yes.'

Unable to say no to the beautiful blond boy who had knocked him for six, Dominic nodded his head.

The Berwick Manor was set in the country lanes in the middle of nowhere. It didn't look like a nightclub, more like a massive country home.

'Weird-looking, ain't it?' Frankie said, as she climbed out of the taxi.

'Frankie, you've left your phone under the seat,' her brother shouted.

Frankie hated taking out a handbag – she felt like a right girlie – so had shoved her phone and fags into a carrier bag. The phone weighed a bloody ton and was a poxy nuisance to lug around, especially if she wanted to dance later on. She snatched at the carrier bag. 'Look after it for me Joey, please?' she pleaded.

Dominic laughed. He liked Joey's sister, she was a top girl. ''Ere, give it to me. I'll keep it safe for you,' he told her.

Frankie smiled. 'If he weren't queer, I'd have gone for him meself,' she whispered to Joey.

'Shut up,' Joey said, as he pushed her towards the entrance.

Inside the place was rocking and Frankie's eyes lit up. 'This is amazing,' she said as she stared at the funky, trendy people cluttering the dancefloor. The music was different, amazing, and there was a handsome-looking guy with dreadlocks spinning the tunes. Everyone looked so relaxed and happy and Frankie had never seen anything like it.

'Shall I get a drink? Everyone seems to be on water,' Joey said to Dominic.

Older and wiser, Dominic laughed. 'They take Es at these places; water's all they drink.'

Joey stood with a confused expression plastered across his face. 'What's an E?'

'Ecstasy tablets. New things out, they are. They've all been taking them in the City, where I work.'

With ears like a bat, Frankie turned to Dominic. 'What do Es do? Have you tried one? Are they any good?'

Dominic smiled. 'No idea, I've never taken one, but judging by the looks on the faces on the dancefloor, they're all right. The guys I work with reckon they're wicked. Apparently, you get this euphoric feeling when you take them and you just love everybody.'

Wandering back to her friends, Frankie ordered another round. 'Four vodkas with pineapple and two vodkas with orange,' she shouted to the barman.

'Oi, stop pushing in. I was before you,' a voice said.

About to let rip at the lad standing next to her, Frankie looked at him and, for the first time in her life, was totally lost for words. He was as fit as a fiddle, had dark, floppy hair and the brightest green eyes she had ever seen.

'What's up? Cat got your tongue?' he asked her, laughing.

'Go on, you go first,' Frankie mumbled. She couldn't look him in the eye – he was drop-dead gorgeous and making her insides go all funny.

'I'll have two lagers mate, four bottles of water and whatever this lady wants,' the lad said.

Struggling to find her voice, Frankie turned to him. 'I'm fine. I have my own money and I've got to get a round,' she mumbled.

The lad laughed as he waved a big wad at her. 'Can't a man buy a lady a drink? I'll get the round,' he insisted.

With her eyes desperately searching for her brother and their mates, Frankie was annoyed that she couldn't see them. 'Whatever, just hurry up, I've lost the people I'm with,' she told him.

The lad chuckled. 'Ungrateful little filly you are, ain't ya?'

As his face broke into a cheeky smile, Frankie smiled back. He had the most perfect teeth and appealing face she had ever seen.

'I definitely recognise you from somewhere. Do you come down here all the time?' he asked her.

Frankie shook her head. 'Nah, first time I've been here. I like it though, it's proper.'

The lad laughed. 'Hark at you – proper! I bet you're a right little handful, ain't ya?'

Frankie swallowed her drink and then necked her brother's double. Suddenly full of Dutch courage, she gave it back to the lad. 'Who do you think you are, you cheeky bastard? Actually, you do look familiar, like something out of a horror movie,' she said giggling.

'You all right?' Joey said reappearing.

Frankie handed him the drinks. 'Sorry, I forgot to get your one. Where are Dominic and the girls?'

'We're over by the dancefloor. I've still got a drink, so don't worry about mine. Are you sure you're OK?' Joey asked, looking at the boy standing next to her.

Frankie nodded. 'I'm fine. I'll be over in a minute.'

The lad smiled as Joey walked away.

'That ain't your boyfriend, so who is it? Your brother?'

Frankie nodded. 'How did you know he weren't my boyfriend?'

The boy smirked. 'Too normal. You go for tough boys, a bit like meself!'

291

Frankie grinned at his cheekiness. 'You're so full of yourself. Has anyone ever told you that?'

The lad chuckled. 'Every day, sugar pie. I swear I know you from somewhere. What's your name?'

'Me name's Frankie. What's yours?'

The lad shook her hand. 'Extremely pleased to meet you, Frankie. I'm Jed. Jed O'Hara.'

TWENTY-EIGHT

As the recognition hit her, Frankie nearly dropped her glass in shock. 'I think we have met before, at a party when we were young,' she mumbled.

'What party? Where?' Jed asked her.

'I'm Frankie Mitchell. Eddie Mitchell's daughter. I can't remember where the party was, but I think your dad and my dad made you and my brother fight with one another in a boxing ring. I can't remember exactly what happened, but I think you beat my brother, 'cause my mum was hysterical.'

Jed laughed. 'I know your face, but I don't remember the fight. My father made me spar with so many kids over the years, I sort of lost count.'

With her heart pounding, Frankie gratefully accepted Jed's offer of another drink. 'Let me take these drinks back to me mates – they'll think I've gone missing,' she said.

'You go and tell your brother that you're OK, and we'll meet back here in five minutes. I'll buy you another drink then. The music's proper loud, ain't it? We can go outside and talk,' Jed said, grinning at her.

'Who's that boy? How do you know him?' Joey asked, as Frankie appeared by his side.

293

'We've met before,' Frankie replied casually.

This was neither the time nor the place to mention the name Jed O'Hara. Joey was a drama queen at the best of times. 'Where are the girls?' Frankie asked Joey.

Joey pointed towards the dancefloor. 'Dom's such a show-off, he's teaching them some new moves. I'm gonna join 'em – you coming?'

Frankie shook her head. 'I'm gonna stand at the bar and have a drink with that boy I know.'

Joey smirked. 'You like him, don't you? It's written all over your face.'

'No, I don't. I'm just chatting, that's all,' Frankie said agitated.

Joey was full of suspicion as he watched his sister walk away. They knew all the same people and he wondered where Frankie knew the lad from.

'Are you OK?' Dominic asked, as Joey joined him on the dancefloor.

'Yeah, sort of. Do us a favour, Dom, you're taller than me. Keep an eye on Frankie, she's standing up the bar with some bloke with dark hair. I don't like the look of him. I don't know why, but keep watch for me.'

'Frankie will be fine. You're just being overprotective, as any decent brother should,' Dominic whispered in his ear.

Frankie felt like an idiot as she stood up at the bar alone.

'Wanna dance?' some spotty-faced jerk in dungarees asked her.

'Fuck off,' she replied angrily.

'Worried I'd forgotten about ya, was ya?' said a voice beside her.

Jed's confidence was appealing and Frankie couldn't help but giggle. 'I was hoping you had. I prefer him over there,' she said, pointing at Mr Dungarees.

Jed laughed. 'Let's go outside, we can have a proper chat. I can't hear meself think in here.'

As she followed Jed outside, Frankie was nervous, but also excited. The Berwick Manor was remote and, apart from a few revellers and a mass of parked cars, the outside was a kind of ghost town.

'Follow me,' Jed said, leading her away from the car park.

After a five-minute walk, Jed grabbed her hand and sat down by a tree. Not backwards in coming forwards, he pinned Frankie down on the sweet-smelling grass and plunged his tongue down the back of her throat.

Frankie succumbed to his kiss and then, as realisation kicked in, pushed him away. 'I thought you wanted to talk,' she said defensively.

Jed smiled. Her face was even prettier when she was angry. His mum was always trying to fix him up with fellow travelling girls. He'd slept with loads, but none of them had captured his heart. They were too common and tarty for him. Not like Frankie – she was feisty and beautiful.

Jed held her hand. 'Sorry about that. I didn't mean to be forward, but I had to kiss you. I remember you now. You were the little rawnie who stole my heart at Pat Murphy's party. Memory like an elephant, me. I think you came to me dad's house once and I sat in a car with ya.'

Frankie didn't remember going to his house. 'How comes we ain't bumped into one another over the years, then? Your dad lives near me, don't he?' she asked.

'I moved away. Me old mum caught me father at it, so we went to live in Basildon. Didn't like it there much, although there was a good nightclub down the A127. Elliot's it was called, but I think it's shut down now. Shame, I could have taken you there for our first date.'

Frankie smiled. This boy was gorgeous. 'What you trying to say? Do you want me to go out with you?' she asked shyly.

Trying his luck again, Jed chuckled as he held her down. As he lay on top of her, he knew she was aware of his erect penis rubbing against her. 'I'll take you anywhere you want. I'll treat you like a proper princess. Come out with me tomorrow.'

Frankie had never felt so sexual in her life. Richard Jones at school had tried to rub himself against her once. She had frozen and then punched him in the cock. Richard had screamed in agony and had never spoken to her again. With Jed it was different. His eyes, his cheeky smile, his erection – she was hooked by it all.

'I can't come out tomorrow. It's mine and Joey's sixteenth birthday today and me parents have organised this boring family barbecue for us.'

Feeling himself getting a little bit too excited, Jed rolled off her. 'What about Sunday? Meet me Sunday.'

Frankie nodded. 'OK. Where and when?'

Jed laughed. She wanted him and he knew it. 'I've gotta mobile phone. I'll give you me number and you can ring me tomorrow. Anyway, tonight's not over yet.'

As he kissed her again, Frankie felt an unusual sensation wash over her. She had always known she wasn't gay, like her brother, but most of the boys she had met had done nothing for her.

'Just stroke it for me,' Jed panted, placing her hand on his big, hard cock.

Frankie felt the fullness of it through his jeans. She had

296

never really touched one before and it was massive, like a snake.

'Do you wanna see it?' Jed asked her.

'Frankie, are you out here? Frankie, where are you?'

'Shit – it's me brother,' Frankie said. She pushed Jed away, stood up and pulled herself together.

'I'm over here, Joey. Just having a chat. I'm coming back in now.'

Joey glared at Frankie as she reappeared looking dishevelled. 'What have you been doing?' he whispered accusingly.

'Nothing. Don't fucking start on me. You bat the other way, remember?' she spat back at him.

Annoyed, Joey grabbed Dominic's arm. 'Come on, leave her to it. We're going back inside,' he said.

Jed held Frankie's hand as they walked towards the entrance of the club. 'Dordie! Is he the other way, your brother?'

Frankie shook her head. 'Not as far as I know. He's had loads of girls,' she lied.

Chuckling, Jed tilted her chin and kissed her with a passion. 'I'll think you'll find he is, Frankie. I reckon that geezer with him is his boyfriend.'

Frankie shrugged. She wasn't about to start discussing her brother's private life with anyone.

As soon as they re-entered the Berwick, Jed went to get some more drinks and Frankie searched for Joey. 'What you got the hump about? Where have the girls gone?' she asked as she caught sight of him.

Joey spoke abruptly to her. 'The girls have all gone to a party in Dagenham. They met some lads they knew. What was you doing with that boy? You were doing something, Frankie.'

'Having a fucking kiss and cuddle, is that all right? Don't go all psycho on me, Joey. I'm sure if I can accept the way you are and what you get up to, then you can accept that I'm only human, too.'

Feeling a bit silly, Joey hugged her. 'I'm sorry, Frankie. You've never really had much track with boys and I was just worried about you. Who is he, anyway? He don't come from round here, does he? He's got a funny accent.'

Too frightened to spill the beans, Frankie lied. 'His name's John and I know him through an old friend of mine. I'm not sure where he comes from, but I think he's from up north or somewhere.'

'Me and Dom have had enough of it here now. We might go back to the B&B. Are you coming? You can bring John if you like. Dom's got some drink,' Joey said, hoping she had forgiven him.

Frankie smiled. 'Give us five minutes and I'll ask him if he wants to come.'

Jed laughed as Frankie repeated the story. 'So I've gotta pretend I'm called fucking John, now, have I?'

'Please. I've been thinking about that party years ago, and you knocked Joey out, if I remember rightly. I don't want him to remember who you are.'

Desperate to get the beautiful Frankie alone in a bedroom, Jed promised he would keep his trap shut. 'I'll just say goodbye to me mates, give us a minute,' he told Frankie.

'Where are your mates? Shall I come with you?' Frankie asked him.

'My mates are vultures. They'll take one look at you and they'll all want you for themselves. Stay here and wait for me,' Jed told her.

'Are you ready?' Joey said, spotting his sister standing alone.

Frankie looked around. Jed had been gone ages now and she was worried he'd had a change of heart. As she saw him bowling towards her, relief flooded through her body. 'Here he is,' she told her brother.

Outside the Berwick, Dominic jumped in a taxi.

'I've got me pick-up truck here. Come with me,' Jed told Frankie.

Unable to say no, Frankie told Dominic and Joey to go on ahead and climbed into the Toyota Hilux.

As Jed expertly swung out of the car park and followed the taxi, she smiled at him. 'How old are you? When did you pass your test?' she asked him, impressed.

Jed laughed. 'I'm younger than you, you dinlo. Us travelling boys don't need driving licences. We're taught from an early age how to drive. I've been tugged before – got away with it, I did. I told the gavvers I was me brother. Me cousin gets hold of bent insurance certificates. Filled it out meself, I did. The gavvers are mugs, they know nothing.'

'What's gavvers mean?' Frankie asked, bemused by his slang.

'The police, you dinlo,' Jed said laughing.

The B&B was a shit-hole bang opposite the A13. It wasn't built to be paradise, but to serve a purpose for workmen and party-goers.

'We'll go in me brother's room. His mate, Dom, has got a load of drink in there,' Frankie informed Jed.

'You go and grab the drink off them. I wanna spend some time alone with you, Frankie. We can't chat properly in front of your brother.'

Dominic handed Frankie a bottle of vodka and two cartons of orange juice.

'Are you sure you're gonna be OK, Frankie? Please

don't do anything you'll regret in the morning,' Joey begged her.

Headstrong, Frankie waved away her brother's fears. 'Yous two have a good time. Don't make the walls shake,' she giggled as she shut their door.

Taking a deep breath, she entered the other room.

'Come here, sexy,' Jed said, smiling at her.

As Frankie got under the flimsy quilt, she realised that Jed had taken his jeans and pants off. 'Stop it,' she squealed as he put her hand on his penis. She had never felt a naked one before and it reminded her of the raw jumbo sausage that her dad cooked at barbecues.

Laughing, Jed poured out two large vodkas and handed her one. 'You ever tried an E?' he asked her.

Frankie shook her head. 'I've heard about them, though,' she replied casually.

She had to sound knowledgeable; she didn't want Jed to think she was some stupid schoolgirl.

Jed lent out of the bed and pulled a small plastic bag out of his jeans. 'I've gotta couple here. Shall we do one?' he asked her.

'I dunno. I've got to be home early,' Frankie said awkwardly.

Jed put one on his tongue and washed it down with vodka. 'Come on. It's your birthday – enjoy yourself,' he urged her.

Desperate not to look boring, Frankie took the white tablet from him and swallowed it.

'There's my girl. American burger, that is. They're the bollocks, they are. Make you feel horny, they do.'

Frankie poured herself another vodka and orange. The tablet looked just like a paracetamol, and she was sure it wouldn't do much to her.

Jed had a portable radio in the front of his truck and

300

had brought it up to the room with him. 'I need a slash, find a station,' he asked Frankie, as he put his jeans back on.

Frankie got off the bed and felt herself go all weird. She felt happy, but very sick at the same time. As Jed came out the toilet, she raced towards it. 'I feel funny, I think I'm gonna be sick,' she mumbled.

Jed chuckled. 'Bring it up. Looks like seaweed, it does. Once you've spewed, you'll feel fine.'

Frankie's heart was pounding as she looked at the weird-coloured stuff that had come from her stomach. 'Wow,' she said out loud. Jed wasn't wrong, she now felt amazing.

Bounding out of the bathroom, Frankie grabbed his hand. 'Turn the music up, let's dance,' she screamed.

Frankie and Jed's high lasted all night.

At 6 a.m. Jed urged Frankie to lie on the bed with him. 'I want you to be my woman, Frankie,' he told her earnestly.

As his tongue connected with hers, Frankie let out a moan.

'Let me fuck you,' Jed whispered in her ear.

Frankie shook her head. She might be high, but she still knew what was right and wrong. 'I do like you, Jed, but not tonight, not yet. I've only just met you.'

Jed couldn't help himself. He usually got his own way with every bird he went for. He held his penis in his hand and tried to guide it inside Frankie.

'No! I said no,' Frankie said angrily.

'Just let me put it in. If you don't like it, I'll pull it straight back out again,' Jed pleaded with her.

As he tried to enter her, Frankie pushed him away. She wasn't ready for this; it wasn't right.

301

'Please, let me do it,' Jed begged her.

'No. I said no and I mean fucking no,' Frankie told him.

'Just wank me off then, please,' Jed said, grabbing Frankie's hand.

Fuming, Frankie squeezed his balls as hard as she could.

Jed let out an almighty yelp. 'Why did ya do that?' he shouted.

'I've had enough now, Jed. I'm going home,' Frankie said, as she jumped out of the bed

'I'm sorry. I couldn't help meself. You make me so horny. Let me drive you home,' Jed begged her. He liked this girl: she was so different from the others who always spread their legs so easily.

Frankie shook her head. 'You stay here. I have to go home with Joey. My parents will go mad if we come home separately.'

Searching for the pen he always carried on him, Jed grabbed Frankie's hand and wrote his number on her arm. 'Please ring me, Frankie. I'm sorry if I was a bit forward, but it was only because I like you so much. Come out with me on Sunday? I'll treat you like a princess, I promise.'

Frankie's emotions were out of control. Meeting Jed had blown her mind, and her sensible side told her he was very wrong for her indeed. 'I don't know, Jed. My dad and your dad don't get on. It ain't gonna work,' she told him bluntly.

Jed walked towards her and hugged her in a way she had never been hugged before. 'Trust me, we'll make it work. Fuck our dads, who cares what they think? I like you, you like me and nothing else matters. Let's try and make a go of it, eh? What do you say?'

302

As Jed grinned, Frankie's heart pounded. He wasn't just trying it on – he actually was into her. With the E frazzling her brain, Frankie didn't know if she was coming or going. How could she be with Jed? He had just tried to shag her without her consent. Desperate to get away from him, she picked up her jacket.

'Goodbye, Jed. It was nice meeting ya. Take care of yourself.'

TWENTY-NINE

Jessica breathed a sigh of relief as she heard the front door close and the twins creep up the stairs. Joey had rung home last night, as promised, but it still hadn't lessened her worry. She could never relax when the kids stayed out, and she'd lie awake imagining all sorts. Hearing a strange whining noise, she nudged her husband.

'Ed, wake up. One of the dogs sounds like it's crying. Go and make sure it's OK.'

'All dogs whine. It'll be fine, Jess,' Eddie said grumpily. He had been in a deep sleep and wasn't happy being woken.

'Ah, listen to the poor little mite. Go and see to 'em, Ed. They might want to go out to do toilets. You brought them home. Go on, up you get.'

Mumbling obscenities to himself, Eddie threw on his trackie bottoms and stomped downstairs.

The twins lay top-to-toe in Joey's bed. Neither of them were sleepy and they were whispering excitedly about the previous evening. As Frankie gabbled on, Joey sat up and stared at her. 'You've taken something, ain't you? Your pupils look massive and you're talking all weird.'

'No, I ain't,' Frankie said defensively. She could still

feel the effects of the ecstasy tablet, and still felt quite high.

'You're lying. Did that fucking John give you drugs?' Joey asked, his temper rising.

'Sssh, Mum and Dad will hear. Do you wanna cause a riot? If you must know, I had half of one of them Es in the Berwick. Jed never gave it to me, somebody else did.'

Joey couldn't believe how stupid she had been. If their parents found out, the pair of them would be grounded for life. 'Don't ever do that again, Frankie. You don't know what's in the bloody things. And who's Jed? I thought the bloke you was with was called John.'

Frankie took a deep breath. She couldn't tell anyone who Jed was – not yet, anyway. 'I said John. You must be hearing things,' she told Joey.

'Are you gonna see him again?' Joey asked.

'I don't know. I need to get some sleep now, I'm going back to me own room,' Frankie replied haughtily.

Joey grabbed her arm. 'You haven't told me what happened yet. Did you do anything with him? You didn't have sex with him, did you?'

'No, of course I didn't,' Frankie replied, pulling her arm away. Joey questioning her was making her feel paranoid and she needed to be left alone. 'I'll tell you all the gory details later,' she whispered, as she shut his bedroom door.

Frankie walked into her own room and quietly closed the door. She sat down at her dressing table and studied herself in the mirror. She looked out of it; her eyes were the giveaway. 'Shit,' she mumbled, as she remembered the barbecue that was planned for later.

She cursed herself for having taken the bloody tablet in the first place. How was she meant to sit and be normal in front of her parents and grandparents when she felt totally out of her nut? She crawled into bed and shut her eyes. Jed's face was at the forefront of her mind. He had been too forward for her liking, but no boy had ever made her feel the way he had.

Frankie had taken Jed's number, but she hadn't given him hers. She shut her eyes and pictured Jed's face. He had eyes that twinkled when he smiled. She loved his lopsided grin, his dark, wavy hair. Even his funny accent set her pulse racing.

Thinking of his rock-hard penis, Frankie shuddered with excitement. Jed might be bad news, but she had to see him again. It was the only way to get him out of her system.

Joyce and Stanley arrived promptly at one on the dot. 'Are Raymond and Polly here yet?' were the first words out of Joyce's mouth.

'No, they're coming later,' Jessica said, ushering her parents into the lounge.

'Where are the twins?' Stanley asked.

'In bloody bed. Went out with their friends last night, they did, and they're still in the land of nod,' Jessica replied in annoyance.

'What the hell is that?' Joyce screamed as two bundles of fluff jumped onto her lap.

Eddie smiled at his mother-in-law's horrified expression. 'Meet Buster and Bruno, Joycie, the new additions to the Mitchell household.'

Begrudgingly stroking their heads, Joyce was appalled as Buster got a little overexcited and urinated on her dress. 'Oh, look at me new frock! Get 'em off of me. Quick, take 'em away!' she screamed.

Stanley and Eddie looked at one another and burst out laughing.

'Don't worry, Mum, I'll get a cloth. It'll come out – it's only a little splash,' Jessica said, glaring at the men.

Eddie followed Jessica into the kitchen. 'I've got a bit of a confession to make, babe. I rang me Uncle Reg yesterday and invited him over for the barbie. I felt a bit guilty 'cause I ain't seen much of him recently. I didn't think he'd accept, but he rang me back and said Paulie and Ronny are coming too.'

Jessica was not impressed. 'Oh, Ed, it's meant to be the kids' birthday party. They barely know your family.'

Eddie hugged his wife and kissed her on the forehead. 'I'm sorry, it just escalated and I could hardly say no. Come on, cheer up. I picked another few trays of meat up, so we've got plenty of grub. It's only one day, Jess, we can get through it, me and you.'

Jessica sighed. Eddie's family turning up was the last thing she needed, but she could hardly tell him to uninvite them at this late stage. For years, Eddie had welcomed her family with open arms, so it wouldn't exactly hurt her to entertain his for once. She smiled at him. 'Don't worry, Ed. We'll all have a great day. Can you pour Mum and Dad some drinks while I go and wake our lazy children?'

Joey got showered and dressed, then sat on Frankie's bed while she got ready.

'Do my eyes look OK now?' she asked him. She had managed to doze off for a few hours and felt a damn sight better than she had earlier.

'You don't look as bad as before. In fact, you look much better,' Joey told her honestly.

'What time did you tell Dom to arrive?' Frankie asked him.

Joey felt himself shudder. Inviting Dominic had seemed a good idea last night when he was inebriated, but in the cold light of day, he was now shitting himself. 'Wesley's picking him up in a cab from the B&B. I wish I hadn't invited him now. You don't think Mum or Dad or our mates will clock on, do you, sis?'

Frankie shook her head. 'Dominic looks as straight as a die and if he's coming with Wesley, no one will bat an eyelid.'

Joey breathed a sigh of relief. 'Who did you invite? I asked a couple of other boys in the Berwick. I hope they don't turn up – I barely know them.'

Frankie laughed. 'I invited Stacey, Demi and Paige. I can't remember who else, I was a bit pissed. We better warn all of them not to mention the Berwick Manor. Mum and Dad think we went to Stacey's after the pub, remember?'

'You tell the girls to keep schtum and I'll tell the lads. Did you invite that John?' Joey asked.

Shaking her head, Frankie applied some lipgloss. 'Nah. I'm not even sure if I'm gonna see him again.'

'Frankie, Joey, everyone's waiting for you down here.' Jessica yelled. She was getting more annoyed by their no-show by the minute.

'Come on,' Joey said, dragging his sister away from the mirror.

Considering it had poured with rain the day before, the weather was glorious. There wasn't a cloud in the sky and the sun was scorching.

Eddie sat out in the grounds with his uncle, brothers and Dougie.

'Where's Raymondo?' Paulie asked.

'He'll be here soon, so will Gary and Ricky,' Eddie replied.

Desperate to meet her son's posh girlfriend, Joyce was up and down like a yo-yo.

308

'Will you sit down and come away from that bloody window, woman,' Stanley scolded her.

Joyce gave him one of her looks. 'No, I won't. Now shut your face, you miserable old goat, and drink your bleedin' beer.'

Gary and Ricky arrived and handed Jessica a big bunch of flowers. 'We brought the twins something, but these are for you,' Ricky told her.

'You shouldn't have. Your dad's in the garden. Thanks, boys,' she said, kissing them both on the cheek.

Joey hovered nervously in the hallway.

'What's the matter, love?' Jessica asked him.

'Nothing. Just waiting for my friends to arrive,' he replied anxiously.

'You're acting like a right twerp. Have a couple of drinks, for fuck's sake, else you'll give yourself away,' Frankie whispered to him.

'All right if me and Joey have another drink, Mum?' Frankie said, already topping up their glasses.

'I suppose so. It is your birthday party, but don't go too mad. How was your night out? You haven't said much about it,' Jessica asked.

As she screwed the lid back onto the vodka bottle, Frankie smiled. 'It was a bit boring, to be honest, Mum.'

The ringing of the doorbell stopped Jessica from prying any more. 'Get that, Joey!' she yelled.

Joey's heart leaped as he answered it. 'Come in, Dom. All right, Wes? Say hello to me mum, boys,' he said, as calmly as he could.

Jessica kissed Wesley, then turned her attention to Dominic. 'Nice to meet you, at last. I know my Joey spends hours talking to you on the phone, but we haven't met before, have we?'

'No, Mrs Mitchell,' Dominic answered politely.

Jessica was shocked by Dominic's appearance. He was obviously into bodybuilding or something and looked years older than Joey or Wesley.

Dominic had been in this situation in the past with other boyfriends' parents. He knew exactly how to play it. 'Your Joey likes coming out with me, Mrs Mitchell. We pull so many girls, we're babe magnets, aren't we Joey?' he joked.

Joey nodded dumbly.

Frankie's pals arrived shortly after Joey's. 'Where did yous sneak off to last night? Joey said you went to a party in Dagenham,' Frankie asked them.

'Our night was probably boring compared to yours. The party was crap. Who was that boy you were with?' Stacey pried.

'He was gorgeous,' Demi added.

'I've never seen you behave like that before, Frankie. You looked well loved-up with him, you did,' Paige giggled.

'Oh, I've known him for years. It's a long story, I'll tell you later. Don't mention him in front of my parents and don't mention the Berwick Manor. If any one asks, we went to the pub, then back to yours, Stacey.'

Joyce heard a car engine and almost flew towards the window. 'Here they are. She's pretty, Stanley. Looks posh, she does. A bit thin. I'll have to get Raymond to bring her around ours. I can soon fatten her up – looks like she needs a good dinner, she does.'

Stanley scowled at his wife. She had just moved quicker than his bloody pigeons could. 'For Christ's sake, Joycie, don't start with your comments and embarrass our Raymond, will you?'

Joyce looked at Stanley as though he were something

on the bottom of her shoe. 'Since when have I ever embarrassed anyone?' she asked innocently.

As her son and Polly walked towards her, Joyce smiled at the girl and, unable to stop herself, did a little curtsy.

'Whatever are you doing, Mother?' Raymond asked her.

Joyce ignored him. 'Pleased to meet you, Polly. My Raymond's told me so much about you. This is my husband, Stanley. Stanley, stand up and shake Polly's hand.'

Jessica stood in the doorway with Vicki. Unable to stifle their laughter, they fled back to the kitchen. Raymond followed them.

'Mother's off her fucking head. Pour Polly a glass of red wine, sis. I'll have a beer. This is gonna be a nightmare, I just know it.'

'Get us another lager, Ed. You got any stronger than five per cent?' Ronny asked his brother.

Eddie had put a load of cold beers in a black dustbin in the garden and filled it with blocks of ice. 'I dunno what's in there. I'll have a look for you,' he said.

Ronny raced towards the bin in his wheelchair. 'I'll have the Stella. Five point two, that is,' he said snatching two cans.

Eddie sat back down. He and Paulie had just been discussing their father's murder.

'So, where do we go from here? I've chased up Dad's old contacts in the filth and they still reckon they ain't got nothing. They said they never found as much as a fingerprint,' Paulie said.

Eddie felt the usual fire in his belly as he discussed his father's death. He had spoken to every underworld contact he knew ten times over, and no one had heard anything. The Old Bill still reckoned it was something to do with the kids that had been hanging around the area, being a nuisance, but Eddie wasn't so sure. How could a bunch of kids bludgeon to death a gangland legend and not leave a fucking clue?

Eddie swallowed his beer in one go. 'I'll pop round to see all Dad's neighbours again this week. I'll knock on every door for miles if I have to. Some cunt must know, or at least have heard something.'

Paulie nodded. 'It just don't seem fucking feasible, none of it, does it?'

Eddie stood up. He needed a refill. The conversation was making him thirsty. Face etched with anger, he faced his brother. 'Don't worry, Paulie. I'll find out who did it and, when I get me hands on the cunt, I will torture him for weeks. I'll starve him, burn him, cut him, then pull all his teeth and fingernails out, one by one. By the time I've finished, whoever did it will wish they'd never been born!'

Jessica was sweating in the dress she had on. She went upstairs to get changed into a vest top and shorts. She would have liked to have put on her bikini and jumped into the swimming pool, but didn't feel comfortable in front of Eddie's family. She had noticed Ronny leering at her in the past, and was sure he was a pervert.

Vicki giggled as Jessica sat down next to her. She had mixed them up some cocktails and they had been having a right old laugh at the expense of Eddie's family. 'Shut your legs, Jess. Quick, the pervert's looking over,' Vicki said laughing.

Jessica glanced at Ronny out of the corner of her eye. She had dark sunglasses on, so he couldn't see her looking at him. 'I never liked him when I first got with Eddie. He was really jealous of our relationship,' she told Vicki.

'Is his wife here?' Vicki asked.

'No, of course not. Sharon's not his wife, she's his girlfriend, the poor cow. Neither Paulie nor Reg have brought their other halves, either. I reckon they keep all their women shut in cupboards indoors. The only time I've ever seen 'em out is at weddings or funerals.'

Vicki smiled. 'I wouldn't put up with that, would you? I mean, I know Dougie usually leaves me and stands with the men, but that doesn't bother me. I wouldn't be left indoors all the time, though, would you?'

Jessica shook her head. 'That's one thing I must say about my Eddie. He can be a sod at times, but he's always put me and the kids first. He's a real family man, he is.'

Glancing back at Ronny, Vicki started to giggle again. 'Do you reckon his todger works if he's paralysed?'

Jessica burst out laughing. 'Shut up, Vicki, for Christ's sake. You've just put me off me piña colada.'

Joyce couldn't help herself. Every time Polly and Raymond walked away, she reappeared by their side like a shadow. 'So, how long has your father been in the jewellery business, Polly? Raymond says he has lots of shops. How many exactly has he got?'

Sighing at Polly, Raymond linked arms with his mother and gently led her away. 'Mum, you're going a bit over the top now. Polly's come here to socialise, not be interrogated. Sit down and have a drink with Dad. You can meet Polly another time. Perhaps I'll bring her round yours one day or something.'

'That'll be nice, dear,' Joyce said, smiling.

Spotting what her husband had done, Joyce's smile disappeared. 'What the bloody hell have you got on your bonce? Take it off, Stanley.'

'It's only me handkerchief. The sun's burning me scalp. It's all right for you, you've got hair,' Stanley moaned.

Joyce snatched the handkerchief off his head. 'What

313

will Polly think? You look like something out of *It Ain't Half Hot Mum*, you silly old bastard!'

Stacey, Demi and Paige sat with their mouths wide open as Frankie told them all about her liaison with Jed.

'So, was his willy big?' Demi asked.

'I suppose so. I dunno – I've never seen a real one before,' Frankie replied giggling.

Seeing her brother, Dominic and Wesley heading their way, she told the girls to say no more.

'I really like that Dominic. Can't you put a word in for me?' Stacey begged her.

If only she knew, Frankie thought as she nodded her head. 'I'm going to the toilet and then I'll get me dad to put some music on,' she told the girls.

Eddie was busy on barbecue duty. 'All right, sweetheart? Tell yours and Joey's mates that the food's ready now,' he told Frankie.

Frankie gave him a hug. 'What's that for?' he asked.

'Dunno. 'Cause I love you, I suppose,' Frankie replied guiltily.

'Who's that geezer standing over there with you? The tall one with the dark hair. Looks older than your crowd,' Eddie asked. He didn't trust strangers, especially in his house.

'Oh that's Wesley's mate, Dominic. Me and Joey know him well, he's a really nice person, Dad.'

Satisfied with Frankie's explanation, Eddie winked at his daughter and held up a burnt-looking steak on a large fork. 'Grub's up, everybody,' he bellowed.

Frankie went upstairs, sat on her bed and searched through her purse. When she'd come in this morning, she'd written Jed's number on a piece of paper, then washed it off her arm. She was tempted to ring him and arrange a date for the following day. Staring at his number, she switched on her mobile. Should she? Shouldn't she?

'Hello, yous two,' she said, as Buster and Bruno came tottering towards her.

Shoving the piece of paper into her bedside drawer, she switched off her phone and went back to the party.

Jessica had prepared three massive bowls of salad. She had also made coleslaw and warmed up lots of garlic bread. 'Help yourselves – there's plenty more in the kitchen,' she urged everybody.

As Jessica sat down to eat hers, she studied her son from behind her glasses. She was intrigued by what she saw. The way he and Dominic were looking at one another wasn't normal. They looked at each other the way she looked at Eddie.

As the two lads walked towards the barbecue, Jessica noticed Joey slyly pinch Dominic's bum.

'Oh my God,' she said out loud.

'Whatever's wrong? Are you OK, Jess?' Vicki asked concerned.

Jessica chucked her plate on the grass and jumped out of her seat. 'No, I'm not. In fact, I think I'm gonna be sick.'

THIRTY

Eddie waved goodbye to the last of the guests and shut the front door.

'Are you OK? You've been ever so quiet and you look really pale,' he asked Jessica.

'I've got a terrible migraine. Are Gary and Ricky still here?' Jessica replied.

Eddie nodded and gave his wife a big cuddle. 'I thought it was a great party. Even Ronny behaved himself and that's a first.'

Jessica nodded. 'I was enjoying it earlier, before I came over bad.'

'The twins got some nice presents, didn't they? Did you see their faces when your mother brought the cake out and made everybody sing "Happy Birthday". They were well embarrassed and their friends were taking the right piss out of 'em.'

Jessica kissed Eddie on the lips. 'I'm going to bed now. You sit up and have a nightcap with Gary and Ricky. I'll tidy up in the morning, when I feel a bit better.'

'Sweet dreams,' Eddie whispered lovingly.

Jessica barely slept at all that night. Her mind was in turmoil as she tried to convince herself that Joey was straight and she was wrong. She pictured herself at Joey's age. She had been knocking about with her old friend, Mary, then. Had they ever pinched one another's bottoms for a laugh, or looked at one another romantically. No, they hadn't.

As much as she hated to admit it, Jessica wondered if, deep down, she had always known that Joey was different. He had brought girls to the house over the years and had even introduced them as his girlfriends, but Jessica had never been fooled.

Seeing him with Dominic earlier – the closeness between them, the affectionate glances – was proof of something she had desperately tried to avoid. Joey was still her son. She would love him whatever he was, but Eddie certainly wouldn't. One sniff of her son's sexuality coming out into the open and there would be murders, literally.

Two doors away, Frankie was also unable to sleep properly. Every time she shut her eyes, Jed O'Hara's face disrupted her thoughts.

At 8 a.m., she got out of bed and took the piece of paper out of the drawer. She switched on her mobile phone. It was so early, he probably wasn't even awake yet. Punching in his number, she held her breath. Her heart was beating like a drum and, as he answered, she could barely speak through nervousness.

'All right? It's Frankie,' she mumbled.

Jed laughed. 'You took your time ringing me, didn't ya?'

'You're awake, then?' Frankie said stupidly.

'Of course I'm awake, you dinlo. I'm talking to you, ain't I?'

Sensing her apprehension, Jed smiled. He often had this effect on women and he was used to it. 'What you up to? Meet me in half-hour,' he told her.

Frankie nearly dropped the phone in shock. 'It's only

317

just gone eight. I haven't had a shower yet. I need some time to get ready.'

'Well, make it an hour then. Shall I pick you up from outside your house?' Jed asked.

'No. Don't pick me up from here. Where else can I meet you?'

Jed chuckled. He was dying to see Frankie again. 'You know where my house is, don'tcha? Just before you get there, in the direction you're coming from, there's a lay-by on the left. I'll meet you there, say half-nine.'

Frankie smiled. 'See you then.'

'And Frankie, don't put on too much make-up. I wanna see that pretty face of yours.'

Frankie felt faint as she ended the phone call. She didn't have a clue what to wear and had very little time to get ready.

Hearing Frankie switch the shower off, Jessica got out of bed. Joey and Frankie were as close as close could be, and if anyone knew his sordid secret, it was Frankie.

She gently tapped on her daughter's bedroom door.

'This is all I fucking need,' Frankie muttered, as she chucked half her wardrobe onto the floor.

'Can I come in, love?' Jessica whispered.

'Yes,' Frankie replied angrily.

Jessica sat on the edge of Frankie's bed. Her daughter wasn't the earliest riser on earth and she wondered what was so special about today. 'You're up early. Going somewhere nice, are you?'

With time running out, Frankie decided her acid-washed jeans and denim jacket would have to do. Her black suede ankle boots and black basque were enough to tart the outfit up. She didn't want to look like a tomboy. 'I'm going out with the girls. It's Stacey's cousin's birthday and she's having a barbecue,' Frankie lied.

Jessica knew when Frankie was lying, but said nothing. Whatever she was hiding couldn't be any worse than Joey's little secret, and Jessica was more worried about her son than her daughter. 'Has, erm, Joey said anything to you recently about his life? He hasn't confided in you about anything unusual, has he?'

'Like what? What you talking about?' Frankie replied casually.

Jessica was a bit lost for words. Say Joey hadn't said anything to Frankie, or she had made a mistake. 'Has he got a girlfriend?' Jessica blurted out.

Aware that her mum was on her brother's case, Frankie said very little. 'I dunno. We're not together all the time, Mum. He ain't said nothing to me, but if you're so interested in Joey's love life, you best ask him yourself.'

Jessica nodded. The twins were as thick as thieves and, chances were, even if Frankie did know something, she wouldn't tell anyone. 'So where does Stacey's cousin live, then?' she asked, changing the subject.

Frankie let out a bored sigh. 'I don't know. Stacey never told me. Now, can you leave me alone, Mum? I'm trying to get ready and you're making me late.'

With a heart full of worry, Jessica apologised and walked away.

Frankie checked her appearance, grabbed her purse and ran down the stairs. She wanted to warn Joey about the conversation she had had with her mother, but he was fast asleep and she didn't have time to arse about. Debating whether to take her phone with her and ring him, she decided against it. The poxy thing was a nuisance to lug around and she had nearly lost it twice the other night.

Running into the kitchen, Frankie took a large gulp of vodka out of the bottle. 'No, doggies, no,' she said,

319

as Buster and Bruno tried to clamber up the leg of her jeans.

'All right, Frank? What you doing?' Ricky asked.

Startled, Frankie dropped the vodka bottle and it smashed to smithereens on the stone kitchen floor. 'You scared me. I didn't realise you were still here,' Frankie replied.

'Me and Gal slept in the lounge. Drinking a bit early, ain't ya, girl?'

Shooing the dogs out of the kitchen so they didn't cut their paws, Frankie looked at Ricky with pleading eyes. 'Look, I'm meeting a boy and I don't want Mum and Dad to know. Can you clean that mess up for me? I'm running late.'

'What's going on? Was something smashed?' Jessica shouted out from upstairs.

Ricky smiled at Frankie. 'Sorry, Jess, it was me. I went to make a coffee and knocked a bottle of vodka off the kitchen top. You go back to bed, I'll clean it up.'

Frankie hugged her half-brother.

'Do you wanna lift?' he asked her.

'No, I'm fine. Thanks Ricky, you've just saved my life.'

As Frankie ran down the drive, she nervously glanced back at the house. She usually got cabs wherever she went and prayed that no one was watching her.

Frankie's heart leaped as she heard a loud tooting coming from behind her. She was afraid to look around. Surely it wasn't her dad?

Aware of a gold four-wheel drive pulling up beside her, she glanced apprehensively at it.

'Get in, Frankie,' Jed ordered her.

Frankie did as he asked. 'Sod you, you frightened the bloody life out of me. Whose car's this? Where's your pick-up truck?'

'At home. Can't take a beautiful girl out in a pick-up truck, can I? This Shogun's mine as well. Bought it off some old mush me dad knows. Got it for a good price, I did.'

Frankie was impressed. None of the boys she had ever mixed with could even reach the pedals on a motor like this, let alone own one or drive one. 'Where are we going?' Frankie asked, trying to sound relaxed.

'Cambridgeshire,' Jed replied coolly.

Frankie looked at him amazement. He had to be joking, surely. She didn't even know where Cambridgeshire was, but it sounded a long way away. 'You are having a laugh, aren't you?'

Jed stopped at the red traffic light. He leaned towards her and softly kissed her on the lips. 'No, I'm not having a laugh. It's where my family comes from. You'll love it. It's absolutely beautiful, Frankie, just like you are.'

As his piercing green eyes gently teased her, Frankie looked away. The effect he had on her was abnormal and she barely knew what day it was.

'I'm just gonna fill up with diesel. You want anything to eat or drink?' Jed asked her.

Frankie shook her head. Sod the food and drink, all she wanted was him.

Eddie, Gary and Ricky did most of the tidying up. 'You have a break, Jess, we'll do all the dirty work and you can add your magic touch at the end,' Eddie insisted.

With her mind in no-man's-land, Jessica politely asked her parents if they would mind if they didn't stay for dinner.

'Of course not. We know you're not yourself, love,' Stanley said kindly.

Joyce wasn't so understanding. She loved being in this nice big house and was in no rush to head back to her

321

own rabbit hutch. 'Me and your dad will stay here, Jess. You have a lie down. I'll cook the dinner today.'

Jessica blatantly refused. She had enough problems without having her mother driving her bloody mad. 'Look, I'm sorry, Mum, but go home, please. I'm really not up to it today. You can come over again next week, and I'll do you dinner then.'

Annoyed, Joyce stomped upstairs to pack her overnight bag. 'I've got no meat out the freezer, so me and you will have to starve, Stanley,' she shouted loudly.

Stanley hugged his daughter. 'Take no notice. You know what she's like.'

The drive to Cambridgeshire didn't take as long as Frankie thought it would. Jed took her down by the Fens and showed her where his dad and grandfather had both been brought up.

'I really miss my grandad. He was a good old boy,' Jed said, urging Frankie to sit down next to him. He wondered if she knew that her grandad had shot his grandad, but he said nothing. He didn't want to pry, unsettle her; it wasn't the done thing.

Frankie sat with her back against the bark of the tree and smiled. 'It is lovely here. It's so peaceful,' she said.

Telling Frankie to lie across his knees, Jed ran his fingers through her hair. 'We can live here one day. Imagine, me, you and our chavvies. It would be proper, wouldn't it?'

'What's a chavvie?' Frankie asked him.

'Kiddies. Our babies,' Jed said, laughing.

Wrapping her arms around his neck, Frankie pulled him towards her and kissed him passionately.

'No trying it on with me and don't you dare touch me cory. I'm not that type of boy, you know,' Jed said teasing her.

322

Frankie giggled. 'Is your cory what I think it is?'

Jed pointed at his erection. 'It's a big cory, ain't it? Ere cacker, I'm sorry about trying it on with you the other night. Them Es make me horny, I shouldn't have done that. I was out of order.'

As Jed took her in his arms, Frankie clung to him for dear life. He had a wonderful smell, a manly aroma, and she couldn't get enough of him.

Jed stood up and grabbed her by the hand. 'Come on, before I get overexcited. Let's go to a pub, I'll buy you a roast dinner.'

Joey was still in bed and Jessica was desperate for time alone with him. 'Ed, you and the boys have worked so hard this morning. Take Gary and Ricky to the pub and buy them a few beers. Go on, I insist.'

Eddie put an arm around Jessica's shoulder. 'This is the type of woman you wanna end up with, lads. She's one in a million,' he said proudly.

Gary laughed. 'Come on Dad, quick, before she changes her mind.'

As soon as the men had left the house, Jessica took a deep breath and went upstairs. 'Joey, wake up love,' she said, as she knocked and then entered her son's bedroom.

'All right, Mum? What's the time?' Joey mumbled, his eyes still half shut.

'It's gone one. Can I have a little chat with you, darling?'

The seriousness of his mum's voice made Joey's eyes open wide. 'What's the matter? Has something happened? Where's Frankie?'

Jessica sat on his bed and clutched his hand. 'Nothing's wrong. Frankie's gone out with her friends. You dad's not in, he's up the pub and Nanny and Grandad have gone home. It's just me and you, Joey, and we need to have a little talk, love.'

Joey wasn't silly. He sat himself up. She knew; he knew that she knew. 'What about, Mum?' he asked nervously.

Jessica smiled. 'About you and Dominic. About what's going on.'

Joey tore his eyes away from her. What was he meant to say. It was embarrassing. He could talk to Frankie about his sexuality, but not his mum.

Understanding his dilemma, Jessica spoke softly to him. 'It's OK. I'm not annoyed. Whatever you are, or might be, is fine by me. I love you, Joey, you're my son, and I'll always love you, no matter what.'

Shocked by his mum's understanding attitude, Joey's lip wobbled, then the tears came. 'I'm really sorry, Mum. I've tried to like girls, but I can't. I've always known I liked boys, ever since I was little. Even when I was about nine or ten, I remember fancying that bloke out of *The Dukes of Hazzard*,' he admitted.

'Sssh, it's all right, baby. Don't cry, Joey, please, or you'll make me cry, too.' Jessica handed him a tissue. 'So how long have you been seeing this Dominic? Is it serious between you? Or it is just casual?'

'We haven't been seeing one another long. I really like him, though, Mum. It's the first proper relationship I've had. I'm not going through a phase, I know I'm not.'

Jessica smiled. 'And Dominic likes you, too. That's how I found out, I saw the way you were with one another yesterday. It reminded me of how me and your dad were when we first got together.'

Joey gave a half-smile. 'You and Dad are still like that now. So, Frankie never told you, then?' he asked.

'No. I did ask her earlier, but she denied all knowledge. I take it that she knows?'

324

Joey smiled. 'She's the only one who does know. I haven't told anyone else, I swear I haven't.'

Tilting Joey's chin towards her, Jessica stared into his eyes. 'Now listen, my darling, and listen carefully. You must never bring Dominic to the house again and you must never go out with him around this area. If anyone finds out, Dad will lose the plot. Where does Dominic live?'

'The Angel, Islington,'

'Well, from now on, you'll have to meet him where he lives or somewhere miles away from here.'

Joey nodded. 'What will happen in the long run, though, Mum? I mean, if we stay together, I can't keep Dominic a secret for ever, can I?'

'You can and you will, Joey. You have to, you have no choice. Believe me, son, if your dad finds out, he will not accept it, not in a million years.'

Feeling anxious, Joey squeezed his mother's hand. 'Be truthful with me, Mum. Please don't lie. If Dad did find out, what do you think he would do to me?'

Jessica felt her eyes well up. 'My guess would be, he'd disown you. As for Dominic – remember, your dad's got a temper. Who knows that he might do to him? Your guess is as good as mine, Joey.'

THIRTY-ONE

The following morning, Jessica felt under the weather, so Eddie offered to run the kids to school.

'You look peaky. Stay in bed. I've gotta go out anyway. Dad's solicitor rang me, he wants to see me urgently and I promised Auntie Joan I'd take her shopping. Her old legs are playing her up a bit, bless her heart.'

'Thanks, Ed,' Jessica mumbled, as she ran to the toilet to be sick.

Joey poked his head around Frankie's bedroom door. His sister had got in late the previous evening and she knew nothing about the conversation with his mum. 'Take some normal clothes in your bag. I need to talk to you. Let's bin school today and go to the pub instead. We'll just tell Mum we got our days mixed up and thought we didn't have to go in,' he whispered.

Frankie smiled as she stuffed her jeans and T-shirt into her school bag. Thinking of Jed, she tucked her mobile phone in as well. She would ring him later and, if he wasn't busy, maybe they could meet up again.

Eddie dropped the twins off at school and headed straight towards Whitechapel. He had arranged to meet his dad's solicitor at two o'clock, so had plenty of time to take Joan shopping beforehand.

326

'Eddie! Come in, boy. I've made you a nice bread pudding, your favourite.'

Eddie kissed her. Joan was looking ever so old and frail these days. Making a mental note to visit her more often, he followed his aunt into the kitchen. 'So how's tricks? What you been up to?' he asked.

'Not a lot, love. Don't get out much now, to be honest. So many muggings and stuff round here now. Old Maisy Miller got followed into the post office and had her pension snatched last week. Three blacks it was. Wicked bastards they are. We should never have let 'em into the country, you know.'

Realising she was about to get on to the famous Enoch Powell speech, Eddie cleverly changed the subject. 'How's that mate of yours doing now, Auntie? Molly something or other. You know, the one whose son was giving her grief?'

'Molly Jenkins, you mean. Yeah, she's fine. Keeps well away from her now, her Michael. Had an unfortunate accident, he did. Rumour has it, he got beaten up and lost his thumb in the process. Makes you wonder if someone knew what he was doing to his poor old mum, doesn't it?' Joan said, with a twinkle in her eye. She wasn't stupid. She had known when she told Eddie about Molly that Michael would soon experience a nasty little accident of some kind.

As the kettle on the stove began to whistle, Eddie smiled. 'When I take you shopping, I'll buy you a new kettle, Auntie, something a bit more modern.'

'No, you won't. Nothing wrong with this one. The tea don't taste the same when the water's boiled by them bleeding electric things. Tastes like fucking rat's piss, it does.'

Eddie chuckled. Joan might be looking old and frail, but she certainly hadn't lost her spirit.

* * *

327

Frankie and Joey sat at a corner table in the Albion. 'So, is that it? Didn't she say anything else?' Frankie asked, amazed.

Joey shook his head. He had just been telling his sister about the chat he'd had with his mum the previous day. 'She just said that Dom must never come to the house again and not to meet him in Rainham any more. She said I'd be better seeing him in Islington.'

Frankie smiled. 'Well at least you ain't gotta worry about Mum finding out any more. One down, one to go, eh? When you gonna tell Dad?'

'Don't take the piss, Frankie, it's not a bloody joke,' Joey said, annoyed.

Frankie went up to the bar to get some more drinks. As she returned, Joey turned the tables.

'Well, what about you then? Where was you all day yesterday? Sucking Johnny-Wonny's cock, was we?' he asked her.

Desperate to unload the burden of who she was really seeing, Frankie leaned towards him. 'If I tell you something, Joey, you must promise me that you'll never breathe a word to anyone. Not even Mum must know this.'

Joey was intrigued. 'Go on,' he urged his sister.

'John ain't who I said he is. His name's Jed and I didn't wanna tell you because he's Jimmy O'Hara's son.'

Astonished, Joey stared at her and waited for her to laugh. It was a joke, surely – it had to be.

'Well, say something then,' Frankie urged.

Realising Frankie wasn't mucking about, Joey shook his head. 'Ain't that the boy who beat me up when I was little?'

'Don't be a drama queen, Joey. He didn't beat you up. I'm sure Nan or Grandad told me once that Dad forced you get into a boxing ring with him. It wasn't Jed's

328

fault, you were both little kids. It was Dad's fault if it was anyone's.'

Joey didn't know an awful lot about his father's business, but one thing he did know was there was a long-running feud between the O'Haras and his family. 'Frankie, you've gotta stop seeing him. Dad will go mental – he'll kill you if he finds out.'

Frankie shrugged. 'Well, he'll kill you if he finds out about Dominic, won't he? At least we'll both be dead, eh?'

Joey sipped his drink. 'It can't be serious, you only met Jed on Friday. Why don't you just nip it in the bud while you still can. You're a pretty girl, Frankie, there's plenty of other boys to choose from.'

Frankie shook her head vehemently. 'I don't want any other boy, I want Jed. I spent the whole day with him yesterday and it was fantastic. I know I ain't known him long, but I love him, Joey, I know I do.'

Knowing how strong-minded Frankie was, Joey nodded dumbly. She had always stuck by him. She had accepted his sexuality and accepted Dominic. 'Look, Frankie, I'm your brother and I love you. If this Jed makes you happy, then I'm happy for you.'

Frankie pulled her phone out of her bag. 'If I ring him and tell him to come down here, will you mind? I really want yous two to get on. Jed's brilliant, honest, he's a scream and I know you'll just love him, Joey.'

Joey nodded. 'Love him' was a bit strong. He had already met Jed on Friday night and wasn't over impressed by what he saw. 'Was it him that gave you that E, Frankie?' Joey asked.

'No. I got it off someone in the Berwick. Please don't start with all the questions, Joey. You won't get on with him if you start accusing him of things he hasn't done.'

Frankie put the phone to her ear. 'Jed, it's me. What you up to? I'm in the Albion.'

Joey guessed by the big grin that spread across his sister's face that Jed was coming to meet them.

After being dragged around the supermarket by his aunt, Eddie dropped her off and headed to Wanstead. His dad's solicitor, Larry, had been a friend of the family for years. As bent as a nine-bob note, Larry knew every trick in the book and was the perfect brief for anybody not quite legit.

Walking into the restaurant, Eddie asked the waiter if Larry had arrived yet. 'No sir, but your table's ready. Would you like to sit down or have a drink at the bar?'

Eddie ordered a drink and sat at the table. Larry had attended his dad's funeral, but had then sodded off on a three-month cruise. 'Look, there's no rush. We'll sort me old man's estate out when you get back,' Eddie had told him.

Unbeknown to Eddie, his dad had paid for the cruise and ordered Larry to book it as and when he died. Harry's orders were, 'Don't let Eddie know immediately. Leave it three to six months, at least.'

'Eddie, how are you? Any news yet? Larry asked him as he sat down opposite.

Shaking his head, Eddie shouted for a bottle of champagne to be brought over. 'No news at all. Fucking useless, the filth are. They couldn't catch a cold, the cunts. I'm gonna start rooting around meself again, see if I can do a better job. I've asked around the under- world, but no one's heard a dickie. It's a mystery, Lal, it really is.'

Feeling a bit melancholy, Larry quickly changed the subject. He had liked Harry Mitchell very much. He was

330

one of life's characters. His death was an awful shock and Larry hated talking or thinking about it.

Eddie studied the menu.

'The lobster's good in here,' Larry told him.

Eddie ordered them both lobster and sipped his champagne. His father had always told him that he hadn't bothered making a will. 'What's the point? I've got three sons and it will all be split equally. I know you'll look after Reg and Joanie for me and I want the grandkids to be seen all right,' Harry had instructed Eddie.

Bored with listening about Larry's holiday, Eddie spoke bluntly. 'So, have you found out what the old man's estate was worth?'

'I sure have. All in all, including the house your dad was living in, it's worth around the three-million-pound mark.'

Eddie didn't bat an eyelid. The old man had always had an eye for a pound note and three mill didn't shock him at all. In fact, knowing his dad, he wouldn't be surprised if there was more. When he was a kid, he had once caught his dad digging a hole and putting big silver tins in it. 'What's that, Dad?' he'd asked innocently.

'Money, son. Never let the authorities know what you've got. Always bury the bastard. You might not understand now, Eddie, but you will one day, when you're older,' was his dad's reply.

'You don't seem very shocked, Eddie. I mean, considering the size of the house your dad lived in, it's a rather large amount, don't you think?'

'The old man could have bought a big fuck-off mansion years ago, Lal. If I had a pound for every time I tried to persuade him to move, I'd be the richest man in England. He would never leave that house in Canning Town because

331

me mother had lived there with him. Said it made him feel close to her, he did. When he got murdered that night, do you know what the bastards did? Dad kept the house as a shrine to Mum. Whoever done him in smashed every photo he had of her, and Paulie reckons they even took a couple as souvenirs. That's what makes me think it wasn't kids. I'll catch whoever it was one day, Lal, and I swear on my parents' grave, I will fucking kill 'em with me bare hands.'

Over in Rainham, Joey felt uncomfortable as his sister and Jed behaved like the lovesick teenagers they were. He had never really seen his sister kiss a boy before, and watching Jed stick his tongue down her throat was making him shudder. 'Are we ready to order?' he asked, agitated.

Jed laughed. 'You're not jealous, are ya? Don't wanna kiss me yourself, do ya?'

Joey looked at Frankie in horror. Surely she hadn't told him.

Jed stood up. 'I'll go and get another round of drinks and order some food,' he said.

'You ain't fucking told him, have you?' Joey spat at Frankie.

'Of course not, you idiot. He asked if you and Dominic were at it the other night and I denied it. I told him you've had loads of girlfriends. He's just mucking about with you, 'cause you shared the room with Dom.'

'If you ever tell him, I will never speak to you again,' Joey hissed.

Jed swaggered back to the table. 'I ordered about ten different dishes. You can just take your pick,' he said, laughing.

Frankie thought Jed was joking until the barmaid kept

coming up with plates of food. 'Why did you buy all this? It's such a waste of money,' she told Jed.

Jed put his arm around her shoulder and gave her a penetrating stare. 'You didn't know what you wanted, so I bought you the lot. Anyway, I've got loads of wonga. Next weekend, I'll take you shopping and buy you some gold. Whaddya want? Earrings? Bracelet? A chain? I'll even buy you a diamond if you want one.'

About to eat a chip, Joey clocked his sister's gooey expression. She was putting him off his lunch. In fact, he felt physically sick. As the happy couple locked tongues once more, he voiced his opinion. 'You're so embarrassing – the whole pub is looking at us. Instead of mauling one another in public, go and get a fucking room.'

Back in Wanstead, Larry savoured the last mouthful of lobster and wiped his mouth with a serviette. He waited for Eddie to finish his meal, then cleared his throat. 'The reason I asked you to meet me here today is because I have something to tell you, Eddie.'

Delving into the inside pocket of his jacket, Larry handed him a letter. 'Your dad gave me strict instructions that you were to read this. He told me to leave it a certain length of time before I gave it to you. I need to pop outside to make a few phone calls, so I'll leave you alone for a few minutes.'

Eddie tore the letter open. His dad's handwriting had never been the best and he hoped he could understand the bastard thing. As luck would have it, it was typed.

Dear Eddie,
Obviously, if you're reading this, it means I've popped me clogs. Sorry if this letter feels like

333

I've come back to haunt you, but there are a few things I need to tell you, son.

Firstly, I want to tell you how much I love you and how proud I am of you. Paulie and Ronny never quite made the grade and, even from an early age, I knew you were gonna be the star of the show. You didn't let me down. Everything I had worked so hard for, you improved on, and that pleased me more than you'll ever know. You may wonder why I'm telling you this, now I'm brown bread, but I couldn't say it while I was alive. I was never very good with words and, apart from when I was with your mother, I've never been able to show my feelings.

Aware of getting emotional, Eddie paused and took a sip of his drink. He took a deep breath, then continued to read.

The second thing I want to say to you son, is don't end up alone. You and Jessica are the equivalent of me and your mum. Look after her, boy, and don't ever let her down.

Thirdly, I have some instructions for you. Dig about six-foot deep under the apple tree at the bottom of my garden and you'll find plenty of hidden treasure. I want you to keep this to yourself. Don't tell your brothers or anyone, as it's all meant for you.

Last, but not least, I made a will in 1987. I've left a substantial amount for Paulie, Ronny, Gary and Ricky, but the bulk I've left to you. You're the only one I can trust to do the right thing with it, Eddie, and I want you to look after the following people for me:

Reg
Auntie Joan
Auntie Vi
Sylvie (she was a good friend to me)
all the grandchildren
Uncle Albert
Raymondo
and John (from the Flag)

Make sure all me old neighbours are OK, Ed. Especially old Iris next door and Cyril Miller over the road. (Them two ain't got a pot to piss in, bless 'em.)

Well, that's about it, son. You look after yourself now and make sure you look after that wonderful family of yours.

Love always, Dad

P.S. Hopefully, Ed, my death was a quick heart attack in the Flag or I croaked it in my sleep. If by any chance it wasn't natural and some bastard took me out, I put my trust in you to get revenge for me.

With tears streaming down his face, Eddie kissed the piece of paper and put it in his pocket. 'I will, Dad, I promise,' he whispered.

THIRTY-TWO

Eddie instructed Larry to inform his brothers of his father's wishes. He then sat back and waited for the inevitable fall out.

It was Ronny who rang first. 'A hundred fucking grand! That's all me and Paulie have been left. It ain't fair, Ed, we know he's fucking left it all to you. You're some snake in the grass, you are, ain't ya?'

Eddie did his best to calm his brother down. 'Look, none of this is my fault, Ronny. I didn't even know Dad had made a will.'

Ronny was spitting feathers. 'Didn't know! Don't lie to me, you cunt. I bet the two of yous cooked it up between you. What about his house? He left you that and all, has he? There's me ended up in a fucking wheelchair because of him and you're the one reaping the rewards.'

Not wanting to have this conversation over the phone, Eddie told Ronny that he would meet him and Paulie later that evening in the Flag.

'Cunt!' Ronny screamed as he slammed the phone down.

Guessing what the phone conversation was all about, Jessica wrapped her arms around her husband's toned waist. Harry's wealth and generosity had been a shock to her, but she was thrilled for Eddie and the children's sake. 'You won't have to work so much now. Why don't you stop doing what you're doing, Ed? I'm always afraid that one day you might not come home again. With all that money, you can set up a legitimate business. If you get someone else to run it for you, you can spend more time with me and the kids,' she told him.

Eddie waved away her fears. 'No one's gonna hurt me, Jess. Anyway, I like what I do and I'm not a man who can sit on his arse all day. The kids are all grown up now and me and you spend every weekend together as it is.'

Kissing his wife on the forehead, Eddie gently released her arms from around his waist. 'I'll probably be home late tonight, babe. I've got some business to attend to with Raymond and I've gotta face the wrath of Pinky and Perky down at the Flag.'

Eddie's humour never failed to make Jessica smile. 'Love you,' she shouted, as he closed the front door.

Hearing their father's car pull off the drive, Joey and Frankie came downstairs. Their exams had now started and, as neither of them were taking very many, they only had to attend school on certain days.

'Yous two are all glammed up. Where you off to today?' Jessica asked them.

'Southend,' the twins replied in unison.

Jessica smiled. She loved the hustle and bustle of Southend on a sunny day. When she was young, her mum and dad used to take her and Raymond there for a day trip. 'Now be careful. Are you going with all your friends? How are you getting there?'

'There's a big crowd of us going, Mum. We're all travelling together by train, so we'll be fine. I'll look after Frankie,' Joey said reassuringly.

Jessica smiled. Joey was such a sensible boy. She had

now got over the initial shock of his little secret, and loved him more than ever. A beautiful person inside, he was just different, that was all.

'Do you need any money?' Jessica asked. She had forbidden Eddie to tell the twins about his windfall. They were leaving school soon and she wanted them to get a job and make their own way in life.

'We don't need no money, Mum. We've got a load left from our birthday,' Frankie replied honestly.

As the cab tooted outside, Jessica gave them both a kiss. 'Don't forget to bring me back a stick of rock,' she shouted as she waved them off.

Shutting the front door, Jessica sighed. She had been desperate for some time alone all morning. Riffling through her handbag, she found the pregnancy test. Three mornings in a row she had been as sick as a dog. At first, she had thought it was the shock of finding out about Joey, but now she wasn't so sure. Jessica took the white stick out of the box and studied the instructions. When she was pregnant with the twins, this type of technology probably hadn't even existed.

Realising that the test only took five minutes, Jessica smiled. The quicker she got the answer she wanted so badly wanted, the better.

'Oi, oi!' Jed shouted, as he picked up Frankie in the lay-by near his house.

Frankie smiled as she got in his red pick-up truck. 'Where's your Shogun?' she asked him.

'Me dad's got to drive up north. His motor's been playing up, so he borrowed mine.'

Cupping Frankie's face with his hands, Jed gently kissed her. 'Whaddya wanna do today then?'

Lying to her mum had given Frankie ideas. 'Can we

338

go to Southend? I haven't been there for ages and it's a lovely day for the seaside.'

Jed laughed at her way with words. 'I'd take you to the moon and back if you asked me to, Frankie.'

With the help of Raymond and a JCB, Eddie set to work at digging up his dad's garden. Apart from Jessica and her brother, Eddie hadn't told a soul about his dad's letter and its contents.

'You all right, boys? I've got some cold Guinness in the fridge if you want one,' shouted Iris from next door.

Sweating his cobbs off, Eddie gratefully accepted her offer.

'Your turn, Raymond, I'm fucked,' he said.

Eddie had thought it would only take a couple of hours to find what he was looking for. He had been wrong. The ground was rock hard and the digger he had borrowed was pony.

'Thanks, Iris,' Eddie said, as he grabbed the two cold cans.

'Why you digging up the apple tree?' Iris asked nosily.

'Me dad planted it for me mum when she was alive. He always said to me, "When I die, son, I want you to dig up the tree and replant it in your own garden,"' Eddie lied.

He had concocted the story earlier. 'If any of the neighbours ask, we're digging up the tree and replanting it at mine. After we've found what we're looking for, I'll ring up Davey Brown, get him to pick it up and dump it somewhere for us,' Eddie told Raymond.

'It will die if you dig up its roots. It won't grow properly again,' Iris said suspiciously.

Eddie smiled. 'It was me dad's final wish, so I'll do me best to save it,' he assured her.

*   *   *

339

In the trendy Liverpool Street wine bar, Joey smiled as Dominic excused himself to make an important phone call. Joey had come up to meet him for lunch and his boyfriend was taking the rest of the afternoon off so they could spend some time together.

As Dominic returned to the table, he tenderly rubbed Joey's leg. 'I've just booked us a posh hotel for the afternoon,' he said, as he brushed his hand teasingly over Joey's thigh.

Thrilled that he was in an area where nobody knew him and he could be himself, Joey squeezed Dominic's hand. 'Let's finish our drinks and go there now,' he said excitedly.

Standing not twenty feet away was an extremely interested spectator. Darren Palmer was the son of one of Ronny Mitchell's friends. He recognised Joey, knew exactly who he was – they had been at junior school together. He also knew who Dominic was, as his mate worked with him in the City and referred to him as the bum boy. Watching the two queers walk out of the pub, Darren almost flew to the phone box.

''Ere, Dad, you'll never guess who I've just seen. Eddie Mitchell's son, Joey, was all over some bender called Dominic. They were virtually at it in the pub – they were fondling and all sorts.'

As they ended the call, Terry Palmer couldn't stop smiling. He had never liked that flash bastard, Eddie Mitchell. Paulie and Ronny were good lads, but Eddie was too far shoved up his own arse. Joey Mitchell, a poofta. Whoever would have thought it, eh? You just couldn't make it up!

Punching in Ronny Mitchell's number on his mobile, Terry Palmer could barely speak through laughing.

* * *

Southend was heaving with people and Frankie wished she had suggested somewhere else.

'What's up? Not bored with me already, are ya?' Jed teased, knowing full well she wasn't.

Frankie smiled. They had played in the amusement arcades, strolled along the beach, eaten fish and chips and Jed had even won a big teddy bear for her, which they were carrying with them. 'Shall we go somewhere quieter, where we can be alone?' Frankie asked him.

'We can get some booze and I'll book us a room, if you like,' Jed suggested.

Desperate to get intimate with him, Frankie grinned. 'I'd like that Jed, I really would.'

Unable to lift the large silver chest, Eddie urged Raymond to give him a hand.

'Christ almighty! It looks like something out of *Gulliver's Travels* – the bastard thing's fucking heavy,' Raymond moaned.

'Quick, cover it over with them sacks,' Eddie ordered, as he spotted Iris in her garden again.

Lugging it into his father's house, Eddie noticed the nosy old cow peering over the fence. 'Just clearing up all the branches, Iris,' he shouted.

Once inside the house, Eddie flicked the lid of the chest open.

'Well, fuck me,' Raymond said, looking at Eddie in astonishment.

Lifting the guns out one by one, Eddie studied them. Hand, machine, shot: there was every gun going. He stared at the jewellery. Sovereigns, ingots, rings, chains: there were hundreds of different pieces.

Raymond picked up a black velvet bag and opened it. 'Jesus, Ed, you've got a load of diamonds 'ere, mate.'

Eddie smiled. His old man was a wily old bastard and he didn't know whether to laugh or cry. 'Pick out something for yourself, Ray, and take something nice for Polly.'

Raymond shook his head. 'They're yours mate, don't be silly. I don't want nothing.'

'Take it, Ray. Me old man wanted you to have something, I know he did,' Eddie insisted.

Knowing how forceful Eddie could be, Raymond picked out a pretty ring for Polly and a chunky one for himself. He put them in his pocket and turned to Eddie. 'What you gonna do with the guns? You can't leave 'em here.'

Eddie shrugged. 'I'll take the diamonds and jewellery home and put them in the safe. The guns can be hidden down the salvage yard for now. Let's shoot straight there. We can come back here tomorrow and tidy stuff up. I've gotta come back anyway; I wanna ask around, see if anyone's got any more information about Dad's murder.'

'What shall we do about the digger? Have you gotta take it back today?'

Looking at his watch, Eddie cursed. He had told Ronny he would meet him and Paulie at seven and it was already six o'clock. 'The digger's fine, it can stay here till tomorrow. I think I'm gonna ring Paulie and Ronny and meet 'em tomorrow instead. If we clean up here in the morning, it'll give us plenty of time to talk to the neighbours, then we'll go to the Flag after that.'

Raymond agreed.

'I'll tell you what. I dunno about you, but I could kill a couple of beers. Why don't we drop the guns off, then stop at a boozer where no one knows us?' Eddie suggested.

Raymond laughed. 'We could walk into a boozer in Timbuktu and people would know us, Ed.'

Eddie chuckled. 'Come on you tosser, help me get this chest in the motor.'

Frankie laughed as Jed pressed the 'play' button. He was such a sod. In the hotel reception, he had seen a girl carrying a tape recorder. 'Oi, pretty lady, let me buy that off you,' he'd said.

The girl had looked at Jed in amazement. 'It's only a cheap one,' she'd replied.

'How much do ya want for it?' Jed had asked.

'I don't really want to sell it,' the girl had said.

Jed had put his hand in his pocket and waved some money in her face. ''Ere you go. Take fifty quid for it.'

The girl had snatched the money, handed him the battered old tape recorder and disappeared before Jed could change his mind. Jed had then gone outside to his truck and reappeared with a selection of cassettes, which they were now playing.

'Why did you pay all that money for this rubbish?' Frankie asked him. She loved it really. Jed was so impulsive, and the way he was filled her with intense excitement.

''Cause I didn't want you to be bored. You don't wanna be stuck in a room all day with no music, do ya? My old tape recorder's fucked. Dropped it on the floor, I did, and now it won't work any more.'

Frankie smiled. Christ knows where Jed got all his money from. He had plenty and chucked it about like there was no tomorrow. 'Do you mind if I ask you something?'

'Ask away,' Jed replied, grabbing her hand.

'Where do you get all your money from? Does your dad give it to you or do you sometimes go to work?'

Jed turned the music up, took Frankie in his arms and made her dance with him. 'I never went to school. Been

343

working since I was eight years old. I'll never be poor, I can turn me hand to lots of things.'

'Like what?'

'I sell horses, motors, caravans, diggers. You name it, I can get it and sell it. I'll be cakeo one day, Frankie. You stick with me and you'll be rich as well.'

Frankie tightened her grip on him. 'What is this rubbish music? Ain't you got any acid house?' she asked him.

Jed tilted her chin towards his. 'Who needs all that house music crap when you've got country and western? That shit's only all right if you stick a pill down your throat, but country music is proper. You listen to the words. Every song tells a story, Frankie.'

Frankie listened and by the time Tammy Wynette had reached the chorus of 'Stand By Your Man', she and Jed were in bed together.

Unaware of what his daughter was up to, Eddie was on his way home. 'I won't be long, darling. I've just gotta drop Raymondo off first. I'll be about fifteen minutes,' he told Jess.

Jessica ended the call. Grinning, she put Eddie's dinner in the oven. She had been doing buttons all day waiting for her husband to get home. Desperate to tell someone her news, Jessica had rang Vicki and told her. 'Please don't say a word to Doug. I only found out this morning and I haven't had a chance to tell Eddie yet,' she begged.

Vicki was thrilled for herself and her friend. She was over five months now, and it was great that she and Jess would both be mums together.

As the Guns N' Roses song was played on the radio, Jessica turned it up full blast. She wasn't usually a fan of rock music, but the song was called 'Sweet Child O' Mine', and Jess couldn't resist joining in with the chorus.

Back in Southend, Jed was having trouble inserting his penis inside Frankie. 'Are you OK?' he whispered as he finally entered her.

'I'm fine,' Frankie lied. She felt as if her insides were being ripped to shreds.

'I love you, Frankie,' Jed told her as his movements got faster and faster.

'I love you, too,' Frankie replied, wincing.

Suddenly he made a groaning noise and rolled off her. 'What's up? Have I done something wrong?' she asked, concerned.

Propping himself up on his elbow, Jed rubbed her clit with his finger. 'Nothing's up. I've already come, you dinlo,' he said laughing.

As Frankie's breathing started to quicken, Jed moved his finger faster and faster. 'Ahh, Jed,' Frankie panted, as she grabbed his head with both hands. This felt nice, much more pleasurable than him being inside her. She reached her orgasm, yanking his head.

'Fucking hell. You nearly broke me neck,' Jed teased.

Frankie let out a happy sigh. She really had found the man of her dreams.

Hearing Eddie's car pull up on the gravel, Jessica flung open the front door.

'What's this, a welcome committee?' Eddie joked.

Jessica took his hand and dragged him into the lounge. She handed him the glass of champagne she'd already poured and told him to sit down and drink it.

As Buster and Bruno bounded into the room, Jessica shooed them out. This was her and Eddie's moment.

'What's occurring?' Eddie asked. He had sort of already guessed, but didn't want to spoil her plans to tell him herself.

'You'll never guess what I found out today,' Jessica said excitedly.

'I've no idea,' Eddie lied.

'I'm pregnant, Eddie. We're having that baby,' Jessica screamed.

Still caked in mud from earlier, Eddie stood up and lifted her into his arms. 'I love you so much, Jessica Mitchell. I really, really do.'

THIRTY-THREE

At seven o'clock the following evening, Eddie and Raymond pulled up outside the Flag in Canning Town.

Eddie had asked around half the neighbourhood earlier but, apart from what he already knew, no one had any more information about the night his dad died. Frustrated by the lack of progress he'd made, Eddie wasn't in the best of moods.

'There must have been bangs, crashes and fucking screams. Me poor fucking dad was tortured. Some cunt must have heard something, surely,' he said to Raymond.

Raymond shrugged. He had no answers. Poor old Harry's death was a complete mystery to all and sundry.

'How's Jess?' Raymond asked, changing the subject.

The mention of his wife's name lifted Eddie's mood. Jessica had told him to keep her pregnancy quiet until she had seen her doctor and knew how far gone she was. She didn't even want the twins or her parents to know just yet. Desperate to tell at least one person, Eddie smiled.

'Keep it to yourself, but we're gonna be parents again. Found out yesterday, Jess did. She's over the bloody moon; we both are.'

Thrilled at the prospect of becoming an uncle once more, Raymond grabbed Eddie around the neck with his right arm. 'You're a dark horse, you are. I'm surprised at your age you can still get it up, you cunt.'

Laughing, Eddie pushed him away. 'Remember, not a word to anyone. Jess ain't told your mum and dad yet, so don't put your foot in it, for fuck's sake.'

Paulie and Ronny were sitting at their usual table. Both had faces like smacked arses. As Eddie walked in, he heard a few sniggers. He took no notice, walked up to the bar and ordered himself and Raymond a drink.

'What you having?' he shouted over to his brothers.

'Are you sure you can afford it?' Ronny asked sarcastically.

Eddie sat down and tried to make the two of them see sense. 'Look, I know you're both upset, but I'll always see you all right. If you need any money, just ask me and I'll give it to you. Dad left me strict instructions: he wants me to look after a few people, make sure they're comfortable. He left me the bulk, 'cause he knew he could trust me to carry out his wishes.'

'You're a lying cunt. Don't take me and Paulie for mugs. You can stick your handouts where the sun don't shine,' Ronny spat at him.

Eddie turned to Paulie. He had always been the more sensible one out of the two. 'Is that your opinion as well, Paulie? Is it?'

Not able to hold Eddie's gaze, Paulie stared at his lap. 'I want out, Ed. I want out of the business and out of your life. We're meant to be brothers and all you've ever done is stitch me and Ronny up. Well, it's gone too far now. Me and Ronny have discussed things and neither of us want any more to do with you.'

Eddie looked at Paulie in amazement. He guessed that he might have a cob on, but he had never expected this. They had always worked together; how could he even

348

think of walking away? 'Don't be so childish, Paulie. Dad wouldn't have wanted this. We're Mitchells, we're meant to stick together. What do you wanna leave the firm for? It's stupid, I knew fuck-all about Dad's will. It was his wishes, not mine.'

Desperate to say his pre-planned speech, Ronny piped up. 'For years we've lived in your shadow, Ed. You were always the old man's favourite – you spent half your life licking his arse. Why should you dish out the orders, eh? What makes you so fucking special? Me and Paulie have had it with you. We're setting up on our own. We'll find our own clients and do a bit of sharking ourselves.'

Eddie looked at Ronny with contempt. As usual, his eyes were gone and his speech was slurred. Unable to stop himself, Eddie laughed in Ronny's face. 'Well, I wish you every success, Ronny. I'm sure people will be quaking in their boots when they're threatened to pay up by an alcoholic cripple.'

Overcome by jealousy and hatred, Ronny picked up an empty beer bottle and aimed it at Eddie's head. As the bottle brushed against his hair and whizzed past him, Eddie jumped up to retaliate.

'Leave him – he ain't worth it. Come on, Ed, let's get out of here,' Raymond said, holding Eddie back.

Sitting back down, Eddie looked at Paulie with pleading eyes. 'You're making a big mistake, bruv, you really are.'

As Paulie looked at the floor, Eddie shook his head, stood up and walked away.

Ronny called Eddie's name. He hadn't played his ace card yet and he was gagging to do so. 'Oh, and by the way, big man. Your son Joey's a fucking bum boy. Got a boyfriend, he has. Sucks cock and takes it up the arse regularly, by all accounts.'

As Eddie lunged at Ronny, the barmaid let out a

piercing scream. John, the guv'nor, was on holiday, and she didn't know how to deal with such violence.

Picking Ronny up by the neck, Eddie lifted him out of his wheelchair and threw him as hard as he could against the wall. 'You fucking lying cunt, I'm gonna kill you!' he shouted.

To save Ronny's sorry arse, Paulie and Raymond joined forces. When angry, Eddie was so strong he was almost impossible to control.

Eddie bent down and held Ronny around the throat as if to strangle him. 'How dare you fucking bring my kids into this, you cunt!' he screamed.

'It's true. Ask Terry Palmer. Ask his son. I'm not lying, Ed, I'm not,' Ronny said, choking. He was frightened now, really frightened.

Managing to pull Eddie away, Raymond dragged him outside the pub. 'Let's get out of here, mate. I think the barmaid's called the filth,' Ray told him.

Eddie said nothing. Chucking his keys at Raymond, he got in the passenger side and slammed the door. 'Are you OK?' Raymond asked him as they drove along in silence.

'No, I'm fucking ain't,' Eddie yelled. 'As for my so-called brothers, I hope they both rot in hell. I never wanna see either of them ever again!'

Jessica sat in the kitchen with a massive smile on her face. She and Vicki were discussing baby names and they had completely different ideas on the subject.

'Angel's a lovely name for a little girl,' Vicki insisted.

Giggling, Jessica put the kettle on. Eddie would have a fit if she called their kid Angel.

'I think you should opt for an American name if you have a boy. Me and Dougie quite like Troy, so what about you calling yours Travis?' Vicki suggested.

Jessica smiled. 'I've already promised Ed that if we have a boy, we'll call it Harry in memory of his dad.'

As the front door slammed, Jessica ran into the hallway. 'Oh, it's you, Ed. You're early, love. Do you want a cup of tea?'

'Where's Joey?' Eddie shouted.

Jessica's heart went over as she noticed that Eddie's face looked as black as thunder. She knew, without a doubt, that he had been told something. 'Vicki's in the kitchen,' she said, as brightly as she could.

'Get rid of her,' Eddie spat.

Jessica ushered her friend outside and apologised profusely.

'I wouldn't like to be in Joey's shoes. What's he done?' Vicki whispered.

'I bet he's been bunking off school again and Ed's just found out,' Jessica lied.

As she shut the front door, Jessica felt physically sick. She had to play it cool; it was her duty as a mother to protect her son. 'Whatever's the matter?' she asked Eddie.

'Where is he? Is he out with his fucking boyfriend, is he?' Eddie screamed, grabbing his wife by the shoulders.

'Boyfriend? What are you talking about? You're hurting me, Ed, stop it, please.'

Eddie let her go. Leaning with his back against the wall, he put his head in his hands and slumped to the floor. 'He's gay. Our Joey's a fucking queer, that's what the word on the street is. Do you know anything about it, Jess? If you do, tell me. I want the fucking truth.'

Jessica shook her head furiously and proclaimed her son's innocence. 'Don't be so ridiculous, Eddie. Our Joey's got a new girlfriend – he really likes her, he does. He was only telling me about her yesterday. He wants us to meet her. He asked me if she could come round for tea.'

'Are you sure he ain't fucking lying to you?' Eddie asked.

'Of course he's not lying. Someone's winding you up, Eddie. Who told you? Who's spreading these lies?'

'Ronny told me. Terry Palmer told him. Everyone's been told. As I walked in the Flag earlier, every bastard was sniggering at me.'

Jessica knelt in front of her devastated husband. 'How can you believe anything that comes out of Ronny's mouth? He's jealous of you, he always has been. He's making up these awful lies because he can't deal with your dad leaving you all that money. He wants to get back at you, Ed, and he'll resort to anything to do so.'

Eddie shrugged. 'I'll go and see Terry Palmer, see what he has to say. Don't look so worried, I ain't gonna hurt him. I just want solid proof.'

'It's all lies. I know my own son, Eddie,' Jessica insisted.

Eddie shrugged. Joey had always been different – too different for his liking. 'He is fucking effeminate, Jess. Let's face it, Joey's never been like Gary and Ricky, has he? Even as a kid, he was frightened of his own shadow. I mean, he dresses strange and sometimes I look at him and think that he should have been the girl and Frankie the boy. She's got bollocks, Frankie has, but not Joey. He's not normal, Jess, I've always known it, but I kept me trap shut for years for your fucking sake.'

With tears rolling down her cheeks, Jessica did her best to hold her own. 'Of course he's not like Gary and Ricky, or you and your brothers. I didn't want him to end up in your world, it was me that forced him to be different. I mean, come on, as much as I think the world of Gary and Ricky, their mum was an alkie, that's why they're rough around the edges. I brought Joey up differently. He's soft, gentle, with a heart of gold, and I instilled that into him. He might be unusual, but that doesn't mean he's gay, Ed. It's just different mothers, different upbringings, that's all.'

Holding out his arms, Eddie snuggled up to his wife. 'I'm sorry if I hurt you. I just lost me rag.'

'Promise me, Eddie, that you won't say anything to Joey. He's in the middle of his exams, it's not fair on him. You know how he takes things to heart – he'll be traumatised.'

'I swear I won't say anything to him,' Eddie said honestly. He had no intention of giving Joey a warning. If what was being said was true, he would catch him at it and when he did, he would throttle both him and his fucking boyfriend.

Terry Palmer lived alone in a council flat in Beckton. Terry had once been a man of substance, but since his wife had stung him for all he had, his life had gone completely downhill.

Opening another can of Special Brew, Terry focused on the television. He was watching the film *Once Upon a Time in America*. 'Go on, get in there,' Terry said, laughing.

Terry fancied himself as a Robert De Niro type. He and Rob were two of a kind, they sang from the same hymn sheet.

As the buzzer rang, Terry opened the security door automatically. His son, Darren, often stayed of a night, so he left the front door on the latch for him and sat back down. Engrossed in the bit where De Niro actually rapes the bird, Terry barely looked up as the front door closed. 'I'm starving – you brought any grub home with you, Dal?' he shouted out.

'The Chinese was shut, so I brought this round to fill you up,' Eddie whispered, as he yanked Terry's head back and stuck the barrel of a gun down the back of his throat.

Not knowing that her husband was currently playing cowboys and Indians, Jessica tried Joey's mobile number repeatedly. Eddie had popped out to take the dogs for a run and she desperately needed to warn her son. 'Please answer, son, please answer,' she prayed out loud.

Finally, God looked down on her.

'Whatever's wrong, Mum? Has something happened? I'm busy,' Joey exclaimed in annoyance.

Joey had just been having a bit of the other and the constant ringing of the phone was preventing him from reaching a climax.

'Joey, you need to come home right now, son. Your dad knows. Someone told him about Dominic. Now, don't worry, I've got you out of it, but I've told him you've got a new girlfriend. Ring up a girl mate and bring her round tomorrow for tea.'

Joey's hands shook so much he could barely hold the weight of his phone. 'Who am I gonna ring? Apart from Frankie's mates, I don't really mix with any girls.'

Jessica spoke forcefully to him. 'I don't care who you ring or who you know, Joey, but make sure you bring a girl round here tomorrow. I've just stuck my neck out for you and if your father finds out I'm lying, he'll throttle the pair of us.'

Joey stared at his penis. His erection had deflated so

much that it now resembled a burst balloon. 'OK, Mum, I'll find a girl. I'll do it,' he promised.

With eyes as wide as flying saucers, Terry Palmer tried to speak, but couldn't. The gun was hurting his throat and was choking him. Aware of his own urine running down his legs, he began to beg.

Eddie slowly withdrew the gun from Terry's throat. Smiling, he pointed it at his bollocks instead. 'You got something to tell me about my Joey, have you, Terry?'

Petrified, Terry shook his head. 'I don't know anything, honest I don't. Please don't hurt me, Eddie, please.'

Eddie pulled back the catch. 'Tell me what your son saw, else I'll kill you. I want the truth and I'll know if you're lying, you cunt.'

Terry's mouth was as dry as a bone. It was a struggle to swallow, let alone talk. 'I need a drink,' he gasped.

With the gun still fixed on Terry's meat and two veg, Eddie handed him his can of Special Brew. 'Drink that and talk, you prick,' he ordered.

Covering his prized possessions with both hands, Terry blurted out all he knew. 'Darren saw Joey. He was with a bloke called Dominic in a wine bar in Liverpool Street. Him and your Joey were groping and kissing and stuff. Please don't hurt me, Eddie, none of this is my fault. My son saw them, not me.'

Eddie stared deep into Terry's eyes. 'Why did you tell Ronny? You knew what would happen.'

'I'm sorry, Eddie. I'd had too much to drink. I didn't think. I'll ring Ronny now, tell him Darren got it all wrong. I'll say it was someone who looked like your Joey.'

Eddie took the silencer out of his pocket and attached it to the gun.

Realising what Eddie was doing, Terry fell to his knees

and begged. 'I am so sorry. Don't kill me, Eddie. I'll move – you'll never see me again – but please, I beg you, please don't shoot me.'

Eddie Mitchell had never been a man to be dissuaded by tears and apologies. With little emotion, Eddie held the gun to the right side of Terry's temple.

Seconds later, he pulled the trigger.

THIRTY-FOUR

The twins took their last exam in June and both Joey and Frankie whooped with joy as they walked through the school gates for the very last time. They had never really caught up from all the time they'd had off, but had completed all their homework and done their very best.

'How do you think you did?' Frankie asked her brother.

'Shit,' Joey replied. He had always hated maths and, even if he hadn't have bunked off, was sure he'd have still failed.

Noticing her brother looking a bit downcast again, Frankie did her best to cheer him up. Ever since their mum had warned Joey that his father was on his case, Joey had been down in the dumps. 'Why does life have to be so awkward, sis? I've only been able to see Dominic three times in the last month.'

Frankie linked arms with her brother. 'Look, it won't be for ever. You said you want to work in an office. If you get a job up town as an office junior or something, you can see Dom all the time. You can meet for lunch, then shag his brains out after work.'

Joey smiled. 'I suppose so.'

The twins had taken four exams each. Academically, Frankie was probably the brighter of the two. Trouble

357

was, she had never particularly liked school, which resulted in her never fulfilling her potential.

'Look, if you're missing Dominic that much, why don't you invite him out tonight? Dad ain't gonna know anyone in the Berwick Manor, is he? Mum and Dad think we're staying round our friend's anyway. You and Dom can book a room somewhere. Having a bit of the other might cheer you up a bit.'

Joey playfully thumped her. He was tempted, but unsure. 'It's too dangerous, Frankie. I promised Mum I wouldn't see Dom locally and if she finds out, she'll kill me.'

Frankie had always been the daredevil out of the two of them. 'Don't be such a wuss. Ring Dominic, enjoy yourself. Live dangerously, Joey, I most certainly do.'

Joey laughed. Dangerous was his sister's middle name. 'How are things going with Jed? Is it still serious?'

Frankie's face broke into a big, silly grin. She had seen Jed almost every day since they had met and she worshipped the ground he walked on. 'I love him so much, Joey. When I'm old enough, I'm gonna marry him and have loads of kids.'

'That'll please, Dad,' Joey said sarcastically.

'I don't care. Sod Dad! It's my life and I'll do what I want with it.'

Walking around Tesco, Jessica smiled as she checked her shopping list. Positive she hadn't forgotten anything, she made her way to the checkout.

Sunday was to be a special day for her and all the family. Her parents, Raymond, Polly, Gary and Ricky were coming over for dinner. Jessica had chosen to do a roast. She had bought two big ribs of beef and all the trimmings to go with it. It was going to be a double celebration.

Her parents and everybody else thought they were coming just to celebrate the twins leaving school, but Jessica was now ready to announce that she was pregnant.

Apart from Eddie and Vicki, Jessica still hadn't told a soul, not even the twins. She had been desperate to get over the dreaded twelve-week mark before she announced it to the world.

Jessica thanked the cashier and walked towards her car. She loaded her shopping into the boot and leaned against it for a breather. The sun was shining, life was good and she was so excited about her future. Thankfully, the Dominic episode had now blown over with Eddie. Joey had brought a girl round for tea and Ed had believed their relationship was kosher. Jessica smiled. She couldn't wait for the new baby to arrive and at times like these she felt like the luckiest woman alive.

Eddie stood in the hallway of the pub's living quarters. He counted the money and nodded. 'All right, Alec, it's all here. See you same time next month.'

With all debts and protection money collected, Eddie gave Gary and Ricky a ring to see if everything had gone smoothly their end. Since Paulie had left the firm, Eddie had split the collections in two. He and Raymond did one half of their patch and Gary and Ricky the other.

'All done, Dad. Everything went as sweet as a nut,' Gary told him.

'Good lads. You and Ricky out on the town again tonight?'

Gary laughed. 'Going to a rave out Watford way.'

Eddie raised his eyebrows at Raymond. He was far too old to understand all this rave lark. Sometimes Gary and Ricky would go to one and not come home for two days.

'Well, have a good time, and don't forget Sunday, Gal,

will you? Jessica's cooking a special meal. It's a double celebration. Make sure you and Ricky are there by three at the latest.'

'What's the other celebration, then? I thought we were just celebrating the twins leaving school,' Gary asked.

Eddie chuckled. 'There's more to it than meets the eye. You and Ricky behave yourselves and I'll see you both on Sunday.'

Ending the phone call, Eddie turned to Raymond. 'Shall we have a couple of pints somewhere?'

Raymond shook his head. 'Polly's off work today, so I'm gonna meet her up town. She wants to do a bit of shopping.'

Smirking, Eddie nudged him. 'Ain't shopping for engagement rings, are we, Raymondo?'

'Not yet. Don't worry, you'll be the first to know if and when we do,' Raymond replied, chuckling.

Desperate to cure his dehydration, Eddie passed his house and carried on through the lanes. He had a couple of phone calls to make and couldn't make them indoors.

The Optimist was a pub only a few minutes from his home. He pulled into the car park and strolled inside. 'Pint of Kronenberg,' he said to the barmaid.

Taking his drink outside, Eddie sat at one of the wooden tables. He was sweltering, but there was no way he would take his shirt off. He hated it when he saw geezers in pubs with no tops on. People had no decorum these days, no respect. Ed had a fit body and he wouldn't do it. These arseholes that chose to strip half naked were always big fat pricks with bellies like darts players.

Eddie rang home first. He needed to make sure all was OK. 'All right, Jess? I'll be home soon, love. I bet the twins are happy, aren't they? Are they home yet?'

'Yeah, they're playing with the dogs in the garden.'

'Give 'em a shout, Jess, I wanna talk to 'em.'

Bewildered, Jessica called the kids. Eddie never usually asked to speak to them on the phone.

'What's up, Dad?' Frankie asked.

'Bet you and Joey are over the moon, ain't ya? No more school, eh? You still going out celebrating with your mates tonight?'

Frankie giggled. 'Over the moon's putting it mildly. Yeah, we're still going out. There's loads of us, so it should be a really good night.'

'Where you off to – the pub?'

'Yeah, probably the Albion,' Frankie replied. She didn't want him knowing that they were hanging out at the Berwick Manor.

'Ask your mum if she wants me to bring home a take-away.'

Frankie did as she was told. 'No, it's OK, Dad. Mum's already cooked something.'

Eddie ended the call and quickly made the other. When he had first heard the rumours about Joey, he had done nothing, apart from blowing Terry Palmer's brains out.

Palmer's murder had been all over the local news. The Old Bill had even come to the house, but Jessica had given him an alibi by saying he was at home all evening and hadn't left her side. When the police left, Jessica had questioned him herself. 'You were just out with the dogs, weren't you, Eddie? Swear to me that you didn't kill that man.'

'I swear on our unborn baby's life, I was out with the dogs,' Eddie insisted.

He actually wasn't lying. When he had murdered Terry Palmer, Buster and Bruno were in his motor outside Palmer's flat. The dogs were his accomplices.

Jessica never mentioned the incident again and neither

did he. He had no worries about Paulie or Ronny saying anything to the filth. His brothers might be jealous wankers, but they were no snitches. Grasses didn't exist in the Mitchell empire; never had and never would.

Eddie had bided his time, watching Joey closely. He had never mentioned his son's sexuality to Jessica, Raymond or anyone since that day. Jessica must have thought he had forgotten all about it, especially since Joey had brought the pretend girlfriend home, but nothing could be further from the truth.

The thought of his son being a raving iron was eating away at Eddie's insides and he needed to know if it was true. After a lot of thought, he had scoured through the Yellow Pages and hired a private detective. He had been careful. He picked one miles away, a woman called Gina, and provided her with a false name. He called himself John Smith.

'A mate of mine's got this problem. His daughter's dating some kid called Joey and he thinks the lad could be playing her about. My pal's got a few bob and his daughter's quite a plain girl. He reckons this Joey's only with her because she's worth money. He's even heard a rumour that this Joey lad's gay.'

Gina had guessed that Eddie's pal was actually himself. She often had clients come to her with cock and bull stories. At the end of the day it was none of her business. Her only concern was doing her job properly and getting paid. Gina had had more John Smiths on her books than she could remember. It was a very common name that people chose to use. She had never had a John Smith like this one, though. This one was mind-blowingly handsome, with sexuality oozing from every pore.

As Gina answered the phone, Eddie spoke quietly but clearly. 'Me pal's just rung me. Joey's blown his daughter

362

out tonight, so can you follow him? If you see him looking intimate with another geezer, he wants you to follow them wherever they go. He needs you to get Joey's mate's full name and address.'

Gina smiled at the gruff, sexy voice. 'OK, Mr Smith. Does your friend want me to follow Joey from his house in Rainham?'

'Yeah, he does,' Eddie replied. He had already given Gina £500 quid upfront to gain her confidence. He had promised her another £1,500 once she came up with the information he wanted. 'If me mate owes you any more dough, let me know and I'll run it down to your office.'

'No, it's fine at the moment. Tell your friend that he's still in credit, Mr Smith.'

Eddie arranged to call her the following day and went to get another pint. So far Gina had followed Joey three times, but had come up with nothing. It was only a matter of time, Ed thought, as he sat back down. He would eventually find out the truth and when he did, there would be murders – literally!

Frankie was having a fantastic time in the Berwick Manor. She and Jed had swallowed ecstasy tablets earlier and, after feeling sick, she had just come up on it.

As Inner City's 'Good Life' came pumping out of the speakers, she dragged Jed onto the dancefloor.

Seeing Dominic talking to his school friends, Joey quickly dragged him away. 'Are you OK?' Dominic asked, concerned.

'Not really. I'm paranoid in here. It's too close to home for my liking.'

Dominic smiled. 'I've stacked our room up with alcohol. I've got some puff as well. Shall we take a rain check?'

363

Desperate to kiss Dom more than anything else in the world, Joey managed to stop himself. 'I'll just go and find Frankie, tell her we're leaving,' he said excitedly.

Joey found his sister on the dancefloor. Whispering his plans in her ear, he returned to Dominic and ushered him out of the packed, smoky club. Outside was desolate and Joey had the devil inside as he dragged Dom around the side of the building. It had been over two weeks since he had touched or even kissed him.

Both boys were totally unaware of the dark-haired woman sitting in the black Nissan Micra. Seeing the boys get into a minicab, Gina put her camera on the passenger seat. Mr Smith would be thrilled with the photographs she had just taken. All she had to do now was find out Joey's friend's full name and address, and her work would be complete.

Jed O'Hara had his own trailer on his father's land. He had often asked Frankie to stay there in the past, but she had always refused. Tonight, however, with the ecstasy tablet clouding her judgement, Frankie was up for an adventure.

As Jed parked his Shogun on his father's drive, he took Frankie by the hand.

'Oh, my God! What the fuck is that?' Frankie said, as she spotted an animal with horns walking towards her.

Jed giggled. The Es they had taken were fucking strong. 'It's a ram, you dinlo. What the fuck did you think it was? An elephant?'

Frankie was laughing hysterically as they traipsed across the field. Jed opened the door of his trailer and they fell into one another's arms. The sex on an E was sensational, and they were at it hammer and tongs for hours.

Finally, Frankie gently pushed Jed away. She was sore down below and needed a break. 'Can I have a look around?' she asked him. So far, all she had seen of the trailer was the bedroom.

Jed poured them both a pint of water and smiled as she took in the surroundings. Frankie had no knowledge of travellers before she had met Jed and the way they lived intrigued her. 'Why have you got so much china?' she asked him.

Jed laughed. ''Cause me mother decorated it for me. She collects china and because she's run out of room indoors, she now stores it in mine.'

Frankie stared intently at the plates decorating the wall. They were beautiful and had horses pulling pretty little gypsy carts.

'You ever been on a horse and cart?' Jed asked her.

Frankie smiled. 'No. Why? Have you?'

Jed chuckled. 'Course I have, you dinlo. I used to race the bloody things. I tell you what, daylight's breaking now. Shall I harness one up and take you out for a ride?'

Frankie burst out laughing. 'Go on, then, let's do it.'

At 5.30 a.m., Jed and Frankie trotted off down the road. 'Hey up,' Jed shouted as he whipped the filly on the arse.

'I love where you live. Your life's so exciting, Jed. My house is so boring – it's nothing like yours.'

Jed held both reins in his right hand. He put his left arm around Frankie. 'Move in with me?'

'I can't. My dad will kill me,' Frankie replied immediately.

'Tell him about us. I ain't frightened of your father and neither should you be. He's gonna find out we're together one day, ain't he?'

Frankie sighed. 'Yeah, I know, but not yet. You don't know my dad – he'll go mental, I know he will.'

365

Approaching a bend, Jed held the reins back in both hands. 'Trot on,' he said, making a funny clicking noise with his mouth.

Thinking of her dad gave Frankie the heebie-jeebies. Say he drove along and saw her? Feeling worried all of a sudden, she laid her head on Jed's shoulder. 'I'm cold. Can we go back now? I haven't got to be home yet. We can go back to bed if you like.'

Jed turned his head and kissed her gently on the lips. 'I bet you marry me within a year. I'll bet you anything you like.'

Frankie burst out laughing. Jed oozed so much confidence. He had such a glow, you could almost warm your hands on him. Poking her tongue out, Frankie snatched the reins out of Jed's hands.

'Trot on,' she yelled. 'Trot on!'

Jimmy O'Hara had never been a man to lie in bed of a morning. His Alice was the same and they had their own little routines. Alice would get up like a good wife should and clean the house till it sparkled. Jimmy would feed the animals and do the dirty jobs, which men were supposed to do.

As he saw the horse and cart pull onto the drive, Jimmy's eyes widened. He had been aware of a horse trotting about earlier, but thought he had dreamed it. Seeing Jed jump off the cart, he threw down the bucket he was holding and moved nearer to see who the pretty little filly was. He had seen the girl before, she definitely looked familiar, but she didn't look like a travelling girl. His Jed was a dark horse. Jimmy had guessed by Jed's recent behaviour that he had met a bird he liked, but Jed had said very little about her.

Jimmy sneaked around the back of his house so he

366

could get a closer peek. Seeing Frankie not twenty yards from him, realisation crept in and Jimmy smiled with such gusto, it nearly pushed his teeth out. 'It's fucking Eddie Mitchell's girl,' Jimmy whispered as he ducked down, desperate not to be seen.

As Jed shut the door of his trailer, Jimmy stood up. Unable to stop himself, he laughed out loud. Eddie Mitchell was one flash bastard, and wiping the smile off his smarmy face would make Jimmy the happiest man in the universe.

THIRTY-FIVE

Eddie was in a foul mood the following day. 'Where's the twins?' he asked Jess.

Jessica shrugged. 'They're not back yet. I think they stayed round their friend's house.'

Ed glared at her. 'Whaddya mean, you think? It's your duty to know where they are. I've told you time and time again to keep tabs on 'em. You're far too fucking lenient, Jess.'

'I do keep tabs on them, but just lately they've been a bit secretive. I've a feeling our Frankie's got a boyfriend and Joey's covering up for her,' Jessica said honestly.

'Your parenting skills leave a lot to be desired. Best you find out what Frankie's up to, 'cause if she comes home pregnant, I'll crucify her and fucking blame you,' Ed shouted as he slammed the kitchen door.

The twins finally arrived home at Saturday teatime. Desperate to know the truth about Joey, Eddie tried to call Gina, but her mobile was switched off. 'Bollocks,' Ed shouted, chucking his phone against the wall. The not knowing was torture. At least once he had some proof, he could do something about it.

On the Sunday morning, Jessica had a list of jobs for Ed to do and it wasn't until lunchtime, when her parents arrived, that Eddie had a chance to escape. 'Right, I've vacced your car and tidied up the garden. You're OK with your parents for a bit, ain't ya? I'm gonna take the dogs out for a run.'

Jessica gave him a dubious look. He never usually took Buster and Bruno for a run. The last time he had, there had been a murder and the police had come knocking on the door. 'You're not going far, are you? How long will you be?' Jessica asked him suspiciously.

'I dunno. For fuck's sake, Jess, I've worked me bollocks off all morning. Give us a break, will ya?'

Jessica felt uneasy as he left the house. She could always tell when Eddie had something on his mind and she was sure he was up to no good. He'd been in a funny mood for days now and certainly wasn't his chirpy self.

Bored with sitting with Stanley, Joyce walked into the kitchen. 'Let me help you, dear. Shall I peel some potatoes or veg for you?'

'You go and sit in the lounge with Dad. Everything's under control, Mum.'

'I can't sit in there with your father. Been doing my head in all weekend, he has. Just got himself a new cock, ain't he? It's all he talks about. Called it Willie, he has, as a tribute to Willie Carson. I mean, how can you call a cock Willie? Ain't normal, is it, Jess?'

Jessica burst out laughing. Her mother was hilarious and she didn't even realise it.

'There you are! Is Joey still in bed?' Jessica asked, as Frankie suddenly appeared.

Kissing her nan, Frankie flopped onto a chair. She

didn't want to be stuck in all day – she wanted to be out with Jed, but wasn't sure how to broach the subject. 'Joey's getting up now, Mum. I know we're having dinner and all that, but do you mind if I go out afterwards?'

Jessica felt her hackles rise. Frankie was always out lately and Jessica barely saw her. Sometimes she stayed out all night and Jessica had a feeling that she had met a boy and was up to Christ knows what. 'Will it hurt you to stay in for one day? Gary and Ricky are coming over, so are Raymond and Polly. This is meant to be a celebration for you and Joey leaving school.'

'Yeah, I know and I do appreciate it, but it's one of my friend's birthdays today and we're all meant to be going bowling. Please say I can go, Mum. I haven't got to go till after dinner.'

'Do as you like, Frankie, I don't care any more,' Jessica said bluntly. Her daughter was a selfish little cow and she was beginning to lose patience with her behaviour.

As Joey walked in, Frankie slunk into the lounge to see her grandfather.

'Mum, Joey, go and sit in the front room. I'll be in meself in a minute,' Jessica said. Her kitchen was enormous, but somehow people still managed to get under her feet.

Stanley told the twins all about his new cock. 'My Willie's a beauty. Faster than the speed of light, he is. My mates down at the pigeon club are so jealous. Two of 'em have already tried to buy him off me. They say he's the best cock they've ever seen.'

Frankie giggled. 'I'm sure Joey would like to see him, Grandad. He likes pigeons, especially cocks. Don't you, Joey?'

'Really? Why don't I pick you up in the week, Joey? You can come round and see him,' Stanley enthused.

'That would be lovely, Grandad,' Joey lied, glaring at his sister.

Deciding to get his own back, Joey turned to his nan. 'Do you think our Frankie looks like a gypsy, Nan? We was in a pub the other day and this travelling girl came up to us. She said she was positive that our Frankie had a bit of gypsy in her.'

Joyce was furious. 'Of course she don't. Christ, she don't wanna look like one of them tinkers. Never trusted the bastards, I ain't. Years ago, when your mum was little, I had one knock on me front door. She was selling lucky heather and when I refused to buy any, she told me that bad luck was coming my way. The next morning, I got up, tripped down the stairs and broke me bloody arm. Even to this day, I swear she put a curse on me. Evil bastards they are. If you have the misfortune of meeting one again, don't have nothing to do with 'em, will you?'

Joey smirked at his sister. 'Of course not Nan. We wouldn't dream of having any dealings with gypsies, would we Frankie?'

Eddie Mitchell tied the dogs to the wooden table and went inside the Optimist to get a drink. His mouth was as dry as a nun's crotch and he didn't know whether it was due to the hot weather or the impending phone call he had to make.

Eddie thanked the barmaid and went back outside. Buster and Bruno were lying on their backs having their stomachs tickled by some old boy in a trilby hat.

'Good guard dogs you're gonna be,' Eddie muttered, as he walked towards the table. He had been training them to growl and bark at strangers, not lie on their backs with their legs up in the air.

'Beautiful day, isn't it?' the man in the hat commented to Eddie.

'Wonderful, mate,' Eddie replied sarcastically. He was too worried about his gay son to get involved in pointless small talk.

As the man walked away, Eddie downed his whisky chaser in one. His heart was pumping nineteen to the dozen at the thought of what he might be about to hear. He rang Gina's number and took a deep breath as she answered.

'Well?' he asked, trying to sound calm.

'I have all the information you wanted, Mr Smith, including photographs.'

'What did you find out?' Eddie asked abruptly.

'I'll tell you everything when we meet up. I did an eighteen-hour stint to find out all the information you required. I now need to arrange collection for the remainder of the money I'm owed.'

'Can I meet you now? Please, my mate's desperate to find out the score,' Eddie pleaded

'Well, it's a bit awkward. I have to attend a function at three o'clock at a friend's house.'

'I'll meet you now. Anywhere that suits you. I'll pay you extra, make it worth your while.'

Gina sighed. Mr Smith was a very generous but difficult client and, due to her crush on him, she couldn't say no. 'My friend lives in Benfleet. Do you know the Tarpots? I can meet you there at two-forty-five.'

'I'll be there,' Eddie responded immediately.

Overcome by anxiety, Eddie got himself another pint and a whisky chaser. He didn't know what he was going to say to Jessica. With everyone due around for dinner, she was bound to go apeshit at him.

As Buster and Bruno tried to clamber up his leg, he

sipped his drink and stroked their heads. 'Why is my life so fucking difficult, boys? Yous two have got it easy. When I die, I'm coming back as a fucking dog!'

Jessica basted the roast potatoes and slammed the oven door shut. Where the bloody hell had Eddie got to?

'All right to get another beer, Jess?' Gary asked.

'Help yourself, love. Can you make sure everyone's got a drink for me? Christ knows where your father is. He was only taking the dogs for a run and he's been gone nearly two hours. I can't do everything, Gary. I'm trying to cook the bloody dinner.'

Gary squeezed Jessica's arm. 'You just concentrate on the food and I'll deal with everything else. Once I've sorted the drinks out, I'll give the old man a ring, see where he's got to.'

'Thanks, love. I already tried to ring him twice, but he's not answering his phone,' Jessica said gratefully.

Shouting at the dogs to stop yelping, Eddie sped down the A13. Aware that his phone was ringing yet again, he answered it. 'Where are you, Dad? Jess has got the right needle,' Gary informed him.

Eddie didn't want anyone to know where he was going. 'I've lost one of the dogs, Gal. Buster bolted into the woods and I'm hunting for him now.'

'Me and Ricky'll come and help you find him,' Gary offered.

'No, don't worry. I've got a couple of dog walkers helping me. Look, do us a favour, son. I don't wanna upset the kids, so tell Jess on the quiet. I won't come back till I've found him – he can't have gone far.'

Gary ended the call and went to find Jessica to explain. 'I can't understand why he took 'em out in the car in the first place. We're inundated with fields around here. Where has he taken them?'

Gary shrugged. 'He didn't exactly say, but he mentioned the woods.'

Jessica thanked Gary and began cutting the meat. Her husband's story sounded a little bit too far-fetched for her liking.

Not sure where they were supposed to be meeting, Eddie rang Gina as he drove into Benfleet.

'Follow the road straight down and the pub comes up on your right. I'm sitting in the car park in a black Nissan Micra,' Gina told him.

Eddie spotted her immediately and parked right next to her. 'What have you got?' he asked, as he squeezed his big frame into her small passenger seat.

Gina handed him Dominic's name and address. 'Your friend's suspicions were correct,' she said, getting straight to the point.

'Where's the photos?' Eddie asked, his heart feeling like a lump of lead.

Gina handed him a sealed envelope. 'Your friend might want to look at these in private, Mr Smith,' she said diplomatically.

Eddie nodded and handed her a wad of money. 'There's sixteen hundred quid there. Fifteen that I promised you and a oner on top for meeting me today.'

'You've paid me far too much. Please, take some back,' Gina urged. Her heart was beating like a drum, as she'd never been so close to him before.

Eddie opened the car door. 'You keep it, love, but promise me: what you saw, you'll never breathe a word. My pal's an important geezer and he wouldn't be happy if any of this got out.'

'You have my word and my word is my bond. I can guarantee you, your friend has nothing to worry about. I work in a very clandestine manner, Mr Smith.'

Watching Gina drive away, Eddie decided to head back nearer to home before he opened the envelope. He would probably write his Land Cruiser off down the A13 if he opened it in Benfleet. Dreading what the contents held, Eddie started the engine and sped off like a loony.

Annoyed that her day had been thoroughly spoilt, Jessica barely touched her dinner.

'You not hungry, Mum?' Joey asked, concerned.

'No, love. Has everyone finished? I'll take the plates out.'

'Would you like me to give you a hand?' Polly asked politely.

'That's a first. You don't usually lift a cup,' Raymond joked.

With Polly's help, Jessica cleared the table and organised the dessert. If Ed wasn't home by the time the strawberry pavlova was eaten, then sod him, she would announce her good news alone.

'I don't want afters. Is it all right if I go out now, Mum?' Frankie whinged.

'No, it's not. Sit down and shut up for five minutes,' Jessica spat back.

'I don't think I like that, dear. What's it called?' Stanley asked, pointing to the dessert.

'Pavlova! You always have to be awkward, Stanley, don't you?' Joyce said.

'Don't worry, Dad. I've got a blackberry crumble as well. Just waiting for it to warm up. I forgot to turn the oven back on again.'

375

Half an hour later, everybody was full to the brim.

'Thanks, Jess, that was lovely,' Ricky remarked as he helped his stepmum take the dishes out to the kitchen.

'So, how's your father's business doing, Polly? Has he been affected by this recession at all?' Joyce asked nosily.

Stanley felt sorry for his son's girlfriend. For the past hour, all Joyce had done was give her the third degree. 'For goodness' sake, woman. Can't you change the subject?' he said bravely.

'Shut up and mind your own business,' Joyce snapped back.

Jessica handed two bottles of champagne to Ricky and told him to open them. Handing everybody a champagne flute, Jessica topped up their glasses.

'Is this to toast my wonderful grandchildren?' Stanley asked, winking at the twins.

Jessica smiled. She felt sad that Eddie wasn't here to join in, but Frankie was waiting to go out, so what could she do?

Urging Joey and Frankie to stand up, Jessica grinned at them. 'My little babies have now left school and are about to start looking for jobs. To Frankie and Joey – we all wish you every success in your future,' she proclaimed.

'To Frankie and Joey,' everyone repeated.

Frankie knocked her champagne straight back. She was aching to see Jed. 'Can I go out now, Mum?' she asked cheekily.

Jessica hated giving speeches. Eddie was good at them, but she wasn't, and even felt nervous in front of her close family. Urging Frankie to sit back down, Jessica cleared her throat. 'I've got some news of my own. I know Mum and Joey have both commented on me putting on a bit of weight recently. Well, there is a reason for this. I'm pregnant! Eddie and I are going to be parents again, and

Joey and Frankie are going to have a little brother or sister.'

An expert at overacting, Joyce leaped up and down like a kangaroo. 'That's wonderful. Oh Stanley, we're gonna be grandparents again,' she squealed with delight.

'Congratulations, dear,' Stanley said in a monotone voice. He still didn't like Eddie – never had and never would. He loved his grandchildren, though, and would certainly welcome another.

Joey turned to Frankie and pretended to put his fingers down the back of his throat.

'It's disgusting. How old are they? I hope they don't expect us to wipe its arse and babysit, 'cause I won't,' Frankie whispered to her brother.

Aware that the twins' reaction hadn't been one of utter joy, Jessica spoke softly to them. 'You'll always be Mummy's favourites. You were my first born,' she assured them.

'Ain't you a bit old?' Joey asked her bluntly.

'Don't expect me to look after it,' Frankie chipped in.

Jessica smiled. They were probably a bit jealous, bless them. She was sure they would get used to the idea once the baby was born, and would make wonderful siblings for him or her.

'Go on, you can go out now, Frankie. Are you going out as well, Joey?'

'Yep,' Joey said, as he shoved Frankie out of the room. A screaming brat in the house was the last thing either of them needed.

Raymond hugged his sister. 'Me and Polly are thrilled for you,' he said kindly.

'Who wants more champagne? Me and Ricky are gonna be bruvvers again and that deserves a celebration on its own, don't it, bruv?' Gary said.

Ricky agreed and gave Jessica a squeeze. 'Gal, ring Dad again, see where he is,' he ordered his brother.

Not wanting anyone listening in, Gary wandered out into the garden and rang his dad's number. Unbeknown to Jessica, he had been ringing him for the last hour, but couldn't get any response. The more he thought about the Buster story, the more he knew his dad had been lying. 'What the fuck is going on?' Gary said out loud, as once again he received no answer. Unbeknownst to Gary, Eddie was back in the Optimist. Finishing his fourth pint, Ed untied the dogs' leads. He was dreading looking in that envelope. He knew by Gina's voice and face that the contents were bad news, but it was now or never and he had to know the truth.

Lifting the dogs into the back of the Land Cruiser, he sat in the driver's seat and ripped the envelope open. As Eddie stared at the picture of his son kissing Dominic, he repeatedly smashed his fist against the steering wheel. Taking a deep breath, he looked at the rest. The worst one was the last one. His son, his own flesh and blood, had his hand placed on Dominic's cobblers.

Aware of a watery taste in his mouth, Eddie opened his door and retched his guts up.

Conscious of a couple looking at him, Eddie started the engine and sped off. He stopped in a lay-by in the middle of nowhere and got out of the motor again. Furious, he banged his head against the passenger door.

'Fuck, fuck, fuck!' he screamed.

Distraught, Eddie got back into the motor. Fishing through his pockets, he found Dominic's address. Islington, the bastard lived, and his name was Dominic King.

Eddie restarted the engine. 'More like Queen, not fucking King,' he mumbled.

Heading towards another pub, Eddie took deep breaths. He couldn't go home yet; he needed to calm himself down first. He musn't let Jessica, Raymond or anyone clock onto his findings. He had to act normal, it was the only way.

Tomorrow he would pay this Dominic a visit. He would give him King – he would dethrone the cunt.

THIRTY-SIX

Jessica was furious with her husband's behaviour and, as he made an appearance the following morning, she neither glanced at nor spoke to him. He had eventually come home around midnight. She had been in bed, but had heard the dogs barking and him staggering about downstairs.

She knew he was drunk. It wasn't often Eddie got like that now, but she could always tell when he was by the amount of noise he made and the length of time it took him to reach the top of the stairs.

Something was troubling him, she knew that. Eddie hadn't been himself for weeks and Jessica wondered if he had raked up some new information about his father's murder. He hadn't even slept in their bedroom, but had gone into the spare room.

As Jessica banged the kettle against the worktop, Eddie stopped eating his cereal and tried to cuddle her. 'I'm sorry about yesterday. It took me hours to find Buster and then something else cropped up. I'll make it up to your mum and dad, I promise. Got a lot on me plate at the moment, I have, Jess.'

Jessica was angry. Men were so full of themselves at times. 'And so have I, Ed. I've got a lot on my plate, as well. Have you forgotten that I'm carrying our third child? I'm sick of clearing up after everyone here. The twins don't lift a finger and since you brought them dogs home, the place is a tip. Full of hairs, it is, and I now have to clean twice a day, instead of once. Also, I'm worried about Frankie. I know she's turned sixteen now, but I don't like her staying out all night. I'm sure she's got a boyfriend she's not telling us about. I asked her outright the other day, but she denied it, of course.'

Eddie felt the hairs on the back of his neck stand up. He had enough problems with Joey without Frankie being at it as well.

Joey walking into the kitchen stopped the conversation dead. 'Morning Mum, morning Dad,' Joey said brightly.

The sight of his son put Eddie off the remainder of his cornflakes. Joey disgusted him and he would never forget those photographs as long as he lived.

'Do you want me to make you some breakfast, love?' Jessica asked Joey.

'Not really hungry, Mum. You got any fruit? I fancy a banana.'

Remembering the snap where Joey had his hand around his boyfriend's nether regions, Eddie threw his cornflakes into the bin and stomped upstairs.

'What's up with him? Yous two had a row?' Joey asked his mum.

Jessica shrugged. 'I don't know what's the matter with him. Don't worry, it can't be anything to do with you, Joey. If Dad had found out anything about Dominic, he'd have said something to me, I know he would. Maybe it's to do with Grandad Harry. Perhaps he's heard some rumours about what happened to him, or something.'

Joey hugged his mum. He had always been closer to

her than he had to his father, and since she had supported him over his sexuality, he loved her more than ever.

'If I ask you something, Joey, will you tell me the truth?'

'Of course, what do you want to know?'

'I know Frankie's got a boyfriend and I want to know why she's being so secretive about him.'

Joey didn't know what to say. He couldn't drop Frankie in it, so made up the first excuse he could think of. 'Frankie gets embarrassed, Mum. All she's told me is his name. She's never had a proper boyfriend before, so I think it's all new to her. His name's John, apparently, and I'm sure in time she'll bring him home so we can all meet him.'

Jessica pushed Joey's hair off his forehead. He was such a sensitive boy and had a gift for putting her mind at rest. 'Where you off to today?' she asked him.

'I'm going shopping in Romford. Its Dom's birthday next weekend and he's taking me to a posh restaurant to celebrate. He bought me a lovely bracelet for my birthday, Mum. I've hidden it upstairs, but I'll show you it later,' Joey whispered.

Jessica smiled. Her son was in love and, in her own way, she was pleased for him. She would rather Joey be in love with a girl, but he was sixteen now and old enough to make his own choices in life. 'I wish you every happiness, Joey, I really do,' Jessica whispered back.

Aware of Eddie's footsteps approaching, Jessica told Joey to sit down and eat his banana.

'I'm going out now. Got a lot of work on today, so I dunno what time I'll be home,' Eddie growled.

Not able to be in the same room as his son, Eddie turned on his heel without waiting for an answer. The quicker he got out of the house, the less physically sick he would feel.

*   *   *

Frankie woke up feeling like nothing on earth. She was meant to be going over to Kent with Jed to drop off a horse that he'd sold, but she felt too ill to do so. She rang him up to explain. 'I'm so sorry, Jed. I've been as sick as a pig. Do you feel OK? I think that Chinese we ate last night was a bit dodgy.'

Jed laughed. 'You see me, Frankie – never had a day's illness in me life. I ain't even on no doctor's books. I've told you before, you don't eat enough meat. Meat makes you strong, makes you healthy, it does. Fit as a fiddle, I am.'

'How long will you be in Kent for? Can I see you when you get back?' Frankie asked, changing the subject. Talking about meat was making her feel worse than ever.

'Well, if you ain't coming, I might have to take me other bird with me, so I might not be back till tomorrow,' Jed goaded her.

Knowing he was only winding her up, Frankie managed a smile. 'Don't muck about, you tosser.'

'I'll be back this afternoon. I'll ring you when I'm through the tunnel. Tell your mum and dad you're staying at your mate's tonight and stay at mine.'

'OK,' Frankie said immediately. Even though things were getting awkward at home, with her mum asking all sorts of questions, she still couldn't resist spending the night with him. Waking up with Jed in the morning was the best feeling in the whole wide world. Frankie said goodbye to him and struggled onto the landing.

'Mum, I feel really ill. I've been sick twice, I think I've got food poisoning. Bring me up some medicine, will you?' she shouted.

When the kids were younger, Jessica used to be frantic if they had any kind of illness. Since they had got older, she didn't worry too much. She was sure that alcohol played a part in many of their little off days. They drank like fish indoors, so Christ knows what they were sinking when they were out gallivanting with friends.

Fishing through the cupboards, Jessica took a box of tablets upstairs. 'I've got some Setlers. Take two of them,' she said, handing Frankie the box.

Seeing how washed-out her daughter looked, Jessica sat down on the edge of her bed. 'You're having too many late nights and you're drinking too much, that's your trouble. You're only sixteen, Frankie, your body can't cope with being abused on a regular basis.'

Frankie took the tablets, and then lay flat on her back. She felt like death warmed up and a lecture from her mother was the last thing she needed. 'I'm staying round Stacey's tonight, but I promise I won't drink,' Frankie lied.

Jessica squeezed her daughter's hand. 'Don't fib to me, Frankie. I know you've got a boyfriend and I know you've been spending a lot of time with him. If I've accepted Joey's relationship, what makes you think that I wouldn't accept yours? You've left school now, so you're entitled to have a boyfriend. Why don't you bring him round for tea one day, so me and your dad can meet him?'

Overcome by anxiety, Frankie burst into tears and put her head under the quilt. 'Just leave me alone and go away,' she yelled.

Shaking her head in disbelief, Jessica said no more. She stood up and left her daughter to her tantrum.

Sitting outside the pub in Islington, Eddie sipped his drink and stared at the flats across the road. For the last hour he had been watching every bastard that entered the building and there was still no sign of gay boy Dominic. He had buzzed number fourteen earlier, but there was no

384

reply. He guessed Dominic was working. He was a lot older than Joey and, from what he could remember of seeing him at his house, the boy seemed intelligent and well dressed.

Eddie sighed. If Frankie had brought Dominic home, he would have been reasonably happy about it, but not fucking Joey.

Thinking back to when his son was young, Eddie knew that the signs had always been there. He had wanted to stick his oar in years ago and toughen the kid up but, frightened Jessica would leave him again, he had kept his trap shut. Ed had let Jessica bring the twins up in the way she thought was right and now he could have kicked himself.

A son needed a dad to take him in hand, show him what the world was all about. Eddie had missed out on all that with Joey. He had been out working a lot and Jessica had cracked the whip, not him. Trouble was, she hadn't cracked it hard enough. Lost in his thoughts, Eddie almost did a double take as he saw the tall, dark-haired geezer letting himself in the security door.

'Who's a pretty boy then?' Eddie mumbled as he walked back into the pub for a refill.

Dominic had been indoors just over an hour when the buzzer sounded. He hated travelling on the underground; all those sweaty people made him feel grubby and he had just got out of the bath. Throwing on his white dressing gown, Dominic rushed to answer the door.

'Hello, who is it?'

'Royal Mail, mate. I've got a delivery for you.'

Dominic was perplexed. He had nothing on order, to his knowledge. Suddenly it came to him. Joey must have sent him an early birthday present. His boyfriend was such a sweetie sometimes, he really was.

As Dominic opened the front door, the force of Eddie's fist sent him the full length of the hallway. As his dressing gown flew open, he quickly tried to cover his glory. 'What do you want? Please don't hurt me.' he sobbed as he recognised Joey's father.

Eddie shut the door. 'You got a stereo, Pretty Boy?' he asked.

'It's in the l-l-living r-r-room,' Dominic stammered. It wasn't just his voice that was shaking, his whole body was quivering like an unset jelly.

Eddie made Dominic get up and turn the stereo system on. 'Find a decent radio station, like that new one, Capital Gold. Turn it up loud, then kneel on the floor,' he ordered.

'I don't k-k-know the frequency,' Dominic whimpered.

Eddie forced Dominic to lie flat on his face next to the stereo. Ed liked to whistle while he worked and Capital Gold played all the oldies that he liked. Putting his boot on the back of Dominic's neck to stop him from moving, Eddie found what he was looking for.

'A Whiter Shade of Pale' by Procol Harum was playing and as Eddie turned Dominic over, he thought how appropriate the song was. The colour of Pretty Boy's face was whiter than fucking snow.

'Please d-don't kill me. I p-p-promise I will never see Joey again, if that's what you w-w-want,' Dominic begged, terrified.

Eddie smiled. 'Got any beers?' he asked.

'In the f-f-fridge.'

'If you move, I'll kill you,' Eddie told him.

Bringing in a pack of four, Eddie handed one to his son's lover. 'Drink it,' he said, as he sat on the sofa.

As Dominic got up to sit on the armchair opposite, Eddie threw an unopened can at his head. 'Get down on the floor, you cunt. I never said you could get up, did I now?'

'Sorry. I'm so sorry,' Dominic pleaded, as he lay on his front.

Eddie sipped his lager. Trust Pretty Boy to only have Carlsberg. Weak person, weak lager.

'Turn over on your back,' Eddie ordered him.

Shivering, Dominic clutched his dressing down around himself and did as he was told. He was so petrified that his voice had temporarily gone on holiday.

Finishing the lager, Eddie crushed the can in his right hand and smiled as Dominic flinched. 'Do you know what this song's about?' Eddie asked him.

Capital Gold was now playing the Bee Gees' classic, 'Gotta Get a Message to You'.

'No. I don't k-k-know m-many oldies,' Dominic managed to whisper.

'It's about someone who's gonna die and wants to send a message to their loved ones,' Eddie informed him.

'Please d-d-don't kill me. I bbeg you,' Dominic pleaded. 'I p-p-promise, I'll do whatever you ask.'

Knowing that Dominic was telling the truth, Eddie decided to give him just one last little scare. He had no intention of killing him. After the unfortunate Terry Palmer incident, he had to let his bullets lie low for a while. Eddie didn't fancy a stretch inside. Not only that, Jess leaving him would break his heart, and she was worth more to him than Pretty Boy was.

Taking the carving knife out of the inside pocket of his leather jacket, Eddie bent down. 'Open your dressing gown,' he demanded.

Dominic's hand shook like a leaf as he tried to undo the belt, but couldn't. Not one to see a man struggling, Eddie did the honours for him.

'Please, no!' Dominic screamed, holding his hands over his penis and shaking his head from side to side in fright.

As Eddie looked at Dominic's flaccid dick, he tried to erase his son from his mind. One thought of Joey wanking it or sucking it, he would chop the bastard thing off in a flash.

As Dominic screamed in anticipation, Eddie turned the radio up a bit louder. The geezer was a typical weasel, and Eddie didn't want the neighbours knocking on the door.

Lifting Dominic's cock up with the knife, Eddie held the blade to it and stared deeply into his victim's eyes. 'You ring Joey tomorrow and you tell him it's all over. I want you to let him down as kindly as possible, just say he's too young or something. If he won't accept that, you tell him you've met someone else.'

'I will, I will, I p-p-promise,' Dominic wept.

Eddie smiled at Dominic's anguish. Unable to resist terrorising Dominic even more, Ed flopped his penis over and made the slightest of cuts on the tip. 'You see that? Look, it's your blood.'

'I can't look. I c-c-can't, I've got a phobia of b-b-blood,' Dominic whispered.

'Well, I'll tell you something, shall I? If you ever set foot within a hundred yards of my son again, I will hunt you down and chop that little knob of yours off for you. Then I'll pick it up with me bare hands and ram it straight down the back of your throat until you choke on it. Now, do we understand one another?'

'I u-u-understand. I'll tell Joey t-tomorrow. You h-h-have my w-word,' Dominic sobbed.

With a wry grin on his face, Eddie wiped the blood off his knife onto Dominic's dressing gown. He then turned the radio up full blast and calmly left the flat.

THIRTY-SEVEN

From the moment Joey received the phone call from Dominic, he was totally inconsolable. He couldn't eat or sleep, and for the next forty-eight hours refused to get out of his bed.

By day three, Jessica was really worried about her son. She had told Eddie that Joey had the flu, but with his constant tantrums and tears, it was getting harder for her to cover for him. As luck would have it, Eddie had been at work for the last couple of days and hadn't asked too many questions. Today, he was at home and Jessica was dreading him being there.

A while back when Eddie had hit the roof over the Dominic rumours, Jessica had told her husband that Joey had a new girlfriend. Fortunately, Joey had taken her advice and brought a girl around for tea. The doubts about Joey's sexuality had ceased to exist since that day and Jessica didn't want the worry of anything fresh coming out into the open.

Having now forgiven Eddie for disappearing last Sunday, Jessica smiled as he sat down at the kitchen table next to Frankie. 'Who's hungry? I've got a fresh crusty loaf and a nice bit of butcher's ham if anyone wants a sandwich,' Jessica said.

'I'll have ham and tomato,' Frankie said immediately.

'I'll have the same,' Eddie said, tickling his daughter to annoy her.

'Stop it, Dad. You're hurting me,' Frankie giggled.

'I'm not stopping till you tell me and your mother who this new boyfriend of yours is. What's the big secret? He ain't my age, is he?'

As Frankie wriggled on the floor to get away from her father, Eddie kneeled on her arms so she couldn't move. 'Seize,' he ordered Buster and Bruno, who tried to lick her to death.

'Get off, Dad,' Frankie yelled as the dogs slobbered all over her face.

'Not until I know who this geezer is. I'm your father, I have every right to know. If it weren't for me, you wouldn't even be here,' Eddie taunted her.

'He's not your age and his name's John. I met him down the Albion. Now, get off me, Dad, seriously, you're hurting my arms.'

Joining in the fun, Jessica repeatedly hit Eddie with the tea towel. 'Come on, enough's enough,' she said laughing.

Frankie ate her sandwich in silence. Life was becoming more awkward by the day for her.

'Why don't you ask your boyfriend if he wants to come round for dinner tonight, love?' Jessica enquired.

Sick of being interrogated and not having a good enough answer, Frankie stood up. 'Just leave me alone, the pair of you. John and I aren't even serious yet, so why do you have to poke your noses in and try and spoil everything for me?' she yelled, running up the stairs.

Eddie ran into the hallway. 'Best you and that brother of yours stop going out partying all the time and look for a fucking job instead,' he shouted up the stairs after her.

390

Ed had only been mucking about with her, the miserable little cow.

'Don't shout at her, Eddie. I think she's got her period or something,' Jess told him.

'I couldn't give a fuck what she's got! I'm not having all this for much longer, Jess. They both wanted to leave school at sixteen, so now they can go and get a fucking job. I was ten years old when I started work and I've always worked since. They're a lazy pair of bastards. All they do is doss about – they don't lift a finger in here. Going out on the piss all the time ain't gonna get 'em far in life. Once they've spent their birthday money, that's it, they ain't getting no more. They expect continuous handouts and it's as much as they can do to say thank you. Well, I'm putting me foot down from now on. Too soft we've been with 'em, and this is the fucking result of it.'

Aware that Ed's eyes had started to cloud over, Jessica quickly changed the subject. 'I'm sure I felt the baby moving this morning, Ed. It's the first time, I've really felt it. Shall we go shopping tomorrow? We can get the cot and a few other bits.'

The mention of his unborn child put a smile back on Eddie's face. He put his arms around Jessica from behind and gently fondled her stomach. 'How about we choose some wallpaper and stuff and I'll make a start on changing the spare room into a nursery.'

Jessica turned around and threw her arms around his neck. 'Oh, Ed, that sounds wonderful.'

Frankie sat on the edge of her brother's bed. 'You can't carry on like this, Joey. Why don't you ring Dom? Talk to him.'

Joey's eyes filled up with tears once again. 'I've tried. He keeps putting the phone down on me. I can't understand it, we were getting on OK. Dominic always treated me well. He loved me, I know he did, and last week he even spoke about me moving into his flat sometime soon. It doesn't make sense, Frankie. He hasn't even been out to meet anyone else, yet he said he's fallen for some other bloke.'

'You don't reckon it's got anything to do with Dad, do you? Maybe he found out and threatened him or something.'

Joey shrugged. 'I doubt it. Surely Dad would have gone mental at me if he knew something. I wonder if Dom's met someone at work; maybe a new bloke's just started there or something.'

'Why don't you go up to where he works. Wait outside the building, you can see for yourself then. I'll even come with you, if you want.'

Joey and Frankie's conversation was ended by a gentle tapping on the bedroom door.

'I've made you a nice ham sandwich and cup of tea. You can't keep starving yourself, Joey, you need to eat something, love,' Jessica said, walking into the room.

Jessica was as surprised as anyone that her son's relationship had fallen to pieces but, in a way, she was relieved. At least she didn't have to worry about Eddie finding out now.

Joey refused the sandwich. 'Go away, Mum. I'm not hungry,' he cried.

He couldn't bear to speak to anyone apart from Frankie.

Eddie crept up the stairs and stopped halfway, listening to the conversation.

Jessica lifted up the plate and handed it to Joey. 'Please, just eat half for Mummy.'

'Stop treating me like a fucking child. I don't want the poxy sandwich. Go away and leave me alone. If you keep on at me, I'm gonna kill myself.' Joey screamed as he knocked the plate out of her hand.

Hearing the plate smash, Eddie saw red. How dare he talk to his mother like that? The queer little ponce. Opening Joey's bedroom door, Eddie picked up half the sandwich off the floor.

'Eat it, you cunt,' he ordered.

'Stop it, Ed!' Jessica screamed.

'Leave him alone, Dad,' Frankie yelled.

Overcome by a vision of Joey having a big dick in his mouth, Eddie held back his son's head and shoved the sandwich in there. 'Eat it, fucking eat it!' he yelled.

As Joey began to make choking noises, Jessica pummelled Eddie with her fists. 'If you hurt him, I'm leaving you,' she screamed hysterically.

Frankie jumped on top of her brother to shield him from their father. 'Get off him, you bully,' she shouted.

'You're no son of mine. Never was and never will be,' Eddie spat as he left the room.

Making sure that Joey was not hurt in any way, Jessica left him with Frankie and chased her husband down the stairs. 'How dare you treat our son like that? What's got into you, Eddie? If you ever lay your hands on him again, we're finished.'

'What's got into me? I'll tell you what's got into me, shall I? How do you think that him sucking blokes' cocks makes me look, eh? Every time I look at him, he makes me feel sick. I'm ashamed to call him my son. You knew all about it, didn't you? You knew he was at it with that Dominic and you allowed it to continue. What type of mother does that make you, eh?'

Jessica looked at Eddie in amazement. He had obviously known about Dominic all along. 'It was you that ended their relationship, wasn't it? What did you do, beat

Dominic up? Threaten to kill him? Violence is all you know, isn't it, Eddie? Well, that might be part of your world, but it's not part of mine. I'm a good mother and I love my children whatever they are.'

Eddie gave a sarcastic laugh. 'Yeah, and you've done a fantastic job, ain't ya? We've got a daughter out on the piss all night, shagging Christ knows who and a son who's away with the fucking fairies. Well done, Jess, what a wonderful job you did. You see, when our next baby is born, I'm taking over the parenting and I mean that, Jess. Our next kid will be raised my way.'

Jessica burst into tears, 'You can be such a nasty bastard at times, Eddie, you really can.'

Eddie picked up his keys. Usually, whenever Jessica turned on the waterworks, it tugged at his heartstrings, but not today. He was furious with her for allowing Joey to carry on seeing Dominic, fucking furious. 'I'm going down the pub, don't wait up,' he said, as he slammed the front door.

Hearing their dad's car pull off the drive, Joey and Frankie both ran downstairs. They had been earwigging and had heard every word.

'Well, at least I now know why Dominic finished with me. I'm just relieved he's not in love with someone else. I'm gonna meet him from work next week, tell him I know that my dad paid him a visit. Maybe we can sort things out. What do you think, Mum?'

Jessica smiled sadly. Joey had caused all this fracas, yet he was only bothered about himself. Frankie was the same – in fact, she was probably even more selfish than Joey was. Perhaps Eddie was right. Maybe she was a terrible mother and should let him bring up the next child, the way that he saw right.

'Are you OK, Mum?' Joey asked, aware that she was looking at him strangely.

'Not really. I'm going to have a lie down.'

Without even glancing back at her children, Jessica tearfully left the room.

Not that far away, someone else was planning to cause a spot of bother. Jimmy O'Hara was well aware that Eddie Mitchell had been creeping into one of their local pubs recently. Michael Murphy was a cousin of Patrick's and he spent half his life propping up the bar of the Optimist.

Three days ago, on finding out his son was dating Frankie Mitchell, Jimmy had given Michael a ring. 'As soon as Eddie Mitchell comes into that pub again, call me. I'll make it worth your while, Mickey boy,' Jimmy told him.

Jimmy was feeding his chickens when his mobile phone rang.

'Jimmy, it's Michael. Eddie Mitchell has just walked in.'

Jimmy smiled as he dropped the food and ran towards his pick-up truck. It was finally time for a bit of action.

Eddie munched on a packet of dry-roasted peanuts and gulped back his pint. As his phone rang, he answered it and was surprised to hear Jessica on the other end. 'What's up?' he asked abruptly.

'Oh, Ed, I'm sorry. I'm having a lie down and I've been thinking about what you said. I have been too easy on the twins, I know I have. I'm gonna toughen up, you know. What you said this morning about them getting a job makes sense. They have too much time on their hands and I think a bit of responsibility would do them the world of good.'

Eddie smirked. He just loved being proved right. 'No more hiding things from me about Joey, Jess. He either starts dating girls or he stays fucking celibate. I'm not having him make a fool out of me again. I'll disown him next time and sling him out the house, I swear on my life, I will.'

'Please don't say things like that, Ed. Things are awkward for Joey, and I still think you were out of order earlier. You nearly choked the poor little sod. He's probably just going through a phase, I'm sure he'll grow out of it.'

'Well, if he don't, he'll be moving to the fucking Hebrides or somewhere,' Eddie said angrily.

'All right, Eddie? Can I get you a drink, mush?'

Telling Jessica they would talk later, Eddie ended the call and stared at Jimmy O'Hara's ugly face. 'No, I'm all right, thanks,' Eddie replied.

As O'Hara walked to the bar, Eddie cursed himself for drinking locally. 'This is all I fucking need,' he muttered. He couldn't just get up and walk out – he would make himself look like a right mug. Letting the pikey bastard know that he bothered him was the last thing Eddie wanted.

'So, how's business?' Jimmy asked as he sat down opposite Eddie.

'Yeah, going well. What about you?'

Jimmy smiled. 'Good. I don't do so much meself now. I'm happy pottering about at home doing a bit of buying and selling.'

'How's your wife?' Eddie asked politely.

'My Alice is fine. She's a good woman, she is. What about your Jess?'

'Pregnant,' Eddie said smugly.

'Well, I'll be blowed. So is my Alice,' Jimmy told him, smirking back.

About to make his excuses and leave, Eddie was shocked to see the barman bring over a bottle of champagne and plonk it on the table. 'I never ordered this,' Ed said immediately.

'I did. With our families getting it together, I thought me and you should have a little celebration,' Jimmy said grinning.

Eddie looked at him in bewilderment. Surely Ronny and Paulie hadn't joined forces with the O'Haras. If they had, it would be the worst mistake they had ever made. He would be straight up the Flag and would kill the pair of them with his bare hands. 'Whaddya talking about?' Eddie asked.

'Don't you know?' Jimmy asked, chuckling.

Eddie was getting annoyed now. He hated being in the dark about anything, least of all with Jimmy O'Hara. With his expression getting darker by the second, Eddie felt his bottom lip curl up. 'Know fucking what?'

Jimmy was loving every minute of it. Mitchell was already losing his rag and he didn't even know the full story yet, the mug.

Jimmy smiled. 'Your Frankie and my Jed. Well loved-up, they are. Your daughter's always staying on my land in his trailer. Probably at it like rabbits as we speak – you know what these kids are like.'

Unable to stop himself, Eddie leaped up and grabbed O'Hara by the throat. 'Don't lie. This ain't fucking funny, Jimmy. Whatever problems we've had in the past, it's nothing to do with my daughter.'

Michael Murphy walked over. 'Are you OK, Jimmy? What's the problem?'

Jimmy knocked Eddie's hand away and poured two glasses of champagne. He hated the stuff, but had bought it out of devilment. Sipping the shit, Jimmy smiled. 'On my Alice's life, I'm not joking. My Jed and your Frankie are inseparable. They was even out five o'clock the other morning riding up and down on the horse and cart. Let's not argue, Eddie. I mean they'll probably end up getting married, so we have to try to get along for their sake!'

Eddie picked up his glass of champagne and threw the contents into Jimmy O'Hara's unsightly face. 'Over my dead fucking body,' he spat, as he stormed out of the pub.

Approaching his Land Cruiser, Eddie took his frustrations out on the driver's-side door. 'I'll kill the little pikey cunt, I'll fucking kill him,' Ed yelled as he repeatedly kicked the metal as hard as he could.

Aware of Jimmy watching him out of the window, Eddie jumped in his motor and zoomed off.

Eddie was absolutely livid. O'Hara had almost creamed himself while telling him the story. Loved it, the arsehole had, and Eddie sensed that it was probably true. It all made sense. The secrecy, the lies and an invisible boyfriend with a fucking pseudonym.

As he drove for miles, Eddie felt like he had taken a dozen punches from a heavyweight boxer. He had no idea where he was going, the thought hadn't entered his head. Spotting a pub, Eddie swung into the car park. He had to catch Frankie red-handed before he could do anything about it, but there was no point in him following her. She was too cute and he couldn't risk alerting her that he knew.

Making up his mind, Eddie took the business card out of his pocket and punched the number into his phone. 'Gina, it's John Smith. I've got another job for you, but I need you to do it first thing tomorrow.'

'I can't do it tomorrow, Mr Smith. I have another assignment I'm working on, but I can probably do it on Wednesday for you.'

Eddie hated people saying no to him. When he wanted something done, he wanted it immediately. 'Look, this is urgent. I'll give you a thousand pound a day for however long it takes. The house you followed the boy from, I need you to follow his sister.'

Unable to resist the money or the handsome Mr Smith, Gina succumbed to his persuasion. 'OK, I'll do it.'

THIRTY-EIGHT

Unable now to stand the sight of either of his kids, Eddie rang Jessica to check whether they were at home or not.

'They've gone out and both of them said they won't be back till late. Why are you asking, Eddie? What's wrong?' Jessica could tell by the sound of his voice that something terrible had happened.

As Eddie walked into the house, Jessica noticed the look of despair etched across his face. 'Get me a drink and pour yourself one, too. Trust me, you're gonna need it,' Ed told her.

Jessica poured Eddie a large brandy and herself a white-wine spritzer. She had never been a fan of drinking alcohol while pregnant, but she told herself that one wouldn't hurt.

Eddie downed his drink in seconds and immediately got up and poured another. He turned to Jessica, his face contorted with pain. 'I've just found out why our daughter has been so secretive about this boyfriend of hers. Talk about fraternising with the enemy. Guess who she's dating, Jess. Go on, fucking guess.'

Worried, Jessica shrugged. Frankie told her very little and she didn't have a clue. 'I don't know, love, honest I don't. Who is it?'

400

Walking towards the fireplace, Eddie picked up Frankie's latest photograph and smashed it against the wall. 'Jed O'Hara. Our wonderful fucking daughter has been staying on Jimmy's land while shagging his pikey cunt of a son. I'm not having it, Jess, I won't fucking allow it, and tomorrow, when I have the proof in my hands, I will fucking do something about it.'

A couple of miles down the road, Joey had cheered up immensely since finding out that Dominic had only binned him because of his father's interference.

'So, what do you reckon, Frankie? Shall I wait outside Dom's office tomorrow? Or should I give him a few more days to calm down? What would you do if you were me?'

Not hearing a word her brother was saying, Frankie stared vacantly out of the pub window.

'Frankie, whatever's the matter with you today? You're staring into thin air like a tit in a trance.'

'I'm sorry, Joey, I was miles away. What were you saying?'

Knowing his sister better than she knew herself, Joey moved next to her and put a comforting arm around her shoulder. 'What's up? I know you're not yourself. Have you had a row with Jed?'

Frankie shook her head. 'No, it's not that.'

'Well, what is it, then? You know we can tell one another anything.'

Without warning, Frankie burst into tears. 'Oh, Joey, I'm in a right mess. Please don't tell anyone, but I think I might be pregnant.'

Joey looked at his sister in astonishment. 'For fuck's sake, Frankie, please tell me you're joking.'

'I'm not joking. My period's late, and after we were chatting in your room this morning, I was sick twice.'

Joey held her in his arms. Frankie had always been there for him throughout his dramas, and now she needed him to do the same for her. 'Sssh, stop crying. We'll sort this, Frankie, I promise.'

'How? I can't tell Mum and Dad – they'll kill me,' Frankie wailed.

Joey wiped her eyes with his cuff. 'You stay in here and get us another drink and I'll walk down the road and find a chemist. I take it, you haven't done a test yet?'

Frankie shook her head. 'It was only when I was sick earlier that I thought about it. I checked my diary and my period is over three weeks late. I'm so frightened, Joey. I can't tell Jed – say he says he don't want a baby? He might finish with me or something, and I can't lose him. I love him too much.'

Joey soothed her until she finally stopped crying. 'Don't cry, Frankie. You're probably worrying over nothing and it's just coincidence. I mean, you're not stupid. You and Jed have been using something, haven't you?'

Embarrassed, Frankie averted her eyes and stared at her lap. 'Not all the time. Jed didn't like using the rubbers – he said they made his cory itch,' she mumbled.

Annoyed by his sister's naivety, Joey stood up. The quicker he went and got this bloody test, the better. 'I'll tell you something, Frankie, Jed will have more than an itchy cory to worry about if the test's positive. Can you imagine Dad finding out that him and Jimmy O'Hara are about to become family? There'll be murders, Frankie, fucking murders and I hope, for your sake, it's a false alarm, I really do.'

As Eddie knocked back drink after drink, Jessica vacced up the broken glass. The photograph of Frankie was ruined and she had slung it in the bin. 'I know this is hard for you, Eddie, but you won't find your answers in the bottom of a glass. Who told you all this, anyway? It wasn't Ronny again, was it?'

'No, it wasn't fucking Ronny. I haven't heard from him or Paulie since that day in the Flag when I found out our son likes taking it up the arse. What have we done so wrong, Jess, tell me? We've got two kids, one gay and the other screwing pikeys. They've had a privileged upbringing and this is how they repay us. Well, not any more, Jess. I'm putting my fucking foot down from now on and if they don't do as I say, I want the pair of them out of this house immediately.'

Jessica didn't know what to do for the best. There was no reasoning with Eddie when he was in this kind of mood and she was afraid what he might do when the kids came home.

'So, who told you then?' she asked solemnly.

'Jimmy fucking O'Hara. I got it straight from the horse's mouth. I'll kill that boy of his, on our baby's life, if he's touched our Frankie. I'll fucking kill him, Jess.'

Frightened by Ed's demeanour, Jessica tried to hug him, but he pushed her away. 'Please don't talk like that, Eddie. You're scaring me. I'll have a chat with Frankie when she gets home. For all we know, it might not even be true.'

Eddie stood up and snatched at his keys that were on the table. 'Frankie needs a good hiding, not one of your little chats. All this is your fault, Jess. You've been so fucking lenient with 'em, they've ended up with no morals whatsoever. I'm off out and don't expect me home tonight. I'm sick of the sight of this house and I'm sick of the sight of everyone that lives in it.'

As Eddie slammed the front door, Jessica and the glass both shuddered.

*   *   *

Frankie did the pregnancy test in the pub toilets. Too nervous to get the result for herself, she came out and thrust the stick into Joey's hands.

'Urgh, it's all wet. It ain't got your piss on it, has it?' Joey whinged.

'Stop being such a fucking pussy! It only takes five minutes. You check the result for me, I can't do it – I'd do it for you.'

The twins sat in silence. The five minutes seemed more like an hour to both of them. Frankie glanced at her watch. 'Go on, then, check it now.'

'What exactly have I got to look for?' Joey asked.

'If there's a blue line, I'm pregnant and if it's clear, then I ain't.'

As Joey studied the stick, Frankie shut her eyes and said a silent prayer. Her brother's voice interrupted her before she even had time to finish her conversation with God.

'Fucking hell, it's got a blue line. You're pregnant, Frankie, you're pregnant!'

Jessica sipped a cup of tea and weighed up all her options. She could stay at her mum and dad's house, but she didn't want to involve them in this. Her mum always gave unwanted advice and Jessica knew deep down that her dad had never really taken to Eddie. Another option was to stay around Vicki's, but again, Jess didn't want to involve her and Doug either. The problems with the twins were bad enough without the whole world finding out about them.

Finishing her cuppa, Jessica chose option number three. She would ring Raymond and ask him to stay round at hers. Jessica trusted her brother more than anyone and if he came over, at least she wouldn't be alone in the house.

Raymond was having a meal with Polly and her parents when his phone rang. He excused himself and took the call outside. 'What's up, sis?'

'Oh, Raymond. Please can you come round? Something bad's happened and I don't know what to do.'

Raymond sighed. He'd had to shoot away often recently and he didn't want Polly getting sick of his lifestyle and dumping him.

'I'm a bit busy at the moment, Jess. Can't I come round tomorrow?'

Jessica started to cry. 'I don't know how to handle this alone, Raymond. Eddie's found out that Frankie's been seeing Jimmy O'Hara's son and he's gone off his head. I'm frightened to stay here on my own, in case Ed comes back drunk and starts trouble.'

Raymond knew only too well that anything to do with Jimmy O'Hara was enough to tip Eddie over the edge. 'Stay calm, sis. I'll be round within the hour,' he told her.

Ignoring her brother's advice not to tell Jed about the baby, Frankie rang her boyfriend and told him to meet her at the pub. Finding out the test was positive had prompted her to be straight with him. She loved him and just hoped Jed loved her as much as he said he did.

'Just get rid of it, Frankie. We've still got some of our birthday money left. I'll help you pay for an abortion. Mum and Dad will never have to know,' Joey begged her.

Frankie shook her head. 'No, it's not fair, Joey. This is as much Jed's baby as it's mine. I can't get rid of it without telling him. I love him and I couldn't do that to him. For all I know and you know, he might want me to keep it.'

About to plead with Frankie once again, Joey saw Jed walk in and quickly shut up. As her boyfriend walked towards her, Frankie felt her whole body shake from head to toe. She couldn't tell him here. The pub had been almost empty earlier, but now was quite busy.

Jed was more perceptive than most boys his age and he immediately clocked the twins' serious demeanour. 'Blimey, what's up with yous two? Look like you've seen a ghost, the pair of yous do,' he said, smiling.

Telling Joey to stay put, Frankie dragged Jed outside. 'Can we talk in the motor? Where you parked?' she asked him.

Jed led her to his new pick-up truck and opened the door for her. 'Do you like it? Four grand, I give for this. Bought it yesterday, I did, off some old grunter.'

Barely noticing the black metal monster on wheels, Frankie nodded dumbly.

Lifting her chin up, Jed was surprised to see tears in her eyes. 'What's a matter? Not dumping me, are ya?'

Frankie shook her head. She had never felt so nervous in her life and Joey looking out of the pub window wasn't helping matters.

'Jed, I'm pregnant,' she whispered.

Jed burst out laughing. 'Is that why you're crying, you dinlo?'

'I'm scared, Jed. We're so young, what are we gonna do?' Frankie asked, crying even more.

Jed took her into his arms and kissed her tears away. 'Look at me, Frankie,' he ordered her.

Frankie did as he asked and was surprised to see him grinning. 'It's not funny. You're acting as though you want the baby.'

Jed chuckled. 'Of course I want the baby. I love you, Frankie, and we'll get married, if you want.'

'Married!' Frankie exclaimed excitedly.

Jumping out of his seat, Jed ran around the other side

406

of the truck and dragged Frankie out. He sat her on the tail of the truck and got down on one knee.

'There's people watching now, so don't make me look a cory. Marry me, Frankie – I love you.'

Young, naive and hopelessly in love, Frankie said an immediate yes, without thinking about the consequences.

As Jessica finished explaining the full story, Raymond sat silently, sipping his beer. He knew more than anyone how much Eddie hated Jimmy O'Hara and he couldn't believe, if true, how Frankie could have been so bloody stupid.

'He swore on our baby's life that if it was true, he'd kill this Jed. What am I gonna do, Ray?' Jessica sobbed.

Hugging his sister, Raymond was more worried about his brother-in-law. Eddie was the most hot-headed person he had ever come across and he dreaded what he was capable of doing to the O'Haras. The problem was, they were no mugs themselves, and if another feud broke out between the two families, everybody's lives, including his own, would be in danger.

'Let me have a drive around, see if I can find him, Jess. I tried to ring him on the way here, but his phone was switched off.'

Jessica grabbed hold of her brother's hand for dear life. 'Please don't leave me here alone, Raymond. The twins will probably be back soon and if Ed comes back and you're not here, I'm frightened of what he'll do. He could be anywhere. He said he wasn't coming home tonight, so you won't know where to find him, anyway.'

Seeing how shaken up Jessica was, Raymond agreed to stay. None of this shit could be doing her pregnancy any good and he was worried if he left and Eddie came home and created a scene, she might have a miscarriage.

*   *   *

407

Unaware of what was happening at home, Joey looked at his sister in total and utter disbelief. 'You can't get married! You're only sixteen.'

Frankie smiled at Jed as he came back from the bar with a bottle of champagne and three glasses. ''Ere you go. Get this down your neck,' Jed said, as he handed a glass to Joey.

Joey had always been frightened of his sister's lover, so he chose his words very carefully. 'I'm sorry, Jed, I've nothing against you, mate, but my parents are gonna go mental. It's bad enough Frankie's pregnant, but marriage – there's no way my dad's gonna let that happen.'

Jed didn't seem worried in the slightest as he threw a loving arm around his wife-to-be. 'It's got fuck-all to do with your dad. If he don't like it, it's tough shit. Me and your sister wanna be together, and that's all that matters,' Jed said, smiling at him.

'But if you say you're getting married, Frankie, Mum and Dad will chuck you out,' Joey pleaded. He was desperate to make her see sense.

'Look, Joey, as much as I love you, I think I'm gonna have to move out anyway. Jed said I can live in his trailer with him on his dad's land until he buys us somewhere of our own,' Frankie told him.

Seeing her brother's eyes well up, Frankie squeezed his hand. 'Don't get upset, Joey. I'll only be five minutes away and you can come over whenever you want.'

'Course you can,' Jed chipped in. Frankie's brother wasn't his cup of tea. It was obvious the mush was as queer as a nine-bob note, but if Joey visiting made Frankie happy, then it was OK by him.

The thought of life indoors without Frankie was unbearable for Joey. 'When are you thinking of moving out?' he asked.

408

Frankie was adamant as she answered. 'I'm gonna go home in the morning and tell Mum and Dad everything. If it all kicks off, which it's bound to, then I'm going straight away. I'm sorry, Joey, but this is my life and if Mum and Dad can't accept Jed or the baby, then I'm leaving tomorrow, for good.'

THIRTY-NINE

The following morning, Eddie woke up with a sore head, stiff neck and a mouth like a camel's arse. He had spent the night at his salvage yard and had slept on the uncomfortable leather chair. Annoyed with himself for getting so drunk, he walked over to the sink, cupped some water in his hands and washed his face. He'd had the day from hell yesterday, but was now feeling guilty for taking it out on Jessica.

Spotting his car keys lying on the floor, Eddie turned the cabin upside down searching for his mobile. Gina would be ringing at some point today and he needed to find the bastard thing. With no joy, he ran out to his motor and was relieved to see it lying on the passenger seat. He tried to switch it on, but the bloody thing was dead. 'You stupid fucking cunt,' he said, cursing himself.

Still in a complete daze, Eddie nearly forgot to lock the Portakabin up, but remembered just in time. He needed to get home to sort things out with Jessica. Maybe Jimmy O'Hara had been winding him up, although he doubted it very much. Too cocksure of himself, O'Hara was, to be lying.

410

Eddie started the motor and glanced at his watch. Today would probably drag on forever, but at least by nightfall he should know the truth.

Jessica had lain awake all night and had got up at the crack of dawn. Neither Eddie nor Frankie had come home last night and she was worried sick about both of them. Not knowing what to do with herself, Jessica made Raymond a fry-up, then busied herself with the house-work. In times of need, she always turned to her chores to help her; she found them therapeutic.

At 7 a.m., Jessica could stand the suspense no longer and gently tapped on Joey's bedroom door. Her son had arrived home late last night and informed her that Frankie was staying at a friend's house. Jess had tried to question him, begged him to talk to her, but Joey had burst into tears, then locked himself in his bedroom and refused to come back out.

'Joey, it's Mum. I desperately need to talk to you, love. It's not about you, it's about Frankie. She could be in a lot of trouble and I need your help to stop anything silly from happening.'

Joey got out of bed and unlocked his bedroom door. He was furious with Frankie for what she had done and was planning to do. He was also annoyed with her for leaving him in the shit to deal with the aftermath of her stupidity.

Noticing her son was all puffy-eyed, Jessica tenderly rubbed his arm. 'Are you still upset over Dominic?' she asked kindly.

Joey said nothing as he flopped back on his bed. Every time Dominic's name was mentioned, it felt as if a dagger was being jabbed through his heart. He missed

411

him dreadfully and with all that had happened with Frankie, he needed to see him and be comforted by him, not talk about him.

Jessica cleared her throat. 'I know about Frankie and Jimmy O'Hara's son. Your dad knows as well and, as you can imagine, he's none too pleased. For your sister's sake, Joey, I need to know everything. Is it serious? Does she see him much? Are they sleeping together? Tell me all you can, Joey, it's important that you do.'

Joey looked away from her. It was Frankie's job to tell their mum, not his. 'She's coming back this morning, Mum. You can ask her for yourself.'

'So, it is true, then? Jimmy O'Hara told your dad yesterday and I wasn't sure if he was winding him up. What's his name, Joey?' Jessica asked softly. She had to bluff to get the truth out of him.

'His name's Jed. You should remember him, Mum, he's the one that Dad stuck me in the boxing ring with when I was little. Now, if you don't mind, I'm busy. I have to go somewhere myself. Anything else you need to know, Frankie will tell you. This is none of my business.'

Jessica sat with her mouth open. She hadn't realised Jed was that terror of a child who had knocked her son out cold. 'Are you going anywhere nice?' she asked. She couldn't think straight, this was all too much for her.

'Nowhere special. Please, Mum, just leave me alone. I need to have a shower and get out of this house.'

With the weight of the world on her shoulders, Jessica closed Joey's bedroom door and went downstairs.

Aware that his sister looked upset, Raymond hugged her. 'Shall I see if I can find Eddie?' he asked her.

About to answer, Jessica ran to the window as she heard a car pulling up outside.

'Speak of the devil, eh, sis?' Raymond joked, as he went outside to speak to his brother-in-law.

'Is everything OK?' Raymond asked him.

'Not really, but I'll know for definite later. Did you stay here with Jess last night?' Eddie enquired.

Raymond nodded. 'She was a bit upset and rang me. Listen, Ed, I know the score, Jess told me about Frankie and O'Hara's boy. If anything kicks off and you need backup, I'm there for you, you know that.'

Eddie put his arm around Raymond's shoulder. 'Cheers, mate, much appreciated.'

Raymond laughed as Eddie lifted a massive bouquet out of his boot. 'Fucking hell, they ain't for me, are they?'

'Get over yourself, you fucking tosser. Listen, Ray, can you do me a big favour? I've got a gut feeling today's gonna be a bad day. I've got a bit of running around to do, but do you think you can stay here? I don't wanna leave Jess and the kids on their own.'

Raymond immediately agreed. 'Frankie ain't here though, Ed. She never came home last night.'

Eddie felt his pulse start to quicken. 'If I find out she's in that pikey's fucking caravan, I'll kill him, then kill her,' he told Raymond.

Aware that Eddie's eyes had turned cloudy and angry, Raymond led Eddie back to the house. 'Just calm down and go and see Jess. You going off your head ain't gonna do her pregnancy any good, is it?'

Eddie handed Raymond his phone and he told him to put it on charge and make himself scarce for five minutes.

Jessica was in the front room and didn't look up as her husband walked in.

'Jess, I'm so sorry for having a go at you. None of this is your fault, I know it's not. You know the old saying, "You always hurt the ones you love"? Well, I don't mean

413

to, but I suppose because we're so close I take my frustrations out on you.'

Jessica had never been one to carry on an argument. She had only ever done that once with Eddie, when he had shoved Joey into that boxing ring and she had gone back to her mother's for a few days.

As Eddie knelt in front of her, Jessica smiled. 'Look, I'm on me fucking hands and knees, begging your forgiveness. Don't tell anyone, will ya? Got me reputation to think of, ain't I?'

Jessica looked at the beautiful flowers and hugged Eddie as he sat down next to her. 'I've been so worried about you. I thought you'd gone round the O'Haras and done something stupid. Please don't drink that Scotch any more. I can smell it on your breath,' she pleaded, burying her head in his neck.

Eddie stroked her long blonde hair. 'I'm sorry, babe, and I swear I won't touch another drop of Scotch. Raymond said Frankie never came home last night. Do you know where she was?'

'Joey came back and said she stayed at her friend's house. She was probably round Stacey's,' Jessica answered, trying to smooth the situation over.

'Listen, Jess. I promise you that whatever Frankie's up to, I'll try and deal with it in the nicest way I can, but if that don't work, then I'm gonna have to go one step further. Do you understand what I'm saying?'

Jessica clung to her husband for dear life. 'Yes, Eddie, I understand,' she whispered.

Not too many miles away, in Upney, Stanley was in a deep sleep and totally oblivious of his wife prodding and poking him.

Annoyed that he was glued to that stinking armchair

of his and snoring like a pot-bellied pig, Joyce bent down so that her mouth was only an inch away from his ear. 'Stanley', she screamed as loudly as she could.

Stanley shot up in such shock that he lost his balance and fell head first out of the chair. 'You stupid bloody woman. What did you do that for?' he grumbled as he rubbed his right elbow.

Joyce couldn't help but giggle. Stanley looked so funny lying on the carpet in a heap. 'I want you to get yourself ready, Stanley. We need to drive over to our Jessica's. Something's not right, she's got problems, I know she has. Our Raymond was over there last night and Jess barely spoke to me on the phone this morning.'

'Probably something to do with that dodgy old man of hers. Ain't got himself nicked, has he?' Stanley muttered, standing up.

'Now, don't start all that. We've no idea what's wrong yet. I know my Jess and she sounded to me like she'd been crying. For all we know, Stanley, it could be something to do with the baby,' Joyce told him.

'Shouldn't we ask if it's OK for us to visit? We can't just turn up,' Stanley said. Fortunately, he wasn't as nosy as his wife.

'No, because Jess'll say no and then we'll never find out what was wrong in the first place. Now go and get changed, quick as you like,' Joyce said.

'I'm all right. I'll go like this,' Stanley said miserably.

'No, you bloody well won't. Them trousers have got pigeon shit all over 'em. Go upstairs and put your nice grey ones on.'

Stanley tutted, but knew better than to argue. 'What am I meant to say to Jock? I'm meant to be meeting him at eleven to fly our pigeons,' he moaned.

Joyce shook her head furiously. 'You and Jock can get

415

your cocks out any day. Now, chop-chop, Stanley. I'm not one to be kept waiting, you know that.'

'Wicked old witch,' Stanley spouted as he stomped up the stairs.

Back in Rainham, Frankie's heart was beating nineteen to the dozen as she crouched down behind the big bush in her next-door neighbour's front garden. 'Move over a bit, Jed. Your legs are sticking out, someone will see you,' she told her boyfriend.

Jed shook his head in disbelief. He loved his woman very much, but sometimes she had the brains of a rocking horse. 'I'm telling you, Frankie, this is a stupid idea. Does it matter if your dad's there? He's gonna find out when your mum tells him, anyway. We should have done things my way, instead of sitting here like a pair of dinlos.'

Frankie said nothing. Jed had wanted to drive over to her parents, face them and tell them the news together, then load all her belongings onto his truck. Petrified of the fracas that was bound to happen, Frankie put her foot down. She had no doubt whatsoever that her dad would barricade her in the house, then smash both Jed and his new pick-up truck to smithereens.

Hearing the sound of an engine starting up, Frankie peered through the bushes just in time to see her dad's Land Cruiser pull off the drive. 'Right, me dad's gone out. The only people in the house are me mum and possibly me Uncle Raymond. His car's on the drive and I don't think he was with me dad,' she told Jed. She knew Joey was out, as she had seen him jump into a cab about half an hour ago.

'Please let me come with you, Frankie. We're getting married; your mother's gonna think I'm a right div if

I don't face her like a man,' Jed pleaded, as Frankie stood up.

Frankie shook her head. 'You don't wanna come in while me Uncle Raymond's there. He's me father's henchman, so he's bound to kick off. I promise you, once the initial shock's worn off, you can meet me mum. Today, though, I need to talk to her alone.'

Watching Frankie walk away, Jed made a decision. He didn't like the sound of Uncle fucking Raymond and if Frankie weren't back in half an hour, he was going in there, whether his girlfriend liked it or not.

As Frankie walked up the drive, her mind was a whirlwind of emotion. She felt guilty at letting her parents down, but her love for Jed was far too strong for her to put her parents first.

Frankie let herself in with her key.

'There you are. Where have you been?' her mum asked, obviously relieved to see her.

'Mum, I need to talk to you,' Frankie mumbled.

'You OK?' Raymond asked, poking his head into the hallway.

Frankie nodded. 'Fine, thanks. I just need to talk to Mum in private.'

Knowing when he wasn't wanted, Raymond retreated back into the lounge.

'Come on, we'll sit in the kitchen, I'll shut the door,' Jessica said. She knew by Frankie's face that whatever she had to say was very serious and she was dreading hearing it.

Not usually one to eavesdrop, Raymond knew he had little choice. Eddie would want to know what was going on and, for all their sakes, he had to find out. Taking his shoes off, Raymond crept into the hallway and placed his ear against the door.

'What is it, love?' Jessica asked as Frankie began to cry.

'You know that boy I've been seeing? Well, I didn't bring him home because his dad's Jimmy O'Hara. His name's, Jed, Mum, and he makes me so happy.'

'Don't cry. I sort of already knew,' Jessica said, cuddling her.

'There's more, Mum, and you're not gonna like the rest.'

'Go on,' Jessica said, her heart in her mouth.

'I'm pregnant and we're getting married,' Frankie stated. Blurting it out was the only way she could say it.

Feeling her legs turn to jelly, Jessica grabbed one of the wooden chairs and slumped down on it. 'Oh, my God! You can't be, Frankie. You're only a baby yourself.'

Frankie fiercely wiped her tears away. She needed to stand up for herself, be strong, not weak.

'I'm not a baby, Mum. I'm sixteen and I know my own mind. Dad's gonna hate me, I know he is. That's why I'm leaving home today.'

Unable to stop himself, Raymond burst into the kitchen. 'You're going nowhere, Frankie. You dad'll be home soon and he'll sort this mess out.'

Frankie stood up, her eyes blazing. 'You can't tell me what to do. I'm sixteen and I can legally leave home if I want to.'

She turned to her mother. 'Let's not forget, Mum, you were only one year older than me when you got pregnant with me and Joey. You married Dad and had us, didn't you? Why should things be different for me? I love Jed and I will always love him.'

Raymond glared at his niece. Without knowing it, the stupid, brainless girl had just revived the feud that he and

418

everybody else had been dreading. 'I'll tell you why things are different for you, Frankie – because you're with Jimmy O'Hara's son, you idiot. This is gonna break your dad's heart and cause so much fucking trouble. Don't you realise what you've done? Are you that fucking stupid?' Raymond yelled.

'Please stop arguing,' Jessica sobbed.

Having changed lookout positions, Jed was now in Frankie's back garden and could hear almost every word.

'Who do you think you are? Go fuck your grandmother, you cheeky cunt,' Jed shouted, flinging open the back door.

As Raymond went for her boyfriend, Frankie screamed.

Jessica tried to grab hold of her brother. 'Stop it, will you? Violence isn't the answer,' she wailed.

'Come on, Frankie, leave your stuff here, I'll buy you more. We're going,' Jed said, grabbing her hand.

Raymond took hold of Frankie's other arm. 'She's going nowhere, not till her dad gets home. Get upstairs, Frankie, your boyfriend's leaving now.'

Frankie was hysterical as her uncle got Jed into a head-lock and marched him out of the front door. As Raymond slammed the door and walked back inside, he tried to stop a hysterical Frankie following Jed.

'You're going nowhere, you stupid little cow,' he spat at her.

Jed had never been frightened of anyone in his life and he certainly wasn't frightened of Uncle fucking Raymond. 'I'm not leaving here without Frankie,' he shouted, as he repeatedly booted the front door.

'Lock the back door and shut all the windows,' Raymond ordered his tearful sister.

Like a raging bull, Jed tore a big branch off a tree and

419

put it straight through one of the windows. 'Frankie, Frankie! Don't take no notice of your wanker of an uncle. Come on, hurry up,' he yelled.

Ordering Jessica to make sure her daughter stayed inside, Raymond ran out to his motor. He always carried a base-ball bat for emergencies and this was definitely one of them.

'I ain't frightened of you, you fucking dinlo,' Jed shouted at him.

Confident that he could fight Raymond off, Jed changed his mind as soon as he spotted the baseball bat coming his way.

'You go near Frankie again and I'll fucking kill you,' Raymond screamed, as he chased Jed down the driveway.

Streets ahead of him, Jed couldn't resist turning round and doing a wanker sign. 'Shut up, you muggy cunt,' he said, smirking.

Incensed, Raymond carried on chasing him.

Never ones for perfect timing, Joyce and Stanley chose that exact moment to turn into the driveway. Joyce looked at Stanley to make sure her eyes weren't deceiving her. 'Was that our Raymond chasing someone with a baseball bat?'

Stanley nodded dumbly. He was far too shocked to speak.

Joyce got out of the car and did a little jog back to the entrance of the driveway. 'Raymond! It's your mother. Get your arse back here. What do you think you're doing?' she screamed.

With her son nowhere to be seen, a furious Joyce stomped back to the car. 'Come on, Stanley. Don't just sit there, we need to find out what's going on.'

As Stanley got out of the car, he felt nauseous. He hated trouble of any kind and certainly didn't want to be involved in it.

420

Jessica opened the front door. 'What's going on?' Joyce asked, as her daughter fell sobbing into her arms.

Frankie knew that this was probably her only opportunity to escape. Desperate to get away, she sprinted past her mum and nan and sent her grandfather flying as he tried to walk through the front door.

Losing his balance for the second time that day, Stanley landed on his arse. 'Gorden Bennett!' he exclaimed as he tried to get up again.

Jessica could barely speak for crying. 'Frankie's pregnant. Eddie's gonna kill her. What am I gonna do, Mum?' she said between sobs.

Joyce sat Jessica on the sofa. 'Now, come on, dear, stop all that crying. Everything will sort itself out,' she said gently.

'It won't. She's pregnant by the gypsy boy down the road and Eddie's had a feud with that family all his life,' Jessica wept.

Aware of his balance letting him down once more, Stanley fell onto the sofa in utter shock.

'Gypsy? What do you mean? Is that who our Raymond was chasing?'

Jessica nodded. 'Jed's a gypsy boy. All his family are travellers.'

Seeing her husband's face go deathly white, Joyce felt her own turn the same colour. 'Oh, my Gawd. I feel ill,' she gushed.

With his baseball bat still in his hand, Raymond ran back to the house. He had chased Jed for about a mile, but the cocky little bastard was as fast as a whippet and he hadn't got anywhere near him. Out of breath, Raymond ran into the house and put his hands on his knees.

'Where's Frankie?' he asked panting.

Jessica burst into tears again. 'She's gone. She ran off and I couldn't stop her.'

Ignoring his parents, Raymond picked his mobile phone up off the table and ran out the back. Willing the phone he was ringing to answer, he breathed a sigh of relief when it did.

'Ed, it's me. Something terrible's happened. You need to come home right now.'

FORTY

At ten to one, Joey left the coffee shop and crossed the busy main road. Dominic took his lunch break at one o'clock and, although dreadfully nervous, Joey couldn't wait to see him.

Joey had travelled up by train and, while pretending to read the paper, he'd had a long, hard think about his future. Living at home without Frankie by his side really didn't appeal to Joey. He loved his mum, but his sister was the only one who really understood him.

As Dominic walked through the huge glass doors, Joey's heart skipped a beat.

'What are you doing here?' Dominic hissed at him.

'I need to talk to you,' Joey pleaded.

'I've already told you, I've met someone else. Now please just leave me alone,' Dominic told him.

Upset by his ex-lover's reaction, Joey followed him as he walked off in the opposite direction. 'I know you're lying, Dom. I found out the truth and I know my dad came to see you. Please, let's go for a drink so I can say my piece. Ten minutes of your time, that's all I ask.'

Dominic had never felt so petrified in his entire life as the night Joey's father had paid him a little visit. He still couldn't sleep even now, and every time he closed his eyes, he could feel the tip of that knife on the base of his helmet.

Deep down, Dominic still adored Joey, but he wasn't about to tell him that. He couldn't – it was too dangerous. 'Ten minutes, then I want you and your thug of a father out of my life for good,' he said venomously.

Eddie took the phone call from Gina, which confirmed what he had already been told.

'I'm still in the vicinity. I've taken loads of photographs. Do you want me to meet you now, Mr Smith?'

Guessing that Raymond's phone call had something to do with Frankie, Eddie asked Gina to do him a big favour. 'Look, I don't care how much this costs. I want you to keep my friend's daughter and the bloke she's with in your sights. Anywhere they go, I want you to follow 'em. Can you do that for me?'

Gina smiled. She would literally do anything for the gorgeous Mr Smith. 'Of course I will,' she told Eddie.

Desperate to get home, Eddie ended the call and pressed his foot hard against the accelerator. He had been on his way to pick up some money off a geezer in Kent, when Raymond rang him. He had immediately turned around and headed back towards Rainham. Unfortunately, it had taken him ages, as there'd had been an accident at the Dartford Crossing.

Eddie breathed a sigh of relief as he finally pulled into his driveway. Raymond had been reluctant to talk on the phone and all the way home Eddie had been going over what might have happened. Eddie had never been a person to be kept in the dark and the suspense was fucking killing him.

Eddie opened the front door. 'Well, what's going on?'

he yelled, as he saw Jessica, Joyce, Stanley and Raymond sitting in the living room with faces like ghosts.

Jessica burst into tears. 'You tell him, Ray, I can't do it,' she sobbed.

'Fucking tell me then!' Eddie screamed at Raymond.

'Sit down, let me pour you a brandy,' Raymond said.

Eddie was getting more wound up by the second. 'Fuck sitting down and fuck the brandy. Just spit it out, will ya?'

'Frankie's pregnant. She's left home and says her and Jed O'Hara are getting married,' Raymond told him.

Eddie couldn't have been more shocked if an elephant had walked into the lounge. 'What? Over my dead body. Who told you this?'

Seeing the cold, calculating look in his son-in-law's eyes, Stanley felt his bowels loosen, and made a quick exit.

'Where you going, Stanley? Why are you walking funny?' Joyce yelled at him.

'I need the toilet,' Stanley replied, as he did a clenched-arse shuffle down the hallway.

'There's something wrong with that man,' Joyce commented.

Raymond glared at her. 'For fuck's sake, Mother, shut up,' he said as he turned to Eddie.

'Frankie told us. She came home after you went out. He was with her, that Jed, cocky little bastard he is. I chased him off with a baseball bat. I'd have mullered him if I'd have caught him, Ed, but he ran as fast as a grey-hound chasing a rabbit.'

Unable to stop himself, Eddie flew into one almighty rage. 'I will fucking kill that scumbag pikey cunt. Come on Ray, me and you are going over to the house. I want my daughter home and I want her home now!'

Eddie stormed into the kitchen like a bull in a china shop. 'This should do the trick,' he spat, as he grabbed hold of a carving knife.

'Please, Eddie, don't go round there,' Jessica screamed, as she got down on her hands and knees and clung to his legs.

'Jess, get off of me. This is our daughter we're talking about, and I need to put a stop to this shit right now. May God be my judge, she ain't having that pikey cunt's kid. I'll rip it out of her with me bare hands if I have to,' Eddie shouted.

'You'll get arrested. Please, Raymond, do something. You're the only one he'll listen to,' Jessica screamed.

As Eddie stormed out of the house, Raymond caught up with him and grabbed him by the shoulders. 'Listen to me. Jess is right, this ain't the way to do things. For fuck's sake, use your brain. It's broad daylight. If you go round there and stab the cunt, you'll spend the rest of your life in the nick. Think about Jess. You've got a baby on the way.'

Realising Raymond was right, Eddie threw the knife on the gravel, sank to his knees and cried tears of pure anger.

Less than half a mile away, Jed paced nervously up and down his trailer. His old man had gone away to a horse fair for the weekend and his mother was staying at her sister's.

'What's the matter, Jed?' Frankie asked, giving him a hug.

'Us travellers are psychic, Frankie, and I've got a bad feeling about us staying here alone. If me dad was here, we'd be all right, but he ain't.'

'What we gonna do then? I need some clothes, Jed, and underwear.'

Jed squeezed Frankie and rocked her from side to side. 'I think we should get out of here. Me dad's got a trailer in his salvage yard in Tilbury. We can stay there till he gets back from the horse fair. I'm not frightened of no one, Frankie, but we should get away and let things calm down a bit. Don't worry about clothes and stuff. I'll stop on the way there and take you shopping. Trust me, my nan sensed stuff happening and I'm the same.'

Frankie smiled. Life was one big adventure with Jed and he made her feel so safe and loved. 'Are you sure everything's gonna turn out all right, Jed?' she asked him.

Jed tilted her chin. 'I know everything's gonna be OK, but I also know the quicker we get out of here the better.'

As they drove out the gates, neither Jed nor Frankie noticed the woman clocking them in the little black Micra.

Oblivious to what was happening to his sister, Joey was trying to iron out his own problems. Unable to stop his emotions, he hugged Dominic for what would probably be the last time and could only watch as he walked away. As Dominic turned around and waved, Joey stood rooted to the spot for a few minutes. Devastated, he then found the nearest pub to down his sorrows.

'I want a triple vodka, with ice and a dash of lemonade,' he told the barman.

Finding a quiet table, Joey flopped onto a seat. What his father had done to Dominic was despicable and unforgivable.

Joey had never been that close to his dad. He had always known deep down that his dad preferred Gary and Ricky. It didn't really bother him. Even when he was a child, he had sensed that his dad saw him as a disappointment, the weakest link, and he had just got on with things in his own little way.

Another thing that Joey was always aware of was that his father was a villain. Frankie and he had both clocked on when they were about ten years old and spent many a night giggling about what their school teachers might say.

Although not a big fan of his father, Joey had never imagined him as a violent, nasty, vicious bully. Dominic wasn't lying, Joey knew that, and he was flabbergasted by his dad's behaviour. To force his way into Dom's flat with a knife was bad enough on its own. But then, to make him lie naked on the floor while threatening to chop his penis off was the most callous act that Joey had ever heard of.

'You will always hold a special place in my heart and I will always love you, Joey. But, promise me, for my safety, you won't contact me again,' Dominic had begged him.

Finishing his drink, Joey slammed the glass on the table and stormed out of the pub. He couldn't wait to get home and tell his mum the story. She was married to an animal who had a screw loose and she had every right to know the truth.

As Joey got on the train, his thoughts turned to his sister. If his dad was capable of doing what he had done to Dom, Christ only knows what he was capable of doing to Frankie's boyfriend. Joey had no idea if Frankie had told their parents after he had left this morning, but he knew he had to warn her. He didn't particularly like Jed, but at this moment in time he preferred him to his sadistic headcase of a father.

As the train stopped in a tunnel, Joey listened intently as an announcement was made: 'Due to signal failure, there will be a short delay.'

'Shit,' Joey muttered. He needed to get home – and

428

fast. Jed could be in serious trouble and he had to warn Frankie immediately.

After his minor show of emotion, Eddie had now got his act together. Just in case things turned sour, he needed to get anything dodgy off the premises. 'Right, stick the jewellery and diamonds in that sports bag, Ray. Get that picture down from in the front room as well. That's hooky – came out of an art gallery, I think.'

As his son reached above his head to take the painting off the wall, Stanley looked at his wife in horror. 'I always said Eddie was a crook, didn't I?' he whispered.

'Why don't you just shut the fuck up,' Joyce said, punching him in the arm.

Jessica was having a lie on the bed and Joyce was worried about her. She had almost fainted earlier with bad stomach pains, but had begged her mum not to tell Eddie.

Joyce turned to Stanley. 'I think him and our Raymond are going out somewhere. Do you think I should tell Eddie that Jess ain't well?' she said in hushed tones.

Stanley shrugged. He hated this house, hated Eddie and couldn't wait to get home to his pigeons.

As Buster and Bruno came in from the garden and leaped on him with muddy paws, Stanley stood up. 'Our son and son-in-law are probably just popping out to rob a bank, dear. I'm going outside to have a cigar. I need some fresh air and I can be lookout for the police arriving,' he said sarcastically.

'You are one miserable old bastard,' Joyce told him, as he left the room.

Upstairs, Jessica was wide awake and crying on her pillow. She had had pains and twinges all day. Unbeknown to her family, she had rung the hospital earlier.

'You haven't lost any blood at all?' the nurse had enquired.

'No, but I sort of passed out,' Jessica had replied.

'You'll be fine. You've just been overdoing it. All you need is rest,' the nurse insisted.

Hearing the front door slam and an engine start up, Jessica got up and walked over to the window. Seeing her husband's Land Cruiser roar away, she ran downstairs. 'Mum, where's Eddie gone? Is Raymond with him?' she asked, panicking.

Joyce smiled and patted the seat next to her. 'Sit down and I'll make you a nice cup of tea. Raymond's with Eddie, they've gone to the pub. Ed wanted to come up and tell you but I told him not to. I thought you were asleep.'

Picking up the house phone, Jessica rang her husband's mobile, just to check her mother's story.

'I'm fine, Jess. I've calmed down now, honest. Me and Raymond are going out for a few pints,' Eddie assured her.

Jessica was relieved. He sounded OK. 'Promise me, Ed, you won't get on the Scotch,' she begged him.

'I promise, and I love you,' Eddie replied.

Jessica felt her body relax as she sipped the strong, sugary tea.

As Joey burst into the room, Jessica knew her day was destined to end as badly as it had begun. 'Mum, I need to talk to you alone,' her son insisted.

Jessica stood up. Joey was visibly upset, so she led him upstairs, away from his grandparents.

Stanley, who had followed his grandson into the house, looked at Joyce. 'No wonder them kids have got problems. There's more dramas going on than *Dallas* in this family. Our Jess should never have married Eddie,

I told you that years ago, but you wouldn't listen, would you?'

Joyce pursed her lips. 'I should have never married you, but I did. Now, just sit down and shut your bastard trap.'

As Joey sobbed his heart out, Jessica did her best to comfort him.

'I can't understand what you're saying. What did Dad do?'

'He broke into Dominic's flat, made him lie on the floor naked and threatened to chop his penis off and shove it down his throat. Dom won't see me no more, Mum, he's too scared. And now I'm worried about Frankie. If Dad did that to Dominic, what will he do to Jed?'

Jessica felt the hairs on her body stand on end. She suddenly didn't feel as if she knew her loving husband at all. 'We need to ring Frankie and warn her, Mum. Dad's capable of anything, I just know he is. Dominic told me that Dad even made a little cut on the end of his penis, then he laughed as he wiped the blood all over his dressing gown.'

Jessica felt physically sick as she told Joey to search his sister's bedroom. Frankie hadn't taken her mobile with her and they needed to find Jed's number to ring him. As Jessica felt a sharp twinge in her stomach, she lay on her bed and prayed. 'Please God, keep me and my children safe. Amen,' she whispered.

A few miles down the road, Eddie and Raymond were doing a bit of digging. After leaving home, they had purchased a bottle of Scotch and a bag of ice, and headed straight to Ed's salvage yard.

'That's deep enough,' Eddie said, handing Raymond the haul they had dug up from his father's house. Eddie knew it was about to all go off, and he didn't want anything dodgy indoors in case the rozzers came sniffing around.

'What about the painting?' Raymond asked.

'I'll deal with that. You OK for a minute? I've gotta make a couple of phone calls. If you need me, I'll be in the cabin.'

Pouring himself a large Scotch, Eddie drank it, then rang Gina's number. 'Well, are they still in Rainham?' he asked.

Gina smiled when she heard Eddie's voice. 'No, they're in Tilbury. Earlier they went shopping, bought clothes and a sleeping bag and now they're in an old trailer on what looks like some kind of scrapyard.'

'Get yourself home now. Can you get back there first thing tomorrow? I might need you to watch them all day. Money's no object, you know that.'

Gina was usually very professional, but couldn't resist letting her guard down for once. 'I'll do it on one condition, Mr Smith.'

'What?' Eddie asked.

'That you buy me dinner as a thank you.'

'You've got a deal,' Eddie lied. He had no intention of taking Gina anywhere. Not once had he ever even thought of cheating on Jess, and he wasn't about to start now.

'I've gotta go now. Get there at six,' he said, ending the call.

Eddie refilled his glass and studied the guns that he and Raymond had dug up earlier. He had no idea where his father had got the machine gun from. He held it in his hand and smiled. It felt good, it felt right and, providing everything went to plan, it would spell the end of Jed O'Hara, once and for all.

FORTY-ONE

Opening her eyes, Frankie nudged Jed. They were snuggled up together in a sleeping bag, but the bed they were lying on smelt musty and damp. 'Jed, I need to get up. Move over, will you? The smell of this bed's making me feel sick.'

Jed unzipped the bag so Frankie could climb over him. Unbeknown to her, the trailer they were staying in used to be his little shagging den. When his mum and dad split up, Jed had kept in close contact with his old man and when he was thirteen, his dad had given him the key to this place.

'It's got everything you need in there, boy. Anytime you wanna pull yourself a little gorjer bird, take her back there,' he told him.

Within a month of being given the key, Jed was making regular use of the trailer. He had been knocking about with his cousin, Sammy Boy, at the time and, between them, they must have brought a thousand birds back. Jed smiled. He and Sammy boy had had some good times here. None of the birds had meant anything to them, it was all just a bit of fun. Jed had changed since he'd met Frankie. He had never been in love before, but Frankie had cast her magic spell over him. He was content now and other girls didn't interest him in the slightest.

'Jed, what's in this little box room that's locked? Have you got the key? Can I have a look in it?'

About to say yes, Jed remembered what was in there. 'Shit. I've gotta get rid of that stuff,' he mumbled. 'It's a load of old rubbish in there, Frankie. It's me dad's stuff, he don't like anyone going in there,' Jed lied. Frankie would have a fit if she knew what was really in there. If she ever saw those photographs, that would be the end of their relationship. Cursing himself for being so slap-dash, Jed made a mental note to burn the photos as quickly as possible. He had only kept them as souvenirs and should have got rid of them yonks ago.

He got out of bed and slung on his clothes. Frankie smiled as Jed put his masculine arms around her. 'What we gonna do today? Can we get something to eat? I'm starving,' she asked.

'I'll tell you what, why don't we go and get a Maccy D's? And then later, when it's dark, I'll clear me dad's shit out of that spare room and we can make ourselves a nice romantic campfire to sit round.'

Frankie kissed him. She had not sat around a camp-fire since she was a kid. Her dad used to make a big thing of Bonfire Night when she and Joey were little. 'Perfect,' she said.

As he shut the trailer door, Jed smiled. Later, those photos would go up in smoke and then his beautiful girl-friend would never be any the wiser.

With his brain doing overtime, Eddie got out of bed as soon as the birds began to sing.

'Can't you sleep, love?' Jessica asked softly.

Eddie sat on the edge of the bed and held his arms

434

out for a hug. 'Listen, I can't rest not knowing what our Frankie's up to. Today I'm gonna bring her home, Jess, and I need you to do me a favour. I don't think there'll be any trouble, but I don't want you here until she's home. I want you to take Joey and stay at your parents' for a couple of days.'

Jessica moved from her husband's grasp. 'How are you gonna bring her home? You're not gonna do anything silly, are you, Eddie?'

'Of course not. Me and Raymond know exactly what we're doing. I swear to you, Jess, all I want is our baby home, safe and sound.'

Unable to stop thinking about what Joey had told her, Jessica got more involved than usual. 'What about Jed? What are you planning to do to him? I know you better than you think, Eddie, and if you hurt that boy, then I'm leaving you for good.'

Eddie looked at Jessica in amazement. Her leaving him was never going to happen. 'What the hell are you talking about? Has someone been telling tales about me, or what?'

Jessica shook her head. She had promised Joey that she would never repeat what he had told her. 'If you say one word, Dom will be as good as dead, Mum,' Joey had begged her.

'I'm just worried, Ed. No one's said anything to me, but I know what you're like. When you're on that Scotch you're a different person. Just promise me that you won't hurt Jed.'

Eddie crouched down, took her hands in his and looked as sincere as a child. 'I swear to you, all I'm gonna do is buy off that boy. I want Frankie home and him out of her life. If I pay him enough, he'll move on and he won't come back. These pikeys are fly-by-nights, Jess. They ditch one bird, then they're with another five minutes later. He won't return searching for our Frankie, not if the money's good enough, I bet ya.'

Jessica sighed. She wanted to believe Eddie, but didn't know if she could any more. 'It's not as easy as that, Eddie. What about the baby? You seem to have forgotten that Frankie's pregnant. If Frankie wants to keep the child, Jed's bound to want to see it at some point.'

Every time Frankie's baby was mentioned, it was a struggle for Eddie to keep his temper intact. 'That pikey piece of shit probably already has about ten kids dotted about the country. That's what they're like, all fucking inbred. None of 'em go to school and the only thing they learn is to fuck one another. Pat Murphy reckons Jimmy O'Hara's wife, Alice, is his cousin, so that says it all! I dunno about you, Jess, but I refuse to let my daughter live in that community. Now, are you going to your mother's with Joey, or what?' Ed asked angrily.

'Yes. I'll get up now, wake Joey and we'll get going.' Jessica said sadly.

Annoyed with himself for shouting at her, Eddie held Jessica tightly. 'I'm sorry, babe. You know what I'm like. I'll ring you when I've sorted things, then you can come home.'

Staring into his cloudy eyes, Jessica knew he had bigger plans for Jed than he had admitted. She was worried now, really worried. The last thing she wanted to do was betray Eddie, but she knew she had to do something. Feeling terribly guilty, she pecked him on the lips. 'I love you,' she told him.

Thankful she was OK about his plans, Eddie smiled at her. 'And I love you too, babe.'

Jed laughed as Frankie polished off her second egg and bacon muffin. 'Sure sign you're eating for two. You'll be as fat as a bull soon, you will.'

436

Frankie playfully punched him. When she had first got with Jed, his warped sense of humour used to give her the hump. Now she just joined in with him. 'I don't care if I get big and fat. If you don't want me, Jed, there's loads of others that will.'

Jed grabbed Frankie's face and, not caring about the other diners watching, stuck his tongue down the back of her throat.

'Do you mind? That's disgusting,' said a grey-haired woman sitting nearby.

Jed grabbed Frankie's hand. They had eaten all their food and were ready to leave, anyway.

Never able to resist a parting shot, Jed grabbed the woman's hand as he walked past her, and guided it towards his penis. 'You're only jealous, you old grunter. You want me and me cory for yourself, don't ya?' he taunted her.

'Management! I demand you call the police. Never in my life have I been so insulted,' the woman screamed.

Pissing themselves with laughter, Jed and Frankie ran from the restaurant.

Eddie was sitting opposite Raymond in Rosie's Café along the A13.

'Yous two are looking as handsome as ever, may I say,' Rosie shouted out to them.

Rosie was a plump woman in her late fifties and Eddie always had a laugh with her. Rosie had a personality to die for and the biggest pair of tits he had ever seen in his life. 'Rosie, put them knockers away, shut your trap and cook my fucking bacon,' he shouted back.

Turning back to Raymond, Eddie filled him in on the plan. 'So what we're gonna do is turn up there when darkness falls in two separate motors. I want you to run in with a baseball bat and, if Jed starts, clump him over the head with it. Then I need you to drag Frankie out the trailer, shove her in the car and take her home.'

Raymond shook his head. 'That ain't gonna work. Your Frankie's like a wild fucking cat. You don't honestly think she's gonna come out gracefully and sing to the radio on the way home, do ya?'

'I've brought a load of rope with me. I know she's my daughter, but you're gonna have to tie her up. There's a gag in me boot: stick that on her as well,' Eddie told him.

Raymond's face was a picture. 'So where do you come into all this? And what am I meant to do with her when I get her home? What's Jess gonna say when I bring her daughter home looking like an escape artiste?'

Eddie smirked. Raymond had cottoned on to his sense of humour over the years – so much so that he could probably give Eddie a run for his money now. 'I've sorted everything. When you get home, Gary and Ricky will be there. I didn't really want to get 'em involved in this one, but I had no choice. You can leave Frankie with them, they'll take care of her. Then I want you to drive back to Tilbury to help me clear up what's left of Jed.'

'Surely Frankie's gonna realise you've killed him. She's got a will of her own, that girl. Say she starts blabbing to someone?'

'She won't. I'm gonna tell her I gave Jed ten grand to get out of her life. He put it in his pocket and ran like a racehorse, I'll tell her,' Eddie said confidently.

Raymond had his doubts about the story. 'She ain't stupid, your Frankie. You don't wanna underestimate her, Ed.'

'She'll be fine in time. Obviously, she's gonna be upset at first, but once I persuade her to get rid of the baby, she'll get over it. Hopefully, one day she'll meet a nice bloke, have his kids and thank me for her lucky escape.'

Not agreeing with Eddie's way of thinking, Raymond changed the subject. 'If you shoot Jed in the trailer, we're gonna have to burn it.'

Eddie smiled. He was clever and had thought of everything. 'I'm gonna burn the trailer, but not Jed. You know what the filth's like, they'll find his teeth and work out it's him. When you drive off with Frankie, I'm gonna kill him, then wrap his body up in plastic. I've got a hooky motor to use. When you come back, we're taking the body over to Flatnose Freddie. Freddie disposed of many bodies for me dad over the years, and our pikey friend, Jed, is going into his big cement mixer. "Freddie," I said, "the boy's a traveller, he's used to open space." "Don't worry, Eddie, I'll prop him up in one of the flyovers I'm building. He's out in the open for ever then," Freddie assured me. Then Ray, we'll burn the motor.'

Raymond said nothing as he sipped his tea. Eddie's plan was good, but not infallible and Raymond had a terrible feeling that something was about to go very, very wrong.

A couple of miles away, Jessica paced up and down the living room. Joey had just left to stay with his grandparents. 'Please, Mum, I wanna stay with you. What are you gonna do? Please tell me,' her son begged her.

Jessica had waved away his fears. 'Mummy's not doing anything for you to worry about. All I'm going to do is ring Jed and speak to him and Frankie. If I can meet up with them, maybe between us we can sort things out,' she told Joey honestly.

'Please let me come with you. I miss Frankie so much,' her son pleaded.

Knowing that Joey was an emotional wreck and certainly no tough cookie, Jessica refused. 'You stay at

Nan and Grandad's and as soon as I've met up with Frankie, I promise I'll ring you and tell you everything.'

With Joey now safely out of the house, Jessica rang Jed's number. Joey had found it the day before; it was written on a piece of paper in Frankie's bedside cabinet.

As Jed answered the phone, Jessica spoke calmly and rationally. 'Please don't put the phone down, Jed. It's Frankie's mum and I want to help you.'

'We're fine. We don't need your help,' Jed said coldly.

'Listen, Jed, and listen carefully. I need to meet up with you. Eddie's on the warpath and I'm worried about your safety. I swear he doesn't know that I'm ringing you and if you see him, please don't tell him.'

Jed swerved onto a kerb and, holding his phone between his legs, repeated the conversation to Frankie. Although Frankie used to be a daddy's girl, she knew that her mum was the one she could trust. 'Let me speak to her,' she urged Jed.

Reluctantly, Jed handed her the phone. 'Mum, what's up?'

Jessica repeated what she had already told Jed. 'I'm really worried, Frankie. Your dad's planning something stupid, I saw it in his eyes.'

'Well, he won't find us,' Frankie said adamantly.

'Aren't you at Jed's house?' Jessica asked surprised.

'No, we're miles away. It's remote where we're staying, sort of in the middle of nowhere.'

'Please Frankie, tell me where you are and I'll come over and sort things out. I understand how you feel about Jed and the baby, I really do. I felt the same about your dad and you and Joey when I fell pregnant. I want you to be happy, Frankie, and if you want to marry Jed and have his baby, then it's fine by me. We still need to convince your father, but if I can come over and speak to you and Jed, between us we can make things right.'

Frankie held her hand over the phone and spoke to Jed. 'Look, I know she's not setting us up, my mum's not like that. We can't stay away forever, Jed. I miss Joey and I'm gonna want contact with him. If anyone can make my dad see sense, it's my mum. Please Joey, give her the address and let her come over.'

Against his better judgement, Jed told Jessica where they were staying and told her not to drive there until it got dark. 'And don't come in your own car. Borrow one off someone else, or we ain't got a deal,' Jed told her as he abruptly ended the call.

'Thanks, Jed,' Frankie said, squeezing his hand.

Jed snatched his hand away. ''Ere, cacker, you've done a wrong 'un there, Frankie, I'm telling ya. I've got a terrible gut feeling that tonight is gonna be one almighty disaster. Things ain't gonna go cushti, I just know they ain't.'

FORTY-TWO

Eddie and Raymond sat in a grotty pub in Tilbury. The weather was awful. It was meant to be midsummer, but the rain was bouncing off the ground.

'How did you know that Frankie and Jed were in Tilbury?' Raymond asked, sipping his pint.

'I hired a private detective. I need you to go and pay her for me tomorrow. She's got the hots for me, so I ain't going meself. I can't anyway – I'll be too busy indoors sorting Frankie out. I'll ring Jess tomorrow morning, get her to come home. She'll know what to do.'

'Are you gonna tell Jess the same story as you're telling Frankie?' Raymond enquired.

'Of course. No one must ever find out the truth. I'm not even gonna tell Gary or Ricky. The less anyone knows, the better with this one.'

'Do you want another pint?' Raymond asked.

'Nah. I'll just have an orange juice. We've got a big night ahead of us and we need our wits about us,' Ed replied.

Raymond felt himself shudder. Kidnapping Frankie, murdering Jed – something didn't feel right. Even the weather seemed against them. 'Be careful, Ed. Something feels wrong about all this to me.'

Eddie laughed. 'You know your trouble? You worry too much, Raymondo.'

Jessica sat in Vicki's house drinking a strong black coffee. Her nerves had been shattered last night, which had led to her feeling faint and weak.

'So, is Joey at home?' Vicki asked concerned.

'No, me dad picked him up earlier. He didn't want to go – he wanted to stay with me – but what could I do, Vicki? It's not right, him being in the house with all this going on.'

Vicki gave her best friend a hug. Jessica told her everything and vice versa. They trusted one another implicitly and what was said between them, was never repeated to either of their husbands. 'So, how exactly is Ed going to get Jed to stay out of Frankie's life?'

Jessica shrugged. 'Ed says he's going to offer Jed money to stay away. The thing is, Vicki, I think Jed and Frankie are truly in love. If Jed knocks back Eddie's offer, then I'm petrified of what might happen next. I need to sort it, but Jed said I can't take my own car.'

Vicki said nothing. She had heard loads of rumours about Eddie Mitchell over the years and knew he was ruthless and dangerous. 'Look, you can take my car. If anyone can sort this mess out, then it's you, Jess. And don't worry too much about Eddie – he'll be too frightened of losing you to do anything stupid.'

Jessica's face momentarily lit up. 'Do you really think so, Vicki?'

Vicki smiled. 'Of course I do.'

Lying was Vicki's only option. She could hardly tell her best friend that Eddie would stop at nothing to get what he wanted. What Jessica didn't know couldn't hurt her, and as her friend, it was Vicki's job to protect her from the awful truth.

Back in Tilbury, the bonfire was burning brightly.

'Do us a favour, Frankie. Most of this wood's wet. Go and see if you can find some dry bits,' Jed told her.

Frankie stared at the fire. 'It's burning OK. Do I have to, Jed?' It gave Frankie the heebies where they were staying and she didn't fancy walking around in the dark on her own.

'No one's gonna abduct you, you dinlo. The only reason the fire's burning is 'cause I cleared some of me dad's old tut out of that room. I've got nothing left to burn now.'

As Frankie walked off, Jed ran into the trailer, grabbed the incriminating photographs and threw them onto the fire. 'Burn, you bastards,' he mumbled, prodding them with a stick.

By the time Frankie ran back, the evidence was in ashes. 'All right? Where's the wood?' Jed asked her.

Frankie fell into his arms. 'I saw a rat and I hate them. It was staring at me, Jed.'

Jed held her tightly. 'I can't stand 'em either. Longtails, I call 'em. Evil little bastards, they are.'

'You don't think there's any watching us now?' Frankie asked him.

'Look, there's one there,' Jed yelled, making Frankie jump out of her skin.

Jed laughed. 'Come on, let's go inside and have something to eat. You can tidy up a bit before your mum gets here.'

Two miles down the road, Eddie could feel his adrenalin levels rising. 'This orange juice is making me feel

444

queasy. Get us a large Scotch, Raymondo. Get yourself one an' all.'

As Raymond went up to the bar, Eddie gave Gina a call. 'Well, are they still there?'

'Yes. They've lit a fire outside, so I think they're settled for the night.'

'You can pull off now. My colleague will settle up with you tomorrow. I know we agreed on a price, but I've stuck a few hundred quid in extra for all your hard work.'

'Thank you, Mr Smith, that's very kind of you, but I would rather be taken out for dinner,' Gina said boldly.

'I'm very busy at the moment, but as soon as I get a bit of free time, I'll call you,' Eddie lied. He had to keep her sweet, as he didn't want her blabbing. 'And Gina, not a word to anyone. My friend's a very violent man and if any of this got out, it would make him very angry,' Eddie said threateningly.

'I understand,' Gina replied.

'Well, I've gotta go now. It's been a pleasure doing business with you,' Eddie said, before ending the call.

Raymond handed Eddie his drink. 'Who was that on the blower?'

'The private detective. I've just sent her home. It's getting dark now, so I suggest we have a couple more drinks, then make our move.'

Oblivious of what was about to happen, Jed and Frankie were munching crisps and discussing baby names. 'Whaddya think of Chantelle for a girl?' Frankie asked.

Jed turned his nose up. 'Don't like it, sounds like a fucking porn star.'

'Well, you think of some, then. You ain't liked any of mine so far,' Frankie said sulkily.

Jed pushed her onto the bench settee. 'Getting the hump, are we?' he said, tickling her.

As he kissed her passionately, Frankie immediately responded. 'I really do love you,' she told him as he pulled away.

Jed smiled. He needed to butter her up to ask his next question. 'Frankie, if we have a boy, can we call him Butch, after my grandad? I know you never met him, but he was a good old mush and I was always close to him.'

Frankie paused before answering. She didn't particularly like the name, but it obviously meant a lot to Jed. 'I don't see why not, but let's decide for definite nearer the time,' she said smiling.

Jed grinned as he cuddled her. Baby Butch would be the most idolised kid in the travelling community. His grandfather had been a legend amongst their own and by giving his son the same title, the name Butch O'Hara would carry on for years to come.

Frankie stood up and peered out of the window. 'I'm sure I just saw headlights. Go outside and have a look, Jed, it might be my mum.'

Seeing a figure walk towards her, Jessica turned the beam down and squinted. She had had terrible trouble finding her way here and had stopped on numerous occasions to ask for directions.

Jessica breathed a sigh of relief as she realised the boy must be Jed. At one point, she had wondered if he and Frankie had sent her on a wild goose chase, and was so glad that they hadn't.

'Just park down the road somewhere. It's a bit muddy, but you'll be OK, won't ya?'

Jessica looked at her feet. In her frantic state of mind, she had forgotten to put her shoes on and was only wearing carpet slippers. 'I've got me slippers on,' she told Jed awkwardly.

'Wait there,' Jed said, as he legged it back to the trailer.

'What's up? Was it me mum?' Frankie asked. She had been looking out of the window, but it had started raining heavily again and she couldn't see a thing.

'Yeah, it is. Give us your trainers, Frankie. Your mum's got her slippers on and it's like a swamp out there.'

Frankie giggled. 'I'm a size three and me mum's a size six. They won't fit her.'

Jed took them off of her anyway and ran back out to Jessica. 'Try them,' he said.

Unable to get them on, Jessica handed them back to him. 'Don't worry. If my feet get soaked it won't kill me, will it?'

Jed gave a half-smile. 'Just follow me and run. I've got a heater inside. I'll try and get the slippers dry for ya before you drive back.'

Frankie felt nervous as her mother stepped into the trailer. 'This is cosy,' Jessica said politely, hugging her daughter.

''Ere, put these on,' Jed said, handing her his socks and dealer boots to wear.

'Thanks, love,' Jessica said gratefully, as he put her slippers on top of the heater.

'Make Mum a cup of tea,' Frankie urged Jed.

Jessica squeezed her daughter's hand. 'So, how are you? Why aren't you staying at Jed's house?'

'Jed's dad and mum aren't there. His dad's gone to a horse fair and his mum's at her sister's. We was gonna stay there, but Jed said we'd be safer staying here until his dad gets back.'

'Were you worried about your dad?' Jessica asked.

Frankie nodded. 'What we gonna do, Mum? Me and

447

Jed don't wanna have to live like this. I'm happy and I want everybody to be happy for me. I want you, Joey and dad to all be part of me and my baby's life.'

Seeing tears roll down Frankie's face, Jessica felt her own eyes well up. 'Frankie, I promise you that I'll do my utmost to make your dad see sense. I can see that you and Jed are in love and I want to support both of you and the baby. With me being pregnant as well, our babies can be playmates, Frankie. I can babysit whenever you want. If you and Jed want to go out, I can –'

Handing Jessica her tea, Jed shut her up in mid-sentence. 'Look, I know you mean well, Mrs Mitchell, but unless you sort that husband of yours out, none of that shit's gonna happen, is it? I ain't having Frankie upset while she's carrying my child, so if things ain't smoothed out fast, I'm taking Frankie away and none of yous will ever see her again!'

Crawling along in the rain, Eddie stopped the motor, got out and jumped in the passenger seat of Raymond's motor. 'Right, that's the place down there on the left. You know what you've gotta do, don'tcha?'

Raymond nodded. 'Take this just in case,' Eddie urged as he handed him a small gun.

'Whaddya want me to do with that?' Raymond asked.

'Nothing, it's just for back-up. Now remember, Ray, be as threatening as you can when you get there. If the door ain't open, then smash the fucking windows. You'll have to hit 'em hard, 'cause it's probably that plastic shit. That cocky pikey cunt is bound to stick up for himself and I want you to clump him as hard as you can with the bat. Knock him out, so he don't wake up. Now, you go first and when I see you've got Frankie and driven off, I'll go in and finish off the job.'

448

Raymond felt sick as he drove towards the trailer. Usually violence didn't bother him. He could kill a man in the blink of an eye, but not when it involved his own family. He didn't like Eddie's plan one little bit, but he was too frightened to argue. When Eddie Mitchell made his mind up to do something, there wasn't a man in the world who could change his mind.

As the tyres screeched to a halt outside, Frankie screamed, grabbed her mother and got down on the floor. Jed took the knife he always carried out of his pocket and stood by the door.

'Open this fucking door – now!' Raymond screamed menacingly as he smashed the baseball bat against it.

'Oh, my God! It's Raymond. Your dad's gonna kill me. What am I gonna do?' Jessica whispered, sobbing.

'Quick, hide in that room, Mum. There's a gap under the bed,' Frankie urged her.

As Jessica crawled into the bedroom, she shuddered as she heard the window go through. 'Please God, don't let anyone get hurt. Please God, don't let anyone get hurt,' she repeated over and over again.

Frankie screamed as Raymond threw himself against the door and it flew open. 'Leave us alone. Go away!' she screamed.

Desperate to be the big hero, Jed lunged at Raymond with the knife. 'You fucking mug!' Raymond yelled, easily knocking it out of Jed's hand.

As Jed picked the kettle up, Raymond obeyed Eddie's orders and clumped him over the head with the baseball bat. He could have hit him harder, but guilt stopped him from doing so. All he wanted to do was stun Jed; it was Eddie's job to do anything else.

Jed wasn't stupid, so he fell on the floor and played dead.

'Jed! Jed!' Frankie screamed hysterically.

As Raymond walked towards her, Frankie went for him. 'Get off of me! I hate you and my dad. I wish you were both dead,' she yelled, pummelling her fists against his chest.

Raymond took the rope out of his pocket and carried out the instructions he had been given. 'It's all right, Frankie, all I'm doing is taking you home,' he said, as she repeatedly kicked and punched him.

'Jed, wake up, please wake up,' Frankie cried.

As Raymond bent over with his back towards him, Jed held his forefinger to his mouth to tell Frankie to be quiet and to let her know he was all right. I love you, he mouthed to her.

Frankie bit Raymond's hand, as he tried to gag her. Raymond felt terrible. He was cut out for most things, but not this shit. He was mad to have let Eddie talk him into this. He should have been a man and refused.

Jed lay still as Raymond finally managed to tie and gag Frankie. He cursed himself for not bringing a proper weapon with him. Pretending he was knocked out cold was all he could do. Raymond was double his size and was armed with his infamous baseball bat, and Jed knew that Frankie needed him alive, not dead.

Jessica was frozen with shock. She couldn't breathe, move or anything. Her daughter's screams had been awful. She had wanted to get up and help her, but she had been paralysed by fear and couldn't. She felt faint again, really ill.

Seeing Raymond bundle Frankie towards the car, Eddie picked up the machine gun and studied it. He had never used one of these things before, but he was sure he could handle it.

As Raymond's car pulled away, Eddie got out of his

car and took a pop at one of the nearby squashed cars. Perfect, he thought, as the bullets landed exactly where he aimed them.

Hearing the fun being fired, Jed quickly got up. It was obvious what was coming next and he knew he had no choice other than to leg it. Raymond had smashed a couple of windows in the trailer and, realising the gunshots were coming from the front, Jed squeezed himself out of a back window and literally ran for his life.

At the sound of the gun being fired, Jessica lost consciousness. Out for the count, she was totally unaware of her husband's footsteps nearing.

In the back of Raymond's car, Frankie was desperately trying to pull the gag off her mouth. She had seen her father waiting in the shadows as Raymond had lifted her into his motor, and not only was she worried about Jed, she was also concerned about her mother.

Realising Frankie was making all sorts of funny noises, Raymond stopped the car. He had to check she was all right in case she couldn't breathe properly. 'Are you OK? Can you breathe?' he asked as he pulled the gag off her.

'You stupid fucking idiot. I saw me dad outside and Mum's in that trailer.'

'What?' Raymond asked incredulously. Frankie was winding him up – she had to be.

'I swear on my baby's life, Mum's in there. She came to see me to sort stuff out. When she heard your voice, she hid under the bed.'

Realising that Frankie was telling the truth, Raymond felt all the hairs on the back of his neck stand up. 'Jesus! No!' he screamed, as he spun the car around and raced back to the scene of the crime.

*   *   *

451

Eddie smiled as he saw the dealer boots poking out from under the bed. He would have liked to have tortured the little fucker for a while, but he really didn't have the time. Poor little Jed must have crawled in here after Raymond clumped him over the bonce. Smiling, Eddie prepared his speech.

'Bye-bye, Jeddy boy. This is what you get for crossing me,' he said as he let fly with the machine gun.

With blood splattered all over himself and the walls, Eddie decided enough was enough. He was extremely thirsty and decided he needed to have a little refreshment before Raymond got back. The cleaning-up process was much harder work than just killing people, unfortunately.

Eddie went to the fridge and was pleased to find a can of lager. 'Cheers, you little gyppo cunt,' he toasted, as he sat down on the old sofa.

Sipping his beer, Eddie took a good look at the surroundings. 'So this is how pikeys live, is it?' he said cuttingly.

Smirking, Eddie slurped his beer. Frankie wouldn't thank him for a while, but he had literally saved his daughter from a life of hell. Any man in his position would have done the same as he had. Every father in the world only wants the best for their daughter, don't they?

As the sound of brakes screeched outside, Eddie shot up like a jack-in-the-box. Raymond wasn't due back yet, so who the fuck was this?

Eddie picked up the machine gun and lifted back the old net curtain. As he saw Raymond running towards him, Eddie guessed there had been a hitch, but still breathed a sigh of relief. Flatnose Freddie would have thought he was taking the right piss if he had turned up with a boot full of bodies instead of just one.

'What's up?' he asked as Raymond let himself in.

'Where's Jessica? Have you seen her?' Raymond asked frantically.

'Of course I ain't seen her. She's round her fucking mother's,' Ed replied, looking at him as though he was mental.

'No, she ain't. Frankie said she was here, she came to see her,' Raymond said nervously.

'Well, she ain't here now, is she?' Eddie said, fuming that his wife had gone behind his back.

'Where's Jed?' Raymond asked, as a sudden feeling of dread washed over him.

'Having a little rest under the bed. Don't worry, Ray, I've put about two hundred bullets in him, so he's hardly likely to jump out on us,' Eddie said, laughing.

Raymond yanked open the bedroom door and breathed a sigh of relief as he saw a pair of boots poking out from underneath the bed. 'Thank God. You did see his face, didn't you, Ed?' Raymond asked confused. He could have sworn that Jed was barefoot when he had left.

'You ain't losing the plot, Ray, are you? You clumped him, he crawled under the bed. I came in, shot the cunt, job done. So what is your problem?'

Raymond felt ill as he turned to Eddie. 'Ed, Frankie reckons Jess crawled under the bed and was hiding there.'

Eddie stood up. 'My old woman don't walk around in dealer boots,' he said, as he strolled into the bedroom.

Grabbing hold of the ankles, Eddie was shocked as the boots came off in his hand. Seeing a pair of perfectly manicured feet, Eddie sank to his knees. 'No, no, it can't be! No!' he shouted.

Raymond pushed him out of the way, grabbed the legs and dragged the body out. As Eddie screamed out his wife's name, Raymond started to sob.

'Jessica, Jessica. I'm so sorry, I love you. Why did you come here? Why?' Eddie howled, cradling her bullet-ridden body in his arms.

Raymond was too stunned to speak. He could barely believe that his beautiful, vivacious sister was the bloodied corpse he was looking at. Jessica's body was lacerated beyond recognition. Her beautiful blonde hair was matted with blood and her face looked contorted with shock.

'Oh my God, Eddie. What have you done?' Raymond whispered.

Sobbing like a baby, Eddie clung to his wife's lifeless limbs. Raymond tried to drag Eddie off his sister and, as he did so, Ed started to yelp like a wounded animal. Raymond stared at Jessica's face once more, then bent over and vomited.

As Raymond's gun fell out of his pocket, Eddie immediately picked it up. Without Jessica, his life was nothing and he knew he could never forgive himself or get over what he had done. 'It's all right, darling. I'll look after you and our baby. I'm coming with you,' he said, as he pointed the gun towards his temple.

'No, Ed! No!' Raymond yelled, as he lunged towards Eddie.

Outside in the car, Frankie was still tied up. She was frightened, thirsty and desperate to know what was going on. As she heard the gunshot echo in the wind, she let out a piercing scream.

'Jed! Mum! Where are you?' she sobbed.

FORTY-THREE

Raymond crouched down. He had managed to knock the gun away from his brother-in-law's head, but it had still gone off and had whizzed through Eddie's shoulder. 'Stay with me, Ed. I'm calling an ambulance right now,' Raymond urged him.

Eddie lay moaning and groaning. He was conscious, but not really with it. 'Let me die. I want to die,' he muttered.

Ignoring his pal's wishes, Raymond dialled 999. 'Get me an ambulance. Two people have been shot,' he yelled, as the woman asked him which service he wanted.

Taking off his jacket, Raymond laid it over his sister's mutilated body. 'I love you, Jess,' he said, tears rolling down his face.

Knowing that the police were going to have a field day, Raymond's instincts kicked in and he ran outside to untie Frankie.

'What's happened? Is Jed alive?' his niece screamed.

By now Frankie was absolutely hysterical and Raymond had never felt so guilty in his life as he tried to calm her down. 'Jed's fine, he got away. Now listen Frankie, and listen carefully. The police and ambulance will be here in a minute. You say nothing to them, OK? All I'm gonna say is me and you drove over here to look for your mum.'

'I'm telling them everything. You and Dad are animals and I hate you both,' Frankie bellowed.

Raymond slapped his hand around her face. She was in terrible shock and needed to snap out of it, else they were all going down. 'You say nothing, Frankie, do you hear me? Nothing.'

'Where's my mum? I want my mum,' Frankie sobbed.

Untying the last bit of rope, Eddie held his distraught niece in his arms. How was he meant to tell her that her dad had killed her mum? As the sound of sirens approached, he pleaded with Frankie to do as he had asked. 'There's been an accident, Frankie. I'll explain later. Don't say anything to the police,' he said, as he jumped out of the car.

Both the police and paramedics were taken aback by the sight that greeted them. They were obviously trained to deal with these situations, but neither service had ever seen a woman with so many bulletholes in her body. Eddie was now out for the count, and was bleeding profusely.

'Is he still alive?' Raymond asked, as Eddie was rushed into the ambulance.

'He's still got a pulse, but we need to get him to hospital immediately. He's lost a lot of blood,' the paramedic replied.

Seeing the stretcher being brought out of the trailer, Frankie lost the plot. 'What's going on?' she screamed, as she got out of the car and ran towards the amubulance.

As Frankie tried to dart inside the trailer, a policeman grabbed hold of her. The police had been so shocked by the scene they had encountered, they hadn't even realised Frankie was there. 'Where's Jed? Where's my mum?' Frankie yelled.

'You can't go inside. It's a crime scene,' the policeman told her gently.

Raymond led his inconsolable niece back to the safety of the car. He had to tell her the truth before the coppers did the honours. Sitting Frankie in the passenger seat, Raymond crouched down and held her hands. 'Mummy's dead, Frankie. I'm so, so sorry,' he said, as another ambulance and more police back-up arrived.

'Mum's not dead. What about her baby? She can't be dead,' Frankie whimpered.

'It was an accident, Frankie. I'm sorry,' Raymond responded, hugging her fragile body in his arms.

As white as a ghost, Frankie shook like a leaf. 'I want my mum, I need to see her!' she screamed hysterically.

The police came over to tell Raymond and Frankie that the ambulance was waiting to take them to hospital. 'You'll be treated for shock. We're going to need to take statements from both of you later,' an officer informed Raymond.

Raymond nodded. He had already told the police that he had brought Frankie here to see her mum and found Jessica and Eddie both shot. 'It's obvious someone wanted to kill them, and thought they'd succeeded,' he told the shell-shocked copper.

'I want Joey. Ring Joey for me,' Frankie wailed, as she was helped into the ambulance.

Raymond sat opposite her with his head in his hands. How the hell was he meant to tell his mum and dad that both Jessica and the baby were dead?

Unaware of the carnage, Jed was sat drinking a beer and soaking his sore feet in a trailer over in Basildon. Fearful of losing his life, he had run for miles barefoot. He had heard the gunshots as he had scarpered across the fields, but had no idea of what had actually happened. Finally, he had come to a main road, had found a phone box and rung his cousin, Sammy Boy. His feet were ripped to pieces and when Sammy arrived to collect him, he could barely speak through the pain.

'Do you want another beer? How do ya feel now?' Sammy asked him.

Gratefully accepting the can, Jed opened it and drank most of the lager in one go. 'I feel like shit, but I need to find Frankie. I want you to drive me to her house and if she ain't there, then you'll have to take me back to Tilbury.'

'It's a bit risky if they've got shooters, ain't it?' Sammy asked him.

'If Frankie ain't indoors, I'll go to mine and get one of me dad's guns,' Jed replied.

Sammy handed him a fresh pair of socks and some trainers. 'Come on then, let's go.'

Many miles away, Joyce, Joey and Stanley were all of a panic as they headed towards Basildon Hospital.

'There's been a terrible accident – you need to come quick. Frankie's asking for Joey, so bring him with you,' was all Raymond had told them.

Joey couldn't stop crying, 'Whaddya think has happened, Nan?' he wept.

'I don't know, darling,' Joyce said, squeezing his hand.

Raymond was pacing the corridors when he spotted his parents walking towards him. The doctors were worried about Frankie. She had been that hysterical, her blood pressure had shot through the roof and they had now given her a sedative to calm her down.

Joyce and Stanley glanced fearfully at one another as they spotted the huge police presence. 'Is it Jess? Has she lost the baby?' Joyce sobbed, as she was led into a nearby relatives' room.

A sombre-looking policewoman urged them all to sit down.

458

'Where's Frankie? Is she OK?' Joey asked, shaking.

Raymond begged the policewoman to let him break the terrible news to his family.

'What's going on, son?' Stanley asked, his face stern.

Raymond let out a cry. 'Jessica's dead,' he sobbed.

'Dead! What do you mean, she's dead?' Joyce asked incredulously.

'There was a shooting. No one knows exactly what happened, but Jessica's dead and Eddie's being operated on as we speak.'

As Joey let out a piercing scream, Joyce collapsed with shock. Stanley stood up and, as his legs buckled, sank to his knees. 'I always knew that bastard would be the death of my Jessica, I always knew it,' he howled.

Nearby, in the operating theatre, Eddie's heart had just stopped beating. 'Cardiac arrest. Start resuscitation,' shouted one of the surgeons.

Everybody crowded round. It was touch and go for Eddie Mitchell.

Still unaware of the chaos, Jed and Sammy Boy headed straight to Frankie's house and were surprised to see her driveway swarming with police officers. Jed told Sammy to stay in the car.

'Wait here while I ask the gavvers what's going on,' he said as he slammed the car door.

'You can't go in there. No one's allowed in there,' said a copper, standing by the gate. He had been ordered to guard the property while his superiors searched for clues.

'What's happened? I need to see my girlfriend, she lives here,' Jed said bluntly.

'There's been an accident, that's all I can tell you,' the copper replied.

Jed was never one to be fobbed off. 'Me and my girlfriend are getting wed. She's having my baby, so I need to know she's all right. Can you try and find out where she is for me?'

Turning his back to Jed, the young officer spoke into his walkie-talkie. His girlfriend was also pregnant, so he felt some empathy towards Jed. 'Your girlfriend's OK. She's at Basildon Hospital.'

Jed sprinted back to the car. 'Basildon Hospital, as quick as you like,' he yelled at his cousin.

Back at the hospital, Joyce had been treated for shock. Seeing Joey and his father in absolute pieces, Raymond left the room. Their tears were pure and raw and Raymond felt as guilty as hell.

Outside, he punched the wall. He couldn't live this life any more. He pictured Jessica's face. It seemed so surreal that he would never see her or hear her infectious laugh ever again. Memories of the past came flooding back to Raymond. He remembered Jess struggling to learn to ride her bike without stabilisers. How she took the piss out of his obsession with Marc Bolan. She'd been so supportive when he'd joined that band, and even stuck up for him when he'd worn eyeliner. Raymond sat on a plastic chair and toyed with his emotions. Grassing Eddie up to the police was a no-go. Many people would have done, but not Raymond – he was too loyal. He knew how much Eddie had loved Jessica. It was an accident, a mistake. Ed's life would be destroyed after this. It was a pure mishap and Raymond would never tell a soul about the horrendous true happenings. As long as Frankie and Jed kept quiet, the police would just think that Jessica and Eddie had been attacked by somebody else.

Seeing a copper staring at him, Raymond went back

inside the hospital. Joey was curled up on the floor like a baby. 'Get up, Joey, come on, mate,' Raymond said, crouching down next to him.

'Leave him alone. This is all your fault, you and that other fucking hoodlum. With the lives you and him led, something like this was always bound to happen and it did, to my beautiful Jessica, who did nothing to deserve it. I hate what you've become, Raymond, and I'm ashamed to call you my son. Get out. Go on, get out, I never want to see your face again,' Stanley shouted, pushing his son towards the door.

Shocked at the venom in his usually mild-mannered father's voice, Raymond ran from the room.

With no room in the hospital car park, Sammy parked his motor in one of the spaces marked for staff only.

Jed had had his thinking cap on during the journey. He guessed from the police presence at Frankie's that something sinister had happened, so he had prepared himself a story. 'If the gavvers say anything, then I'm gonna say that you picked me up from Tilbury at six o'clock this morning. Me dad'll go mental, 'cause he owns that fucking land. Me truck's there and it's registered in his name, so the gavvers are bound to wanna question him. Thank God I burnt them photos yesterday, Sam. Can you imagine the can of worms they could have opened?'

'Are you sure you burnt 'em properly?' Sammy asked worried.

'Positive. I checked,' Jed replied confidently.

'Can I go and see my Joycie?' asked a red-eyed Stanley.

'And can I see Frankie now?' Joey asked, distraught.

Neither asked about Eddie, as neither really cared how he was.

461

The nurse nodded. 'Take no notice if they're still woozy. It will just be the medication we've given them,' she told them.

Joey sat down next to his sister's bed. 'What happened, Frankie? Talk to me,' he pleaded, as he stared into his sister's haunted eyes.

Frankie squeezed his hand. She wanted to tell him the truth, tell him that Raymond had kidnapped her, but she was still sedated, in shock, and unable to speak properly.

A few doors away, Stanley clutched Joyce's hand. She was still sound asleep, but Stanley was sure she could hear him. 'You should have listened to me all them years ago, Joycie. If Jess hadn't married Eddie, we wouldn't be mourning our daughter's death. We should have put our foot down when she was seventeen and she first met him. I always knew he was a villain, a wrong 'un, and still I let her marry him. How are Frankie and Joey ever gonna get over this, eh, Joycie? Their lives are ruined and so are ours. I hope that bastard doesn't wake up. He deserves to die, not our Jess. I hate him, Joycie, I really do.'

Joyce's eyes flickered open. 'You were right all along about him, Stanley. I'm just sorry I didn't listen to you,' she mumbled.

Unable to read properly, Jed kept stopping staff to ask them whether he was going in the right direction.

'Go straight down the end of this corridor, then turn left,' a nurse told him.

As Jed and Sammy ran around the corner, they came face to face with Raymond. 'Where's Frankie? What's happened?' Jed asked him.

Raymond led Jed away from the Old Bill.

'This is all your fault, you pikey cunt. My sister's dead

because of you. What are you doing up here anyway? Just do one, will ya?' Ray said viciously.

'If you don't tell me what's happened, I swear I'll cause a fucking riot,' Jed yelled.

Seeing the Old Bill had reappeared, Raymond realised that he had no option but to tell him. 'Frankie's not injured, but her mum's dead. Eddie's been shot as well. I don't know how he is 'cause no one will tell me.'

Jed looked at Raymond in astonishment. 'What happened? How did Jess die?'

'I don't fucking know,' Raymond spat.

Seeing a copper walk over to them, Raymond put his arm around Jed's shoulder. 'Say nothing about what went on. Go and see Frankie and make sure she keeps schtum as well,' he whispered.

Jed nodded and went in search of his girlfriend. The copper walked up to Raymond. 'Your brother-in-law's OK. I think he's in recovery.'

Raymond took a deep breath. 'Thanks for letting us know.'

'How is she, Joey?' Jed asked as he sat on a chair next to Frankie.

'She's sedated. She's still in shock. What are we gonna do, Jed? My mum's dead,' Joey sobbed.

As Jed stood up, Joey threw himself into his arms. Jed didn't know what to do. He was positive Frankie's brother was an iron and he didn't really want to touch him. 'Move out the way, Joey. I wanna talk to Frankie,' he said awkwardly.

As Jed held her hand, Frankie opened her eyes. 'I'm sorry about your mum. I'll look after you from now on, I promise I will. Is the baby OK? Have they checked you out?'

463

'I'm having a scan in the morning. Please don't leave me, Jed, stay here with me,' she whispered.

'I'm going nowhere,' Jed assured her.

Eddie Mitchell woke up in the early hours. At first his brain was fuzzy, but within minutes he remembered everything. 'Jessica! Jessica!' he cried, the tears rolling down his cheeks.

The Irish nurse walked over to him. 'You're going to be OK, Mr Mitchell. You had a nasty bullet wound and lost a lot of blood, but you're in the best place here. We'll have you back on your feet in no time.'

'Are the police still here?' Eddie asked groggily.

The nurse nodded. Eddie was in a private room and the police were waiting outside the door. 'Can you tell 'em to come in. I have a confession to make,' Eddie whispered.

Raymond stood outside smoking another cigarette. The whole episode had been a nightmare and had made him take stock of his life. He had already planned what he was going to do. He was going to propose to Polly, settle down and go straight. What he had seen in that trailer had put him off violence for life and he would never forget the sight of his sister's mutilated body lying on that floor for the rest of his days.

'Are you OK, Uncle Raymond?' Joey asked, as he walked up to him.

Joey felt like a spare part now that Jed had arrived, and he couldn't wait to leave the hospital and grieve in peace. Raymond put his arm around Joey's shoulder. 'I think I should ring your uncles Paulie and Ronny to tell 'em what's happened. They can tell Reg and Auntie Joan. They're all gonna find out, anyway.'

464

Joey nodded dumbly. His mum was dead and nothing else really mattered any more.

Sergeant Lineker could barely believe his ears as Eddie Mitchell confessed to murdering his own wife.

'So, it was mistaken identity? You thought that Mrs Mitchell was somebody else?'

Propped up against his pillow, a tearful Eddie nodded. 'My daughter's pregnant. She's only sixteen and I went there to shoot her boyfriend. I didn't know that my wife was there and when I saw this big pair of dealer boots poking out from under the bed, I assumed it was Jed, Frankie's fella. My Jessica and me were so happy. She was pregnant again and we were over the moon. I loved her more than anyone or anything,' Eddie said.

Sergeant Lineker glanced at his colleague. A full confession was the last thing they had expected to come out of Eddie Mitchell's mouth. 'You get some rest. You need to speak to your solicitor tomorrow. We'll set the wheels in motion.'

As the two coppers left the room, Eddie covered his face with his hands and howled. He had never admitted to a crime before in his life, but this was different. He had murdered his own wife and unborn child in cold blood, and spending the rest of his life in prison was what Eddie felt he deserved.

Stanley walked back into the room where his wife was. 'The doctor said that we can go home soon,' he told her.

Joyce sat up and clung on to her husband for dear life.

'Come on, let it all out,' Stanley said, as she sobbed on his shoulder. He felt like crying himself, but had to be strong for her sake.

'What are we gonna go without her, Stanley? She was my life,' Joyce wept.

Stanley felt his eyes welling up. 'I really don't know, but we'll manage somehow, darling.'

'I'm gonna pop outside with Sammy to have a fag. Shall I bring you a coffee back?' Jed asked Frankie.

Frankie nodded. 'See if you can find Joey for me. He can sit with me while you're gone.'

Jed nodded and left the room.

'Your sister wants you,' he told Joey as he walked past him.

Outside, Sammy handed Jed a cigarette. 'I might shoot off in a minute. Will you be all right here on your own?'

'I'll be fine. Frankie will probably be allowed to go home in the morning, so I'll stop here with her,' Jed replied.

Sammy shook his cousin's hand. 'You know where I am if you need me. Ring me tomorrow,' he said, as he went to walk away.

Jed grabbed hold of him. 'Sam, that thing we done, you must never tell anyone, especially not now. Promise me you won't?'

'I swear, you have my word,' Sammy replied.

Jed leaned against the wall as his cousin walked away. Thank God he'd had the brains to burn them photos he'd stolen as souvenirs. No one but him and Sammy knew the truth. He hadn't even told his dad.

Jed smiled as he thought back to that night. Murdering Harry Mitchell had been all his idea. He had planned it with precision and, due to his cleverness, they'd got away with it.

In Jed's eyes, Harry Mitchell had deserved to die. Butch, Jed's grandfather, had had his life ruined by

466

Mitchell. Butch had never recovered from being shot in the foot. He walked with a severe limp from that day onwards and spent the latter part of his life living as a recluse.

Jed had plotted the operation from start to finish. He'd recruited Sammy's younger brother, Billy, and his pals to act as decoys. Six times Jed had driven them over to Harry's and paid them fifty quid to cause mayhem. The boys had no idea what Jed was up to. He'd told them that the man had knocked him for money.

'See that house over there, number thirty-one? I want you to hang about outside and make a nuisance of yourselves. Make sure all the neighbours see and hear you, but keep your hoods up at all times so they can't see your faces. You've gotta shout, scream, throw stones, knock on the doors. I need you to be as noisy as you can,' Jed ordered.

On the night of the murder, Jed had paid the boys their money, driven them back to Essex, then he and Sammy Boy had returned to Canning Town. They knew Harry was in, as they'd seen the lights go on and off earlier.

Jed had chosen Christmas Eve for a reason. He knew there'd be loads of noise on the streets, therefore Mitchell's shouts and screams would blend in with those of drunken revellers.

At eleven o'clock, Harry's house was in complete darkness.

'Let's give it an hour, make sure the old shit-cunt's asleep,' Jed told Sammy.

Sitting across the road in the back of a hooky van, Jed and Sammy amused themselves by secretly poking fun at the merry worshippers heading off to midnight mass. At a quarter to twelve, Jed checked the coast was clear and told his cousin to follow him.

'Right, put your gloves on and your hood up. Time to give old Harry boy his Christmas present,' Jed whispered, as they crept through the alleyway that led to Harry Mitchell's back garden.

Jed knew they'd have no problem gaining entry. He'd done his homework and was aware that Mitchell left the louvres open in the conservatory to let his cat in and out. Jed then expertly removed the louvres one by one, climbed in, then urged Sammy to do the same.

Jed waited until he got to the lounge before he switched his torch on. Spotting the photos of young Harry with a pretty woman, Jed smiled. 'Once we've finished him off, we'll take a couple of them pictures as souvenirs. We need to rough the place up a bit, make a mess, but we'll have to do it quietly,' Jed whispered.

Gesticulating for Sammy to follow him up the stairs, Jed clutched his baseball bat tightly in both hands. He'd waited a long time for this moment and felt high on adrenalin.

Harry's snoring sounded like a pig snorting and Jed grinned as he tiptoed towards his bedroom. The door was open, and as Jed stood over the sleeping man, he was filled with a mixture of excitement and hatred. Glancing at Sammy, he lifted the bat in the air and smashed it as hard as he could over Harry's head.

Instinct took over and a dazed Harry staggered out of the bed and lunged at Jed. 'Who are you? What the fuck do you want?' he shouted, as his feeble punches failed to connect.

Jed hit Harry once more and laughed as he fell to the floor. 'Not as strong as you thought you were, eh?' he goaded.

'Tie up his arms and legs then shine the torch on him,' Jed told Sammy.

Recognising the accent was that of a traveller, Harry knew he was in trouble. For many years he'd slept with a gun under his bed and his only hope now was to make a grab for it. With the two blows he'd received to his head, Harry was no match for his fit young attacker. Clocking Harry's hand creeping under the bed, Jed repeatedly stamped on it with his right foot.

As Harry felt his wrist snap, he screamed out in pain. Sammy tied Harry's arms up, 'Who are you? One of the fucking O'Haras? I'm warning you – you kill me and my Eddie will break every bone in your useless pikey body,' Harry shouted.

Jed laughed as Sammy tied Harry's legs up. Harry reminded him of an oven-ready chicken, 'Sorry, did I forget to introduce myself? I'm Jed O'Hara, Butch's grandson, and this is my cousin, Sammy. I take it you remember my grandfather?'

Annoyed that Harry didn't reply, Jed booted him in the head. 'Answer me, you old shit-cunt.'

Harry was in so much pain he could barely speak. 'What happened with your grandfather was business, nothing personal,' he croaked.

'I'll give you fucking personal,' Jed spat, tying the gag around Harry's mouth.

Jed could sense Harry's despair. Watching him choking, trying to say something, Jed loosened the gag.

'Please don't kill me. I beg you not to. If you kill me, you're signing your own death warrant. The feud between our families ended years ago. To start it up again now will cause an absolute bloodbath.'

Jed tightened the gag once more. He had to finish what he'd come here to do. 'My grandfather turned into a hermit because of you. You killed his spirit and now I'm gonna kill yours. So go fuck your grandmother.'

As Jed lifted up the baseball bat, Harry began to wriggle like a fish out of water.

'Hurry up, Jed. Finish him off and let's get out of here,' Sammy urged his cousin.

Jed looked into Harry's petrified eyes and smiled. 'Happy Christmas. I hope you rot in hell,' he whispered, repeatedly smashing the bat over Harry's skull.

As blood sprayed everywhere, Sammy felt queasy. 'Come on, Jed, that's enough,' he said.

Even though he knew Harry was dead, Jed couldn't stop. His victim's head was already bashed to a pulp, so Jed started to smash the bat against his teeth.

Frightened, Sammy grabbed Jed and pushed him against the wall. 'Whaddya doing? The old cunt's been dead five minutes. We need to get out of here, Jed. If we don't, we're both looking at prison.'

The word prison seemed to snap Jed out of his violent trance. Checking he'd left no clues in the bedroom, Jed followed Sammy downstairs.

'Open a few drawers and throw some stuff on the floor. It has to look like a burglary,' Jed said, as he stuffed some photos inside his jacket.

Ten minutes later, with the house looking completely ransacked, Jed and Sammy climbed out the same way they'd got in.

'Excuse me. Do you know what the visiting hours are?'

Jed's daydream was ended by the woman standing in front of him. 'Sorry. What did you say?'

The woman repeated her question.

'I've no idea. Ask a nurse,' Jed told her.

Taking the last drag on his fag, Jed flicked the butt into the air. Everything had turned out OK in the end. Harry was long gone, Jessica was dead, Eddie was looking at a life sentence, which meant Frankie and the baby were all his.

Unable to stop himself, Jed began to laugh. He couldn't wait to tell his father that Eddie Mitchell had tried to shoot him, but instead had killed his own wife. For years his dad had banged on about getting his own back on the Mitchells and now, without his dad even knowing, he'd done it for him.

Jed grinned as he strolled back into the hospital. Thanks to him, the feud was finally over.